NO CAT DOOR REQUIRED ...

The steps up to the apartment were at the back of the building. I set the messenger bag down on the floor of the covered porch at the top of the stairs. Herc popped his head out and looked around. "Not a sound," I warned. "Not a meow, not a rumble, not even a burp. Rebecca will be here any minute."

I bent down to close the top of the bag. He jumped out, looked right and left and then disappeared through the door before I could grab him.

Yes, through the closed door.

My heart stopped. I dropped down into a crouch. Hercules was definitely gone, gone through a thick, solid door. That was the other thing about him that I couldn't tell anyone. He could pass through any solid object—doors, six-inch-thick walls, concrete foundations.

I didn't have a clue how he did it. In fact, the first time I'd seen him walk nonchalantly through an inch-and-a-half-thick wooden door at the library, I thought I was having hallucinations or even a stroke. Because cats can't walk through doors or walls ... *can they?*

D0092562

Also by Sophie Kelly

Curiosity Thrilled the Cat

SLEIGHT OF PAW

A MAGICAL CATS MYSTERY

SOFIE KELLY

AN OBSIDIAN MYSTERY

OBSIDIAN

Published by New American Library, a division of
Penguin Group (USA) Inc., 375 Hudson Street,
New York, New York 10014, USA
Penguin Group (Canada), 90 Eglinton Avenue East, Suite 700, Toronto,
Ontario M4P 2Y3, Canada (a division of Pearson Penguin Canada Inc.)
Penguin Books Ltd., 80 Strand, London WC2R 0RL, England
Penguin Ireland, 25 St. Stephen's Green, Dublin 2,
Ireland (a division of Penguin Books Ltd.)
Penguin Group (Australia), 250 Camberwell Road, Camberwell, Victoria 3124,
Australia (a division of Pearson Australia Group Pty. Ltd.)
Penguin Books India Pvt. Ltd., 11 Community Centre, Panchsheel Park,
New Delhi - 110 017, India
Penguin Group (NZ), 67 Apollo Drive, Rosedale, Auckland 0632,
New Zealand (a division of Pearson New Zealand Ltd.)
Penguin Books (South Africa) (Pty.) Ltd., 24 Sturdee Avenue,
Rosebank, Johannesburg 2196, South Africa

Penguin Books Ltd., Registered Offices:
80 Strand, London WC2R 0RL, England

First published by Obsidian, an imprint of New American Library,
a division of Penguin Group (USA) Inc.

First Printing, September 2011
10 9 8 7 6 5 4 3 2 1

ACKNOWLEDGMENTS

Writing is a solitary occupation, but it takes the hard work of a lot of people to create a finished book. Thank you to my agent, Kim Lionetti, and everyone at Book-ends LLC. Thank you as well to my editor, Jessica Wade, whose skills make me look good, and to Robin Cata-lano, who knows more about grammar than I ever will.

Special thanks go to Police Chief Tim Sletten of the Red Wing, Minnesota, Police Department for generously and patiently answering my questions. Any errors in po-lice procedure are due to my playing with reality.

Thank you to all the readers who have e-mailed or written to let me know how much they like Owen and Hercules and to share their own cat stories.

And, as always, thank you to Patrick and Lauren, who make everything better.

1

It was pretty clear the body wasn't going to go in the back of Roma's SUV. The legs were hanging out, almost touching the driveway.

"Can't we just push him in?" she asked, kicking dirty snow away from the back tires.

"No, we can't just push him in," Maggie said. "That would break his legs." She walked to the other side of the SUV. "Maybe if we put him in feetfirst . . ." She looked at me. "What do you think, Kathleen?"

What did I think? I thought it was freezing. "He still won't fit," I pointed out. "Could we take his legs off?"

Maggie looked at me, aghast. "Take Eddie's legs off? How?"

"I have a hacksaw under the front seat," Roma added oh so-not-helpfully. Because she was a veterinarian she had a number of things in her vehicle that other people didn't.

I gave her a look. "No, I don't mean saw off his legs," I said. "But don't they detach somehow?"

Wrong thing to say. Maggie laid a protective hand on Eddie's thigh. "Do your legs detach?" she asked me.

I exhaled slowly, watching my breath hover in the air. "No," I said, "my legs don't detach, but I'm a human being and Eddie's a mannequin."

"He's a mixed-media assemblage piece," Maggie said huffily.

The real Eddie Sweeney—"Crazy" Eddie Sweeney—was number 22, a six-foot-four forward for the Minnesota Wild hockey team and the pride of the state, born and bred. Maggie had been commissioned to create a display featuring Eddie for this year's Winterfest. I was pretty sure the Winterfest committee had been expecting Maggie's collage panels, not a life-sized re-creation of Eddie in pads and skates. He looked so real, truthfully, that he had given me the creeps the first time I had seen him dressed and sitting in a chair in Maggie's art studio.

"Could we wrap him in plastic and tie him to the roof racks?" Roma asked.

All I could see were Roma's eyes and nose buried under the hood of her heavy coat.

"Realistically, how far do you think we'd get before someone called the police?" I said.

"Good point, Kathleen," she said.

"We can't leave him like this." Maggie looked skyward. "I think it's going to snow."

"There's a surprise," I muttered.

Winter in Mayville Heights, Minnesota, came in three varieties: About to Snow, Snowing, and Get Out the Shovel. I had to concede, though, that the town looked like something out of an old Currier & Ives greeting card. Snow decorated the tree branches, frost sparkled on windowpanes, and there was a complete snowman in every second yard.

It was my first real winter in town. I'd arrived last year at the tail end of the season to be the new librarian and supervise the renovations to the library building for its upcoming centennial.

I looked at Eddie's backside sticking out of the rear of the SUV. "I have an idea," I said. "Roma, can you grab Eddie's left thigh?"

She pushed back her hood. "With pleasure," she said with a grin. She gave Faux Eddie a pat on the behind and caught him by the leg and the waist. I took the other side and we lifted him out of the back of the SUV. Though he wasn't a real body, he was still heavy.

"Now what?" Roma asked.

"Be careful," Maggie said, hovering behind us.

"Open the passenger's door," I told her.

"You can't put his feet in the front and his head in the back," she warned. "Once Roma starts driving he'll slide backward and break."

"That's not what I'm doing," I said. "Trust me."

Maggie was my closest friend in Mayville. We'd met when I'd joined the tai chi class she taught, and bonded over our mutual love of the cheesy reality show *Gotta Dance*. She was a talented collage artist, but I'd never seen her so worked up about a commission.

She chewed her lip for a second, then caught herself. Putting both hands on her stomach, she took several slow deep breaths. "Sorry," she said. "This whole project is making me crazy. Do whatever you were going to do." She reached over and opened the passenger's door.

"What are we doing?" Roma whispered.

"We're putting him in the front seat. You take the shoulders and I'll take his legs," I said. We set Eddie on the front passenger's seat, legs out to the side.

"Turn him around," I said to Roma. She shifted Eddie to face the windshield, while I moved his legs, resting his skates on the floor mat. Then I leaned in and fastened the seat belt. "Ta da," I said, backing out of the SUV.

Roma walked around to the front of the vehicle and looked through the windshield. "He looks so real," she said.

I nodded. "Yeah, he does."

Maggie couldn't help checking the seat belt herself. Roma closed the tailgate, then came around and got in behind the wheel. I climbed in the backseat, sliding over to make room for Maggie.

Roma backed out of the alley and headed down the street. I'd met her at tai chi, too, but the friendship between the three of us had really been cemented last summer when Mags and I had coerced Roma into helping us follow someone, à la Charlie's Angels.

"Thanks for doing this, Roma," Maggie said.

She smiled at us in the rearview mirror. "I don't mind. How often do I get the chance to drive around with a celebrity?" She reached over and patted Eddie's shoulder. "Well, sort of a celebrity."

"Eddie's having the best season of his career," Maggie said. "Forty goals and thirty-five assists so far."

"Really?" I said, working not to let her see me smile.

"And he's probably in the best shape of his career, as well. Did you know he does extra skating drills on his own after practice?"

"I did not know that," Roma said solemnly.

Maggie pulled off a mitten and reached forward to fix the back of Eddie's jersey. "Every single Wild home game has been sold out this season and it's because of Eddie."

I pulled off my own mittens and fished in my pocket for lip balm. "You know, Roma," I said, "I never thought it would happen, but I think Matt Lauer has some competition for Maggie's heart." I saw Roma's face widen into a grin.

"Do you think Eddie can dance?" Roma asked, referring to Matt Lauer's improbable win on the previous season of *Gotta Dance*.

"Gee, I don't know. He does have some smooth moves."

"Ha, ha, ha," Maggie said. "I don't have a thing for Eddie Sweeney."

"Of course not," Roma said. "He's only tall, strong and gorgeous."

Maggie squared her shoulders. "I'm just a fan of Eddie's athletic abilities—that's all."

"Oh, me, too," Roma retorted. "If I were just a little bit younger . . ." She let the end of the sentence trail away, and grinned.

We turned left at the corner and drove down Main Street under the huge Winterfest banner stretched across the road in front of the James Hotel.

"So, how long has Winterfest been going on?" I asked.

"Since I was a kid," Maggie said. "And before that."

Roma nodded. "It started out as an ice-fishing competition back in the forties."

"I didn't know that," Maggie said.

"Oh, yeah. People came from all over the state." Roma put on her blinker to turn in to the community center parking lot. She shot a quick glance back over her shoulder at Maggie. "Which door?"

"The side one, please," Maggie said, shifting to peer through the windshield. "Tell me there's a perfectly good reason it looks like no one else is here."

Except for one light I'd noticed at the front entrance, the building seemed to be closed.

"Sam's been on an energy-saving kick," Roma said. "He can go overboard pretty easily."

Sam was the mayor of Mayville Heights, and Roma was right. His efforts to save energy had gone a little bit too far for some people.

She pulled into a parking spot close to the door and shut off the SUV. "Let's get Eddie inside," she said.

We reversed the process of putting Eddie in the passenger's seat. Maggie went ahead to hold the door for us.

It was locked. "No," she groaned, kicking the door with her heavy boot. "Hey, anybody in there?" she called.

Silence.

"Seven o'clock, Thorsten said. Seven. O'. Clock. Where is he?"

I looked around. Thorsten was the building's caretaker. There were maybe a half dozen vehicles in the parking lot. None of them were Thorsten's.

"Can you hold on to Eddie while I try to find out what's going on?" Maggie asked, pulling out her cell phone.

"Sure," I said. I tucked Eddie's knees against my sides. Roma pulled his body a little closer, wrapping her arms around his chest. I couldn't help wondering what this would look like to anyone walking by.

Maggie punched a number into the phone and took a couple of slow deep breaths while she waited for it to ring on the other end. She made a face. "Voice mail." She waited another moment. "Thorsten, it's Maggie Adams. I'm at the community center and the building is locked. Where are you?" She rattled off her cell number and pressed the END button. "Who else is on the Winterfest committee?" she asked.

"Rebecca," Roma said.

Maggie made a face. "I don't want to bring her down here in the cold."

Eddie was heavy for a guy that was mostly cotton padding. My arms were starting to cramp. "What about Mary?" I said. Mary worked for me at the library.

"Do you know her number?" Maggie asked.

I recited it to her.

"Thanks," she said, putting the phone up to her ear. We waited, then Maggie let out a breath. She watched it slowly dissipate in the frigid air. "Does anyone answer the phone?"

Eddie's back end was hanging dangerously close to a pile of dirty snow. I tightened my grip on his legs.

"Call Oren," Roma said. "He did some work on the ceiling this week, fixing that leak from the ice buildup. He'll have a key." Oren Kenyon was a jack-of-all-trades. He'd worked on the library renovation last summer as well as getting the Stratton Theater ready for the Wild Rose Summer Music Festival.

"Roma, you're a genius," Maggie said, pushing buttons on the phone.

The cold was seeping up through the heavy soles and fuzzy linings of my boots, and the long underwear I was wearing underneath my jeans.

"Oren," Maggie said. "It's Maggie." Quickly she explained the problem. Then she listened, nodding even though Oren couldn't see her. "Thank you so much," she said. "We'll see you then." She snapped the phone shut. "Oren will be here in about a half hour. Do you guys mind waiting?"

Roma shook her head.

"Why don't we go down to Eric's and have hot chocolate while we wait?" I said.

"Excellent idea," Roma said, her voice partly muffled because her face was pressed against Eddie's side. "But what are we going to do with Eddie?"

"Stick him back in the SUV," I said.

Maggie held the passenger's door open and we managed to get Eddie back in the front seat without dumping him in the snow. We piled into the car, and Roma backed out of the parking spot.

"I know it probably looks like I'm being a little obsessive," Maggie said.

I raised an eyebrow in my best Mr. Spock impersonation.

"I just don't want anything to happen to Eddie. He's the biggest piece ever I've done."

Roma looked both ways and pulled out of the lot. "Hey, I don't want anything to happen to Eddie, either. He's the only man in my life right now."

I laughed.

"Oh, sure, Kathleen. Go ahead and laugh. You have two guys in your life."

"I do?" I said. Then I realized she was talking about my cats. "You mean Owen and Hercules? They shed, they don't pay any attention to anything I say to them and their breath smells like sardines."

"And that would be different from a real man how?" Roma asked.

Maggie and I both laughed.

Eric's Place was just up ahead. It was one of the best places to eat in town and was run, perhaps unsurprisingly, by Eric Cullen. His wife, Susan, worked for me at the library.

"Look for somewhere to park," Roma said.

I scanned the street, wondering why there were so many cars on a Wednesday night in February.

Maggie must have read my mind. "Wait a sec. There's an auction going on tonight over at Fischer's Warehouse, isn't there? The stuff from Cormac Henry's place."

I remembered reading about that in the paper. "That's where Mary is," I said.

"Probably Thorsten, too," Roma added.

"There," Maggie suddenly squealed, pointing across the street. Amazingly, there was an empty parking spot in front of Eric's.

Roma scanned the pavement in front of us. "You didn't see this," she muttered. She made a tight U-turn in the mouth of the alley two buildings down from the café, then drove ahead and backed smoothly into the empty space in front of the restaurant. "There," she said to Maggie. "You can keep an eye on Eddie and he won't miss all the fun."

We piled on to the sidewalk and went into the restaurant. It was almost empty. Peter Lundgren was at a table by the end wall, his head bent over a book, probably something to do with World War II history; that was where his reading interests lay. I also knew he liked heavy-metal music, which wasn't what I would have expected of a lawyer.

Claire, my favorite waitress, smiled at us. "Sit any-where," she called, making a sweeping gesture with one hand.

I caught sight of Eric behind the counter.

"Why don't we take a table by the window so we can keep an eye on Eddie?" Roma said.

"Good idea," I said. "I'll be right back. I just need to speak to Eric for a second."

"Hi, Kathleen," Eric said with a smile. He was wear-ing a long apron with splotches of chocolate all over it. That had to be good.

"Hi," I said. "I just wanted to say thank you for the apple cake this morning." Eric liked to experiment with new recipes for the café. Sometimes Susan brought his efforts to work.

"Oh, you're welcome." He pushed back the sleeves of his dark green sweater. "Did you think there was too much cinnamon?"

I shook my head. "No. But if you feel you need to experiment a little more . . ."

"You'll all force yourselves to be my taste testers."

I put my hand over my heart. "We'll make the sacri-fice," I said solemnly.

He laughed, and I headed back to Roma and Maggie, pulling off my old coat. It was warm, but it was an ugly shade of brown. I'd bought it to wear out to Wisteria Hill when it was my turn to help feed the cat colony that lived at the abandoned house. Since I'd paid only five dollars for the jacket at Goodwill, I didn't really care that it wasn't very fashionable. I was pretty sure the cats didn't, either.

Claire came over with an insulated carafe. "Hot choc-olate?" she asked, holding it up.

"Please," Roma said, pulling off her gloves and rub-bing her hands together.

Maggie and I both nodded.

Claire poured three mugs of cocoa. "Marshmallows or cinnamon?"

"Marshmallows!" Maggie and I said in unison.

"Eric made chocolate pudding cake," Claire said with a sly smile. Her red curls were caught in two pigtails and she looked like a mischievous little girl.

Roma was bent over, fixing her boot. "Yes," she said, holding up one hand and waving it.

"That sounds good," Maggie said.

"It does," I agreed.

"It'll just be a couple of minutes," Claire promised, heading back to the counter.

Roma straightened and picked up her mug. "Here's to chocolate and duct tape."

"Excuse me?" I said.

"Chocolate and duct tape," she repeated. "Between the two of them you can solve just about any problem." She stuck out her left leg, pointing to her boot. "See?" There was a piece of gray duct tape stuck to the heel on the inside edge. "I caught that on a spike this afternoon. Couple of pieces of tape and it's fine for now."

I laughed. "Don't tell me you carry a roll of duct tape in your bag."

"I do. And a bag of M&M's." She held out her right hand, palm up. "Duct tape." She did the same with her other hand. "M&M's. If I can't fix whatever's wrong with those two things, I'm going home and getting back into bed."

Claire was coming toward us, carrying a large oval tray. I could smell the warm chocolate. She set a dish of marshmallows in the middle of the table, then slid a bowl of pudding cake in front of each of us.

It tasted even better than it smelled, and it smelled wonderful. "Can I get you anything else?" she asked. All she got for an answer was three grunts. She smiled. "I'll check back in a few minutes."

We ate in silence except for the occasional sigh of pleasure. Maggie set down her spoon first and licked a drop of chocolate sauce from the side of her thumb. "That was so, so good," she said. She pulled a small black notebook from her pocket. "What's the rest of your week look like?" she asked Roma. "I need to take some more pictures of the cats."

Roma wiped her hand with her napkin. "What works for you?" she asked. They leaned across the table, comparing schedules.

Maggie had done a collage of photos of the feral cat colony at Wisteria Hill, where I'd found Owen and Hercules. It hung in the waiting room of Roma's veterinary clinic. Now an animal-rescue organization had commissioned Maggie to create a poster for their spay-neuter program. She was going to take pictures of three new strays that had been left on the doorstep of the clinic last week.

There was a rush of cold wind in my face as the door to the café opened. A tiny, elderly woman stepped inside. Something about her seemed familiar. She hesitated in the doorway, blinking in the light. Was she looking around for someone? I wasn't sure. I touched Roma's arm. "Roma, who's that?" I asked.

She looked up, smiling at the sight of the old woman. "That's Agatha," she said, her smile widening as the other woman noticed her. Agatha didn't exactly smile back, but her expression softened a little. And she ducked her head in recognition. Then her eyes shifted to me and she nodded.

Roma frowned. "Do you know her?"

"Not exactly," I said. "I saw her a couple of times yesterday. When I was shoveling she, uh, she stopped to talk to Hercules. You know what a wuss he is about getting his feet wet."

What I didn't say was that Agatha had picked up my

little black-and-white cat and carried him over to me. Hercules and Owen, like the rest of the cats from Wisteria Hill, were likely feral. I'd found them as kittens, and they typically wouldn't let anyone other than me touch them.

Agatha was slowly making her way over to where Peter Lundgren was leaning on the counter, talking to Eric. I couldn't tell how old she was. She was hunched over with what I guessed was osteoporosis, her face lined with a web of fine wrinkles. She wore what looked to me like an early 1960s vintage red-and-black-plaid mohair coat. It seemed just a bit too big, or maybe the woman wearing it had gotten smaller with time.

Peter straightened and walked over to Agatha, offering his arm to her. She took it, shifting a black canvas bag to her other hand, and he helped her the rest of the way. They clearly knew each other.

"Why have I never seen her before?" I said.

"Agatha had a minor stroke this time last year and fell and broke her hip," Roma said. "She's been in a rehab center in Minneapolis." She glanced over at the counter, where Eric was handing Agatha a brown paper bag and take-out cup. Peter was on his way back to his table. "I didn't think she was coming home and then yesterday I saw her with Ruby."

Like Maggie, Ruby was also an artist. She painted huge abstracts and taught art. And she was the best student in our tai chi class.

The second time I'd seen Agatha she'd been talking to Ruby, as well. They'd been in the parking lot of the library and Agatha had seemed upset with Ruby, the way she seemed to be right now with Eric. He was gesturing at an envelope the old woman was holding. She'd had it the day I'd seen her with Ruby, as well. It looked like the kind of envelope my sixth-grade report card had been in.

Even at a distance I could see Agatha's expression, her lips pulled into a thin, angry line. Eric's face was flushed. He shook his head.

Agatha turned, her shoulders rigid under the out-of-date coat. She made her way back to the door, cup in one hand, bag in the other, the envelope held tightly against her chest with her forearm. It *was* an old report-card envelope, I realized as she passed us.

"She was a teacher," I said.

"Principal, actually," Maggie replied. She checked her watch. "We should get going." She looked around for Claire.

"You know, Agatha kept more than one kid from becoming a juvenile delinquent," Roma said, pushing back her chair and standing up.

Maggie nodded. "Ruby," she said. "And Eric." Claire came over and Maggie took all three checks from her, then held up her hand. "I'm getting this."

"There's two of us," I said to Roma.

She narrowed her eyes thoughtfully. "I think we could take her."

"I want to do this," Maggie said. "Don't argue with me."

Roma and I exchanged glances. "Okay," I said.

Maggie headed for the cash register. "And there's no way that you two could take me," she said over her shoulder.

Through the window I could see Agatha moving slowly down the sidewalk. Roma followed my gaze as she zipped her coat. "Me," she said softly, with a slightly embarrassed shrug.

It took me a moment to get what she meant. "You were a juvenile delinquent?" Roma as a wild child didn't fit with the compassionate veterinarian I'd become friends with since I'd moved to Minnesota.

"Maybe not exactly a delinquent," she said, pulling on her gloves. "But I was hanging out with a bad bunch of kids—sneaking out of the house, smoking, drinking—and I was only fourteen."

"That doesn't sound like you," Maggie said. She'd come back in time to hear the tail end of the conversation.

"That's because of Agatha," Roma said. "She noticed my interest in animals. Also caught me cutting school." She laughed at the memory. "Part of my punishment was cleaning cages three days a week after school at the animal shelter. For an entire month."

We headed for the door. I waved good-bye to Eric, who nodded in return. I turned back to Roma. "I take it the punishment really wasn't much of a punishment."

"I loved it," she said. "Not that I let on. When the month was up the shelter director offered me a part-time job, Saturdays and after school. I didn't find out for years that was Agatha's doing, too. Walking dogs, cleaning cages—I didn't have time to get into trouble anymore."

Maggie flipped up her hood and pushed the door open with her hip. It was achingly cold outside. "Agatha entered a painting of Ruby's in a statewide contest," she said. "She won tuition to a summer art camp."

Roma moved behind the SUV, squeezing between it and the bumper of the half-ton parked behind us. "I know she encouraged Eric's interest in cooking," she said. "He was about fifteen and he did all the food for some big teachers' breakfast."

Raised voices, sharp in the icy air, came up the sidewalk toward us. Roma stopped and craned her neck to see. Maggie leaned back and looked down the street, her hand on the car's door handle. I took a step backward for a better view.

What I saw was Agatha, her tiny, birdlike frame in the too-big plaid coat, still clutching the envelope to her chest. It took a few more seconds to recognize the man towering above her, despite the fact that he was leaning on a cane.

"Is that Harry Taylor?" Maggie asked.

"Uh-huh," I said.

Harry and Agatha's voices, not so much the words as the tone, hung in the frigid air. I didn't need to make out the words to know they were arguing. The old man reached a hand toward the envelope Agatha was holding. She shook her head vigorously, turned and began to make her way slowly along the sidewalk. Harry stayed where he was, leaning heavily on his cane.

I hesitated, looking down the street to where he stood alone on the sidewalk. I didn't want to interfere, but he wasn't well. Old Harry—Harrison—was always with one of his sons, usually Harry Junior—Young Harry—but I didn't see him or the truck anywhere.

"Harry Taylor is as tough as a boiled owl," Roma said, noticing my hesitation.

I let out a breath. She was right. But it was so cold. What was the old man doing out by himself on a night that was so cold? And why had he been fighting with Agatha?

2

"Go," I said, pulling the hood of my parka tighter against my neck.

"We can wait," Maggie said.

I shook my head. "No, it's okay. Go. Don't keep Oren waiting. I just want to make sure Harry's all right."

Roma nodded and patted her coat pocket. "Call my cell if you need anything or you want me to come back and get you."

"Thanks," I said. I hunched into my jacket and headed down to where the old man was standing. It was a clear night, the moon a thin sliver in the inky blue-black sky. Harry turned as I got to him, the expression on his face not surprise, but more like *What took you so long?*, and I had the feeling that he'd known I was up the street and would walk down to him.

"Hello," I said, pushing back my hood.

"You want to exchange pleasantries or go right to the part where you ask me what I'm doing out here when it's cold enough to freeze the brass off a bald monkey?" he asked.

"It is cold," I agreed. "What are you doing out here?"

"Without my keepers?"

"Without a ride."

"Boys are at the auction," Harry said, inclining his

head in the direction of the riverbank. "There's nothing of Cormac's I want. I've got too much junk of my own. So I decided to get some air."

I didn't say anything, but my eyebrows disappeared up under my wool hat. A sudden gust of wind blew a swirl of snow down off the roof of the store we were standing in front of.

Harry gave a halfhearted shrug. "I like snow with my air," he said.

"How do you feel about chocolate with your air?" I asked, offering my arm. "Eric has a pretty good chocolate pudding cake tonight."

"I can be flexible," he said, taking my arm with his gloved hand. "Why don't you walk me up to the restaurant so I don't get into any trouble?" He glanced behind him, but Agatha had disappeared.

"Harry, is everything all right?" I asked.

"Nothing to worry about."

That didn't really answer my question.

"How are your cats?" he asked.

"Fine," I said as we made our way very slowly toward the café. "But Hercules doesn't like the snow."

"There are days I feel the same way," he said. "Boys were after me to go south for a while, sit on a beach and have some fussy little drink with an umbrella stuck in the top. I said it's February. In February you're supposed to be wearing long johns, not some dinky swimsuit stuck up—" He caught himself and smiled. "Stuck up a palm tree."

"That does sound . . . uncomfortable," I said with a grin.

We'd made it to the door of the restaurant. "Thank you, Kathleen," Harry said, letting go of my arm and dipping his head with old-fashioned gallantry. I half expected him to sweep off his hat with its pile earflaps and bow to me. "The boys will be along in a bit."

"All right," I said.

"You figuring on standing here until you see me go inside?"

"That's pretty much my plan." I stamped my feet on the sidewalk. "Sure is cold."

He let out a snort of laughter. "I'm going, I'm going." He waved away my offered hand and reached for the door. "Go catch up with your friends before you freeze something."

"Good night, Harrison," I said.

He gave me a dismissive wave as the door closed behind him.

I pulled up my hood again and started for the community center. Snow crunched under my boots and my breath hung in the air like some sort of smoke signal to lead me.

I looked back. There was no sign of anyone. I hoped that meant Harry really was inside Eric's, waiting for his sons. On the other hand, I knew the old man was perfectly capable of doing exactly what he wanted the second I'd started walking.

Oren's truck was next to Roma's SUV in the lot at the community center. There was no sign of him, or Roma or Maggie or even Eddie, and there were definitely lights on inside. I tried the door. It was unlocked. Kicking snow off my boots, I went in.

The main auditorium was at the top of the stairs. I saw boots to the right of the door; Maggie's Sorels, Roma's pile-lined mukluks with their duct-tape patch, and big black boots that had to belong to Oren. I couldn't help grinning as I pulled off my own boots. That was Maggie, making everyone take off their outside footwear to keep the floor clean, when in a couple of days most of Mayville Heights would be clomping around inside.

Her display was at the far end of the auditorium,

along with a larger exhibit of old photographs. She stood in front of the wall, arms crossed, head cocked to one side. Roma stood beside her. Eddie was on the floor, head slumped forward as though he'd just been checked especially hard into the boards. I looked around, but didn't see Oren anywhere.

Roma caught sight of me and walked over to meet me. I gestured at the wall.

"What is this? The history of Winterfest?" Maggie had been very closemouthed about the project. She'd been sorting through old photos for months.

"Close," she said. "History of sports in Mayville." She gave me a searching look. "Harry okay?"

I nodded. "Yeah. Apparently he was at the auction and got antsy. He's meeting the boys at Eric's."

Roma shook her head. "He's a stubborn old buzzard," she said.

"I know." I couldn't help feeling uneasy. Had the old man stayed at Eric's or was he back outside?

"Is Harry okay?" Maggie asked as we joined her.

"He's at Eric's, probably halfway through a bowl of that chocolate pudding cake, waiting for the guys to finish at the auction." I gestured at the wall. "Mags, this is amazing."

Many of the pictures were black-and-white. They were grouped together with Maggie's unique perspective. Some of them had been hand tinted, and I was pretty sure the backgrounds were all Maggie's handmade paper.

The locker room, where Eddie was eventually going to be sitting on a wooden bench, looked as real as any locker room I'd ever been in.

"The lights are wrong," Maggie said.

"What's wrong with them?" I asked.

She pointed. "One should be focused on that part of the display there, and I was supposed to have two lights here in the locker room and the overall quality is just wrong." She walked over to the wall and glared up at a ceiling fixture.

"Oren went to see if he could find any bulbs in the storeroom," Roma whispered.

It was warm in the community center. I peeled off my coat, setting it on the floor along with Maggie and Roma's things.

Across the room the door to the stairs opened and Mary and Abigail came in, both carrying hangers covered with big orange plastic garbage bags.

I walked over to them. Both women worked at the library for me. Abigail was the earth-mother writer. She'd grown up with five older brothers, so she was confident and unflappable. Mary looked like every stereotype of a grandmother, and was. She was also a championship kickboxer. I'd seen her in competition. First time someone fought with her, they inevitably underestimated her gray hair and grandmotherly look. No one did that twice.

"Hey, Kathleen, what are you doing here?" Abigail asked.

"Helping Maggie finish the display," I said.

"Isn't it wonderful?" Mary said, her apple-dumpling cheeks bright red from the cold.

I gestured to the hangers. "What are you two doing here?"

"We brought the tablecloths. We thought we'd get the tables set up for Friday night," Abigail said. "We're going to be in the kitchen tomorrow night, doing the pies."

"I didn't want to leave everything till the last minute." Mary looked around. "Is Thorsten here? I don't see any tables."

I shook my head. "No, he's not. But Oren's around."

"Even better," Mary said. She turned to Abigail. "Let's get this stuff to the kitchen and finish unloading the car. Then we'll get Oren to open up the storage room so we can get the tables out." She started for the kitchen. "See you later, Kathleen."

"I'll tell Oren you're looking for him," I said. I walked back to Maggie. She had Eddie under the arms, and Roma had his feet. They were trying to get him up on to the locker-room bench, but it wasn't going very well because Maggie was paying more attention to the display than to where she was going with the dummy.

"Maggie!" Roma said sharply. "You almost knocked down that picture with Eddie's right arm."

Maggie turned at the sound of Roma's voice. Too fast, it turned out. Eddie's other arm came swinging up, carried by momentum, and smacked Maggie on the head. Her hand automatically went to the spot. "Ow!" She yelled.

Eddie's upper body hit the tile floor. The shift in weight caught Roma off balance. She went down hard on her backside, Eddie's legs bowing out on either side of her. I scrambled over to them. It probably would've been better if I hadn't laughed.

Maggie rubbed the side of her head just above her ear. "Are you okay?" I said.

"I'm all right." She looked past me at Eddie splayed on the floor. "Is he all right?"

Roma waved a hand. "I'm okay," she said. "Don't worry about me."

"All Eddie's parts seem to be attached, but I think there might be a two-minute penalty for knocking Roma over," I said. "Unnecessary roughness."

I climbed over the dummy and offered a hand to Roma. "You all right?" I asked.

She nodded. "Yeah. Luckily I landed on the part with all the padding."

Maggie was down on her hands and knees, checking Eddie carefully.

"Anything break?" I asked.

She sat back on her heels. "I don't think so," she said. "But one of the shin pads shifted."

"Not a problem," Roma said. She walked over to our coats, fished in the pocket of her parka and tossed a roll of duct tape to Maggie.

"You have a roll of duct tape in your pocket, too?" I said.

Roma grinned. "I told you. Duct tape and chocolate will fix pretty much any problem."

Maggie tore off a couple of pieces of tape and reached up under the dummy's sock. After a minute she smoothed it down and wiggled the leg. "Better," she said. She handed me the roll and smiled at Roma. "Thanks."

I slipped the tape on my arm like a fat bracelet. "Okay, why don't I grab his shoulders?" I said. "Roma, you take his feet, and, Mags, you direct us."

I slid my arms around Eddie, holding him in a kind of backward bear hug. With Maggie directing us and watching for swinging arms, we managed to get Eddie in place on the bench. Roma kneeled on the floor, keeping him steady while Maggie fastened Eddie into position. I glanced behind me. I could see Mary and Abigail moving around in the kitchen. The door to the hall swung open and Oren started across the floor toward us.

He smiled when he saw me. "Hello, Kathleen," he said. "How are you?"

"I'm well, Oren," I said. "Thanks for coming to let us in."

He gave a slight shrug. "Thorsten probably just got caught up in the auction and lost track of time. Have you seen Maggie's pictures?"

"Not yet."

"Would you like to see photograph of my father?" he asked shyly.

"Yes," I said. "Where is he?"

We walked over to the wall. Oren scanned the panels, then pointed to a scrum of young men gathered by the edge of the frozen river, probably for a pickup game of hockey. "That's him on the left."

I could see the resemblance. Oren's father had the same fair hair and rangy build. Oren himself always made me think of Clint Eastwood. "You look alike," I said.

"Everyone says that."

"Where was the picture taken?"

"You know where the marina is?" he said. "Back then they put out a wooden dock in the summer. In the winter the kids—well, the boys," he corrected himself, "played hockey. It was long before they made it deeper for the boats, so the ice froze pretty solid."

I studied the boy in the center of the picture. Like the others, his expression was serious, but there was confidence on his face. I tried to picture time adding lines around the mouth and eyes. I shifted back to Oren's face. "Is that Harrison Taylor?"

Oren nodded.

"I didn't know Harry played hockey."

"Good enough to be invited to the Black Hawks training camp. He helped coach at the high school and junior high."

That was how Harry knew Agatha, I realized, although in a place as small as Mayville everyone pretty much knew everyone else, anyway.

"These photographs are wonderful," I said to Oren. "Are there any of you?"

He shook his head. "I wasn't very athletic."

Oren had been a musical prodigy. He probably hadn't had much chance to play hockey or softball or anything like that.

I remembered then that Mary and Abigail had wanted to get out the tables.

"Oren, I forgot," I said. "Mary and Abigail are in the

kitchen. Could you let them into the storage room so they could set up the tables?"

He nodded. "Sure."

He took a couple of steps toward Maggie and Roma. "Maggie, are you all set?" he asked.

Maggie had her foot up on the edge of the bench, knee jammed against Eddie's back to keep him upright. "I am, Oren," she said. "Thank you for coming down here. I'm sorry I had to bother you."

"You didn't," he said. "I'll be here first thing in the morning if you need to get in to do anything." He smiled at me. "It was good to see you, Kathleen."

It was my opening. "Oren," I began slowly.

He turned to face me. "Yes."

"Yes?" I said.

His smile got a little bigger and he nodded.

"I haven't asked you anything."

"You were going to ask if I'd let you put my father's sculptures on display for the library's centennial celebrations."

"How did you know?"

"When you came out to look at the plan for the gazebo for the library, I think you spent more time looking at the sculptures than the plans."

"People should see his work, Oren," I said.

"You're right," he said. "I'm going to need to take some measurements at the loading dock as soon as Winterfest is over. Is that okay?"

"Yes." I wanted to jump up and down, but I settled for beaming at him.

"I'll be in to the library as soon as Winterfest is over."

I nodded, and he headed for the kitchen.

Roma was still sitting on the floor, one hand on Eddie's thigh, the other on his hip. She looked like a groupie sitting adoringly at the feet of her hockey hero. Maggie was standing on the bench, straddling Eddie.

"What can I do to help?" I asked.

"Could you find me a pair of pliers? I think they're in that box." Maggie pointed at one of the cartons that had been in the back of Roma's SUV.

After I'd handed the pliers to her I wrapped my arms around Eddie to keep him steady so Maggie could have both her hands free. From a distance I probably looked like a groupie, too.

"Why does Eddie smell like Christmas dinner?" I asked.

Roma frowned and pressed her face against Eddie's chest for a moment. "Kathleen's right. Eddie smells like stuffing."

Maggie was bending a piece of wire with the pliers. "It's sage."

"And why does Eddie smell like sage?" Roma asked.

"It helps to keep negative energy away from the project."

Maggie was kind of New Agey about some things. She taught tai chi, believed in the power of karma and had been learning about herbal medicine from my neighbor Rebecca since last summer.

"There," she said, jumping down off the bench and taking a step backward. "Kathleen, you let go first."

I slid my arms free and stood up. Eddie stayed in place.

"Okay, Roma," Maggie said.

Roma stood up, too. Nothing moved. Maggie smiled with satisfaction and started gathering boxes.

"So, will you two be at the Winterfest supper Friday night?" Roma said.

Maggie glanced at me.

"Don't," I warned.

"Don't what?" Roma asked.

"Maggie has the insane idea that I should take a date to the supper," I said.

"A date. Who?"

"Marcus Gordon," I said. Marcus was a police detective and I'd gotten to know him after I'd stumbled upon a dead body last summer. Not my favorite way to meet new people.

"What's wrong with Marcus?" Roma asked.

"He likes you," Maggie interjected.

I crossed my arms and glared at her. "He thought I killed Gregor Easton."

"You weren't really a suspect," Maggie said. "He didn't arrest you."

"That was really romantic of him," I said dryly. I looked at Roma. "Marcus Gordon is not my type." Even though he was tall, good-looking and liked cats.

"I'm not saying marry him," Maggie said. "Or kiss him, or even hold his hand. I'm just saying get to know the man."

She'd been saying that for months.

"Who knows? You might like him."

"Who knows?" I mimicked her voice. "Pigs might fly."

Roma looked at me and burst out laughing. Maggie followed her eyes and started to shake with the giggles. I tipped my head back slowly because there was no way. No way.

Overhead, a fat pink pig floated in the air just above me.

3

Mary stood, trying to look innocent and not quite getting there. There was a twinkle in her eyes and a smile was pulling at the corners of her mouth. In one hand she was holding a thin pink ribbon. The other end was attached to a helium-filled balloon. A helium-filled pig.

"Bad timing?" she asked.

"No, no, your timing was excellent," Roma said. She looked at me and started laughing again.

Maggie had the back of her hand pressed against her mouth. It didn't hide the fact that she was shaking with laughter.

"This is not a sign," I said sternly. I turned to Mary. "Can we help you with your . . . pig?"

"Yes," she said. "It's the mascot of the Horton Meat Company. They're providing the ham for the supper Friday night." She made a face. "Sam promised we'd display the pig during the supper and who knows where else, but I don't know what to do with the thing." She looked at Maggie. "Please, Maggie, do you have any ideas?"

Maggie squinted up at the balloon. "Maybe," she said. "Which door are you going to set up at?"

Mary pointed to the double doors that led in from the front hall.

"Okay, I need to take a look." Mags headed across the floor, Mary and the pig right behind her.

I turned to Roma. "So, aren't you going to say something? You know you want to."

She shook her head. "I think the flying pig pretty much said it all."

I stuck out my tongue, which only made her laugh.

While Maggie walked around in a circle, studying the ceiling by the hall doors, Roma and I gathered the empty boxes, stacking them by the parking lot entrance. By the time we had our coats and hats on, Maggie walked back over to us. I knew by the distracted look on her face that she had more than one idea brewing in her head.

"We'll drop the boxes at your studio and I'll drive you both home," Roma said.

Maggie smiled. "Thanks."

"I think I'll walk," I said, grabbing an empty carton.

"You sure?" Roma asked. "It's cold."

"It's always cold," I said, putting on my boots. "I did paperwork all day and I could use the walk."

"You want to have breakfast at Eric's in the morning?" Maggie asked.

I yawned and nodded at the same time. "Sorry," I said. "Long day."

Maggie turned to Roma. "Can you make breakfast?"

Roma looked up from lacing her boots. "Can't," she said. "I have a couple of surgeries in the morning."

We clattered down the stairs and stepped into the parking lot. I put the box I was carrying into the back of the SUV.

"Thanks, Kathleen," Maggie said, wrapping me in a hug made puffy, thanks to our heavy coats.

"You're welcome," I said. "I'll see you in the morning." I flapped my mittens at Roma. "See you, Roma."

I cut diagonally across the parking lot. I hoped Harry had met up with his sons. And I couldn't help wondering where Agatha had gone. I pulled the hood of my jacket over my hat and stuffed my hands down into the pockets of my parka.

The cloudless sky was shot with stars, but I knew snow was still coming. My left wrist ached with a bone-deep tenderness. I'd broken it last summer, and lately it seemed to ache right before we got snow. I was getting good at knowing the weather in my bones.

By the time I'd made it up Mountain Road I was happy to see my little house. I banged my heels together before stepping into the porch and kicking off my boots. Then I unlocked the kitchen door and stepped inside, flipping on the light. I didn't even have to yell, "I'm home." Owen stuck his furry gray head around one side of the doorway to the living room. Hercules, on the other hand, walked in languidly, as though he hadn't missed me at all; then he sat in the middle of the floor and began to wash his face.

I hung up my coat and set my hat and mittens over the heating vent. Roma's roll of duct tape was still on my arm. I slid it off and stuck it in my jacket pocket.

"How was your evening?" I said to Hercules as I passed him. The little tuxedo cat looked up, almost seemed to shrug and went back to cleaning his face. Owen was still watching me, looking a bit like the disembodied head of Alice in Wonderland's Cheshire cat.

"Want a piece of toast?" I asked.

"Merow?" Owen said.

"Yes, with peanut butter." He came galloping into the kitchen to supervise. Hercules abandoned all pretense of face washing and sat expectantly by the table.

Once the toast was made and generously slathered with peanut butter, I sat at the table and broke off bites for each cat, occasionally taking a bite for myself. Roma had warned me more than once not to give Owen and Hercules so much people food.

In my defense, they weren't exactly ordinary cats and the rules didn't exactly seem to apply to them.

"I saw Harrison," I said, licking peanut butter off my fingers. They both lifted their heads and looked at me. "He's fine," I said. "The boys were at an auction. Harry was . . . well, he was out doing something."

I leaned forward and offered Owen another crumb of toast. He took it from me, set it on the kitchen floor and sniffed suspiciously, the way he did with every piece of food before he ate it.

"Remember the woman from the other day?" I said to Hercules.

He lifted one paw and shook it.

"Yes, the woman who carried you up the driveway so you wouldn't get your feet wet."

Hercules made huffy noises in his throat.

"Her name is Agatha Shepherd. She was Roma's teacher." I yawned. "Roma was a juvenile delinquent," I said. "Well, almost." Owen looked at Hercules. Hercules looked at Owen, and I swear they were grinning just a little. Roma was not their favorite person. Because they'd been feral, just giving them shots and basic medical care was an ordeal. "I figured you'd like that," I said. I probably talked to the cats too much. It wasn't that I really thought they understood me. But they were good listeners.

It made me really uncomfortable to think about Agatha picking up Hercules. The cats didn't normally let anyone other than me near them. If a cat could have a crush on a person, Owen certainly had one on Maggie, but he didn't let her touch him.

The first time I'd met Harrison Taylor, I'd been flabbergasted when both cats had climbed onto his lap. Then Rebecca, my neighbor, told me Harry was dying. It made his encounter with the boys all the more unsettling.

Both Harry and Agatha were old and clearly not well.

Did Owen and Hercules know something, or was I just being paranoid?

Owen reached over and patted my leg with his paw, his way of saying *More toast, please.* I loved the little fur balls, but somehow I couldn't quite believe they knew who was going to live and who wasn't. Granted, they had some unexplainable talents, but I just didn't think that Death Psychic was one of them.

Owen woke me in the morning, about a minute or so before the clock went off. I opened one eye and stared into his wide golden ones. "I'm awake," I said. His response was to head-butt my forehead. There was no point in trying to sneak in an extra few minutes.

I sat up and stretched. "I'm up," I said to the cat, who still stared at me without blinking. "Happy?" It seemed he was, because he dropped back to the floor and padded to the door.

Both cats were sitting by the refrigerator when I went downstairs. I fed them, leaning against the counter as they ate. Owen took a morsel of food from his dish and carefully moved it to the floor, the way he always did. Hercules was about to eat when he suddenly stopped and looked up at me, his eyes going from where I was slouched by the sink, to the table and back to me. He meowed softly, tipping his head to one side.

"I'm meeting Maggie for breakfast."

He looked at the dish of food in front of him and covered his face with a paw.

"Oh, come on," I said. "You know I can't take you to Eric's. How would I explain taking a cat out for breakfast? People would think I was crazy."

Hercules continued to stare at me. Owen being Owen, he didn't pay any attention at all; he continued taking food out of his bowl one bite at a time and then eating it.

"You have a perfectly good breakfast in front of you." I rubbed the back of my neck. I already was a crazy cat lady. Someday, someone was going to catch me having a conversation with the cats and my secret would be out. Of course, as far secrets about the cats went, the fact that I talked to them like they were people was pretty tame compared to some of the other things I was hiding about them.

Deciding he'd won the stare-down, Herc dropped his head and started to eat.

I zipped around the little house, tidying up, while the cats had breakfast. Then I pulled on my boots and jacket and grabbed the broom to sweep away the snow that had drifted onto the back stoop.

Owen came up behind me and started down the side of the house. "I'm leaving in fifteen minutes," I said. His ears twitched, which either meant he'd heard and would be back in time or he'd heard and was ignoring me.

Hercules sat by the door and watched while I brushed the stairs clear. "You need boots," I said. "I bet the Grainery sells kitty boots." The Grainery was where Rebecca bought Owen's favorite catnip treat, Fred the Funky Chicken.

"They sell doggie sweaters." Herc flicked his tail at me in the universal gesture that one didn't have to understand cats to get. And then he turned and walked through the door. Literally *through* the door.

It still made my breath catch. I didn't have a clue how he did it. In fact, the first time I'd seen him walk nonchalantly through an inch-and-a-half-thick wooden door at the library, I thought I was having hallucinations or even a stroke. Because cats can't walk through doors or walls, can they?

Except Hercules could. Owen, on the other hand, couldn't. What he could do was make himself invisible when it suited him. Which was usually when it didn't suit me.

Both cats had some kind of magical abilities. Superpowers, if you will. I had no idea why or how. I had no idea if there were any other cats in Mayville Heights that could do the same thing. It's not exactly something you can bring up in conversation. I couldn't invite Roma over for coffee and then say, "Oh, by the way, any of those cats at your clinic able to walk through walls? Any of them go invisible on a whim?"

I couldn't tell anyone. At best I would look like a mentally unbalanced person, and at worst someone would want to know how Owen and Hercules did what they did. I didn't like thinking about what that might mean. Since I'd discovered what the boys could do, I'd tried to make sure no one else found out about it. Part of me kept hoping I'd discover some logical explanation, maybe some kind of genetic mutation, some leap up the evolutionary ladder. And the longer I lived with the idea the less strange it seemed.

Owen came back a minute or so before I was ready to leave. I heard him yowl at the porch door. When I opened it he darted past me into the kitchen. There was snow on his face. Unlike Hercules, Owen loved snow and had no problem sticking his head in a snowdrift if he thought there was something good in all that white stuff.

"Hold still," I said. I grabbed a towel and wiped his face. He shook his head and took a couple of swipes at his fur with one paw. "You look handsome," I assured him, patting the top of his head. I gave him a couple of kitty crackers and checked the water dishes.

"Okay, I'm leaving," I said. Owen was too busy arranging his kitty treats on the floor to do more than "Murp" in my direction. "Hercules," I called. "I'm leaving." He stuck his head in for a second, then disappeared again.

Locking the back door, I trudged around the house and down the driveway. As I walked down Mountain Road I thought again that I really needed to buy a car.

I'd left my life in Boston to move to Mayville almost a year ago, and I'd also left most of the things I owned. Because the town was small, it wasn't that hard to get around, and all the walking up and down the hill was giving me the kind of thighs I'd always envied in more athletic women. Still, there were days when it felt like I was on the edge of the Arctic Circle as I was walking to work.

Maggie was already sitting at one of the tables by the window when I got to Eric's. She waved at me through the glass.

Surprisingly, Eric wasn't behind the counter, but Claire was working again. She held up the coffeepot with a quizzical look, and I nodded. She met me at the table.

"Thank you," I said, setting my briefcase on the floor.

"Do you know what you want or would you like to see a menu?" she asked.

"I already ordered," Maggie said. "I'm starving. Go ahead."

"Could I have a couple of blueberry pancakes and the citrus bowl, please?" I said.

Claire smiled. "Got it. It'll just be a couple of minutes. We're a little slow this morning. Eric's not here."

"Eric's not here?" I'd never been in the restaurant when Eric hadn't been there.

"He broke a tooth," Claire said, making a face.

"Ow!" I winced in sympathy.

Claire gave me a wry smile. "It'll just be a few minutes," she repeated, heading to another table with the coffeepot.

My right boot was untied. I bent down, redid the laces and shook a clump of snow out of the cuff of my gray pants. "Did you get everything back to the studio last night?" I asked as I straightened up.

Maggie nodded.

"And how late did you stay working?"

"Not that late."

I looked at her.

"Okay, kind of late, but"—she leaned forward—"I figured out what to do with the pig."

"Make a BLT?" I asked.

"Ha, ha," she said.

"So?"

"So I'm not telling you. You have to wait and be surprised like everyone else."

I picked up my cup, lacing my fingers around it to warm them up.

"Can I at least have a hint?"

Maggie leaned back with her own cup. "No," she said. "If I give you a hint, you'll figure it out and the surprise is gone."

I noticed her eyes dart to the window again. "Are you waiting for someone else?"

"Ruby. She's bringing the bulbs I need for the overhead lights, and she has a couple of sets of small lights I think I might be able to use." She glanced at her watch and shook her head slightly. "New boyfriend."

"What?" I said.

"Ruby met someone. She's in the goofy, rose-colored-glasses stage. Remember, when you lose track of time because all you can concentrate on is the guy?"

"Yeah, I vaguely remember some kind of feeling like that," I said, waving my hand dismissively. I drank my coffee and thought about Andrew, who I'd left back in Boston when I left everything else. Andrew with his blue eyes, broad shoulders and great laugh. Andrew, who went on a two-week fishing trip after we'd had a fight and came back married to someone else.

I blew out a breath and blew away the memory. "Who's Ruby seeing?"

"His name is Justin. He was a counselor at an alternative school in Minneapolis. Now he's working on some kind of project to build a wilderness camp for troubled kids."

"I can't picture Ruby getting all dewy-eyed over a guy." Ruby was funny and unconventional. Her hair changed color about every two weeks, plus she had more piercings than anyone I've ever seen.

Maggie leaned over to look out the window again. "Where is—" She didn't finish the thought because the door to the restaurant flew open and a blast of cold air blew over my back. Mags turned from the window, her eyes widened and she set her cup blindly on the table.

Ruby stood in the doorway, flakes of snow swirling around her. Her hair, hot pink this week, was wind tossed, her scarf was twisted and her face was ashen.

"Somebody help me," she said, closing her eyes for a second.

I stood up. "What's wrong?"

She held out both hands helplessly and looked over her shoulder out the door. "I think she's . . ." She shook her head. "She's in the alley. She's not moving."

Everyone was staring at Ruby but no one was moving. I pulled on my coat. "Ruby, who's in the alley?" I said, crossing to the door. "Show me."

She nodded and hurried down the sidewalk, half running, half stumbling. It was slippery and the snow had drifted over the pavement in places.

Ruby led the way into the alley two doors down from the café, and stopped so suddenly I banged into her. She pointed at something with a trembling hand. I put my own hand on her shoulder. "Stay right here," I said. I could see tire tracks in the dusting of snow and crumpled fast-food wrappers.

There was something lying farther down the alley. *A bag of garbage,* I told myself as I eased closer, my heart pounding. A cat. An injured dog. My hands were shaking and I clenched them tightly in my heavy mittens. Then I stopped, because I could see what was on the ground. It wasn't a bag of garbage or a dog that had been hurt. It was a red-and-black-plaid mohair coat covered with a dusting of snow. It was Agatha Shepherd.

And she was dead.

4

Agatha lay partly on her stomach. I tried to stay in Ruby's footprints as I reached the body. It seemed pretty clear, based on the waxy appearance of Agatha's skin and the fact that she wasn't moving, that she wasn't alive, but still I felt I had to check.

I crouched in the snow and pulled off one mitten. Agatha's eyes were closed. I felt for a pulse at her neck. Nothing.

I closed my eyes for a second, silently sending up a prayer that whatever had caused the woman to die had been swift and painless. Then I got to my feet and turned back to Ruby. Maggie was beside her, one arm around Ruby's rigid shoulders. I shook my head, and Ruby sagged against Maggie.

My phone was in my briefcase back in the restaurant, I realized. "Do you have your phone?" I called to Maggie.

She pulled it out of her pocket and held it up.

"Call nine-one-one."

Maggie gave Ruby's shoulder a squeeze, took a few steps away from her and flipped the phone open. Ruby started back toward the body, and I moved to intercept her.

"Kathleen, please, can you help Agatha?" she said, gesturing at the body with a shaking hand.

I caught her by both arms and turned her away. "Maggie's getting help," I said.

"I can't leave her there covered in snow," Ruby stammered, lips quivering.

I started walking back toward Maggie. There were several people at the mouth of the alley. Maggie had her free arm extended, making it clear no one should go any farther.

"The police are on their way, Ruby," I said gently.

She looked at me as though the words had washed over her without registering. "I have a blanket in the truck," she said, swiping at her face. "I'll just . . . I'll just go . . . go get it so we can cover her up." She started to pull away from me, and I tightened my grip on her arm.

"Ruby, we can't do that."

She looked at me, stricken, tears tracing a track down each cheek. "I can't . . . I can't just leave her . . . there, like a . . . like nothing, covered in snow."

I swallowed a couple of times. "I know," I said. "But we can't touch anything, not more than we already have."

Ruby took a shaky breath.

"Did you move the . . . Agatha?" I asked. "Did you pick anything up?"

She shook her head. "I was cutting through the alley because I knew I was late and I'd had to park around the corner. When I saw her and realized . . . it was Agatha, I just ran for help. I didn't . . . I didn't touch anything." She looked back over her shoulder. "Kathleen, are you sure she's . . . ?" She didn't finish the sentence, and I hated having to be the one to destroy that faint spark of hope in her eyes.

"I'm sorry, Ruby. She is," I said softly.

She pressed a shaking hand to her mouth. The hand looked raw and red in the icy air.

Maggie half turned as we reached her. "They're on their way," she said.

I looked from Mags to Ruby and inclined my head in the direction of the café.

"Can you manage?" Maggie asked, her voice just above a whisper, realizing what I wanted.

"Police will be here any minute."

She nodded and moved to circle Ruby in a hug. "C'mon, Ruby. It's freezing. Let's go to Eric's and get some tea."

Ruby hesitated. "I should stay," she began.

"I'll stay," I said. "I promise I won't leave until the police get here."

Ruby looked down the alley again. Her whole body was shaking from shock and the cold.

"There isn't anything you can do for Agatha," I said. "You're freezing. Go with Maggie."

"Okay," she said softly.

Maggie led her away, and I stayed at the mouth of the alley, listening for sirens, my hands jammed in my pockets, shifting from one foot to the other, partly to stay warm and partly to keep the creeping sense of dread I was feeling under control.

It was only a few minutes more when the first patrol car arrived and parked, nose angled across the sidewalk. I recognized the officer who got out. He'd taken me to be fingerprinted after I'd found Gregor Easton's body last summer. He'd also been in the library a lot lately, reading everything we had about the law and law school.

I turned and pointed down the narrow passage. "She's down there."

He nodded. "Please wait here, Ms. Paulson," he said.

I watched him make his way carefully back to Agatha's body. Just as I had, he bent to check for a pulse.

"Good morning, Kathleen," a voice said behind me.

I swung around so quickly I almost lost my balance on the icy pavement. Marcus Gordon caught my arm to steady me. "Careful."

I took a step backward and regained my footing. "Thank you," I said. I tipped my head back to look at him. He seemed bigger than usual in his heavy black parka and black knitted hat. His wavy, dark hair was a bit longer these days—maybe because it was winter?

"What happened?'" he asked, his tone conversational, as though we'd just bumped in to each other on the sidewalk and were discussing all the snow. I knew from experience that once he got immersed in a case, it would be his complete focus and he'd be all business.

"That's Agatha Shepherd," I said, pointing down the alley.

His deep blue eyes narrowed and he leaned around me for a look. The young officer saw him and started toward us.

"She's dead. I couldn't find a pulse." I remembered the feel of Agatha's skin under my fingers, so, so cold.

"How did you find the body?" he asked.

"I didn't," I said.

Marcus held up a gloved finger. "Excuse me a moment," he said. He walked a few steps to intercept the officer. Heads together, Marcus did all the talking, gesturing toward the body. The other man listened and nodded. Finally Marcus walked back to me, moving me to the side with a small touch on my arm.

"So you didn't find the body? What are you doing here?"

"Maggie and I were having breakfast at Eric's. We were waiting for Ruby . . . Blackthorne to join us." I remembered Ruby's face as she stood in the doorway. "Ruby was cutting through the alley," I said. "She found Agatha."

My fingers were cold and so were my feet, despite two pairs of socks. I stuffed both hands in my pockets and shot a quick look back over my shoulder, but couldn't really see anything now.

I looked at Marcus again. "I came back here with Ruby to see if Agatha was alive." I shook my head. "Maggie called nine-one-one, and then she took Ruby back to Eric's. I waited for you."

He nodded. As usual he wasn't writing anything down. "What did you touch?"

"The collar of her coat when I felt for a pulse."

"Is that all?"

"Yes," I said.

A police van pulled up next to the police cruiser. Marcus looked back down the alley again. "That's all for now," he said. "You'll be at the library if I have any more questions?"

I nodded.

"Thanks, Kathleen." He looked at me expectantly. For a second I was confused; then I realized I was being dismissed. He was already shifting into police officer mode. I didn't think he even realized how cold that could make him seem. Without saying anything else, I turned and made my way back to the restaurant.

Maggie and Ruby were at the table. I sat down opposite them, pulling off my coat and hanging it on the back of my chair. "The police are here," I said.

Claire came over unasked and brought a new coffee cup for me. As far as I could see, Eric still hadn't shown up.

I drank from my mug, the warmth from the steaming coffee spreading through my chest. We sat in silence, and finally Ruby looked at me.

Her face was still very pale, but she seemed less distraught, like the initial shock of finding Agatha was wearing off. "Thank you for waiting for the police," she said.

I gave her a small smile. "It was nothing," I said. "Detective Gordon is going to want to talk to you."

Ruby stared down into her teacup. "I thought she was . . . I thought it was a bag of garbage that had blown into the alley," she said. "I didn't know it was Agatha until I got right up to her." She rubbed her finger along the rim of the cup.

Maggie laid a hand on her arm for a moment.

"I don't understand what she was doing in the alley in the first place." Ruby said. She picked up her cup and set it down again without drinking.

Claire arrived then with our food. I'd forgotten that we'd ordered. She set the pancakes in front of me, then hesitated. "I'm sorry for eavesdropping," she said to Ruby. "Eric let Mrs. Shepherd sleep in the back room when it was really cold. I guess she didn't always have enough money to keep her house warm. Maybe that's why she was in the alley." She reached around Ruby and gave Maggie her plate. "If you need anything, let me know."

I slid the butter pats off the small plate they'd arrived on and replaced them with one of the pancakes and a few slices of orange; then I set the plate in front of Ruby. I waited until she speared a bite of fruit and put in her mouth before I picked up my own fork.

"You know she had a stroke," Ruby said suddenly. "That's why she fell. That's why she was in that rehab center in Minneapolis."

"Then maybe it was another stroke," Maggie said. She lifted the lid of her little teapot and looked around for Claire.

"She hated that place," Ruby said. "Maybe she left too soon."

Maggie finally managed to catch Claire's eye. She held up the teapot and the waitress nodded and reached for a carafe of water.

After she'd dropped another tea bag into Maggie's pot and poured the hot water, I touched her arm. "Claire, could I have two large coffees to go, please?" I said.

"Sure. The usual?"

I shook my head. "No. Double cream, double sugar in one, and could you just add a creamer and a couple of packets of sugar on the side for the other?"

"Not a problem," she said. "I'll get them for you when you're ready to leave so they'll be hot."

"Thanks," I said.

Maggie leaned back in her chair. "Ruby," she asked. "How did you get to be one of Agatha's . . ." She hesitated.

"Projects?" Ruby asked.

"Well, I was going to say 'kids,'" Maggie said. "But, yeah, I guess projects."

"Roma said Agatha was the reason she became a vet," I said.

"She's the reason I'm an artist," Ruby said. "She busted me for tagging—spray-painting graffiti on the side of the school." She put down her fork. "I couldn't run as fast as my so-called friends, and it turned out Agatha was pretty fast for what I considered an old lady."

"She nabbed you." Maggie said.

Ruby picked up a slice of grapefruit with her fingers and ate it. "By the scruff of my neck, literally. When I wouldn't rat out the others, she said I could scrub the entire wall myself." Her smile got a little bigger. "When I tried to argue the artistic value of tagging, she made me write a three-page essay explaining my reasoning. She used that and a painting I'd done to get me a place in a six-week summer art camp."

"It sounds like she had a way of figuring out what people cared about," I said.

"Yeah, she did," Ruby said. "She had a way of looking right inside you, into places you didn't show any other person. On the other hand, she could be stubborn. She made me scrub that wall until there wasn't a dab of paint left."

She ran a hand through her pink, spiked hair, and glanced at her watch. Then she turned to Maggie. "I have to open the store." The artist's cooperative both Maggie and Ruby were part of ran a store and gallery in the same building where Maggie taught tai chi.

"Why don't you let me do that for you today?" Maggie said, setting down her cup.

Ruby studied her hands for a minute. "Thanks, but I'd rather do it. I'd rather be busy than keep thinking about what happened."

Maggie nodded. "Okay, but why don't I walk with you? I'm going that way anyway."

I stood up. "I'm going to get my coffee," I said. I gestured at the table. "And I've got this."

"You sure?" Maggie said, reaching for her coat.

"Uh-huh. I'll be right back." The café was beginning to fill up. As I stood at the counter, waiting for Claire, I overheard conversations around me. The news about Agatha was already spreading.

I paid for breakfast and collected my two cups of coffee. Claire had put a couple of sugar packets, a creamer, and a stir stick into a little waxed-paper bag and rolled down the top. She handed me everything. There was a P on one of the lids.

"That one is just coffee," she said. "P for 'plain.'"

I thanked her and walked back to the table. Maggie held the cups while I shrugged into my coat and pulled on my hat and mittens. After I slid the strap of my briefcase over my head, she gave me both coffees. Their warmth seeped into my fingers.

As we stepped outside a man cut across the street, dodging cars. "Ruby," he called. She turned in his direction and her face lit up. When he reached us, he put an arm around Ruby and gave her a quick hug. *This has to be the new boyfriend,* I thought, which Ruby confirmed when she turned back to us.

"Kathleen, this is Justin," she said.

"You're the librarian," he said.

I nodded. "I am."

He stuffed the knitted hat he was holding into his pocket and offered his hand, and I held up the two coffee cups to show I couldn't shake his.

He gave me an easy smile and said, "Nice to meet you."

He was about average height, with longish dark hair slicked back from a widow's peak and angular features. He smelled like hair gel.

"You remember Maggie," Ruby said.

Justin turned to Maggie. "I do," he said. "Hi, Maggie."

"Hi," she said.

"I'm so glad I caught you," he said. "I found those lights you were looking for."

He patted the black nylon bag on his hip. He had a couple of elastics around one wrist and a silver skull bracelet on the other.

Ruby pressed a hand to her head. "I forgot all about them. They're for Maggie."

He opened the flap of his carryall and handed Maggie a plastic bag.

"Thanks," she said.

Ruby glanced down the street and gave an involuntary shiver.

Justin followed her gaze. "What's going on down there?" he asked.

Ruby closed her eyes for a second and took a couple of deep breaths. "It's . . . it's . . . Remember I introduced you to Agatha Shepherd?"

Justin nodded slowly, his eyes narrowed. "Yeah."

"She's, uh, dead," Ruby said.

"Hey, I'm so sorry." He caught one of her hands and

gave it a squeeze. Then he looked from me to Maggie. "What happened?"

Maggie shrugged. "Stroke, maybe. She was old."

Ruby swallowed hard. "I was cutting through the alley, and she was lying . . ." She didn't finish.

Justin folded her into a hug. "That's horrible. What can I do?"

Ruby broke out of the embrace and pushed stray bits of hair out of her face.

"Nothing really," she said. "I'm . . . all right."

The coffee was going to get cold if I stood there any longer. "Guys, I'd better get going," I said.

Ruby turned to me and touched my arm. "Thank you, Kathleen," she said.

"You're welcome." I smiled at Justin. "Nice to meet you."

"Yeah, you, too," he said.

I caught Maggie's eye. "I'll see you at class tonight." She nodded.

I started down the sidewalk while the others headed in the opposite direction, toward the artists' co-op. Officer Craig was standing at the mouth of the alley, which was already taped off and partly blocked with a couple of town sawhorses. There were a few people hanging around watching, but not that many. I eased my way over to the young police officer and handed him the coffee cup and the little bag of sugar and cream. "I thought you might be getting cold," I said.

"Thank you," he said, taking the cup.

"There's cream and sugar in the bag." I held out the other cup. "Would you give this to Detective Gordon, please?"

There was a brief flash of surprise on his face, but it quickly disappeared. "Yes, ma'am, I will."

"Stay warm," I said. It was what everyone said in Mayville Heights in the winter.

I skirted out around the police van, still angled near the curb, and took the opportunity to have a look down the alley. I couldn't see much, just Marcus and a couple of other people standing over Agatha Shepherd's body, which was still lying on the snowy ground. A shiver crept up the back of my neck. Maggie and Ruby seemed convinced that the old woman had had a second stroke. I hadn't wanted to upset Ruby by disagreeing.

I'd seen blood on Agatha's coat and on the pavement. And her arm was twisted at an unnatural angle.

I didn't know what had happened to her, but I was pretty sure it had been violent.

5

Abigail came up the steps just as I was unlocking the wrought-iron security gate at the main entrance of the library. The gate was mostly decorative now that the building had a proper security system. I punched in the code on the keypad and waited for the light to turn green before I opened the doors.

Behind me Abigail turned on the lights. "It looks good, doesn't it?" she said, pushing the scarf off her head. Her hair, a beautiful mix of red and silver, was pulled back in its usual braid. She smiled at me. "I know, I know. I keep saying that, but I can't get over how amazing this place looks now." She gestured to the mosaic tile floor. "Every once in a while I flash back to that bilious turquoise indoor-outdoor carpet that was on the floors."

I rolled my eyes at the memory. "That was pretty bad."

Abigail started for the stairs and the second-floor staff room. I headed up behind her. "You want coffee?" she asked. "I'll start it."

"Please," I said.

I unlocked my office, dumped my bag on my desk chair, hung up my coat and then bent to take off my boots. Something was caught in the cuff of my pants— probably another chunk of frozen snow.

I started to turn the fabric inside out to dump whatever it was onto the floor when I realized it wasn't a dirty piece of snow caught in my pants; it was a broken piece of glass. How had I gotten that stuck in my cuff?

I went to pull it loose and then stopped myself. I'd bent down in the alley next to Agatha's body when I'd felt for a pulse that hadn't been there. There had been tire tracks and other bits of detritus in the sand and snow near the body. Had I picked up the piece of glass there? If someone had run Agatha down, the jagged piece of broken glass caught in my pants cuff could be evidence.

I reached for my bag. I had Marcus Gordon's card with his cell number in my wallet. He'd given it to me the previous summer when my house had been broken into. Now I used the number.

I wasn't surprised to get his voice mail. I left a brief message explaining that I might have found something connected to Agatha's death and then hung up. I pushed back the sleeves of my sweater and turned around.

Marcus was standing in my doorway. Startled, I made a strangled sound halfway between choking and gargling.

"I'm sorry," he said. "I didn't mean to scare you."

"It's okay," I said, leaning back against the desk. "I just left you a message."

He pulled out his cell and flipped it open. "So you did. Was there something you forgot to tell me?"

"No." I pointed to my pant leg. "There's a piece of glass caught in my cuff. I think I might have picked it up in the alley when I bent down to check on Agatha. It wasn't there when I got to the café this morning."

He tipped his head and looked down at me. I was five foot six; he was taller, over six feet, so tall that I always felt little in his presence. "How can you be sure it came from the alley?"

"Because the laces on my boot came undone when I

was at the café and I dumped snow out of that cuff. I would've felt a piece of glass."

"Did you walk over here?"

"Yes," I said, shifting so the edge of the desk wasn't digging into my backside. "On the sidewalk all the way."

He gestured at my leg. "May I?"

"Go ahead."

I put my foot up on the seat of one of the black faux-leather chairs that flanked my desk. "The inside edge of the cuff," I said.

He pulled a thin purple glove from his pocket and put it on. Then he reached into the fold of fabric and carefully pulled out the piece of glass, holding it by the edges with his thumb and forefinger. He had huge hands. He stood up and looked around. "Do you have an envelope to put this in?" he asked.

"I think so," I said. I dropped my foot and squeezed past him to get to my desk drawer. He smelled citrusy—a bit like one of those drinks with a tiny plastic sword skewering a wedge of lime. I shook my head. Why the heck was I smelling the man? Most of the time I didn't even like him.

I held up a business-sized envelope. "Will this do?"

"That's perfect."

I held open the top and he dropped the piece of glass inside; then I handed the whole thing over to him.

He sealed the top and put the envelope into the pocket of his coat. "Thank you," he said.

"You're welcome."

He didn't move.

"Was there something else you wanted to ask me?" I said.

"I just have a couple of questions."

I gestured to the chairs. "Have a seat."

He made a dismissive gesture with one hand. "I'm okay," he said.

I didn't want to sit down if he wasn't and have him looming over me like a cop in an old black-and-white movie, so I stayed standing, as well. "What did you want to know?"

"You were meeting Ms. Adams and Ms. Blackthorne at the restaurant. What time did you get there?"

"I was meeting Maggie," I said. "She told me Ruby was coming, as well, because she had the lightbulbs Maggie needed for the Winterfest display. And as for when I arrived, I'd say about seven thirty. Maggie was already there."

He crossed his arms over his chest. "How long before Ms. Blackthorne showed up?"

I shrugged. "Five minutes, maybe," I said. "Less than ten, for sure. We'd ordered, but our food hadn't arrived and I hadn't finished my first cup of coffee."

He nodded and I guessed he was filing the information away somewhere in his head. "So, you went to the alley to check on Mrs. Shepherd?"

I nodded.

"Why?"

"Why?" I repeated.

He shifted from one foot to the other. "Why didn't you just call nine-one-one, or at least let someone else go take a look?"

I exhaled slowly, trying to get rid of some of the irritation Marcus always seemed to make me feel.

"I didn't know there was a reason to call nine-one-one," I explained. "Ruby was ... upset, and the alley's dark. Maybe she hadn't seen what she thought she had. As for why me"—I gestured toward my boots standing on a square of newspaper under the coatrack—"Maggie had boots with heels, and I didn't. The sidewalk was icy and I could move a lot faster than she could."

He looked at the boots and for a moment I thought he was going to walk over to pick them up. But he didn't. "So, you got to the alley. What did you do then?"

"I could see that there was something on the ground about halfway down. I couldn't tell if it was a person or maybe a bag of garbage that had just blown there."

I folded my own arms across my chest, mimicking his stance. "I told Ruby to stay at the end of the alley while I walked down to see who it was. As I got closer I could see that it was Agatha, and I could see that she was dead."

"How did you know that?" he asked.

"That wasn't my first dead body," I said dryly. "But as I told you, I felt for her pulse."

"Did you touch anything else besides the body?" He unfolded his arms and turned his head from one side to the other to stretch his neck.

"No," I said slowly and clearly. He'd already asked me this, so there was obviously some reason he was intent on going over it again. "I didn't touch anything else. I walked down and back, and I tried to stay in Ruby's footsteps. When I realized I couldn't do anything for Agatha, I went back to Ruby. Maggie was with her, and I asked Maggie to call nine-one-one because my phone was in my briefcase, which was still in the restaurant."

I held up a hand before he could speak. "Ruby was cold and I was afraid she might go into shock, so I got Maggie to take her back to Eric's while I waited for you to show up. That's it."

He nodded again and felt in his pocket for something. "Did you know Mrs. Shepherd?" he asked.

"No," I said. "I'd seen her a few times in the past couple of days, but I didn't know who she was until she came into Eric's last night and I asked Roma—Dr. Davidson."

I thought about Agatha and Old Harry Taylor standing on the sidewalk, arguing. I didn't see how that had anything to do with Agatha's death, so there didn't seem to be any reason to tell Marcus and have him start bothering the old man.

I leaned back against the desk and stretched my legs in front of me, crossing one foot over the other. "Is there anything else?"

He smiled, almost. "I can't think of anything else. Thank you." He touched his pocket. "And thank you for calling me when you found the piece of glass."

I gave him a small smile. "You're welcome," I said.

He started for the door and then stopped and turned back to me. "Any chance you'd be available to help me out at Wisteria Hill tomorrow morning?"

There was still a colony of feral cats living out at the old Henderson estate, Wisteria Hill. Roma had a group of volunteers taking care of them. Marcus was one. So was I.

I ran through what I had planned for Friday morning: laundry, housecleaning—nothing that couldn't be put off. And I have a soft spot for Wisteria Hill. It's where I found Owen and Hercules, or to be more exact, where they'd found me.

I nodded. "I can help you."

He smiled for real then. "Thanks. I'll pick you up about eight, if that's okay."

I still found it disconcerting, the way he could switch from being coolly professional to almost friendly. "It is," I said.

"I'll call you if something changes."

"You mean if you find the person who hit Agatha."

He didn't even blink. "You think someone hit Mrs. Shepherd?" he said, standing there so unconcerned, feet apart with his hands in his pockets.

"I think a car or truck hit her, yes." I pointed at his pocket. "The broken glass, the blood soaked into her coat, tire tracks in the alley. She didn't have a stroke." I straightened and faced him head-on, almost challenging him to tell me I was wrong.

He looked at me for a long, silent moment. "You're very observant, Kathleen," he said finally.

I waited for something else, some admission that I was right, but all he did was pull on his gloves.

"Have a nice day, Kathleen," he said. This time he made it all the way to the door before he turned around.

I was already reaching for my briefcase.

"Kathleen."

I turned.

"Thanks for the coffee."

He was gone before I could say "You're welcome."

I took my laptop and the file about the reference books I wanted to order out of my briefcase and set the bag next to my boots, under the coatrack. Then I walked down to the front desk, where Abigail was sorting the books from the book drop, peering through her rimless reading glasses.

"I let Detective Gordon in. Was that all right?" she said.

"Yes, it was."

"He's kind of cute in a chiseled-jaw, broad-shouldered, Dudley Do-Right kind of way," Abigail said, a hint of a smile making her lips twitch.

"Don't you start, too," I said. "I'm not interested in him. He's not my type."

She held up one hand. "Okay, whatever you say," she said in a tone that meant she didn't quite believe me. "So, what was Detective Do-Right here for?"

"Do you know Agatha Shepherd?" I asked.

"Not really. I know who she is." She looked up, her face serious. "Something happened to her?"

I nodded. "She's dead. Ruby found her body. You know the alley that turns and runs behind Eric's?"

She nodded.

"Ruby was cutting through to meet Maggie and me at the café."

"Poor Ruby," Abigail whispered. "Wasn't Agatha in a rehabilitation hospital? She's only been home for, what, maybe a week?" She shook her head. "It doesn't seem fair. Was it another stroke?"

I flashed back to the dark stain of blood soaked into the plaid mohair coat. "I . . . I don't know," I said. "Detective Gordon didn't say."

"She was a good principal," Abigail said. "She helped a lot of kids." She glanced down the desk and made a face. "Kathleen, I'm sorry I forgot to tell you that Susan called. She won't be in until after lunch."

"Are the twins sick?" I asked. I remembered that Eric hadn't been at the café. It wasn't like either of them to miss work.

"She didn't say, but I'm guessing that was probably it. She sounded pretty frazzled."

"And Eric wasn't at the café this morning. I think Claire said he broke a tooth."

Abigail winced in sympathy. "I can hold down the fort for a while. Kate will be here soon." Kate was our work-study student from the high school.

"You have story time." As well as working part-time at the library, Abigail was also a children's author. She often read some of her own stories to the kids. I never quite knew what was going to happen at story time—one morning I'd come in to find all the children wearing foil hats with pom-pom antennae—and I liked that.

I glanced at my watch. "I'll try Mary."

"Okay," Abigail said as she went back to checking in books.

I went back up to my office and called Mary at home.

"I can be there in about a half hour," she said. "Only

thing you're taking me from is a heap of laundry, and it won't miss me."

I thanked her, hung up and went back down to tell Abigail that Mary was on her way.

It was nine o'clock. Abigail had turned on the rest of the library lights, and I unlocked the front doors. I started going down a mental list of what needed to be done that morning.

"I'll get the rest of the books from the book drop," Abigail said. "Coffee's ready. Strong, the way you like it."

"Thank you," I said. "I've had only one cup this morning."

"Should we unleash you on an unsuspecting world when you're down at least two cups?" she asked, struggling to keep a straight face.

I looked at her thoughtfully for a moment. "No," I said. We both laughed.

Abigail's face grew serious again. "Kathleen, I didn't ask you. Is Ruby all right?"

"She was a little shaky," I said. "She's working in the store this morning and she decided she still wanted to do it. Maggie went with her."

"I'm glad she's okay."

I thought about Ruby standing there, hunched against the cold at the mouth of the alley, trembling with Maggie's arm around her. "So am I," I said.

Abigail brushed off the cover of a big coffee-table book about the Sahara. "It just doesn't seem fair," she said again. "I can't believe Agatha's dead."

There was a crash behind me. I jumped and swung around.

Harrison Taylor was standing there, his face ashen, his cane on the floor beside him.

6

"Harry, are you all right?" I said.

It took a second for him to focus on me. "Oh, yes ... I'm—I'm getting clumsy in my old age." He started to reach for his cane, but I bent down and picked it up for him.

"Thank you, my dear," he said. His color still wasn't good, I noticed as he took the carved, black walking stick from me. He ran a hand over his chin, twisted finger joints pulling at the skin on his hand, which seemed as thin as tissue paper.

"Did I hear you right, Kathleen?" he asked, blue eyes troubled. "Is Agatha Shepherd ... dead?"

I nodded, putting a hand on his shoulder. I was surprised when he lifted his own hand and put it over mine. "I'm sorry," I said softly.

"Me, too," the old man said.

His son came in then. "There you are," he said, a touch of exasperation in his voice. "I went back to the truck and you weren't there."

"That's because I'm here," Harrison retorted.

"I can see that," Harry—the younger—said dryly. "I told you to wait in the truck."

"Well, I'm not six years old," Harrison said. "And I didn't want to sit in the truck."

Harry opened his mouth to say something else, and then it seemed our expressions or maybe the way we were standing registered with him. "What's wrong?" he asked, and all the aggravation was gone from his voice.

I glanced at the old man first. He met my gaze for a moment and looked down. "It's Agatha Shepherd," I began. I gave Old Harry's arm a gentle squeeze and then let go. "She's . . . dead."

The younger man's face paled. "Dad, I'm sorry," he said. "You, uh, worked with Agatha. You knew her."

"I did," Harrison said. I noticed how tightly he was gripping his cane.

Harry Junior took off his cap and ran a hand over his scalp. He looked at me. "What happened?"

I tried not to think about Agatha's body lying in that alley, or her and Harry arguing on the sidewalk, the anger between them crackling in the cold night air. "I don't think anyone knows for sure," I finally said.

He looked at his father. "You okay?"

"I wouldn't mind sitting down," the old man said. "And if that's coffee," he gestured toward Abigail's mug, "I wouldn't mind a cup of that, either."

"You're not supposed to be drinking more than one cup of coffee."

Harrison fixed his gaze on his son. "If I always did what I was supposed to do, you wouldn't be here."

Harry sighed. "You're a stubborn old far—" He looked at me and caught himself. "Man," he said instead.

"Go do whatever it was you came to do," the old man said. "I can stay here with Kathleen. Maybe I'll poke a few books back on the shelf for her."

"I can always use an extra set of hands," I said. I turned to Harry. "Go ahead. We're fine."

He hesitated. His mouth worked, but in the end all he said was, "Fine." Then he turned and went back out the front doors.

"Would you like that cup of coffee now?" I asked Harrison.

"Please," he said. "Before the Food Police comes back."

I gestured across the library to the computer room. "There are a couple of chairs by the window. Have a seat and I'll go get it."

He smiled at me, and I couldn't help thinking how much he looked like Santa Claus with his warm, blue eyes and white hair and beard. If I hadn't seen him arguing with Agatha, I wouldn't have believed it. There was no way an old man who could pass for Kriss Kringle had any connection to Agatha Shepherd's death.

He made his way across the tile floor toward the big windows looking out over the water. I turned to the front desk and mouthed *Watch him* to Abigail, who nodded. Then I went upstairs and poured coffee for Harry. I set the carton of cream, several packets of sugar and a spoon next to the cups on a black plastic tray and carried the whole thing down the stairs.

Abigail was on the phone. "Come get me if you need help," I whispered. She nodded without looking up.

Harry had taken off his coat and hat. I wondered why he had so much thick hair and his son had so little.

There was a low table under the window. I pulled it closer with my foot and then set the tray on top.

Harry noticed the carton of coffee cream. "Ahh," he said, approvingly. "The good stuff."

"I didn't know how you took it," I told him, as he poured cream into the cup.

"A little cream and three sugars," he said, reaching for the paper packets. "Because I'm a sour old coot."

"You are not," I said.

He put the sugar in his coffee, stirred and then took a sip. "Mmmm, that's good coffee."

"Thank Abigail." I told him. "She made it."

"I will," he said.

I took a drink from my own cup. Harrison was right. It was good coffee. I shifted sideways, watching as he settled himself a little more comfortably in the chair. Some inner resilience had taken over.

Balancing the cup on the arm of the chair, he looked at me. "Are you going to ask me about Agatha?" he said.

I wasn't really surprised by the question. "It's not any of my business."

"Not a lot of secrets in a small place like this."

I had to smile at that. Sometimes it was annoying how quickly news spread through Mayville. On the other hand, I was growing to like the fact that people knew me, that I was starting to belong.

The old man studied his left hand for a long moment, and I wondered what he was really seeing—some image from the past? Abruptly, he looked up at me again. "You probably figured out that I knew Agatha pretty well."

The fact that they had been standing on the street in the cold, arguing, did make it pretty clear that Harry and Agatha had been more than casual acquaintances. I remembered Oren saying Harry had coached the junior-high hockey team.

"You were friends," I said.

He took another sip of his coffee. "Years ago, yes. We had a falling-out. We hadn't spoken in years."

Okay, I wasn't expecting that.

"You're surprised," he said.

I twisted the mug in my hands. "A little," I admitted. He didn't seem the type to stay angry for so long.

"I was stubborn. She was stubborn." There was regret on his face and sadness, too.

"Is that what you were angry about last night?" I asked. "That same falling-out?"

His expression changed. For a moment it softened. "I

can't tell you what we were arguing about. I can tell you it had nothing to do with her dying."

I took a long drink from my coffee while I figured out what to say next. "Harry, the police are going to hear about that argument you had with Agatha," I said finally. "I probably wasn't the only person who saw you two."

His jaw tightened. "Kathleen, how did she die?" he asked.

"I don't know."

He stared at me intently. "There's something you're not saying. Don't humor me because I'm an old man."

I swallowed and took a moment to set my cup back on the tray. "Agatha was found in the alley that runs behind the back of the buildings on Main Street."

"Was it her heart, or did she fall?"

I leaned forward in the chair. "I don't know, Harry. Really, I don't."

"But you think you know."

"I only saw her long enough to see for certain that she was . . . gone."

"Good Lord," he muttered. "You think someone . . . I didn't kill Agatha."

I reached out a hand to him. "Harry, I know that," I said. "Maybe . . ." I stopped. I'd been going to say that maybe Agatha had had a stroke. But I didn't really believe that. I leaned an elbow on the arm of the chair.

"Harry, the police are going to have questions. It's their job. Detective Gordon is investigating Agatha's death. He has integrity. Whatever you tell him won't get spread out around town."

Harrison shook his head. "I know you mean well, Kathleen," he said, edging forward in the chair so he could set his own cup on the tray. "But I gave my word and that still means something to me. Agatha isn't here to release me from that promise, so I intend to honor it."

I pressed my lips together and didn't say anything.

"I suppose it seems old-fashioned to you."

It seemed foolhardy to me, but I didn't say that. "I didn't know Agatha," I said. "But from what I've heard, she cared about the people close to her. Roma told me about the kids she helped, how she changed their lives."

He smiled. "It's true. She wouldn't give up on a kid. She was like a dog with a bone."

"So would she want you to maybe get into trouble with the police because of a promise you made to her? Especially when she isn't here?"

He slowly shook his head. "It's not the same thing. Agatha's word was her bond. I may not have always liked that, but I will honor it."

I wasn't going to change his mind. "Then I respect your decision," I said.

"You still think I'm wrong," he countered.

"I think you have to do what you think is right." I reached over and patted his hand. "And I am sorry about Agatha. Truly."

His eyes were sad again. "The last words we had were angry. I do regret that. Maybe that's why I feel I have to keep my word to her. I can't take back what I said."

Just then there was a sound behind us. I turned. Young Harry was standing there. "Time to go," he said.

The old man struggled to his feet. I hovered in case he needed any help, but he waved me away. He struggled into his heavy coat, and handed me his cane while he pulled on his hat. "Thank you for the coffee and conversation," he said.

I smiled. "You're welcome." I handed him back his cane. He started for the door.

"Thanks, Kathleen," Harry Junior said.

"Anytime. I enjoyed the visit," I said.

Once they were gone I took the tray upstairs. By lunchtime I'd finished the final report on the refurbishment of the library and e-mailed it over to Everett Henderson's secretary, Lita. Everett had funded the library renovations as a gift to the town.

Kate knocked on my open door midmorning. She was wearing purple-and-black striped leggings with a long purple sweater and black high-tops that she'd jazzed up with glued-on rhinestones. She had an evaluation sheet from her teacher for me to fill out. "You can fax it back to the school," she said.

I promised I'd get the paperwork to her teacher by the end of the day. I had nothing but positive things to say about her and the work-study program. Kate worked hard, showed up early and was great with the little ones who came to story time. She'd even persuaded me to let her put a camera in the library storage room to shoot pictures of the riverfront for a school art project.

I covered the front desk while Abigail took her lunch, checking out piles of picture books for the four-year-olds who had been at story time. Susan came in about twelve thirty. When she caught sight of me at the desk, for a second she looked . . . guilty? This was the first time she'd missed work, except for a day in the fall when both of the twins had fallen out of the same tree on the same day.

"I'm sorry about this morning," she said, standing in front of the desk, twisting her wedding ring around her finger.

"That's okay," I said, smiling so she'd see I meant it. "How's Eric?"

"Eric?" She swallowed a couple of times. "Oh, he's—he's fine. This didn't have anything to do with him." She made an elaborate shrug. "The twins . . . They ate something they shouldn't have."

"Oh," I said. "Do you want to take the rest of the day? Mary's here and I could get her to stay."

Susan shook her head, which her set her topknot bobbing. Usually Susan had something stuck in it—a chopstick, a pencil, a swizzle stick—but today it looked as if she'd just grabbed an elastic and quickly piled her hair on her head. A few curls were loose around her face.

"It's okay, really. The boys are good." She smiled, but it was forced. "You know how kids are, projectile vomiting one minute and then tearing up the house the next."

She hesitated for a second. I'd never seen her so fidgety. "So I'll just get rid of my stuff," she said. "Do you want me to put the new magazines out?"

"Please," I said. "They're in the workroom."

"Okay."

I watched her head up the stairs, wondering what was really wrong. Something was making her jumpy and evasive. When she'd been talking to me her eyes kept slipping off my face, and her story about the twins having eaten something that made them sick sounded fishy.

Claire had said that Eric hadn't come into the restaurant because he'd broken a tooth. Was that true, or was it something else that had Susan acting funny?

Susan was generally sunny and kind of snarky. Eric, in contrast, was serious and intense. I liked them both and hoped things were okay between them.

It occurred to me then that Susan hadn't said a word about Agatha Shepherd. The alley extended behind the restaurant and on behind the next building. Someone had to have called Eric at home to let him know what happened. Maybe that's why Susan didn't seem like herself. Claire had said Eric sometimes let Agatha sleep in the back of the restaurant. Maybe Susan felt bad. Maybe Eric felt guilty for Agatha being in the alley in the first place.

Abigail came through the door then, snow coating her shoulders and scarf. She stamped her feet on the mat and some of the snow fell off. "It's snowing," she said. "Again." She glanced back over her shoulder. "It's never going to stop, you know." She looked at me again. "I quit, Kathleen. I'm going to move to some island where I don't have to put on four layers of clothing before I go outside."

She grabbed the front of her parka and shook it at me. "I'm a whole person smaller underneath all of this."

"I can see that," I said.

"I'm going somewhere where I can wear a grass skirt and a coconut bra," she continued, kicking the last of the snow off her feet.

"Sounds itchy," I said.

She shot me a withering look and headed for the stairs. "I got splashed twice—*twice*—on my way back. What is it about snow that makes people behave like such jerks?"

It was pretty clear that was a rhetorical question, so I didn't say a word as she clomped up the steps. From what I'd seen it wasn't bad weather that made people behave badly; they could do that no matter what it was like outside.

7

It snowed on and off all afternoon. It was off when Abigail and I came out of the library at just after five o'clock. She gave me a ride up the hill in her truck. With its oversized knobby tires that truck probably could have driven up out of the bottom of the Grand Canyon. I made a mental note that when I bought a vehicle, I would get tires like that. Whatever the heck they were.

Hercules came into the kitchen as I was hanging up my coat. He twisted around my legs, and I bent to pick him up. "Where's your brother," I asked, scratching behind his ear. "He'd better not be sleeping on the footstool. How many times have I told him to stay off it?"

Hercules was suddenly engrossed in something over my left shoulder. I headed for the living room, still carrying the cat, who made garbled noises in his throat like he was trying to clear it.

We found Owen sitting on the rug beside the aforementioned footstool, all round-eyed cat innocence. "I know where you were," I said.

He looked at the footstool and then back to me, the picture of kitty bafflement.

"And you," I said to Hercules. "I'm not fooled by that hacking-up-a-fur-ball routine you were doing." I gave him one last scratch before setting him on the rug. Then I bent down to Owen. "Stay off the footstool," I hissed.

He licked my chin.

Both cats trailed me while I changed my clothes and heated a bowl of chicken soup I'd made over the weekend. I told them about Agatha, about Ruby, about Harry Taylor. Saying it all out loud helped me sort out things in my mind.

I fished chunks of chicken and carrot out of the pot and shared them with the cats. After I'd eaten about half my soup, I set down my spoon and leaned my elbows on the table. Owen immediately looked up from the piece of chicken he was suspiciously sniffing.

"There's something off about what happened to Agatha," I said. Herc looked up from his dish. "Marcus wouldn't say so, but she didn't have another stroke." Owen's ears twitched. "Yes, he has the case, assuming there is a case."

Marcus had been at my house several times last summer. He'd tried to win over the cats—at least Owen. Hercules had pretty much ignored Marcus, but Owen, who could be bought for a handful of kitty treats, had been friendly—well, at least as friendly as he got.

I picked up my spoon again. The cats exchanged looks. Sometimes I thought they were in cahoots with Maggie and her efforts to play matchmaker. I reminded myself that they were just cats.

I scooped up a spoonful of noodles. "All right, I admit he's a good police officer, but he's a frustrating person." What I didn't say was that I'd enjoyed the times during the summer that we'd ended up having breakfast together. Marcus could be funny and charming when he wasn't being RoboCop. If he wasn't a police officer maybe we could be better friends.

I ate the rest of my soup while Owen and Hercules

finished their chicken and carrots, exchanging glances and soft cat mumbles.

"I'm in the room and I can hear you talking about me," I said. That didn't get any reaction. I talked to the cats like they were people, not that I would admit that to anyone. I didn't want to be known as the Crazy Cat Librarian. Part of it was probably living by myself—well, living by myself except for Owen and Hercules. And part of it was the fact that they weren't exactly run-of-the-mill house cats.

They'd helped me figure out what had happened to Gregor Easton last summer. And when the house was broken into, Hercules had gone for help while Owen had helped me knock out the intruder. How exactly could I explain that to anyone without coming across as though I were a few kitty treats short of a batch?

"Okay," I said, getting up to put my dishes in the sink. "Since you like Marcus so much, you'll be happy to hear I'm going out to Wisteria Hill with him in the morning."

Hercules, who had finished eating, walked by me without making a sound, although he did flick his tail at my leg.

"Don't get too excited," I called after him. "It doesn't mean I'm going to go out with the guy." He flicked his tail at me again and disappeared into the living room.

It was snowing lightly as I walked down to tai chi. I rubbed my wrist through the sleeve of my quilted coat. So far it was a better forecaster than the meteorologist on Channel 2, who had predicted clear skies and sunshine through Saturday.

Rebecca was at the top of the stairs outside the studio, changing her boots for shoes, when I got to class. Rebecca was my backyard neighbor, although several feet of snow on the ground meant we couldn't cut across each other's yards right now, so I didn't get to see her as much as I usually did. She smiled and hugged me. I dwarfed her in my huge coat.

"Kathleen, it's so good to see you," she said, standing back to give me the once-over. She'd been out of town and had missed the last two tai chi classes.

"How was your trip?" I asked.

"Wonderful." Her smile got even bigger. "I almost came home with green hair."

I leaned back and pretended to consider it. "Nah," I said, shaking my head. "I think blue is more your color."

She laughed.

"So you got to the hair-products show with your friends," I said. Rebecca had been a hairdresser before she retired.

"I did. Would you believe orange hair is the thing for spring?"

I made a face.

She leaned forward and tucked an errant strand of hair behind my ear. "Your hair is growing out nicely."

Rebecca was slowly fixing a disastrous pixie hairdo I'd come to Mayville Heights with last year. A huge fashion error, it had been part of my plan to show I could be spontaneous. I'd learned I could be spontaneous—if I planned for it.

She waited while I took off my outside clothes and changed my shoes, and told me a little more about her visit with several of the women she'd studied hairdressing with.

I got the feeling the green hair was more of a possibility than I'd first thought.

"I almost forgot," she said suddenly. "I bought a little something for Hercules and Owen." She fished in the pocket of her coat and handed me a brown paper bag about the size of a school lunch bag.

"I suppose it wouldn't do me any good to tell you that you shouldn't have done this."

"Not in the slightest," she said, her eyes crinkling with delight.

I stuck the bag in my coat pocket. "Thank you so much, Rebecca," I said.

"Oh, you're welcome. I miss the boys."

I pulled on my left shoe and stood up, shaking down both of my pant legs. "Owen's been racing around in the snow," I said. "But you know how Hercules is about getting his feet wet. He such a fussbudget."

"Well, I don't know if I'd call him fussy," Rebecca said as we walked into the studio. "I don't like wet feet myself."

"True," I said, giving her arm a squeeze. "But I don't have to carry you across the lawn if there's a little dew on the grass."

Her eyes twinkled again. "Well, Kathleen, I have to say I've always been a bit partial to those chairs the ancient Egyptians used to carry the pharaohs around." She laughed. I loved the sound. Rebecca had a great laugh, and now that she and Everett were together again I got to hear her laugh a lot.

She spotted Roma over by the window. "I need to talk to Roma," she said. "Come stand beside me in the circle when it's time."

I crossed to the table where Maggie and Ruby were standing. "Hi," I said, touching Ruby's shoulder lightly with my hand.

"Hi," she said. She seemed more like herself, albeit a quieter version of herself. Her hair was spiked and she was wearing her favorite CROSS YOUR NUTS T-shirt with black spandex leggings.

I didn't know Ruby nearly as well as Maggie did, but I liked her. She had a kind soul. I still wore the crystal necklace she'd made for me.

"How are you?" I asked.

"Better. Thank you for this morning, for everything."

She stopped and swallowed a couple of times. "I can't believe Agatha's dead. She worked so damn hard so she could come home."

"And she got home." Maggie's voice was steady and reassuring.

That made Ruby smile. "That was Agatha. When she made up her mind to do something"—she laughed—"forget it."

"Oh, so that's where you learned it," Maggie said dryly over the top of her mug of herbal tea.

"Yeah, I guess I did."

It was almost time to start. Maggie took one last drink from her cup and set it down. She held up two fingers to us. The two-minute warning.

"If I can help or do anything, please ask," I said to Ruby. "Do you know about the service yet?"

She shook her head. "David—that's Agatha's son—is in China, of all places. He's a mining engineer. It's going to be a week before he can get here. Part of the road collapsed in a storm where he is. Peter Lundgren is in charge of everything, I guess. He's Agatha's lawyer."

"Lawyers are good at working these kinds of things out," I said.

Maggie moved to the middle of the room.

"Agatha would hate a big, showy service." Ruby said.

"It doesn't have to be that way. Peter was her lawyer. He'd know what she would want." I touched her shoulder again. "I meant what I said. If I can help, just ask."

Her eyes filled with tears. She blinked them away and after a second's hesitation threw her arms around me and hugged me.

I gave her my best everything-will-be-okay smile and tried to ignore the worm of doubt squirming around in my head.

"Circle, please, everyone," Maggie called.

Ruby, as the most accomplished student in the group,

went to stand to Maggie's left. Rebecca was next to Roma on Maggie's right. She caught my eye and patted the air next to her. I slid into place, returning Roma's smile as Maggie started the warm-ups.

I worked steadily during the class as Maggie reminded me to bend my knees and shift my weight at least a dozen times, while Rebecca, who was surprisingly fluid for her age, gave me little bits of encouragement.

I wasn't naturally coordinated, though I had to admit I was getting better since I'd started the class. More than once in the past few weeks I'd caught myself shifting my weight to reach something, instead of stretching too far and losing my balance.

"What do you have planned for tomorrow?" Maggie asked, after we'd finished the complete form at the end of class. "Any chance you could give me a hand changing the lights at the community center?"

I didn't want to tell Maggie I was going out to Wisteria Hill with Marcus. She'd start telling me it was a sign the universe thought we were good for each other. Okay, so she wouldn't rub her hands together and cackle, but it'd be close.

"I have a couple of things I need to do first thing," I said, using the hem of my T-shirt to blot the sweat on my neck. I was the only one who seemed to be sweating so much in class. "When did you want to go do it?"

"Midafternoon."

"I can make that work," I said. "Call me in the morning."

"Okay."

I went out to get my coat. Rebecca was putting on her own things.

"Would you like a drive, Kathleen?" she asked, wrapping a soft rose-colored scarf around her neck. "Everett is picking me up."

"Thank you," I said. "But I have to check in at the library. How is Everett?" I asked, trying not to grin.

Rebecca and Everett had been a couple when they were very young, but had broken up and gone on with their lives. They'd gotten back together during the summer, with a little indirect help from the cats and me. I liked them both and I felt a bit like a fairy godmother invested in the romance. And sometimes they acted like a couple of love-struck teenagers, so it was easy to get caught up in what looked like a happily-ever-after.

"Everett's fine," she said, but she couldn't help smiling that huge smile she got when she said his name.

I couldn't hold back my own grin. "Glad to hear it." I waggled my eyebrows at her.

She shook her finger in a mock reprimand. "Don't start getting ideas. We're taking it nice and slow."

I was actually happy they could take it slowly. Rebecca had needed surgery to remove a small growth back in the fall. Luckily it had turned out not to be serious.

The downstairs door opened and Everett Henderson himself started up the stairs. He looked like the actor, Sean Connery, strong and charming with just a touch of ruthlessness. Rebecca's cheeks flushed pink at the sight of him.

I leaned over and spoke softly in her ear. "Rebecca, if I had a man in my life who made me blush the way you do when you see Everett, I wouldn't take it nice and slow. I'd wrap him in duct tape, stick him on a sled and take him home."

She looked at me, shocked. "Kathleen!" she said, shaking her head.

I tried to look innocent as Everett joined us. "Hello, Kathleen," he said.

I smiled. "Hello, Everett."

"Thank you for the information on the library renovations," he continued. "Lita said you sent it over. She'll call you Monday about a meeting."

I nodded.

He looked at Rebecca. "Ready to go?" he asked, reaching for her hand.

"I am," she said.

"Kathleen, do you need a ride?" Everett asked, turning back to me.

"No, thank you," I said.

They started down the stairs. Rebecca paused on the second step to look back at me. "Give the cats a scratch for me," she said. "I miss them coming across the backyard to say hello."

"I will." I reached for my boots.

"Oh, and Kathleen, I don't need to use duct tape." She winked and disappeared down the steps.

I laughed, pulling on my coat and hat and winding the scarf my sister, Sara, had made for me around my neck.

Mary, wearing a blue sweater with a snowflake design, was at the front desk when I got to the library. She hadn't minded working a split shift. She smiled as I came in through the doors.

"How's your evening?" I asked.

"Surprisingly busy. A gaggle of twelve-year-olds came in to do research for a school history project. Their teacher said they had to use an actual book for the research instead of the Internet." She chuckled and shook her head, her gray curls bouncing. "I introduced them to the mysteries of the online catalogs and then just for fun told them that when I was their age the card catalog was actually on cards."

"And they looked at you like you were a dinosaur."

"One of them actually used the words 'olden days.'" She gave me a wry smile. "But two of them went home with books that weren't on the research list. They just wanted to read."

"I love to hear that," I said.

Mary had the knack for making the library seem like a treasure trove of adventure. She'd tell the story of how she began her competitive kickboxing career by borrowing a book on the subject by mistake. She'd been looking for craft books on making boxes and hadn't been wearing her reading glasses.

"Would you like me to stay?" I offered.

"No." She waved away the idea. "Kate is here. We have it under control. But before I forget . . ." She looked around the checkout desk. "Ah, there it is." She picked up a piece of blue paper. "Detective Gordon called to remind you about Wisteria Hill in the morning."

"Thanks," I said. "I hadn't forgotten."

"How are the cats?" she asked.

Over time, Roma had managed to catch and neuter all the feral cats out at Wisteria Hill, but they were too wild to ever be anyone's pets. A collection of volunteers made sure they had food and water and care when they needed it.

Everett never talked about the abandoned estate. He had to know what was going on, but he didn't say a word about it, and, strangely, neither did anyone else.

"The cats are doing well. Harry's managed to keep the driveway clear and they all seem to be healthy."

Mary gave me a sheepish smile. "Detective Gordon also said to remind you to wear your snow pants."

"Snow pants, parka, wool hat, scarf, insulated mittens, and Sorels. And two pair of socks and long underwear," I recited, ticking them off on my fingers.

She nodded approvingly. "This is not your first rodeo."

"Or my first trip to Wisteria Hill in the winter," I said. Even though I wasn't born and raised in Minnesota, I did know how to dress for winter, though apparently Marcus Gordon didn't think I did.

Mary's expression grew serious. "Kathleen, have you seen Ruby? I heard she found Agatha."

"She was at class," I said, picking clumps of snow off my mittens. "She's all right for the most part. Sad."

She shook her head. "Doesn't seem fair that Agatha would just get home and then . . ." She didn't finish the sentence.

A shiver slid up the back of my neck, like a finger slowly creeping across my skin. Agatha's death had left me unsettled, and I didn't even know her.

"And there are already rumors going," Mary continued, making a neat stack of the book-request printouts by her left elbow. She liked to get things organized almost as much as she liked kickboxing.

"What kind of rumors?"

She made a face and smoothed her gray hair with one hand. "Most common one is that Agatha had a secret fortune."

"I doubt it," I said. "You don't generally get rich being a teacher." I flashed to Eric giving Agatha the bag of take-out food and cup of coffee. "How do these rumors get started?"

"Probably people with too much time on their hands," Mary said tartly. "My grandma always told us kids, 'If you don't have anything to do, go get the pail and scrub brush and I'll find you something to do.'"

"A drop-dead practical woman, from the sound of it," I said.

"Very," Mary said. "She couldn't abide gossip." The smile turned to a grin. "But since Gran is gone, tell me if there's any truth to what I heard about Roma."

"What did you hear about Roma?"

Mary looked around and leaned toward me. "I heard from more than one person that she's seeing someone."

"Someone? You mean a man?"

"No, I mean a grizzly bear," she shot back with exasperation. "Yes, a man."

"Nope."

"You sure?"

"Positive."

Mary looked disappointed.

I tugged my hat down over my ears and pulled on my mittens again. "Since you don't need me, I'm heading home. I'll see you tomorrow."

"Good night," Mary said. The phone rang then and she reached for it.

I put the strap of my bag over my shoulder and headed out. Peter Lundgren was just coming across the parking lot, a couple of library books under his arm. I'd always found him a little imposing when we'd talked in the library. He was a large man who seemed to fill whatever space he was in. But I remembered how carefully he'd walked Agatha over to the counter at Eric's, and I smiled at him as we both got to the bottom of the steps. He nodded and started to move past me. I reached over and touched his arm.

"Excuse me, Peter," I said. "Could you tell me if there are any plans yet for a service for Agatha Shepherd?"

He brushed a few flakes of snow off the top of his sandy hair. He wore it long, almost to his shoulders, a kind of rebel-lawyer look. "I can tell you that there will be some sort of memorial service once her son is back in the country. David wants to plan that himself."

I nodded.

"There should be something in the paper next week."

"Thank you," I said. He was already halfway up the stairs, so I wasn't sure he'd even heard me.

It was snowing lightly, tiny flakes reflected in the pinkish glow of the streetlights like little stars. I started up Mountain Road. The street looked more like a stage set, a picture-perfect town in a picture-perfect scene. Perfect always made me a little antsy.

I couldn't help it. Because of my parents' acting, I'd spent a lot of time in theaters big and not so big. I knew about subterfuge and illusion. I knew things are rarely as they appear on the surface. Other kids had parents that taught them how to ride a bike, manage money or do long division. Not mine.

What I got from my mother and father was the ability to separate fakery from reality, to spot the truth in a sea of fallacy. And that was why I felt so unsettled. No matter what everyone thought and no matter what Marcus Gordon *wasn't* saying, Agatha Shepherd hadn't died from natural causes.

Something bad had happened.

I just knew it.

8

I was dressed and ready with my thermos of hot chocolate when Marcus pulled into my driveway in the morning. It was a clear morning, sharp and biting cold, and the sun seemed far away in the cloudless sky. Hercules sat on the bench, looking out the porch window.

I picked up the stainless-steel thermos sitting on the bench beside him and gave him a quick scratch just above his nose. "Stay out of trouble," I told him. "I won't be long."

He turned back to the window. He liked winter as long as he was only looking at it. It was almost as cold in the porch as it was outside, but I knew Hercules had his own way to get in the house again when he got cold.

I locked the door and headed around the house to the driveway. Marcus was just getting out of his SUV. He wore a blue parka with the hood thrown back, black snow pants, and lace-up boots. His cheeks were red from the cold. Okay, so Maggie was right. He was cute. His blue eyes flicked over my old brown quilted coat and insulated pants, and for a second I had the ridiculously childish urge to strike a model's pose, hands on my hips and feet apart, with a vaguely haughty look on my face. But I didn't. I kept the fantasy to myself and smiled at him instead.

"Good morning."

He smiled back. "Good morning."

I walked around the front of the car and got in the passenger's side. As I fastened my seat belt, I took the opportunity to quickly check out the SUV. It was clean. Not no-cardboard-coffee-cups-on-the-floor-or-junk-on-the-backseat clean. It was how-the-heck-can-he-be-so-clean-in-the-middle-of-winter? clean. The only thing on the backseat was an old gray blanket. The dashboard in front of me was shining—no smudges, no dust, no fingerprints. There was no mug of half-finished coffee in the cup holder.

I clicked my seat belt into place and then set the thermos at my feet. The floor mats looked like they'd just come from the dealer. Okay, so it seemed as though Marcus Gordon was a bit of a clean freak, at least with respect to his personal vehicle. Being a fairly tidy person myself, I couldn't exactly see that as a flaw. I wasn't going to tell Maggie about this. She'd see the clean-car thing as another karmic sign that Marcus and I were soul mates.

He backed out of the driveway and started up the hill. The overnight snow had been plowed and there was sand on the road. As we drove past the road to Oren's place, I made a mental note to talk to him about which pieces of his father's artwork I wanted to display in the library for the centennial celebrations. I still had to figure out how to get the massive metal sculptures from his workshop to the library. I was hoping Harry Taylor would have some ideas on that.

"You're somewhere else," Marcus said.

I turned from the window to look at him. "Excuse me?"

"You were thinking about something else," he said, shooting me a quick glance.

"The library centennial."

"End of May?" he asked, putting on his left turn signal to pull onto the road to Wisteria Hill.

"Close," I said. "End of June. That's the one hundredth anniversary of the original construction being completed."

There was a break in the line of passing cars, and we pulled onto the road. The rear wheels spun for a second on an icy patch and then found traction.

"Are you staying?" Marcus asked.

I'd forgotten that the conversation could take some quick detours with him. I had the feeling sometimes that his mind was three steps ahead of everyone else's. Thank goodness he didn't drive the way he talked.

"I have another year on my contract."

The car in front of us slowed and so did we. Marcus took the opportunity to look directly at me for a moment. "No, I meant are you going to stay beyond that, or are you going back to Boston when your contract is up?"

"I don't know." I adjusted the shoulder belt so it wasn't pushing the hood of my coat against my neck.

That was the truth. I didn't know if I wanted to stay in Mayville or even in Minnesota. I also didn't know if I'd be offered the chance. There was always the possibility that the library board would smile politely, shake my hand, thank me for my service and send me on my way.

And did I want to stay? The decision to apply for the two-year job supervising the upgrade of the library and organizing its centennial had been an impulsive one. Probably the most impulsive choice of my life.

Except it wasn't spontaneous; it was mostly running away, from Andrew—him marrying that waitress had pretty much ended our relationship—and from my wildly unpredictable family, who'd come to expect I'd always be the dependable, responsible one.

But I'd discovered that I liked it here, and I said so.

"You don't miss Boston?"

"Sometimes," I said. "I miss my family. I still have

friends there." I pulled my hat down over my ears. "But I have friends here, too. And I can't exactly picture Owen or Hercules in an apartment in the city."

I'd never be able to hide the cats' little idiosyncrasies in an apartment. And Owen would go nuts if he couldn't stalk around the yard like one of his genetically distant African cousins hunting a gazelle.

"They really won't let anyone else touch them?" Marcus asked. Again, the conversation went off in a direction I wasn't expecting.

I thought about Old Harry and Agatha. I didn't have any explanation for how the boys reacted to them. "Mostly no," I said.

"Do you think it's because they came from Wisteria Hill, because they were feral?" He was watching the left side of the road for the two reflectors Harry had set into the ground to mark the long driveway into the old estate.

"I think that's part of it," I admitted. I did sometimes think Owen and Herc were the way they were because they'd come from Wisteria Hill. There were things about them I just couldn't explain logically. And there was something about Wisteria Hill I couldn't explain, either. Whenever I was out there I always felt as though all my senses were amped up on high alert.

Marcus put on his blinker and started up toward the house.

"Roma thinks they might not have been feral," I said as we bumped up the long driveway. Harry had plowed and sanded, but the track was dirt and gravel and driving up it in the winter was a bit like being stuck in one of those vibrating machines that promises to shake away excess pounds.

We hit a ridge that ran the width of the driveway and my stomach rebounded like a rim shot off the edge of a basketball hoop. I grabbed the seat on either side of me.

"So someone might have left them out here?" Marcus said.

"Yes." I didn't add that if someone had left two tiny kittens at Wisteria Hill, they'd left them to die.

We bounced into a deep well in the frozen ground and the car lurched. "Sorry," Marcus muttered.

"Is it just me or is this driveway getting worse?" I asked.

He gripped the steering wheel tightly as we bounced over and around the last turn. "It's been a colder than usual winter, plus all that rain we had last fall made a mess of this." He pulled into the space Harry had cleared for parking, shut off the SUV and turned to me. "How would you like to talk to Everett Henderson? Maybe he'd agree to have the driveway graded and leveled this spring."

I pulled on my mittens and tugged the scarf a little tighter around my neck. "Sure," I said. "What exactly needs to be done?"

"Wait. You're serious?"

"You're not?"

"I was being sarcastic." A rosy flush spread across his cheeks.

"See? I missed that entirely," I said, trying unsuccessfully not to smile as I got out of the SUV. That got me a smile in return that looked cute with his pink cheeks.

Marcus lifted the tailgate. He handed me a canvas bag with the cat food, dry because the wet froze a lot faster. He grabbed two jugs of water and slammed the hatch shut. Since December Roma had organized extra shifts to make sure the cats had fresh water.

We walked past the old house. It looked sadder and more neglected each time I came out. No one had lived in it for years. No Henderson since Everett's mother. No one at all since the caretakers moved closer to their daughter a couple of years ago.

Everett didn't talk about the estate, ever. It wasn't that he changed the subject. He just didn't talk about it. And because of that there were a lot of rumors about the old place. Some people said it was haunted; others said that the cats were very old and had some kind of magical powers. Roma felt they were most likely descendents of the kitchen cats from the estate.

But most people believed the cats were descended from Everett's mother's cat, Finn. It was commonly believed that Finn had otherworldly abilities. That last rumor worried me. People knew Owen and Hercules came from Wisteria Hill. After Roma told me that she didn't think they had ever been feral, I started telling people that they had probably been abandoned. I didn't want anyone getting the idea my cats might have superpowers.

At one point there had been a push to round up all the Wisteria Hill cats and find foster homes for them. Roma had strongly resisted that, making a point of educating people so they understood that a feral cat was never going to turn into a fluffy house cat, chasing a ball of yarn across the living room floor.

"Do you think it's true?" Marcus asked as we went around to the side of the old carriage house, where the cat shelters and feeding stations were.

"Do I think what's true?" I said, as he held the side door for me.

"Do you think there's something different about these cats?"

I looked back at him and tried not to smirk. "You think they might have supernatural powers?" I waggled one hand from side to side at him. "Or maybe they're shape-shifters?" I stood for a moment, letting my eyes adjust to the dim light.

Marcus closed the door carefully behind us. "No, I don't mean all that nonsense," he said. "But you have to admit, some of these animals have lived a very long time under"—he held out both hands—"some pretty adverse conditions."

Marcus Gordon didn't seem the type to buy in to the woo-woo theories about the old estate or the cats. "You think the cats have some kind of genetic mutation?" I asked. Now that I could see better, I started across the wooden floor to the feeding station.

"Maybe."

My chest tightened. I didn't want him—or anyone else—to get any ideas about Owen and Hercules.

I bent to brush some straw and dry leaves from around the shelf where the dishes would sit, so he couldn't see my face. "So do you think they should be somewhere being studied instead of living here?"

"No, I don't."

I stood up and turned so I could see him now and read his expression. He pulled off his hat. His dark hair stood up at the crown of his head. It made him look like a kid, not like an annoying police officer.

He met my gaze directly. "I think the cats have the right to live where they feel safe. They aren't bothering anyone and I don't think anyone should bother them."

"Wait a second. Has someone been out here again who shouldn't be?" I asked, stuffing my mittens into my pocket so I could open the bag of cat food. "I know Roma made a couple of extra trips out here this week."

"Yeah, I think so." He took the clean water bowls I held out to him. "Monday the outside door wasn't closed properly."

"It could've just been someone being careless," I said, even though I knew none of Roma's volunteers would be careless with the cats' safety.

"Harry saw tracks when he came out to plow."

"What kind of tracks?"

"Snowmobile." Marcus leaned around me, setting the water bowls in place. A couple of times during really bad weather, Harry had used his own snowmobile to come out and feed the cats, but other than that everyone else drove their trucks or SUVs.

"Were the cats okay?" I asked, as he filled the bowls with water.

"As far as anyone can tell. I don't think whoever it was realized the shelters are back here."

The cats' homes—insulated shelters built by Roma's volunteers—were in what she called the cathouse, a corner of the old building that had probably originally been used for storage.

I filled all the food dishes and Marcus and I retreated to the door, where we waited, crouched down on the dusty floor.

"Why would anyone want to be out here, anyway?" I whispered.

His shoulders rose under his jacket. "Who knows? Maybe it was just kids. The rumors are kind of dramatic, when you think about it. What kid wouldn't want to own a cat that was a hundred years old and could turn in to a wolf?"

A flicker of movement caught my eye in the far corner of the carriage house. I put a hand on Marcus's arm to warn him into silence. The cats came into view. The first one was a sturdy black-and-white cat not unlike Hercules, but with more white on his face. The others came behind him, cautiously, one by one.

They'd all come to know the volunteers and realize our presence meant food, and we all knew to stay quiet and still while they ate. Like Marcus, I eyed each cat in turn, looking for any signs of injury or illness.

"Where's Lucy?" he whispered.

I looked around. He was right. There was no sign of Lucy, the matriarch of the feral-cat colony. She was usually the first one who appeared to check things out.

I scanned the space, squinting in the dim light. There

was something—I hoped it was feline—over by one of
the posts supporting the carriage-house roof.

I leaned forward on the balls of my feet, grabbing
Marcus's arm for balance. He really did smell good, like
a fruit salad of orange, lemon and grapefruit. Lucy made
her way slowly across the floor. The calico cat was carrying something in her mouth. Or, to be more accurate,
she was half dragging something.

She paused. Her ears twitched. I didn't hear anything,
but something caught her attention. She looked back
the way she'd come for a long moment. Then, seemingly
satisfied, she turned back around.

And looked directly at us.

I froze, not even breathing for a moment, because I
didn't want to scare her.

The cat put a paw on whatever it was she'd captured
so she could get a better grip on it with her teeth. Then
she started toward us. *Should we move, or would that
startle her and the other cats?* They were all eating, not
even giving her as much as a glance as she passed
them.

Lucy made her way closer. She still had a very small
limp left over from last summer when she'd injured her
leg. And whatever it was she was carrying was heavy,
close to half her size.

It wasn't a bird; I couldn't see any feathers. I could
see a long tail and . . . fur? I tightened my grip on Marcus's arm.

Lucy continued to make her way across the floor.
About six feet or so away from us she stopped, dropped
her . . . catch on the wooden floor and looked at us. Then
she gave the dead animal—I was pretty sure it was
dead—a push with a paw.

It dawned on me that she was bringing us a gift. Owen
and Hercules brought me things on occasion—a drag-
onfly, a dead bird, a very hairy caterpillar. Owen had

once gifted Rebecca with a dead bat that was bigger than he was.

"Thank you, puss," I said softly.

She tipped her head to one side and studied me for a second. Then she bent and nudged the gift a bit closer with her nose. With a flick of her tail she made her way over to the feeding station.

We stayed where we were, silent while Lucy ate. My legs were cramping from being crouched in the cold for so long. I kept one eye on the dead thing, just in case it wasn't so dead after all.

One by one the cats finished eating and wandered away until only Lucy was at the feeding station. Like Owen, she liked to sniff and scrutinize every bit of food before she ate it. Finally she stretched, took a couple of steps away from the food and started washing her face.

I dug my knuckles into the knot in my right thigh. If I hadn't been holding on to Marcus, I would have fallen over. I couldn't help thinking that Lucy was doing this on purpose, knowing we'd have to wait, huddled on the floor by the door until she was finished. From time to time she'd look our way.

Finally she gave one last swipe of her face with her paw. She stretched again and slowly made her way across the floor of the carriage house, back to the shelters. She had the same graceful stride as a lion on a dusty African savannah, and a touch of the same menace.

We could finally get to our feet. I shifted my weight from one leg to the other to stretch out the kinks. Marcus walked over to Lucy's gift. He peered at it and gave the dead thing a push with his toe.

"I think it's just a field mouse," I said. He looked at me, surprised. Had he thought I was going to go all girly on him and scream?

"My parents did a lot of summer theater and every theater had more than just actors in it," I said.

"How nice." He moved around the dead mouse to get the second water jug.

"One summer they did Shakespeare in the park, just at dusk. My mother thought she was sharing a changing area—a tent—with my father." I started to laugh at the memory. "Turns out it was a raccoon, after the ingénue's secret stash of peanut butter cups."

"Oh, come on. You're kidding."

"No." I couldn't keep the laughter from bubbling over. "I don't know who was more surprised, my mother or the poor raccoon. There was a prop sword someone had left behind in the tent. She went after the raccoon with it. He wasn't going to leave those peanut butter cups without a fight."

Marcus was laughing now, arms crossed over his chest. It was easy to like him when he was just being himself. "She chased him, at sword-point, out of the tent and across the grass, right in front of the staging area. And keep in mind she was wearing a lace-up corset and petticoats." I was laughing so hard that I was shaking.

"So what happened?"

"She got the best review of the entire two-week festival. No one knew it wasn't part of the play."

We worked quickly to clean up the feeding station. I gathered the dishes and picked up a couple of pieces of dropped food. Marcus put out more fresh water. I looked around the carriage house one last time. Everything else seemed okay.

"Ready to head back?" Marcus asked.

I nodded and picked up the bag with the food and the dirty dishes. "What about that?" I asked when we came level with the dead rodent.

Marcus made a face. "I don't think we should leave it here. I don't want to attract any other animals." He pulled his hat back on. "I have a shovel in the car. I can at least put it outside, away from the building."

"Good idea," I said.

We walked to the car. The sun was stretching up over the trees. I put the bag in the back. Marcus opened the front passenger's door for me and took a small shovel from the rear.

"Be right back," he said.

I got in the car and peeled off my hat and mittens. In the cup holder between the seats was a pump bottle of hand sanitizer. I used it to clean my hands. It left them smelling faintly of lemons.

Something was digging into my hip. I felt in my pocket. It was Roma's roll of duct tape. I had to remember to give that back to her.

I unscrewed the thermos top. There was a second cup inside the top, like a nested Russian doll. I kept it out for Marcus.

After a few minutes he was back. He set the shovel in the back and closed the hatch. Then he got in the front seat. "Done," he said, reaching for the hand cleaner. He looked at my cup. "Coffee?" he asked hopefully.

"Sorry," I said. "Hot cocoa. Would you like some?"

"Almost as good. I'd love some, please."

I poured him a cup and handed it carefully over to him.

He took a sip. "Mmmm, that's good," he said, his eyes half closed in pleasure at the warmth and taste. "Old family recipe?"

I laughed. "No."

He gave me two eyebrows raised in surprise.

"My mother knows how to make only three things: lemonade, baking-powder biscuits and toast. All my dad can make is a martini."

"Seriously?"

"Seriously. And the toast thing is iffy."

"So how did you learn to cook?"

I shrugged. "How else? The library, and a very nice woman in South Carolina who owned a little theater right on the coast. She taught me the secret to the best chocolate cake."

He smiled at me over the top of his cup. "Which is?"

I laughed. "I'm not telling you. It won't be a secret anymore."

"You at least have to make one sometime and let me taste it."

"Deal," I said.

He finished the cocoa and handed me the empty cup.

"Would you like some more?"

"No, thanks," he said, fishing in his pocket for the car keys. "So, what's the martini like?"

"Martini?" Then I realized what he meant. "Good, as far as I know. I'm not a martini connoisseur, but my friend Lise is and she likes them."

He found the keys then and reached for his seat belt. Mine was already fastened. I finished my cocoa and put the thermos back together. Marcus started the SUV.

"Home, or is there somewhere I can drop you?"

"Home, please," I said. "I don't go to the library until lunchtime."

He backed up the car so we could drive out. "Are you closing the library early because of Winterfest?" he asked.

I nodded. "Lita said everyone will be at the supper at the community center."

"She's right," he said, as we eased our way down the rutted, frozen driveway. "The food is terrific, by the way."

I grinned. "I believe you. I've had Mary's apple pie."

"I'm looking forward to having a slice or two myself tonight."

This was my opening. "Will you be able to make it?" I asked. "Or will the case keep you too busy?"

"You mean Mrs. Shepherd's death?" He slowed to a crawl as we lurched over a particularly large frost heave. "I should be able to make it." He kept his eyes forward, but I noticed a tiny twitching muscle in his cheek.

Change of plans. Subtlety wasn't going to work. "Was she hit by a car?" I asked. Based on what I'd seen, I was still convinced Agatha hadn't died from natural causes.

"The autopsy isn't until later this morning."

That wasn't a yes or no.

We were at the bottom of the driveway. Marcus stopped, the back end of the SUV slipping a little on the ice. "Why are you asking?" he said. "Is there something you didn't tell me?"

"I told you everything that happened yesterday morning." *Just don't ask me about the night before,* I added silently.

We pulled onto the old highway. The sun was behind us, surprisingly warm on the back of my head. Marcus continued to watch the road. "Did you see anything any other time? The night before, for instance."

How did he do that? It was as though he could read my thoughts. I pulled a ChapStick out of my pocket. My lips were suddenly dry and I needed to buy time.

I snapped the cap on the little tube and rolled it over my fingers and back again before I put it in my pocket. The movement caught his attention.

"How did you do that?"

"Excuse me?" I said.

"Flip that lip stuff over your fingers."

I looked down at my hands. "Oh, that. It's just the same as doing it with a quarter."

He let out a breath. "And how do you know how to do it with quarter?"

I felt my cheeks getting warm. "Well, poker," I said.

"Poker?"

"Uh-huh, a lot of poker games happen backstage. Crew, cast. I watched. I learned things."

"So I see," he said, making a left turn onto Mountain Road, slowing a little in the traffic.

I hadn't answered his question. Maybe I was in the clear.

"So," he said, checking the mirrors. "You were going to tell me if you saw anything Wednesday night."

I exhaled slowly. I was making myself crazy trying to protect someone who didn't need protecting. Harry Senior didn't drive. What did it matter if he'd had an argument with Agatha?

"I don't think this has anything to do with Agatha's death," I began, holding up my hand, because I knew he was going to interrupt. "And yes, I know you'll be the judge of what's important and what's not."

He closed his mouth on whatever words he'd been going to say. When he did speak it was only to say, "Go ahead." His tone told me he was already shifting into detective mode again.

"Agatha came in to the café while Maggie, Roma, and I were there. We were waiting for Oren to open the community center for us."

An image of the old woman in the out-of-fashion plaid wool coat flashed in my mind, followed by another image of that same coat, stained dark with blood.

"Eric had food for her. Right after that we all came out."

Marcus said nothing, hoping that the silence would make me say more, I was guessing. I already knew what I was going to say. "Down the street a little I saw Agatha with Harrison Taylor."

"What were they doing?"

"As far as I could tell, talking. I couldn't hear what they were saying."

"That's it?"

"Uh-huh. I did walk Harry to Eric's."

He shot me a quick look. We were almost at my house. "Why did you do that?"

"Because the sidewalk was slippery. Because he isn't a young man."

"So, that's it?" he said. "You saw Mr. Taylor talking to Mrs. Shepherd. You walked him to the restaurant."

"That's it," I said, feeling a knot of annoyance beginning to twist in my stomach. "What? Do you think I ran after Agatha, lured her into the alley, and whacked her with my purse?"

"Did you?"

For a second I thought about whacking him with my mittens. I took a breath and let it out. "No. I didn't."

"I know," he said. "The waitress saw you with Mr. Taylor. So did Peter Lundgren."

"So I have an alibi."

He smiled and turned into my driveway.

I swallowed my aggravation and picked up the thermos.

He shifted in his seat. "Thanks for the cocoa. And for helping me this morning."

"You're welcome," I said a bit abruptly. It bothered me that he didn't trust me, even though I knew it was part of his job not to trust anybody. "Have a good day," I said as I slid out of the car.

Owen was in the kitchen, lying on his side in a square of sunlight, lazily washing his face. "Hey, fur ball," I said as I hung up my old coat. "I forgot last night. Rebecca sent you a present."

At the sound of her name Owen jumped to his feet and trotted over to stand expectantly at my mine. I pulled the paper bag from the pocket of my other jacket, reached inside and fished out a Fred the Funky Chicken. If it was possible for a cat's face to light up with joy, Owen's did.

I took the yellow toy out of the package, then I leaned down and handed it to him. I didn't even bother with my usual "Rebecca spoils you" speech. Owen grabbed the chicken and disappeared around the corner of the doorway.

After a moment Hercules came in from the living

room. He looked back in the direction Owen had gone with his catnip chicken, then looked quizzically at me.

"Rebecca," I said.

Herc yawned. Catnip wasn't his thing.

I held up the paper bag. "She sent you something, too," I said. His head came up, eyes big and green. I held out the bag, swinging it from side to side. "Wanna see?" I teased.

Of course he did, but unlike Owen, Hercules wouldn't want to seem too eager. He walked slowly over to me, glanced at the small, brown paper sack, and then looked around the kitchen like it didn't matter if I showed him or not. I waited until he sat down in front of me before I pulled the sardine can from the bag.

"Merow," he said. He knew what was in the can.

"What do you think?" I asked. "Maybe you should try one, just to make sure they haven't gone bad or anything." I set the sardines on the counter, found a plate, and pulled back the top of the oblong can.

The pungent smell of fish and oil hit me. "They smell like sardines," I said. I used a fork to pull out two tiny fish and put them on the plate. I took it over to Hercules, who was studying his paw, pretending to be indifferent.

He sniffed the little fish and looked up at me. "Yeah, I think they smell okay," I said.

He bent and licked a bit of oil on the plate. And then a bit more, and then he didn't even try to act uninterested. He started eating with a sigh of happiness.

"Do they taste okay?" I asked. The only answer was the sound of him slurping. Better than a yes, I figured.

I was putting the rest of the sardines away when the phone rang. It was Maggie. "Can you still give me a hand this afternoon?" she asked.

"Sure," I said. "What do you need?"

"Mostly another set of hands and eyes."

"I could probably get away around three o'clock." I

looked out the living room window. The sky was still blue, the sun was still shining, my arm didn't ache. There was no snow coming for a while.

"That would be great," Maggie said. "I think Ruby is going to come, as well, and she's in the store until two."

I sank on to the footstool. "How is she really?"

"She's better."

"Marcus had said the autopsy was this morning. I know having some kind of memorial is important to Ruby," I said.

"And Roma and a lot of other people," Maggie added. "Any chance you can get any information from Marcus?"

"I don't think so," I said, brushing a clump of gray cat hair off the footstool. Proof that Owen was sleeping on the thing when I wasn't home.

"I went to Wisteria Hill with him this morning and I didn't find out anything." I held up a warning finger even though she couldn't see it. "And don't start with me," I cautioned. "I went to feed the cats. I don't want to go out with him. I don't even like him most of the time—"

"—and he doesn't even have a library card," she finished.

"Well, he doesn't," I muttered. Did I hear a laugh on the other end of the phone? "He thought I killed Gregor Easton."

"You were never a serious suspect. You weren't arrested."

"He thought I was having an affair with Easton. The man was twice my age."

"But you weren't," Maggie added, ever so reasonably. "Why don't you bug Roma about her love life?"

"You know, there's a rumor going around that she's seeing someone." Maggie said.

"There's always a rumor going around about something," I said. "I heard the same story. The only male she sees on a regular basis is that old horse the Kings bought for their daughter."

Maggie laughed.

"I'll see you at three o'clock."

"See you then," she said, and hung up.

I went upstairs and checked my e-mail. There was one from my sister, Sara. She was working in northern Canada on a film. Sara was a documentary filmmaker, but she paid her bills working as a makeup artist on small, and now increasingly bigger, independent films. In the attached photo she was squinting into the sun, most of her face obscured by the hood of her parka. I peered at the background. There was almost much snow there as there was in Mayville.

There was also an e-mail from my friend Lise, in Boston. *I miss you,* her e-mail ended. *This time next year you'll be home.*

This time next year.

I'd been in Minnesota for almost a year now. That meant I had just over a year left on my contract. What if they wanted me to stay? Did I want to stay? When I left Boston it had been an impulsive decision.

Andrew had married someone else. Granted, there had been a large amount of alcohol involved, but as far as I was concerned, his being married, even if it was to somebody he'd known for just two weeks, meant I wasn't going to be with him anymore.

And while I loved my mom and my dad, and Ethan, my brother, and Sara, they'd always been impetuous and unpredictable. Someone had had to be sensible and practical. Someone had had to make sure there was milk and toilet paper. Someone had had to know how to fill out the myriad of papers in the emergency room. And get supper, even if it was only peanut butter–and-banana sandwiches.

That someone had been me for as long as I could remember. Me, when it was just Mom and Dad and me. Me, when they got divorced and I alternated weeks between them. Me, when they got married again because they couldn't leave each other alone, which is why Ethan and Sara were guests, so to speak, at the wedding.

Coming to Mayville had really been running away. I hadn't expected to make friends. In Boston everyone just assumed that I'd be back when my two-year contract was over.

I tried to imagine not sitting in Eric's with Maggie and Roma, not going to tai chi—I was so close to mastering the complete form—and not walking across the backyard to have iced tea with Rebecca in her gazebo.

And what about Owen and Hercules? Could I take them back to Boston? I tried to picture them in an apartment in the city. Owen, who fancied himself a hunter—the birds had never been safer—would hate it. And how would I get Hercules to stay inside?

I couldn't leave my cats behind. They wouldn't let anyone but me touch them. Well, other than Agatha, who was dead, and Old Harry, who was supposed to be, according to the gossip around town.

And how would I explain to anyone—Roma, Maggie, anyone—about the cats? Roma said they were special, but she meant because of the way they'd attached themselves to me.

As much as I missed watching my parents prepare for a production, or seeing what Ethan had done to his hair, or going to one of Lise's dinner parties, I wasn't sure I wanted to go back to Boston.

That was a surprise.

Something in the hallway caught my eye. Owen was just passing the bedroom door with the funky chicken's decapitated head in his mouth and a blissful look on his face. I couldn't be sure, but he didn't seem to be walking in a straight line. Owen was a little catnip junkie, no matter what Roma said.

I looked at my watch. I had enough time to get the slow cooker started and get to the library early.

I got supper simmering, quickly cleaned up, and hustled back upstairs to get ready for work.

"I'm leaving," I called, pulling on my coat. From somewhere in the house I heard a faint meow—Owen. Then in a moment Hercules appeared. "I'll see you later," I said. He gave me a soft "murp" and disappeared back into the living room.

I pulled on my boots and hat and grabbed my bag. I was locking the door when I realized I hadn't packed a lunch. I looked at my watch. It would be faster to walk down to Eric's Place and get a sandwich than to go back inside and make something. And yes, maybe I would get some of the latest talk about Agatha Shepherd's death, too.

I was three houses down the hill when Harry Junior's truck drove past me, slowed and stopped. He rolled down his window. "Hey, Kathleen, would you like a drive down the hill?" he called.

The sun was bright, but with the wind, it wasn't very warm out. "Yes," I said.

"Hop in, then," he said. He rolled the window back up.

I waited for a minivan to pass in the other direction, then scooted across the street and climbed into Harry's truck. It may have been well used, but Harry took care of the old Ford and the heat was blasting like I was sitting in front of a stoked woodstove.

"Thank you so much," I said, reaching for the seat belt.

"You're welcome." He put the truck in gear, checking the mirrors before he pulled into the street.

I leaned back against the turquoise vinyl seat and let the heat soak through my coat. "I have to buy a car."

"Is there a reason you haven't?"

"Pretty much laziness," I said with a laugh. "I sold my car in Boston, intending to buy one when I got here." I held my hands up to the heating vent. "But it was easy to walk everywhere and, well, you know what they say about good intentions."

Harry smiled. "That I do."

"Are you going to the Winterfest supper tonight?" I asked.

"Absolutely," he said. "The old man hasn't missed a Winterfest supper in"—he paused for a second—"well, ever, except for when he was overseas. As long as he's got a pulse he's going to be there."

"I hope that's a long time," I said.

"Me, too," Harry said. He opened his mouth as though he was going to say something else, but he didn't.

I waited without saying anything myself. Harry would get to whatever it was in his own time.

"Are you headed for the library?" he asked as we got to the bottom of the hill.

"I'm going over to Eric's to get something for lunch," I said. "But here is fine. Anywhere is fine."

"I'm going to the bookstore." Harry put on his turn signal. "It's only one door down."

"Okay," I said. The truck was so cozy and warm that I was happy to stay in my seat for a few more blocks.

"Have you heard anything about Agatha Shepherd's death?" Harry asked.

I looked at him, but he kept his gaze fixed on the road. His tone was almost too offhand. It occurred to me that maybe it wasn't just chance that Harry had been driving by just as I was walking downtown. "I was at Wisteria Hill this morning with Detective Gordon," I said. "He said the autopsy was this morning. That's it."

Harry sighed. "Kathleen, I'm worried about the old man."

I could see the tightness in his face. "They were friends."

"They were," Harry said quietly. We were at a stop sign with no other cars behind us. He turned to me. "They stopped speaking a long time ago."

I struggled for a moment. I didn't want to break the old man's confidence, but it was clear Harry knew something had happened to his father and Agatha's friendship. "He said they had a falling-out," I said finally.

Harry nodded. "He likes you," he said, turning down toward the water.

"I like him."

He pulled into an empty parking spot just a couple of spaces down from the café and put the truck in park, but stared out through the windshield for a moment before he said anything more. "Kathleen, he had some kind of argument with Agatha the other night, didn't he?"

I undid my seat belt to delay answering his question for a moment. "They had a conversation about something. It was very short. Your father was upset, although he tried to hide it. How did you know?"

He held out his hand, turned it over and studied his palm before he answered. "He wasn't himself, even before he heard about Agatha. And Detective Gordon came to talk to him last night." He let out a breath.

"Dad wouldn't tell me what the detective wanted, but he said something about saying things in anger that you can't take back. I figured it had to be Agatha. It was pretty clear you two hadn't argued about anything."

I reached over and touched his arm. "Whatever they were discussing had nothing to do with her death." I gestured to the café with my free hand. "She had a disagreement with Eric right before she saw your father. People argue, Harry. It doesn't always mean anything."

He pulled a hand across the bottom of his face. "He swiped one of my old trucks and drove himself down.

Said he changed his mind and wanted to see what was happening at the auction. He scraped the front fender on something, I think when he was parking. At least he had enough sense to call me from Eric's."

I could suddenly hear my own heartbeat in my ears. Harry Senior was driving Wednesday night. "I didn't know that," I said slowly. "But it doesn't mean he came looking for Agatha."

"Dad has been having these episodes, times when he can't remember where he was or what he was doing." Harry swept his hand over his face again.

"The doctors don't know if they're small strokes, some kind of seizure disorder or even a brain tumor." He shook his head. "Stubborn old coot refuses to go through more tests."

He stared through the windshield. "Kathleen, he had one of those gaps the other night. He hasn't admitted it, but I've gotten so I can pretty much tell when it happens."

Harrison had been driving.

No. I wasn't going there. Whatever had happened to Agatha, Harry Senior had had nothing to do with it. What had Harry just said? *At least he'd had the good sense to call me from Eric's.* I'd walked the old man to the café, and Harry had picked him up there. Agatha had been fine when she'd walked away.

"Harry, Agatha was fine when your father left her," I said. "I saw her head along the sidewalk. And I walked him to Eric's, where you picked him up. I understand that you're worried, but I don't think you need to be."

He looked relieved. "Thanks."

I reached for the door handle with one hand and my bag with the other and got out of the truck, stepping up over the ridge of snow on the sidewalk. I raised my hand in good-bye, heading up the short stretch of sidewalk to the café.

Harry Senior had been driving the night Agatha died.

But I'd walked him here and Harry had picked him up here. Had he stayed here? I closed my eyes for a second. In my mind I could see the blood soaking the plaid coat, and Agatha's arm bent at an unnatural angle. I could see Marcus pulling the shard of glass from my pants cuff. Glass I was pretty sure came from a headlight.

The old man had scraped the fender of the truck on something, Harry had said. My heart started pounding in my chest again.

Something?

Or someone?

9

Claire was behind the counter inside the restaurant. It was too early for the lunch crowd.

"Hi, Kathleen," she said. "What can I get you?"

"Sandwich, I think," I said.

"For here or to go?"

I was tempted to stay and eat, but I needed to get some things done if I was going to get away and help Maggie later. "To go," I said, pulling off my mittens.

She thought for a second. "All right. How about turkey and Swiss with spicy mustard and baby lettuce?"

"That sounds good."

"Sourdough bread?" she asked.

I took a deep breath. The smell of fresh bread made my mouth water. "Yes."

Claire put in the order and turned back to me. "What about a cookie?"

I patted the front of my parka. "If I keep eating your cookies more than just this coat is going to be padded."

"It's a new recipe," she said, her tone wheedling. "Whoopie pie. Soft chocolate cookies, creamy, fluffy filling."

"Stop, stop, stop!" I held up both hands, palms out.

She waited, eyebrows raised expectantly.

"One cookie," I said, and held up a finger for emphasis. "One."

Claire headed for the kitchen, a big grin on her face.

"Where's Eric today?" I asked when she came back with my lunch packed to go in a brown paper bag.

"He's still having problems with that tooth," she said, taking the money and counting change from the till.

I grimaced in sympathy as she handed back my change. "I hope he feels better soon."

"Me, too," Claire said. "Double shifts are killing me. I'm getting too old for this."

I smiled, pulling on my mittens again and picking up my food. Claire was maybe twenty-two.

She leaned across the counter and gave me a conspiratorial smile. "Is it true about Dr. Davidson?"

"Is what true?"

"I heard she's seeing a younger guy, a hockey player. Eddie Sweeney."

Eddie Sweeney? I couldn't help laughing. "Sorry. This time the rumors are wrong."

Claire looked disappointed.

I walked over to the library, noting that the sidewalks had all been sanded and plowed again. Susan was at the front desk. She turned as I walked in. "You're early," she said

"I need to get away for about a half hour or so later on," I said, unwinding my scarf. "So I thought I'd get an early start. Quiet morning?"

She tucked a loose piece of hair behind her ear. Her topknot was kind of sideways. That wasn't like Susan. She wasn't wearing any lipstick, either, and there were crumbs on the front of her chocolate brown sweater. She looked frazzled and distracted.

"Actually it was fairly busy until about twenty minutes or so ago. Even with Winterfest, I guess people are looking for a good book to curl up with in this weather."

Her eyes kept darting to the phone, and she tried but failed to stifle a yawn.

"Is everything all right?" I asked undoing the button at the neck of my jacket.

"I'm just a bit tired," she said, but again her eyes slid off me to the phone. "Eric and the boys all have colds, so I'm not getting a lot of sleep. But, hey"—she gave an elaborate shrug—"what can you expect in this weather?"

Her eyes just couldn't stay on my face. In the almost year I'd known her I'd learned that Susan was a terrible liar and I knew she was lying now. Whatever was happening between her and Eric, she was going to have to work it out in her own way.

"Susan, if you need anything, you only have to ask," I said quietly.

Her cheeks reddened. "I, uh, thanks," she mumbled. She gestured to a stack of books behind her. "I should get back to work."

"I'll be in my office," I said, and headed for the stairs.

Upstairs, I hung up my coat and changed into my shoes. Then I went down the hall for a cup of coffee. Roma was on my case because she thought I drank too much coffee. I couldn't wait to tell her the story that had been spawned from driving around with the Eddie dummy in the front of her SUV. She might not have a love life, but she did have a heck of a rumored love life.

I spent some time in my office, working on the book order and finishing up plans for the spring programs at the library. I worked at the front desk while Mary and Susan had their lunch breaks. Then I took some time to go over the library usage hours.

Library visits were up; so were the numbers of books checked out. I was hoping Everett Henderson and the rest of the library board would be pleased. After all the turmoil associated with the refurbishment of the old building, it made me glad to see that the town was using it.

About two forty-five, I went to the desk. Mary was checking out a man with a stack of books at least ten volumes high.

"Mary, I'm going over to the community center for a while," I said. "I won't be any more than an hour, probably less, and I have my cell."

"Okay," she said. "You're coming to the supper tonight?"

"Absolutely." I zipped my jacket. "I love your pie."

"That's because I bake it with love," she said, trying to look like a sweet, gentle grandma, but not quite getting there with the devilish twinkle in her eye.

"Later," I said, and headed out.

Maggie was on a ladder when I got to the center, taking down a string of lights I hadn't noticed fastened to the ceiling. I dropped my coat and mittens on a chair and hurried over to help her.

"Hi. What can I do?"

She frowned at the ceiling. "Hi. How about grabbing the end of the lights before they bang against the side of the ladder and break?"

I caught the end of the cord, holding it away from the ladder while Maggie finished unhooking the string. That was when I noticed the helium-filled pig. It was floating over the tables, wearing a Minnesota Wild hockey jersey and holding a sign that said BITE ME.

"Interesting choice with the pig," I said.

"Thanks," Maggie said. "Could you hand me those bulbs, please?"

I draped the lights over a nearby chair and grabbed the package of bulbs she pointed to. I got one out of the box and handed it to her. She screwed it in place, then looked at the adjacent fixture, twisting her mouth to one side in thought. I held up my arm, offering another bulb without speaking.

"Yeah," she muttered to no one in particular. She

twisted the second light into place and nodded with satisfaction. We ended up replacing six bulbs before Maggie was completely happy.

"Thanks," she said, scrambling down the ladder. "I
just want to see how this looks." She walked over to the
door and flipped the light switch.

There was a faint pinkish yellow cast to the light on
the locker-room scene. Maggie came back and stood,
studying it, with her arms crossed. "What do you think?"

"It looks kind of like those old fluorescent lights. I'm
guessing that's the effect you wanted."

She nodded. "Yeah, I wanted it to look like a locker
room. She frowned suddenly. "Do Eddie's legs look
right to you?"

"Uh-huh. Why?"

She shook her head and started for the dummy. "No,"
she said. "His right leg is crooked."

I watched her twist the dummy's leg. Even though he
was just a mannequin I caught myself cringing in sympathy.

I was still wearing my hat. I pulled it off and shook
my head as Rebecca came out of the kitchen. She
waved, and I dropped my toque on the chair and went
over to her.

"Hello, Kathleen. What are you doing here?" she
asked. She was wearing a long white apron tied at the
neck and waist and she smelled like cinnamon.

"Just giving Maggie a hand."

Maggie was on her knees now, doing something to
Eddie's knee that would've had him writhing on the
floor if he'd been a real person.

"Have you had a chance to look at the photographs?"
Rebecca asked, gesturing to the display.

"A little," I said. "They're fascinating."

She pressed a hand to her chest. "They take me back."

Behind her Everett appeared in the kitchen doorway.

He was wearing an apron, too. He had a vegetable peeler in one hand and a carrot in the other. "Hello, Kathleen," he said.

Rebecca turned at the sound of his voice and every bit of her face smiled.

Everett held up the carrot. "This is the last one. I think we need to do another bag."

"All right," Rebecca said. "I'll be right there." He lifted the peeler in acknowledgment and disappeared back into the kitchen.

I smiled at Rebecca. "The things we do for love."

Her eyes sparkled and a blush of pink spread across her cheeks. "Isn't it grand?" she said. She gave my arm a squeeze. "I'll look for you tonight."

I watched her go back to the kitchen, hoping I'd be that happy when I reached Rebecca's age.

The door to the hall pushed open and Ruby came in. She looked around, caught sight of me, and hurried across the floor "Am I late?" she asked, yanking off her gloves.

"It's okay," I said. "Maggie's adjusting Eddie's legs."

Ruby looked over at Mags pulling on Eddie's leg like a demented chiropractor, and handed me a canvas bag. "These are the lights Maggie wanted."

"Thanks," I said. I studied her face for a moment. She seemed unsure whether to go or stay. Before I could ask her if everything was all right, Lita poked her head out of the door to the kitchen.

"Ruby, hang on for a moment," she called. "I have something for you." Lita skirted the long tables and joined us. She was carrying a black cloth bag from the grocery store. "I was so sorry to hear about Agatha," she said.

Ruby nodded. "Thank you."

"I know the two of you were close." She held out the bag. "Agatha left this here the night she . . . died. I didn't know what to do with it."

"What is it?" I asked. I remembered Agatha had had the bag at Eric's.

"Just odds and ends," Lita said.

Ruby took the bag, hugging it to her chest. "Thank you," she said in a low voice.

Lita nodded and went back to the kitchen.

Ruby pressed her lips together and swallowed a couple of times. "I'm not very good at this."

"You're doing fine," I said. Agatha's death had hit her hard. Her usual resilience seemed to have deserted her.

"David—Agatha's son—called me. It's going to be at least another three or four days before he can get here."

"I'm sorry."

"He asked me to pick some clothes for her to be . . ." She let the end of the sentence trail off. Then she cleared her throat and continued. "And check on the house." She had to clear her throat again, and I could see the effort it was taking for her not to give in to tears. "I said I would, but when I think about it . . ." She took a shaky breath.

"I'll go with you if that would help."

Ruby looked at me. "Seriously?"

"Yes."

Her shoulders sagged. "That would help a lot. Thank you."

"When do you want to do this?"

"Any chance we could go before the supper tonight?"

"I don't see why not," I said. "The library is closing early because of Winterfest. Where did Agatha live?"

It turned out the older woman had lived close to the Stratton Theater, ten minutes, maybe less, from the library. We agreed to meet just before five thirty.

"It won't take long," Ruby promised, setting the bag on a chair and shedding her coat. She took the lights back from me. "I appreciate this, Kathleen."

"It's not a problem," I told her.

Maggie was standing back studying Eddie again. From where I was standing, his legs didn't look any different from the way they did before she started pulling and twisting them. Ruby walked over, gave Maggie the bag and studied Eddie, too. Whatever it was they were concerned about, I couldn't see.

"Hello," a voice said behind me.

Startled, I jumped.

"Sorry. I didn't mean to scare you." It was Ruby's boyfriend, Justin. He smiled. "Ruby says she's going to stick a warning bell on me. She says I must've been a cat in a past life."

I thought about Hercules and Owen sneaking around the house. They were always catching me unawares.

"Hello, Justin," I said. "Ruby's helping Maggie. She shouldn't be too long."

He pulled off his gloves and stuck them in the pocket of his brown leather jacket. "Actually I was hoping to talk to you. Ruby said you'd probably be here. Could you answer a couple of questions about the reading program you set up at the library?"

I frowned. "You mean Reading Buddies?"

"Yeah," he said. "You got a Franklin grant for that, didn't you?"

"We did," I said.

Reading Buddies was a program we were doing through the schools. It paired kids in kindergarten and grade one with older kids in grades four and five—supervised, of course.

"I've been working on a project to build a camp for at-risk kids. You know, the ones who for whatever reason don't fit in at a regular school." He pulled a brochure out of his pocket and handed it to me. "It'll give them the chance to learn responsibility and life skills." His face got dark. "We have a piece of land, but the funding for the next stage fell through."

"I'm so sorry to hear that."

"People can be shortsighted." His voice was laced with anger. He took a deep breath. "Ruby thought maybe I would be eligible for a Franklin grant."

"Maybe," I said, glancing at the pamphlet he'd just given me. "With a Franklin grant you have to document the need when you apply. They like numbers. They like statistics."

He rolled his eyes. "Isn't it kind of obvious that there are kids living on the street? Kids that need a chance?" He snapped the two elastics around his wrist.

"It's easier for some people to connect with the problem —whether it's kids who can't read or kids who are homeless—if they have specifics."

He sighed and shook his head. "I've been working on this project for over a year. So many pieces of paper, so many trees used, and nothing happens."

His dark hair was slicked back with gel. He smoothed a hand over the top of it, then let out a breath and smiled at me. "I'm sorry," he said. "I get a little crazy about this."

He looked over at Maggie and Ruby. "I'm worried about her," he said quietly.

"She was close to Agatha," I said. "It's understandable that she's upset."

"She's not getting any sleep. She has nightmares," he said shifting restlessly from one foot to the other.

"She found Agatha's body. That would give anyone nightmares."

At that point Ruby caught sight of Justin. She waved to him, said something to Maggie, who was on her way down the ladder, and walked over to us.

"Hi," she said. "Did Kathleen answer all your questions?"

He nodded, reaching to brush something from her cheek. His fingers lingered on her skin for a moment. "Yeah, she did."

I did? I didn't think he'd actually asked any. I touched Ruby's shoulder. "I'll see you later." She smiled and nodded, but her attention had already been pulled back to Justin.

I walked over to Maggie, tucking Justin's brochure in my pocket. "Am I just a bitter, cynical person? Because he gets on my nerves," she said.

I held up my thumb and middle finger about an inch apart. "Maybe just a bit," I said. "I thought you liked Justin."

"I don't dislike him." She leaned in close to me. "He's just so intense," she said, stressing the words the way Justin did when he spoke.

I couldn't help laughing.

Maggie grinned and then her attention went back to Eddie.

"He looks good, Mags," I said.

"Are you saying that because it's really what you think or because you've decided I've crossed the line into Wack-a-doodle Land?"

I waggled one hand at her. "About sixty-forty."

"I can live with that."

She turned her attention to the photo collages. The new lights were clear and natural, a lot more like outdoor sunlight than anything else. Maggie looked up at the ceiling.

"Would it help if I went up the ladder and you nitpicked over how the lights are positioned?"

"Yes." She smiled at me. Sometimes Maggie was like Owen and Hercules; sarcasm was totally wasted on her.

I moved the ladder about a foot to the left, checked to make sure it was steady and climbed up. For the next ten minutes or so I made miniscule adjustments to the lights until Maggie was satisfied.

"That's it," she said, holding out both hands. "I'm not touching anything else. I swear."

Rebecca came across the tile floor, beaming. "Maggie, this is fantastic," she said.

Maggie's cheeks flushed. "Thank you."

"And I love Roma's young man."

"Excuse me?" Maggie said.

Rebecca pointed at the dummy. "That's Eddie Sweeney, right? The hockey player Roma's seeing?"

"Roma's not dating Eddie Sweeney," Maggie said, looking at Rebecca like she had a second head.

"She's been driving around with him all over town."

Maggie looked at me. I looked at her. We both burst out laughing at the same time.

Rebecca looked at us like we were crazy.

"Yes, Roma was driving around town with Eddie," Maggie said, giggling. "But it was this Eddie." She pointed at the mannequin.

Rebecca looked at me. I nodded. "That's how we got him down here," Maggie explained, gesturing with both hands. "He wouldn't fit in my car, so we belted him into the front seat of Roma's SUV."

"And people thought it was the real Eddie," Rebecca said with a laugh.

"I guess we were invisible in the backseat," Maggie said softly to me.

I looked at my watch. "Is there anything else I can do?"

"No," she said, giving me a quick hug. "Go back to the library. I'm headed back to the studio. I'll meet you here about six o'clock."

"Okay," I said.

"Don't eat for the rest of the afternoon," Rebecca said. "They'll be lots and lots of food."

I got my coat and pulled on my hat. Then I headed down the stairs, cut across the lot and made my way to the corner. Waiting for a car to turn so I could cross the street, I noticed Marcus come out of Eric's. He paused on the sidewalk in front of the restaurant, then made his way down two buildings and disappeared into the mouth of the alley.

I waited on the curb for a moment, but he didn't come back out.

This wasn't good. I just knew it wasn't good.

10

We closed the library at five. Susan quickly bundled herself into her coat and boots and left. I pulled up my hood against the slight wind and started down the street toward the Stratton Theater.

It was a beautifully restored building—older than the library. Unfortunately, the first time I'd been inside I'd found a dead body. I'd been back to the theater for the summer music festival, for a couple of plays, a concert and a wonderful production of *A Christmas Carol*. My feelings about the old building were a lot happier now.

Agatha's little house was up a tiny side street just past the Stratton. Ruby was waiting at the end of the driveway, a shopping bag tucked under her arm. She smiled as I walked up to her. "Thanks for doing this."

"I don't mind," I said, giving her what I hoped was a reassuring smile in return.

Someone had plowed the driveway to the tiny brick house and cleared the path and steps. I trailed behind Ruby. Squinting at the door, she felt for the keyhole. I took a step back to get out of the light.

The key turned in the lock. Ruby leaned her weight against the old wooden door. It stuck for a second, then groaned open. I slid my hand around the left side of the frame, feeling for a light switch.

A light came on and I could see into what looked to be the kitchen, up a few steps to the left. I followed Ruby up the stairs, leaving my snowy boots at the bottom.

The kitchen floor was green-and-blue speckled linoleum, very old and faded but spotless. The walls were pale green; the cupboards painted white. The table was a vintage chrome set, blue flowers on a white background circa the 1960s, I guessed.

Other than that there was nothing in the room.

Nothing. No cookie jar on the counter. No calendar on the wall or funny pictures stuck to the refrigerator. Maybe her son had cleared a lot of things out when Agatha went to the rehabilitation center after her stroke.

Ruby looked around the room, lips pressed together.

I touched her arm. "Let's see if we can find the bedroom."

She nodded but didn't speak. The little house was cold. Claire had said Agatha hadn't always been able to afford the heat. It was a wonder the pipes hadn't frozen.

A tiny hallway led out of the kitchen. An upright piano, dark chocolate brown, sat in a niche to the right. The room at the end of the hall looked like it could be Agatha's bedroom. I could see a bed made up with a white chenille bedspread.

Ruby walked slowly down the hall, looking at everything. Clearly she'd never been in the house before. As in the kitchen, there was nothing personal in the hall. The hardwood floor was bare; there was nothing on the walls.

The double bed in the bedroom was made with the precision of a high-end hotel, the spread pulled tightly and with perfectly squared hospital corners. The night table held a clock and a box of Kleenex.

Ruby hesitated and pulled open the closet door in the wall to the left of the bed. The small storage space was organized with the same precision as the rest of the room. Blouses, skirts and dresses were arranged from white to dark. Two pairs of shoes, one black, one beige, sat on a shoe rack on the floor. Several sweaters were folded on the shelf above the rod.

All of the clothing looked old. Not "old" in the sense of worn-out, but in the sense of vintage. It was almost as though Agatha had gotten stuck at some point in time.

Ruby looked into the closet, one hand on the door. Her shoulders slumped. "I don't know what to take."

"Maybe a dress," I suggested.

"Yeah. She wasn't much of a pants person. She didn't think they were very ladylike." She caught the skirt of a black-and-white print, holding out the fabric. "But which one?"

"That's pretty," I said. "But why don't you look at each dress. Maybe one of them will, I don't know, spark a memory."

Ruby did smile then. "That's a good idea." She looked around the room. "Would you see if you can find a suitcase? I don't think the bag I brought is going to be big enough." She hesitated. "And I know no one is going to see, but I don't want things to be wrinkled. Agatha would care about that."

I squeezed her arm. "I'll see what I can find."

Ruby started flipping through the hangers while I took a quick look around the room. There was no suitcase in the corner under the old spool bed. I went back into the hallway.

The living room was to my right. A three-sided bay window with a deep window seat looked out over the street. Like the rest of the house, the furniture here was all old—a maroon sofa and matching chair, plus a gray-and-maroon flowered wingback chair with matching footstool. There was a low walnut coffee table in front of the couch and a matching side table by the wingback. A brick fireplace filled the entire end of the room, the heavy brass andirons in the shape of watchful lions.

The living room was spartan. There were no magazines on the coffee table, no stacks of books anywhere. There were no pictures, no photographs, no artwork. There were no pillows on the sofa, no blanket to curl up in. Everything was functional, but there was nothing that told me about Agatha as a person. Even allowing for the fact that she'd spent the past several months in a rehabilitation hospital, the house still seemed lonely and empty.

I pictured my own house, with kitty treats cooling on the kitchen counter, Owen sneaking onto the footstool in the living room, Herc grooving to Barry Manilow, and pieces of Fred the Funky Chicken always needing to be vacuumed up. I felt sad for Agatha.

I went back out into the hallway, glancing in the bedroom as I passed the door. Ruby had a long-sleeved teal dress laid out on the bed.

The second bedroom in the tiny house was next to the living room. It was big enough for a single bed and dresser and very little else. I opened the closet door and found the suitcases Ruby needed, sitting on a large cardboard box with the name *Ellis* written on the side in spidery handwriting.

There was also men's clothing hanging in the closet. Several gray suits, a navy blazer and a weathered aviator's jacket, sheepskin lined and worn to a chocolaty softness on the outside. With the exception of the jacket, the clothes were very much out of style; in fact, the suit had probably been in and out of fashion several times.

I grabbed the smaller of the two suitcases and took it back to Ruby. She had everything spread on the bed—dress, slip, underwear, stockings, even a lacy, knit white cardigan.

"Here," I said, holding out the blue suitcase. "This should work."

"Thanks, Kathleen," she said. She looked shaky.

"Why don't you let me fold these for you?" I said. "I'm a master at folding and packing. I promise."

Ruby hesitated for a second, then nodded and sat on the edge of the bed.

I folded the green dress and laid it in the bottom of the suitcase. Then I added the sweater, the slip and the rest of the underclothes. "There," I said to Ruby, snapping the suitcase closed. "Ready to go?"

She grabbed the suitcase handle and stood up. A look of panic crossed her face. "Wait a minute," she said. "I didn't get her any shoes." She took a couple of steps toward the closet.

"We don't need shoes, Ruby," I said softly. She looked at me, confused. "Agatha doesn't need shoes," I repeated.

Ruby swallowed, turned her head and blinked away the tears that filled her eyes. I waited silently until her breathing even out. "You're right," she whispered. "For a minute I forgot why we were here."

We went back to the kitchen, turning off the lights behind us. I pulled on my boots and held the suitcase while Ruby stepped into hers. Outside she locked the door, twisting the knob to make sure it was fastened securely.

"It looks so sad," she said.

"I know." I pulled on my mittens. "But don't forget that Agatha was away from here for months."

We walked down the driveway to the street. "Ruby, who was Ellis?" I asked. "Was that Agatha's husband?"

"No," Ruby said. "Ellis was her brother. Ellis Slater. He died, oh, almost twenty years ago. This was his house. He left it to Agatha." She shifted the suitcase from one hand to the other. "Why do you ask?"

"There were boxes in the second bedroom. The name Ellis was on one of them. And there were some men's clothes in the closet."

Ruby gave me a wry smile. "That would be Agatha. Never throw out something that might be useful."

"My father does the same thing." I didn't add that my dad's idea of useful didn't usually meet the average person's idea of what was useful. Which was why every time we'd moved, someone had had to pack the candelabra made from a pair of moose antlers.

We walked to the corner together. "Thank you for coming with me," Ruby said. "I'm going to take this down to Gunnerson's. I want things to be there when she . . . when her . . ." She stopped to clear her throat. "When they're needed." She shrugged. "Silly, isn't it?"

"No," I said. "It's kind." I pulled my hat down over my ears. "Will I see you later at the Winterfest supper?"

She nodded. "As far as I know. I'm meeting Justin later."

"I'll see you later, then," I said. I started for the community center, looking back over my shoulder once to see Ruby heading resolutely down the street for Gunnerson's Funeral Home.

Maggie was at the entrance of the parking lot as I came up the street. She was wearing her purple fake-fur jacket, stamping her feet on the sidewalk to stay warm. She waved when she caught sight of me, and I quickened my pace. "Am I late?" I asked.

"No," she said. "You're few minutes early. Let's go get in line before it gets any longer."

The line at the front door of the community center, of maybe two dozen people, snaked down the street. Maggie and I scurried to get to the end.

The queue moved pretty quickly. We were inside in five minutes, maybe even less. Maggie had money hidden in her glove and paid for both of us before I could even get my wallet out.

"Why did you do that?" I asked, as we followed the crowd to the hall.

"Because you've been doing so much to help me while I've been working on the display."

"I climbed a ladder and adjusted a couple of lights."

She held up a hand. "You did more than that," she said. "How many times did you bring me supper? How many cups of tea did you make? How many times did you listen while I sat in your living room, going on and on about this project?"

I grinned and elbowed her. "You thought I was listening? I don't even think Owen was listening."

She stuck out her tongue. "Even so, I just wanted to say thank you. So let me. It's beans and scalloped potatoes and pie, for heaven's sake. I didn't buy you a car."

"Okay," I said. "Thank you for the thank-you." I looked around. There were at least a couple dozen people checking out Maggie's display.

Maggie had spotted a pair of vacant chairs at one of the long tables. I threaded my way around the chairs and people, trying to keep up with her long legs. A lot of people smiled, said hello or raised a hand in greeting. I was surprised by how good it made me feel, especially after being in Agatha's lonely house.

Mags was standing by the table she'd spotted, a hand on each of the chairs.

"Now what?" I asked.

"Take off your coat and sit down."

I looked around. "How do we get our food?"

"It's coming," she said, setting her fuzzy teddy-bear coat over the back of the chair and pulling off her lime green hat.

I tipped my head toward the back wall. "You have fans," I said.

She looked over her shoulder and then grinned at me.

The person to the right of Maggie leaned around her and smiled at us. His mouth was too full to say anything.

It took a second for me to recognize Officer Craig in his street clothes.

I smiled back.

"How's everything?" Maggie asked the pretty brunet on the other side of Officer Craig.

"Good," she said.

"Your mom's?" Maggie asked, pointing at what looked to be some kind of mustard pickle on the table in front of her.

The young woman nodded.

"Great," Maggie said. "I bought three bottles of her pickles at the market last fall. They didn't last three weeks."

"I know. I ate all the jam she gave me. And when I tried to get another bottle she said I'd have to pay for it. And I picked half those berries."

Just then a woman wearing a long white apron appeared. She was carrying two loaded plates. She set them, hot and steaming, in front of us. Behind her came a teenager, also apron clad, with two glasses of water.

They were the Kings, I realized, mother and daughter. Roma had been out at their place almost every week this winter, looking after the old—too old, it turned out—horse they'd bought for their daughter. I was guessing the teenager was the horse-loving daughter. The I ♥ HORSES T-shirt was a dead giveaway.

She gave me a shy smile and handed over one of the glasses and a napkin-wrapped roll of utensils.

I looked at the plate, unsure of where to start. There were baked beans fragrant with molasses and mustard, a thick slice of ham, crispy golden-topped scalloped potatoes, and a casserole of what looked like carrot and turnip.

I unrolled my napkin and picked up my fork. Maggie was already eating, making little murmurs of enjoyment. She sounded a lot like Hercules had when I'd given him the sardines.

I tried a bite of the casserole. "Oh, wow. This is good," I said out loud. I took another bite. Did I taste just a hint of nutmeg? I couldn't help a grunt of pleasure.

"You're making me hungry," a voice said behind me. Roma was standing between our table and the next, unwinding a fuzzy blue scarf from around her neck.

"Hi," I said.

"Can I squeeze in next to you?" She looked around for space.

Maggie scraped her chair a little closer to Officer Craig, who didn't seem to mind moving closer to his pretty girlfriend. I went in the other direction and then a chair seemed to materialize out of nowhere, handed over the tables to Roma, who smiled a thank-you and pushed into the space we made for her.

"I'm sorry I'm late," she said, pulling off her coat and putting it over the back of the chair. "I had to set a golden Lab's leg."

"What happened?"

"Hit by a car." Roma shook her head in annoyance. "It's slippery. If the dog's running loose and meets a car, the car is the one that's going to come out unhurt." She pushed the sleeves of her sweater back. "Why don't people understand that?"

Before I could say anything, the Kings were back with a drink and plate for Roma, steam rising from the food.

"Thanks," Roma said.

"Are you alone?" Ella King asked with a sly smile.

Roma gave her a puzzled look. "No, I'm with them," she said, pointing from me to Maggie, who was eating like food was going out of style. Roma noticed the teenager then. "Hi, Taylor. How's Horton?"

"He's good," the girl said. "Kind of stiff in the cold, though."

"Yeah, me too these days," Roma said. "I'll be out the first of the week to see him."

Taylor gave her a warm smile. "Thanks, Dr. Davidson," she said.

Roma unrolled her napkin, placed it in her lap and picked up her fork.

"Horton?" I asked, grabbing my knife so I could cut a piece of ham.

"Her horse. *Horton Hears a Who!* Dr. Seuss. It's Taylor's favorite book."

A woman I didn't know passed in front of us in the aisle between our table and the next. "Hi, Roma," she said, with a grin and an obvious wink.

Roma lifted a hand in hello. Her mouth was full.

The other woman looked around. "By yourself tonight?" Before Roma could say anything, the woman's grin got bigger. "Yeah, playing hard to get is a good plan."

Maggie kept her head over her plate and her eyes on her food, but her shoulders were heaving with laughter. It was clear the rumors about Roma and Eddie Sweeney were all over town.

I started on the scalloped potatoes and hoped I wouldn't laugh, too.

Roma set down her fork and slid her chair back a bit. "Spill it," she said.

I leaned over, trying to catch Maggie's eye, but she kept them on her food, stuffing in more beans and shaking with laughter. Roma folded her arms. My food was getting cold and Maggie was letting me sink. Roma waited, staring expectantly at me.

"Well, there's kind of a rumor going around that you're . . . seeing someone."

"Whom am I supposed to be seeing?"

I swallowed. Maggie was not going to rescue me. "Eddie." I blurted.

"Eddie?" Roma said with a frown. "Eddie who?"

Maggie almost choked. Roma thumped her on the

back a couple of times, then turned her attention back to me again. "Eddie who?" she repeated

"Eddie Sweeney," I said staring down at my plate. If I looked at anyone I was going to laugh, too.

Her mouth fell open. "Eddie? The hockey player? Maggie's mannequin?" Maggie looked up at last.

Roma glared at her. "This is all your fault."

"How is it my fault?" Maggie asked, trying to look innocent and not laugh herself silly at the same time.

"I was driving your"—Roma gestured wildly with her hands—"creation around. And now people think I'm having a fling with the real Eddie. I'm old enough to be his"—she paused—"older sister, for heaven's sake."

"Since when do you care what people think?" I asked, wiping mustard from my chin.

"Since always," she retorted.

Maggie lips were twitching. Trouble. "Tell you what," she said. "When Winterfest is over, I'll give you Eddie. Then you really will be a couple."

Roma picked up her fork. She was trying to look mad, but I didn't think she really was. I kept looking at her until she looked at me.

"Every time I let you two in my car, things end up going south," she said. "Every single time."

I realized she was thinking about the time Maggie sort of hijacked Roma and her SUV because we were trying to follow someone.

At the end of the table, beyond Officer Craig and his girlfriend, was a family I had seen in the library a few times, lots of Dr. Seuss and Max and Ruby books. Dad and the four-year-old were doing patty-cake, the girl's blond curls bouncing.

"Patty-cake, patty-cake," the little one chanted, her high, clear voice carrying down the table. But instead of saying, "bake me a man," she said, "make me a man."

Maggie looked at Roma and said, "I did." Then she

put her head on the table and collapsed in laughter. Roma whacked her with a paper napkin and went back to eating.

I decided this would be a great time to go in search of coffee, even though I knew it would make me restless this late in the day. "I'll be right back," I said.

The coffee and tea table was over by the kitchen. I wound my way around tables, smiling and saying hello to everyone I knew. Rebecca and Mary, both in the same long white aprons that all the servers seemed to be wearing, were deep in conversation at the tea table.

I picked up a mug, added sugar and reached for the stainless-steel coffee carafe.

Mary noticed me then. "I'll get that for you," she said, taking the cup from my hand. "Would you like regular, decaf or chocolate hazelnut?"

I wasn't much of a fan of flavored coffee, but maybe just this once.

"Chocolate hazelnut," I said. "Please."

Rebecca lightly touched my arm. "Kathleen, is Justin Anders the young man Ruby's been seeing?"

"Yes, he is," I said, taking my cup back from Mary. "Why?"

"You haven't heard?" Mary asked. "Turns out it wasn't a rumor after all."

"What?" I asked, wondering what new piece of town news they had.

Mary shrugged. "Agatha left Ruby's boyfriend half a million dollars."

11

I glanced from Rebecca, who looked apologetic, to Mary, who could be described only as smug. I set the coffee on the edge of the table. I was afraid I was going to drop it.

"Agatha left money to Ruby's boyfriend?"

"Yes." Mary grabbed the carafe to pour a cup of coffee for one of the servers.

I was dumbfounded. Then I thought about the rumor going around that Roma was seeing an NHL hockey player ten years her junior. "You certain?" I asked. "I didn't realize he even knew her."

Mary handed the cup over to the young server. "Yes, I am."

Rebecca brushed the front of her apron. "The information came from Bridget," she said.

I had forgotten that Mary's daughter, Bridget, was the publisher of the *Mayville Heights Chronicle*. "But half a million dollars? Where would Agatha get half a million dollars?" I remembered the tiny, spare house.

"Agatha was very frugal," Mary said, smiling at another server on her way to the kitchen.

"What about her son? Why would she leave money to someone she didn't know instead of him?"

Mary shrugged. "All I know is some lawyer from Red Wing did a new will for Agatha. She signed it the day before she died."

I shook my head slowly. "That doesn't make any sense. Peter Lundgren was Agatha's lawyer."

"Apparently not anymore." Mary swept a few crumbs off the table.

It couldn't be true. But it was going to hurt Ruby. "This is getting messy," I said to Rebecca.

She patted my arm. "I know."

I picked up my coffee and wound my way back to the table. Maggie glanced over at me as she scraped the last few baked beans from her plate. Something in my face made her take a second look. "What is it?" she asked.

Roma turned to look at me, as well. I pointed toward the tea table.

"According to Rebecca and Mary, Agatha left half a million dollars to Justin."

"Of course she did," Roma said. "And I'm dating Eddie Sweeney." She shot a quick look at Maggie, who blushed just a little. "First of all, Agatha didn't have half a million dollars. She had a teacher's pension and from her day that wasn't a lot of money. And second, if she did have a little money she wouldn't leave it to someone she hardly knew."

"It doesn't make a lot of sense," Maggie agreed.

"The story came from Bridget."

Roma waved her hand like she was chasing away a bug. "Well, Bridget got it wrong or Mary did. Agatha didn't have that much money. She didn't have any money." She pushed her plate away. "It's just a rumor and it's wrong."

"It has to be," Maggie said. "You saw her. Did Agatha look like someone who had a lot of money?"

Actually she had looked like someone who didn't

spend a lot of money. She wasn't buying clothes or things for her house. Maybe she'd amassed a small fortune and no one knew about it. Luckily I didn't have to answer because the Kings were back to collect our plates and deliver slices of apple pie.

I picked up my fork. The pie was better than promised. There was a hint of tartness to the apples, and I could taste the cinnamon and nutmeg. I actually made little groaning sounds as I took a second bite.

Maggie grinned at me over her plate. "I told you it was good," she said.

I licked apple off the back of my fork. "Good?" I said. "I think I know how Owen feels about catnip." I'd had Mary's pie before, but this was warm, with a small scoop of vanilla ice cream melting on top. It was a party in my mouth.

We ate without talking, the pie was that good. I thought about swiping my finger over the plate to catch the last flakes of pastry, but those kind of manners belonged at the home, where only Owen and Hercules could see me. I pushed back my chair so I could stretch my legs.

"I ate too much," Maggie said, patting her midsection.

"Me, too." Roma pulled at the front of her sweater.

"Want to walk over to the Winterfest site and take a look at things?" Maggie asked.

"I can't," Roma said, getting to her feet. "I'm on the cleanup crew."

"Kath?" Maggie looked at me.

"Sure," I said. I was kind of curious to see the sliding hill, the dogsled track and the outdoor rink.

Maggie looked over her shoulder at the back wall. There were dozens of people checking out Eddie and the various photo collages. "Roma just wants to ditch us so she can spend some time with Eddie," she stage-whispered.

Roma rolled her eyes and headed for the kitchen.

We put on our coats, tugged on hats and mittens and headed for the door. There were still people arriving. "You weren't kidding when you said the whole town comes to this thing," I said.

"It's a social event of the season," Maggie said as we made our way down the stairs. "Heck, it's the social event of the *year*, not to mention Mary makes the best freaking pie in the universe." She stopped on the last step to wind her scarf around her neck. "There should be a community supper as part of the library centennial," she said.

"You know, that's a good idea," I said. "I'll mention it to Everett and Rebecca."

We pushed our way out into the cold night air and I was glad to be outside. It had been getting warm and stuffy in the community center. The parking lot was full of cars and trucks and they were also parked down both sides of the street.

We started toward the marina, where all the outdoor Winterfest activities were taking place.

"Are you really going to give Eddie to Roma when Winterfest is over?" I asked.

Maggie laughed. "I don't know. It would be kind of funny to stick him in the waiting room at the clinic for a few days and see what kind of rumors that starts."

I stuffed my hands in my pockets. "I can't believe people think she's dating the real Eddie Sweeney, just because she drove around with a mannequin in the front seat of her SUV."

"So, how do you think the rumors that Agatha left Justin a bunch of money got started?" Maggie asked. She looked both ways for cars and pulled me across the street.

I hesitated. Maggie leaned in front of me. "You don't think it's true, do you?"

"I think it could be, at least partly."

"All right," Maggie began, lowering her voice because of all the people around now. "Where did Agatha get the money? And why did she leave it to Justin?"

I shrugged. "I don't know where she got the money. Maybe she saved it. She didn't seem to be spending much. Maybe she bought Microsoft or Dell stock back in the day." I could hear voices ahead of me and laughter and music.

"Let's say, for the sake of argument, she had the money." Maggie kicked a chunk of frozen snow down the sidewalk. "Why leave it to Justin?"

I gave her the Mr. Spock eyebrow.

"Because of Ruby." Maggie made a face, as if the words left a bad taste in her mouth.

"Exactly."

She kicked the chunk of snow again. It collided with a streetlamp and smashed into small bits of snow and ice. "People are going to talk."

"I know," I said. "And it's going to hurt Ruby."

"You think that's why she's not here tonight?"

"Maybe." We were surrounded by people all heading in the same direction. "Where's everyone coming from?" I asked.

"First you eat, then you come down here and slide until your stomach hurts," Maggie said. "It's a Winterfest tradition."

As we came around a curve in the road by the marina I saw the venue for the first time. The rink was close to the marina itself. There was a fire going in the outdoor pit between the building and the ice. Beyond that I could see the dogsled track. But what dominated the space was the hill.

It was man-made, or, to be more exact, machine-made. There were eight runs: two for the little ones and six for the adults and teenagers. Walk up the ramps on either side, get in line, grab a sled—which looked like a potato sack and probably was—and then slide like stink to the bottom and crash into the bales of hay.

Maggie grinned at me, eyes sparkling.

"No," I said.

"Oh, come on. One time."

I watched Kate, my co-op student, hit a bump and go airborne for a minute. "You want to watch pie come out my nose?" I said.

She pretended to think about that for a minute.

"You can go without me." I said. "I'll stand here and cheer for you."

Maggie made a show of checking her watch. "Oh, darn," she said. "We have to go through or we're going to miss the start of the *Gotta Dance* reunion special." She held up one hand. "Otherwise . . ."

"Well, of course we wouldn't want to miss Matt Lauer demonstrate that it is possible for human beings have two left feet," I said.

"Matt does not have two left feet. He's a fantastic dancer. He won—"

"—the coveted crystal trophy," I finished for her. I'd never quite gotten Maggie's love for the *Today* show host.

"You're just jealous because that piece of beefcake in a loincloth lost."

I blew a raspberry at her. The peace of beefcake she was mocking was Kevin Sorbo, Hercules from the cheesy syndicated series of the same name and the source of my Hercules' name. Not that I admitted it to anyone.

"Where did you park?" I asked as we made our way back through the crowd.

"I'm about half a block up the hill," she said. We dashed across the street and walked back to her little bug.

"You still thinking about buying a car?" Maggie asked as she started the car and cranked up the heat.

"Thinking about it is all I've done."

"You need a truck. Something like Ruby's. Well, maybe less funky."

I thought about Harry's truck, heat blasting from the vents. "Maybe a truck would be a good idea."

"I can just picture Owen and Hercules riding shotgun," Maggie laughed.

Owen and Hercules were waiting in the kitchen when Maggie and I walked in.

"Hey, guys," she said as she pulled off her coat. Hercules watched her, hoping, I guessed, that she'd brought them some kind of treat. Owen walked around behind her, more like a puppy than a cat. I put the kettle on to make tea for Maggie. "Want a date square?" I asked.

"I could eat one," she said. Maggie ate like a lumberjack and was built like a runway model. "I'll put the TV on." She headed for the living room.

Hercules padded over to the counter and looked at me. I slipped him a couple of cheese-and-sardine crackers. "Don't tell your brother," I whispered.

I put the date squares on a plate with a few chunks of mozzarella, which I knew Maggie would sneak to the cats when they all figured I wasn't looking. When the water boiled I made tea, put everything on a tray with a couple of napkins and headed for the living room.

Maggie was on the sofa, feet propped on my leather footstool. Owen was on one side, giving Maggie adoring looks, and Hercules was on the other side, doing his *no one ever feeds me* look. The theme song for *Gotta Dance* was just beginning. I curled into the opposite end of the sofa, setting the tray on the cushion between Maggie and me.

She leaned forward and pointed at the TV. "See?" she said to Owen. "That's Kevin Sorbo. Boo!"

The cat would have booed if he'd been able to.

Maggie gestured to the screen again. "Remember? That's Matt Lauer. Yay!"

"Meow!" Owen said with enthusiasm.

Maggie laughed.

"Sold out for mozzarella," I said. Owen was busy eating the bit of cheese that Maggie had just snuck to him.

I settled back against the cushions to watch the show and I couldn't help thinking how much happier my house seemed than Agatha's. Okay, so there was cat hair on the footstool and some part of a catnip chicken by the stairs. But it felt a lot more welcoming than Agatha's lonely place.

Maggie was leaning forward again, forearms on her knees, discussing the various dancing couples with Owen, while Hercules ate the piece of cheese Maggie had slipped to him.

Thinking about Agatha made me wonder if what Rebecca and Mary had told me could be true. Did Agatha have all that money and had she left it to Justin?

Maggie left when the show ended. We made plans to check out the Winterfest activities Saturday night. Yawning, I put the dishes in the sink. "I'm too tired to tell you everything," I said to Hercules and Owen. "Remind me in the morning."

Owen woke me in the morning by breathing his cheesy, bad breath in my face. Over oatmeal and bananas for me, plus two cups of coffee, and cat food and water for the cats, I told them about the visit to Agatha's house and the rumors about the money. They didn't have any insights, either.

The library was open only until one o'clock because of Winterfest, but it was a busy morning. I stopped for groceries before heading home, slogging up the hill with a heavy canvas bag in each hand. I decided maybe

I could create a workout DVD: the Grocery Bag Workout.

I spent the afternoon cleaning my little house and doing laundry, with Hercules for company. Owen appeared only when the new batch of kitty treats came out of the oven.

Maggie pulled into the driveway at about seven o'clock. She was wearing heavy boots and cherry-colored earmuffs over her mohair hat. It made her look like a fuzzy, red-eared teddy bear.

"Oh, good. You're wearing your snow pants," she said, as I laced up my boots.

"I don't know what you have planned, but I'm figuring a little padding couldn't hurt."

Owen came over for a quick nuzzle. "Stay off the footstool," I whispered to him. His response was to bat an errant piece of hair coming out of my hat.

Maggie parked on one of the side streets, and we walked down to the Winterfest site. There were probably twice as many people as on Friday night. More of the lights were on and I could see the course was even bigger than I first realized. Along with the sliding hill, the dogsled circuit, and the rink, there were a puck shoot and a labyrinth.

Maggie tugged on my sleeve. "Let's do the maze."

From where we were standing, on a slight incline looking down, the maze, built completely out of frozen snow, looked massive and complicated and scary.

"I don't think so," I said.

"Why?" Maggie asked.

"Because I have a bad sense of direction. Once I get in there I'll be wandering around all night. Anyway, I thought you wanted to go sliding." I pointed the hill. "Why don't we do that before the line gets any longer?"

"Good idea."

Saved.

I felt kind of silly, but I didn't want to admit that the maze scared me. It was because of an old movie called *The Maze* that a bunch of older kids had scared me with the summer I was nine and my parents were doing summer stock in a hundred-year-old, supposedly haunted theater. I had nightmares for months after watching that movie on an old black-and-white TV late at night in one of the back rooms at the theater.

Maggie and I got in line for the hill. As we worked our way to the top I realized it was probably a good idea that I was wearing snow pants, sweats, and long underwear. I also realized it looked like a heck of a lot of fun. I turned out to be right on both counts. We slid until my legs began to wobble.

"I can't climb that hill again. I need hot chocolate," I told Maggie, brushing hay and snow off my jacket.

We walked slowly down to the canteen set up by the rink and the puck shoot. I pulled at the front of my parka. I was actually sweating.

"That was fun," I said to Maggie as we stood in line for our cocoa.

"Yeah, you're not a bad Saturday night date," she joked. She looked around. "I haven't seen Roma. Have you?"

"No," I said. "But there's so many people here, it would be easy to miss her."

Lita was working behind the counter. She caught my eye. "What can I get for you, Kathleen?" she asked.

I held up two fingers. "Two hot chocolates, please, Lita."

She poured two cups from a huge insulated carafe and dropped a marshmallow in each one before she snapped on the sippy-cup lids. I paid and moved out of the way, handing one cup to Maggie.

"Thank you," she said, wrapping her hands around the cup and taking a sip. "Oh, that's good."

We walked over to the puck shoot and stood watching for a moment. Maggie elbowed me. "Hey, maybe Roma is with Eddie," she said with a grin.

"How do stupid rumors like that get started?" I said, sipping my hot chocolate.

"There's usually a grain of truth to them," Maggie said. "Roma was driving around with Eddie in her SUV. It just wasn't the real Eddie."

Did that mean there was a grain of truth to the story that Agatha had left a fortune to Justin?

"Hello," someone said. Maggie's face lit up with a slightly mischievous smile and she turned immediately to say hello to Marcus.

I shot her a warning look over my cup, but it was a waste of effort. I turned, "Hi," I said.

Marcus was wearing the same heavy jacket he'd had on at Wisteria Hill, as well as black ski pants and over-sized gloves.

"Have you tried the puck shoot yet?" Maggie asked, gesturing at the game.

He shook his head. "I just got here. How about you?"

"We were on the sliding hill," I said. I held up my hot chocolate. "We came over here to get warm."

Beside me, Maggie took a step forward, and I realized we had somehow ended up in the puck-shoot line. "Maggie, how did we get in this line?" I asked.

She looked around. "I'm not sure." She looked at Marcus. "Do you want to go ahead of us?"

"You're not going to try it?" he asked.

"Maybe when my fingers get a little warmer. I think I need to at least be able to feel them before I pick up a hockey stick."

Marcus looked at me. "Hockey is probably not your sport," he said.

I could hear just a touch of condescension in his voice. At least I thought I could. "I wouldn't want to make you look bad," I said lightly.

He laughed.

I would've let it go. I really would have, if he hadn't laughed. "You don't think I could beat you?"

"I've been playing hockey since I could walk," he said. "It wouldn't be a fair contest."

I handed my hot chocolate to Maggie. "I could play left-handed, if that would make you feel better," I said with a small smile.

We were at the front of the line. The teenage boy running the game handed me a hockey stick and held one out to Marcus. He hesitated.

I had already stepped over the low wooden barrier onto the playing surface. "You coming?" I asked, making sure the challenge was evident in my voice and my posture.

He shrugged, trying to look casual about the whole thing. I could tell from the way he sized up the playing surface and the tightness in his jaw that he wanted to play. Marcus Gordon was competitive.

That was okay. So was I.

The puck shoot was actually more like a game of one-on-one street hockey. The space was snow packed, not too slippery yet. The net was at the far end. Instead of a puck we had a fluorescent pink ball. Marcus took the other stick and stepped onto the snow.

"You have five minutes," the teenager said. He stepped over the barrier, holding the ball for the face-off. I leaned forward, stick on the ground, and Marcus leaned in, as well, a smile pulling at the corners of his eyes and mouth. "Most goals wins," the young man said. "No head butts. No groin hits. Body checks are okay. Like I said, you got five minutes." He held the ball up over his head and dropped it.

I got my stick on it first, faked right, went left and whipped the ball into the net with my blistering slap shot. Behind me everyone cheered. I grinned at Marcus.

He didn't smile back.

It was about to get fun.

He was ready for me on the next face-off. He got the ball first, but when he pulled back his stick to shoot I flicked it away and raced to the net.

Score!

We'd attracted a crowd and they went crazy cheering, and I shamelessly played to them, making a dramatic, sweeping bow.

He beat me on the next face-off, then faked me out by pretending to make a move for the net and instead going backward. It was two-one.

I won the next face-off, literally ducking under him to shoot. Three-one.

Even though I knew I'd won, I went all out the last time. Marcus got the ball first, but when he flicked his eyes away for just a second to set up a shot, I hip-checked him. He lost his balance and toppled over onto the snow.

I went right for the clearest shot. Out of the corner of my eye I saw him stretch his stick across the snow to hook me. I timed it perfectly, jumping dramatically over the stick as it swept across the snow, and then whipped my own stick back and scored just as the buzzer sounded.

As they like to say in hockey, the crowd went wild.

To show I was a good sport I walked over to Marcus and offered him a hand up. Because he was a good sport he took it. We got a round of applause as he got to his feet.

"Wow!" Maggie said, as I joined her after several high-fives and a couple of fist bumps. "Where did you learn to play like that?" She handed me my hot choco-late.

"Yeah, where did you learn to play like that?" Marcus asked, brushing snow off his jacket.

My face was flushed and I was sweating. "Parking lots and back alleys," I said. I took a sip of my hot chocolate as we moved over to let the next players by. It was cold.

Maggie looked skeptical. "Seriously?"

"Seriously," I said. "You know my parents did a lot of summer stock. I hung out with the backstage crew when there weren't any kids to hang out with." I detoured sideways into the canteen line. "They played a lot of street hockey."

"I owe you another one of those," Marcus said, gesturing at my cup.

"No, you don't."

Behind him Mags was glaring at me. We were already in the line and I wasn't going to gain anything by arguing with him, so all I did was smile. "Thanks," I said.

When we got to the head of the line, he bought one hot chocolate for me and a second for himself, after offering Maggie one, too. She held up her empty cup and declined.

Marcus lifted his drink in a toast to me. "You owe me a rematch." Then he smiled at us and said, "Have a good night." And disappeared into the crowd.

Maggie was watching me, hands behind her back. "You're not going to tell me I should've let him win, are you?" I said. She wrinkled her nose at me. "No. That was great."

"So are you going to give me the gosh-you're-so-cute-as-a-couple speech?"

She shook her head as we started walking. "No. I give up."

"Good," I said, taking a drink from my cup. The hot chocolate was steaming.

"You did look good, though, the two of you chasing that little ball."

"Mags," I said. "You'd have better luck getting Roma and Eddie—the real Eddie—together."

She laughed. "I don't think so. I'm already in trouble for getting Roma and the fake Eddie together."

We walked around for a while, mostly people watching. The line was long at the maze and Maggie didn't mention trying it again.

"Ready to go?" she asked after another half hour.

"Yeah," I said. "My fingers are getting numb." We walked back to the car, and Maggie drove me up the hill.

The motion-sensor lights came on as I walked around the house. I could see Hercules sitting on the bench in the porch, watching for me out the window. He waited while I pulled off my gloves and boots. Then I swept him up into a hug, kissing the top of his furry head where the white of his nose met the black fur on his forehead.

"You are so good to come home to," I said. Hercules started squirming, and I set him down. "I know. No mushy stuff."

He shot me a look and took a few washing passes at his face with his paw. "Hey, do I wash off all your kisses?" I said.

I unlocked the door and shed my coat and the rest of my things. There was no sign of Owen in the kitchen. I held my finger to my lips and pointed at the living room, slowly making my way to the doorway. Hercules padded silently beside me. I'd left one lamp glowing on the table by the window.

I peeked around the door, hoping to catch Owen napping on the footstool. No luck.

He meowed hello from where he sat beside the chair. Hercules walked around me, making muttering noises in his throat. I went over to Owen, sat on the footstool and lifted him into my lap. "I know what you're up to," I said as I stroked his soft fur. He was the picture of wide-eyed innocence. "I will catch you," I said sternly. "And when I do, no kitty treats for a week."

His response was to put a paw on my shoulder and lick my cheek. Then he jumped down and walked away. Basically I'd just been given the kiss-off by a cat.

I got up and headed to the kitchen. Hercules and Owen might be very independent, but with a piece of toast and peanut butter, they were putty in my hands.

12

I'd been up maybe fifteen minutes in the morning when the phone rang. There's something about a phone ringing early or late that gives me a jolt.

It was Rebecca. "Morning, Kathleen. I hope it's not too early to call. I saw your light on."

"It's not too early," I said, relieved that it was Rebecca and she sounded just fine.

"Wonderful," she said, and I could hear the smile in her voice. "Everett and I were hoping you'd join us for breakfast, if you don't have the plans or you haven't eaten already."

I looked around the room. Hercules was dozing in a square of sunshine by the door. Owen's head was under the bed. "I don't have any plans. When would you like me?"

"How about now?"

"I'll be there as soon as I get my things on and walk around." There was too much snow to cut through the backyard into Rebecca's yard.

"Just walk up to the Justasons'," Rebecca instructed. "Their boys made a path between our two streets."

"All right," I said. "See you soon."

I hung up, looked down at the faded blue sweater I was wearing and decided I needed to change into something a little more presentable—not that Rebecca or Everett would care.

I pulled down my favorite black turtleneck from the closet shelf. Hercules looked up. "I'm going over to Rebecca's," I said.

He laid his head back on his paws. Owen had come out from under the bed at the sound of Rebecca's name. He stood in front of me and meowed.

"No," I said, fluffing my hair back into place. "You have to stay here."

That got me another loud meow. I glared at him. Hercules opened one eye for a moment to look at us.

Owen followed me down the stairs. He headed straight for the closet where my messenger bag was hanging, sat down and stared at the door as though he could will it open.

"Give it up," I said. "You're not coming."

He didn't even come into the kitchen until I had my things on and my keys in my hand. He walked slowly, tail drooping. Owen was good at guilt trips.

"Look," I said, feeling slightly silly because I was trying to coax a cat into a better mood. "I know you miss seeing Rebecca, but you can't come. How would I explain showing up with you?"

I crouched down. "I'll invite her over. I promise." He twisted his head away when I tried to pet him. "And I'll tell her you miss her." Grudgingly he turned his head back and let me scratch the top. "I have to go," I said, getting to my feet. "I'll be back soon."

I locked the door, pulled on my mittens and headed for the street. *I'm crazy,* I decided. *I've been living alone too long.* Then I remembered Agatha's empty house, and talking to Owen and Hercules didn't seem quite so bad. There were worse things than being the crazy cat lady.

I walked up to the Justasons' house, two above mine. There was the path next to their driveway. It was only the width of a snow scoop, but that was enough. I was on Rebecca's street in less than a minute.

Everett let me in the back door. He looked different in a gray sweater, and, surprisingly, jeans. "Hello, Kathleen. Come in," he said.

Rebecca was at the stove, peeking at something in the oven. She smiled. "I hope you're hungry."

"For your cooking? Always," I said.

Everett took my coat and ushered me into the dining area off the kitchen. The sun was beaming through the windows. "Coffee?" he asked.

"Please."

He gestured to a chair, reached for the coffeepot and poured me a cup.

I added milk and sugar to the blue stoneware mug.

Rebecca came out of the kitchen, carrying a pink glass bowl full of chopped fruit. She set it in the middle of the table.

"How can I help?" Everett asked.

She smiled at him. "Talk to Kathleen," she said, bustling back into the kitchen.

He watched her go, the look on his face making it clear he was crazy about her. Everett had been in love with Rebecca when they were very young and all the time they spent apart hadn't changed his feelings. He turned his attention to me.

"She's glowing," I said teasingly.

"What about me?" he asked, his eyes sparkling.

"You have a twinkle, too."

Rebecca came back with a plate piled high with her cinnamon-raisin waffles. The smell made my mouth water. "Don't wait," she told us. She made one more trip to the kitchen, returning with a glass casserole dish.

"This is a new recipe," she warned. "So the two of you are my guinea pigs."

"I have no worries, my dear," Everett said, spooning fruit on his waffle.

I just nodded. My mouth was already full of waffle and fruit.

Breakfast was delicious, from Everett's coffee to Rebecca's experiment—a casserole of eggs, cheese, potato, onion and ham. The two of them kept me entertained with stories about past Winterfest celebrations.

With my plate clear and a second cup of coffee, the conversation turned to Agatha. "Could she have had as much as half a million dollars?" I asked Everett.

He ran his fingers over his beard. "Yes."

That surprised me. "How?" I asked. "I know she was extremely thrifty, but half a million dollars on a teacher's pension?"

"Agatha was very savvy," Everett said. "She took an interest in business and finance at a time when, frankly, women were considered incapable of it."

Across the table Rebecca nodded in agreement.

I leaned back in my seat. "I understand being frugal," I said. "It's how I grew up. But from what I saw at Agatha's house, she'd gone beyond frugal."

"And you assumed it was because she had very little money," Rebecca said. "So did most people."

"I was surprised she left all that money to someone she didn't know," Everett said. "Although"—he gave a slight shrug—"it is for a camp for troubled kids, and Agatha was a big believer in education being the way to solve most of our problems."

"I'm not surprised," Rebecca said.

"Why?" I asked, leaning forward.

"Out of all the young people Agatha helped—and there were a lot, believe me—she had a soft spot for Ruby."

"I think Ruby felt the same way."

"Ruby's been seeing Justin Anders. He's important to her and so is his project," Rebecca said. "So I think Agatha probably did it for Ruby as much as anything." She looked at Everett. "I'd do anything for Ami."

Ami was Everett's only grandchild and she was very close to Rebecca—always had been. Ami's parents had died when she was a baby, and her grandmother, Everett's wife, had passed away before Ami was born. Although Everett and Rebecca hadn't been in each other's lives, Rebecca, whom Ami loving referred to as Rebbie, had been part mother figure, part grandmother to Ami since she was a little girl.

Everett's face softened, "I know you would," he said. He shifted his gaze to me. "Kathleen, Agatha was demanding and stern, not at all a sentimental person, but she loved kids. She dedicated her life to helping them. It does make sense."

I thought about the affection in Roma's voice when she talked about Agatha. I thought about Eric feeding her, and even Harrison Taylor insisting on keeping his promise to her. I was letting my big-city suspiciousness get to me.

Everett stood to clear the table and I got up to help him. He shook his head. "No," he said. "You're our guest."

I looked at Rebecca. "Then let me help with the dishes." I knew she didn't have a dishwasher.

"Thank you, Kathleen," she said. "But no. Everett will wash and I'll dry." She brushed off her hands, signifying that as far as she was concerned the subject was settled.

Rebecca studied my hair as I fastened my coat. "Your layers are growing out nicely." Maybe we'll trim it in another couple of weeks."

I nodded. We'd been working on shaping my hair as it grew out ever since the summer.

"Come over and see me when you have time," I said. "Owen and Hercules miss seeing you."

"I miss seeing them." She wrapped me in a hug. "I'll be over soon, I promise."

"Owen loved his chicken," I said, "and Hercules was in heaven with the sardines. Thank you again."

"You're welcome," she said, giving me a last squeeze before she let me go.

Everett was already running water in Rebecca's sink. I wondered what some of his business rivals would think to see him up to his elbows in soapsuds and wearing a flowered lavender apron.

"I'll see you later in the week," I said to Everett. He waved a soapy spoon at me in acknowledgment.

I walked back along the path between the two streets. As I unlocked the kitchen door, I could hear the phone ringing. Now, I knew in theory that I shouldn't run for the phone. I knew if it was important the caller would leave a message, but a ringing phone was like a plate of iced brownies—not something I was going to leave alone.

I skidded over the kitchen floor and launched myself across the living room to grab the phone.

"Kathleen, I'm so glad you're there." It was Maggie.

I undid my jacket, pulling out one arm and then switching the receiver to my other hand to pull out the opposite arm. She didn't sound right. "Mags, is something wrong?"

She cleared her throat. "Yes. The police arrested Ruby. They say she killed Agatha."

13

M y knees went rubbery and I dropped into the chair. "What?" I said.

"They arrested Ruby. She was in her studio." Maggie's voice dropped to a whisper. "They put handcuffs on her."

"How long ago did this happen?"

"Um, right before I got here, I guess," she said. "Jaeger Merrill has studio space across the hall. He said it happened ten, maybe fifteen minutes ago."

What was Marcus thinking? "Mags, does Ruby have a lawyer?" I asked.

"I don't think so. And her mom and stepfather are on that cruise."

"I just came from having breakfast with Rebecca and Everett," I said. "I'll call and ask him to recommend a lawyer for Ruby. I'll call you back."

"Okay," Maggie said. "I'm at the studio. Call my cell."

I hung up and dialed Rebecca's number. "Hello, Kathleen," Rebecca said when she heard my voice. "Did you forget something?"

I explained about Ruby. "I don't want to interfere," I said. "But I doubt Ruby has a lawyer and, Rebecca, she couldn't have done this."

"Ruby's a lovely girl," Rebecca said. "She wouldn't hurt a fly, and you're not interfering."

"Do you think Everett could suggest a lawyer?"

"He certainly could," she said. "Wait just a moment."

She set down the phone and I heard murmuring in the background, and then Everett picked up the phone. "Kathleen, are you certain they arrested Ruby?"

"Yes," I said. "Maggie said they handcuffed her."

"I'll send one of my lawyers to the police station," he said. "Don't worry about Ruby. I can't promise you she won't have to stay in custody, because it's Sunday, but her rights will be protected."

"Thank you, Everett," I said, struggling to keep the emotion out of my voice. "I owe you."

"No, Kathleen, you don't," he said. "If you need anything else you call me."

I said I would and hung up.

Owen and Hercules were sitting in front of me, a set of gold eyes and a set of green eyes fixed on my face. "Marcus arrested Ruby," I said angrily.

Hercules gave his head a vigorous shake.

"I don't understand what he was thinking."

I was still wearing my hat and scarf. I took them off and set them on the footstool. "I have to call Maggie back."

Mags answered on the second ring. I explained Everett was sending a lawyer for Ruby.

"Thank you," she said. "When I found out Ruby had been arrested, my mind went blank. What are they thinking? Ruby would never hurt Agatha. Never."

Owen came over and leaned his head against my leg. I stroked his fur. "It's a mistake," I said. "Everett's lawyer will straighten the whole thing out."

"You're right," Maggie said. "This is just some mix-up. Maybe because she was the one who found Agatha. You found Gregor Easton's body and the police looked at you."

Marcus had actually suggested I'd been having an affair with the much older and hugely egocentric composer. But he'd learned he'd rushed to judgment, and he'd learn the same thing about Ruby. I felt myself start to relax.

"Got any plans for this afternoon?" Maggie asked. "If we've done all we can for Ruby, I need to get my mind off things." She was starting to sound more like herself again.

"Nothing special."

"I want to work for a couple more hours, but after that do you want to go skating?"

"Mags, I can't skate," I said.

"How can you be such a good hockey player and not be able to skate?"

"Street hockey."

There was silence for a moment, then she said, "Okay, this is the perfect time to try skating."

"Of course. Only half the town will be down there; nothing embarrassing about that."

"Lots of people to help you," Maggie said.

I lifted Owen into my lap. He nuzzled the phone receiver. "Owen says hello," I said.

"Hey, Fuzz Face. How are you?" Maggie crooned.

Owen flopped across my lap and started to purr. "You're such a suck-up," I whispered to him. "He heard you," I told Maggie.

"Give him a scratch for me," she said. "So, are you coming skating?"

"I can't. I don't have skates."

"I can borrow a pair for you. What size shoe do you wear?"

I could stay home and worry about Ruby for the rest of the day, or go watch Maggie skate and maybe try it myself. "Okay, you win."

I told her my shoe size. She reminded me to bring an extra pair of socks. We settled on the time and I hung up.

I gave Owen a scratch behind the ears. "That's from Maggie," I told him. The purring went up a notch.

I went into the kitchen to make more coffee, leaning against the counter while it brewed. I kept coming back to what Marcus had been thinking.

He wouldn't just arrest Ruby on a whim. He had reasons, evidence. He was clearly interpreting the evidence incorrectly, but he had it. Was it because she'd found Agatha's body?

I'd been there in the alley, too, and unlike the last time we tangled, I didn't seem to be a suspect. Was it the money? It looked like that rumor was true.

When the coffee was ready I poured a cup and pulled out one of the kitchen chairs. Owen was roaming around and Hercules wandered in from the porch.

"When I finish my coffee let's go outside," I said to them. They exchanged glances but ignored me. "You both could use some exercise and so could I. Maggie's taking me skating this afternoon."

Hercules ducked his head and put a paw over his face. Owen yowled as though someone had stepped on his tail.

"Very funny," I said dryly.

With their little melodramatic display over both cats headed for the living room. I jumped up and stood in the doorway. "I was serious. We're going outside. And don't even think about doing an end run around me."

Both sets of whiskers were twitching.

"It's not that cold," I said darkly. "Move your tails." I went for my coffee without looking at them, and when I was ready, they were sitting sullenly by the outside door.

I widened the path around the side of the house, burning off a little of the anxiety about Ruby being arrested. Owen prowled the yard while Hercules sat on the bottom step, looking annoyed. We spent a half hour outside. When we went back in the cats disappeared and didn't come out until lunch, when they tried to mooch some of my sandwich.

The sun was still out as I got dressed to meet Maggie. Hercules paced restlessly around the kitchen as I pulled my wool socks up over my snazzy green long underwear and stepped into my snow pants.

"It's skating, Hercules, not BASE jumping. I'll be fine," I said. He didn't look convinced.

There was a reason I had never skated, I discovered. It was a lot like patting your head and rubbing your stomach—while standing with one foot on a banana peel. At least that's how it felt to me.

There were quite a few people on the ice when I got down to the marina, mostly little kids and a few adults. Maggie was sitting on a wooden bench with her own skates already laced. I dropped beside her. "Hi," she said.

I looked out over the ice surface. "I didn't think there'd be so many people."

"That's okay. No one expects you to audition for *Stars on Ice* your first time out." She pulled a pair of skates out of the bag at her feet. "They should fit," she said.

I undid my boots and pulled on the extra socks I'd tucked into my pocket. Maggie laced the skates for me, wrapping the ties around my ankle at the top and double knotting the bow.

We stepped onto the ice and my legs slid out to the side until I was more than halfway down into a pretty decent split. My arms flailed until I could latch on to Maggie and I did, wrapping both my arms around her waist in an awkward bear hug. I managed to pull myself up, but my ankles wouldn't stop wobbling. The only way to stay upright was to keep a death grip on Maggie and press my knees tightly together. My feet kept trying to slide off in opposite directions. Every bit of coordination I thought I had was gone.

"Take a second to find your balance," she said.

"It's going to take more than a second," I said. I tried to straighten out more, clutching at Maggie's jacket like it was a lifeline, because it was. I got both feet together and pointed in the same direction.

"Link your arm through mine," Maggie instructed.

I pried my fingers from the front of her coat, put my arm through hers, and smiled triumphantly.

And then immediately fell on my snow pants.

Maggie, who had somehow known I was going to fall, had let go of me a split second before I went down.

"Ow!" I said, glaring at her.

She pulled me up and had the good sense not to smile. I found my balance again, and this time I didn't end up on my padding. "Okay, we're going to try a little skating," she said.

"I don't think so," I said. "I think I'll stay right here and enjoy the scenery."

"You can do this." She tugged on my arm, and for a moment I was gliding across the ice.

Although my brain said *forward*, my feet decided to move sideways and independently of each other. I windmilled my arms to try to stay upright. But I didn't.

That was how it was for two turns around the outdoor rink: Maggie alternating between giving me confusing instructions and pulling me back to my feet.

"I have to sit down," I said finally. I was sweating like a bear in a sauna. and I was pretty sure my feet had tied themselves into knots inside my skates. Maggie was more or less dragging me around while I clung to her, bent at a ninety-degree angle at the waist. It was the only way I could keep my feet from sliding off on a tangent. I pretty much looked like Wile E. Coyote on skates.

Maggie steered me over to the bench and I dropped inelegantly onto it. "Go skate," I said, waving her away. "Go."

She went, which meant I could sit and sulk silently for a while.

Mary glided over, stopping with a flourish and a little spray of ice chips. I should've guessed she could skate. She held out a thermos. "Hot chocolate?"

"Yes, please," I said gratefully. Sulking went a lot better with some chocolate.

She sat down beside me, took one of the cups from the inside of the thermos, and filled it about half-full. I inhaled the scent of steaming chocolate.

"Your first time on skates?"

I nodded.

"So what do you think?"

"I think ice is very cold, very slippery and very hard," I said.

"So you had fun, then?" Mary said, her eyes sparkling over her cup.

I gestured at the rink. "How do you all do that so easily?" Maggie was skating backward. Backward, talking to Claire.

Mary smiled. "Back in the dark ages when I was young, all there was to do here in the wintertime was skate and toboggan. If you stayed home someone would find a chore for you to do."

I took another sip of hot chocolate. My fingers were starting to thaw.

"My first pair of skates were hand-me-downs from my older brother," she said. "I had to wear two pair of my father's woolen socks with them to fit. "

I wiggled my toes in my skates. The feeling was coming back to my feet. I looked at Mary. "Mary," I said. "If you tell me you skated to school uphill both ways through waist-high snow, I'm going to whack you with a snowball."

Mary laughed and shook her head. "Of course not," she said. "Snow was closer to over my head."

I snatched a chunk of snow from the ground and threw it at her. It disintegrated against the front of her coat. She just laughed harder.

We watched the skaters zip by, and then Mary's face grew serious. "Kathleen." She hesitated. "You know about Ruby?"

"That she was arrested? Yes." I blew on my hot chocolate and took another drink. "Ruby didn't kill Agatha."

"The police have evidence," Mary said. "They found a glove belonging to Ruby with the body."

"She found Agatha's body. She was upset. She could have easily dropped a glove."

Mary studied her skates for a moment. "That's not the only evidence. Bridget says they have a piece of glass that was found in the alley and paint that matches the paint on Ruby's truck."

It struck me that Bridget was doing too much talking, but I didn't say that out loud.

"The glass is from the kind of headlight Ruby has on her truck and"—Mary cleared her throat—"the headlight is broken."

She wouldn't meet my eyes. "And it looks bad that Agatha left all that money to Ruby's boyfriend," I said.

"Yes, it does."

"What it looks like and what the truth is are not always the same thing. I know Ruby didn't kill Agatha." I finished my hot chocolate and gave the cup back to Mary. "Thank you," I said. "This is probably going to sound crazy, but could Agatha have had any enemies?"

Mary twisted the top back on the thermos, then looked at me and shrugged. "She was an old lady. When she was teaching, sure, there were some irate parents and some kids who didn't like her. She was a pretty strict teacher. But enemies? No." She banged her skate boots together, knocking off the snow that was clinging to the metal blades. "It had to be an accident."

"More proof that it wasn't Ruby," I said. "She wouldn't have left Agatha to die in that alley."

Mary stood up. "I hope you're right." She gave me a finger waggle and skated away with the thermos.

Susan and Eric came skating by then. Each of them had one of twins by the hand. The little guys could skate better than I could. They grinned at me and I waved at them.

Susan gave me a quick smile. Her attention was focused on the boys. Eric didn't look good from a distance and he looked even worse closer. His hair went in every direction around his black earmuffs. His color, even in the crisp, bracing air, was bilious, and he needed a shave. He had more than I'm-a-sexy-bad-boy stubble.

He looked like he'd been on a three-day bender, which wasn't likely, since I'd never seen him drink so much as a glass of wine. He'd been close to Agatha. Having her die in the alley by the restaurant had to have been painful.

I wondered if Eric had heard about Ruby being arrested. If he hadn't, he would soon. And when the newspaper went online after midnight, the whole world would know.

I thought about what Mary had said. Ruby could have easily dropped her glove or even have given both of them to Agatha earlier in the day. As for bits of paint, I didn't know enough about automotive paint to know whether it could be narrowed down to one specific vehicle, although it didn't seem likely.

And then there was that piece of glass that might have come from the headlight of Ruby's truck. Was that the sliver of glass that had caught in the fabric of my pants? Was I, indirectly, responsible for Ruby getting arrested?

Even if, *big if*, the glass had come from Ruby's truck, it didn't mean she'd been driving it. She was pretty generous about loaning the truck. Maggie had borrowed it last summer, but it refused to run for her, which is how we'd ended up on our first "road trip" with Roma.

I leaned forward, chin propped on my hands, and watched all the skaters whiz past. I knew that Marcus was just doing his job, but he was wrong. I'd seen Ruby's face in that alley. I'd seen how stricken she was, knowing that Agatha was dead. That reaction wasn't faked.

I'd grown up with actors. I'd seen them practice. I'd seen them perform. I'd seen every emotion from joy to depression to grief acted out. I've seen it acted well and unbelievably badly. Nothing about Ruby's grief was made-up.

Maggie waved at me from the far end of the rink. In the clump of people behind her one head stuck out.

Marcus.

For a moment I thought about skating down to him and telling him how wrong he was about Ruby. Because of course once he knew he'd apologize and let her go. It was a nice fantasy. Still, I wanted to talk to him.

Maggie was almost level with me now. I struggled to my feet and, legs wobbling, waved my mitten at her to get her attention. She stopped in front of me with a spray of ice chips, just as Mary had done. I teetered toward her.

"You want to go back out?"

"Yes," I said, arms flapping as I stepped over the low barrier between the ice and snow. My feet were seesawing in and out. I grabbed Maggie's arm as though it were a rope and I was going down for the third time.

"Just skate," I said, through clenched teeth. I willed my feet to go forward and they did. Sort of.

"Okay," she said slowly.

We started along the ice. I scanned the crowd ahead of me, looking for Marcus. I couldn't see him, and I knew if I turned around I'd be flat on the ice again. A skater slipped past me on the outside, turning in a smooth arc in front of me.

"Hello, Kathleen."

Of course it was him. He was skating easily, almost lazily backward, and of course at that moment my feet slid out to the sides and I lost my grip on Maggie. I pitched forward, grabbing air, realizing as I went down that I was going to slide through his legs as if we were playing a game of reverse leapfrog.

Crap on toast!

He was grinning, which added insult to injury. Then just before I hit the ice he reached out and caught me under both arms, the momentum pulling me in against him.

Of course.

14

My hands were flat against his chest and out of instinct I clutched his jacket.

"I've got you," he said.

"Kathleen, are you okay?" Maggie asked. She had both of her hands out, as though I were a basketball and Marcus was going to toss me back to her.

"I'm okay."

"Can you stand up?" he asked.

I tipped my chin so I could look at him. "If I could stand up I wouldn't have fallen on you in the first place."

He put his hands on my shoulders and turned me so I was on his left side. "Bend your knees and lean forward," he said. "Just a little bit."

Gingerly I followed his instructions, and my legs stopped quaking as I found my balance.

He looped my left hand around his arm, holding it securely with his other hand. "Better?"

I nodded.

"Okay, now lean on me just a little and push out and back with your outside foot."

We moved forward and I didn't fall down. I tried another push.

"Keep your blade flat on the ice," he said. He turned

his head. "I've got her," he said to Maggie, who just raised a hand and smiled as she skated away.

I was skating. I pushed with my outside foot, and feeling brave and fancy, did the same with my inside foot. I was definitely skating. Someone had a weird sense of humor to make this happen because of Marcus.

I waited until we made one circuit around the ice before I spoke. "You're wrong about Ruby," I said.

He didn't try to pretend he didn't know what I was talking about. "You heard."

"I heard. Ruby didn't kill Agatha." I loosened my grip on his arm. "I was there with her, with the body. She was grief-stricken. She wasn't faking that."

"I can't do my job based on feelings," he said. "I look at the facts, at the evidence."

I took a breath and let it out. It was important to make my case without sounding like a crackpot. "That she was distraught is a fact. Ruby isn't a killer. Look at all the work she does with kids. She was inspired to do that by Agatha."

I took my eyes off the ice for a second to search his face. It was unreadable. I continued. "The piece of glass that I gave to you. Can you prove it came from the headlight of Ruby's struck? Can you prove how it ended up in that alley? Or when? Or how it got stuck in my pants? Can you even prove Ruby was driving her truck that night?"

I shook my head. "Never mind. I know you can't tell me any of that," I said.

Maggie was sitting on the bench now. She waved merrily as we went past her.

"No, I can't." His cheeks were red from the cold.

I pictured Agatha in the restaurant, clutching that old brown envelope so fiercely. I hadn't seen it with her body. "Can you at least tell me if you found an old report-card envelope with Agatha's body?"

He frowned, then recovered and shook his head. "I can't—"

"I know. You can't tell me that, either." And I didn't need him to. That frown was as good as a no.

"It's an open case," he said.

"I'm guessing Ruby didn't have an alibi," I said. "Well, neither did Maggie; neither did I." I stumbled over a divot in the ice, and his hand automatically tightened its grip on my arm.

"Oh, wait a minute. I do have an alibi. Owen and Hercules."

He sighed. From the corner of my eye I saw his jaw work like he was grinding his teeth. "This is a complicated case, Kathleen," he said. "Don't get involved in it the way you did in Gregor Easton's death last summer."

Anger did a slow burn in my stomach and I struggled not to let it into my voice. "You're the one who got me involved in that, because you thought I was having an affair with the man solely because we both lived in Boston at the same time. You were wrong about that, and you're wrong about Ruby."

We were turned away from where Maggie was standing, talking to Rebecca. Anger got the best of me. "You didn't listen to me then and you're not listening to me now," I snapped. I let go of his arm, determined to glide away in melodramatic fashion. Except my glide was off by several feet.

I was heading for a snowbank when Susan grabbed my arm. We spun in a circle, but I managed somehow to keep my balance as Susan stopped me.

"You all right?" she asked. We were face-to-face, Susan holding both my upper arms. "It looked like you were arguing with Detective Gordon about something."

I couldn't see him anymore. "Not exactly arguing," I said. "More like discussing."

She raised her eyebrows.

"Vigorously."

She almost smiled.

"I was trying to point out that his reasons for arresting Ruby weren't very good ones."

The color drained from Susan's face. "The police arrested Ruby? Why?"

She didn't know. How could she not know? I looked at the ice for a second, then looked back at her. "Because they think she killed Agatha."

I thought she couldn't get any paler.

I was wrong.

Susan's mouth moved but no sound came out.

"Susan, I'm sorry," I said. "I thought it was common knowledge by now. I shouldn't have just blurted it out like that."

She shook her head "Oh, no, it's okay. We're a bit out of touch because we've just kind of been staying close to home this weekend. You know, colds and stuff."

Her face was still sickeningly white. "When did they . . . when did they arrest her?"

"This morning."

"She didn't kill Agatha."

"I know. And the police will figure that out, too."

Susan's eyes darted around the crowded rink. "I . . . I better go," she said. "Eric just left for the café, and my mom's on her way to the sliding hill with the boys. I wanted to skate around a couple of times by myself, but I should go help her." She let go of my arms, holding her hands out for a moment. "You okay?"

"Oh, sure," I said. "Go. I'll see you tomorrow."

"Okay," she said, skating away with long strokes.

Of course I couldn't move.

Maggie made her way over to me. "Are you all right?"

"Just get me off the ice, please," I said.

She pulled me to the edge of the rink. I stepped over the boards and collapsed on the bench.

"Is everything okay with Susan?" Maggie asked, dropping beside me.

I sighed. "I don't know. She's been, well, not herself for the past few days. Since Agatha died, really."

Maggie leaned her folded arms on her thighs. "It has to be hard on Eric, Agatha dying. So that has to be hard on Susan."

I nodded. "Speaking of Eric, you want to head over to the café for some hot chocolate?"

"Oh, that sounds good," she said.

I started undoing my skates. I loved Eric's hot chocolate. It was even better than mine. And maybe I'd get a chance to talk to him. Maybe he'd seen or heard something the night Agatha died. Maybe I could come up with something that would help Ruby.

Maggie had her skates off in half the time it took me, so she watched me, head cocked to one side. "Marcus was a pretty good skating teacher," she said.

"Marcus is a dip wad," I said darkly.

"Let me guess. He told you not to play *Law & Order* with this case."

"He has tunnel vision," I said, getting to my feet.

She gave me a hip bump. "He probably says that about you."

We headed up to the street. As we crossed the parking lot we bumped into Roma. Literally. "We're going to Eric's," Maggie said. "Wanna come?"

"Yes." Roma pulled off her crocheted red hat. "I can't feel my toes. I was in that infuriating maze for a half hour. I thought they were going to have to send a scent dog to find me."

I felt the prickle of goose bumps up my spine.

"We were skating," Maggie said. "We haven't tried the maze yet."

And we are not going to, I added silently.

"Where are you parked?" Roma asked. "Because I'm right here."

"I walked," Maggie said.

"Me, too," I added.

"C'mon, I'll drive," Roma said.

I was happy to climb into the backseat of her SUV. My feet hurt. My knees ached. When I moved it sounded like someone deboning a turkey. And when I sat down it was clear I'd bruised my tailbone.

Maggie buckled her seat belt and then leaned forward to look out the windshield. "You giving us a ride isn't going to start a rumor that we're dating, is it?" she said to Roma.

"No, everyone's pretty convinced I'm seeing Eddie Sweeney," Roma said with a smile, putting the car in gear. Her expression changed. "I heard about Ruby."

Maggie nodded. "Kathleen called Everett. He sent one of his lawyers."

"Good. It's ridiculous to think that Ruby would kill Agatha."

We drove slowly up to the café. There were a lot of people on the sidewalk, headed for the Winterfest site. Roma slid into a parking spot as a minivan pulled out.

Our waiter, a high school student with green hair who I knew had an interest in medieval armaments, brought us three mugs of steaming hot chocolate and a bowl of marshmallows.

Eric was behind the counter. He didn't so much as wave, let alone come over. Agatha's death had clearly hit him hard. I didn't want to make him feel any worse, but I did want to talk to him.

I was grasping at straws, because I felt guilty about the piece of glass I'd given to Marcus. But maybe Eric had seen something or even someone and didn't realize it was important.

"I know Ruby seems tough," Maggie was saying. "But that's an act. We were taking summer courses at the university at the same time." She smiled as she remembered. "She was living in this real dive. I mean, the place was falling apart. There was a mouse in her apartment. Anyone else would have moved out, or at least gotten a trap."

"Let me guess," Roma said. "She kept it as a pet."

"And did two paintings of the thing," Maggie said with a smile.

That sounded like Ruby.

Our waiter came back with a carafe of cocoa and we all had a second cup.

I glanced over at the counter, still trying to come up with a way to talk to Eric without being too pushy.

"Why do the police think Ruby killed Agatha?" Roma asked, setting down her mug. "What's her motive supposed to be?"

"Maybe they think it was an accident and she panicked," I said.

"I can't believe the rumor's true. I can't believe Agatha had half a million dollars," Roma said. "You know, a couple of times I paid for a tank of heating oil because I knew she skimped on heat and I thought she couldn't afford it." She gestured to Eric, who was making change for someone at the cash register. "Eric let her stay in his office on really cold nights."

She picked up her cup again. "She lied to us." She traced a square on the tablecloth. "You know, I would have said Agatha Shepherd was the one person who wouldn't lie. Why didn't she spend some of that money on herself?" She looked up at us. "Then she goes and leaves everything to Ruby's boyfriend."

"She had to be suffering from some kind of brain damage from the stroke," Maggie said. Her blond hair was standing up from when she'd pulled off her hat. She looked like a curly blond lamb. "Maybe she'd been having small strokes and nobody knew about it. You've seen those TV shows about hoarders. Only in her case it was money."

Was that why that old envelope had been so important? Was there something inside that had to do with all that money? I wondered what had happened to the envelope. Agatha had had words with Eric over it. And I remembered Harry Taylor's gesturing at it as he stood on the sidewalk arguing with her. It couldn't be connected to her death, could it?

No. What could she have been carrying around in a recycled Mayville school-system envelope that would make someone kill her? Investment statements? On the other hand, the envelope hadn't been with Agatha's body or at her house, as far as I'd seen. And it had been important to her, given the way she held on to it, and it did have some significance to Harry and Eric, because they'd both argued with her about it. Could she have had any other secrets besides half a million dollars?

Across the table, I looked at Roma, who was gesticulating as she talked to Maggie. I didn't want to go home and spend the rest of the day obsessing about Agatha's death.

"Hey, guys," I said. "Why don't you come have supper with me?"

"Yes," Roma said.

"Don't you want to know what we're having?" I asked.

"Do I have to cook anything?"

"No. I have beef stew in the slow cooker."

"As long as I don't have to cook, I'll eat just about anything. Heck, I'd probably eat those smelly crackers you make for the cats."

"Mags?" I said.

"Are you making dumplings?" she asked. "I'll come even if you aren't . . . But are you?"

"Yes, I'm making dumplings."

Roma picked up her cup, drained it and set it back on the table. "Let's roll," she said.

Owen came out at breakneck speed when he heard the back door open. He skidded to a stop, sliding into the leg of the kitchen table when he saw Roma. Tail twitching, he glared at me.

Maggie came in behind us, spotted the cat and said, "Hey, Fuzz Face." Owen's entire demeanor changed. His tail went down and his eyes narrowed with happiness. He made a wide berth around Roma and stopped about three feet in front of Maggie.

"I brought you something," she said, giving the cat a conspiratorial grin. She pulled a little brown paper bag from her pocket. I recognized the logo.

"Maggie, you didn't," I said. "You're as bad as Rebecca."

Owen recognized the bag, as well. He was squirming so much that I thought he would wiggle right out of his fur.

"Ignore her," she said to the cat. She took Fred the Funky Chicken of the bag. Owen shifted from one foot to the other. Maggie set the yellow catnip chicken on the floor and pushed it toward him. He pounced on it, picking it up in his mouth. As he turned to take off with it, he gave Maggie an adoring look. Again he made a wide berth around Roma, glaring at her and me as he went by.

Hercules appeared in the doorway then. He didn't even look at Roma, acting as though she wasn't there. Instead he looked at Maggie. "I didn't forget you," she said, reaching into the bag again.

"You've lost your mind," I said, crossing my arms and shaking my head. Hercules walked over to her, obviously curious about what Maggie had brought him. I was curious, too. Herc was the type of cat who didn't go for toys.

"I had to get some wine," she said. "And then I saw the chickens and that made me think of Owen. And how could I get something for him and not get something for this one?" She gestured at Hercules, who modestly ducked his head.

"Oh, for heaven's sake," I muttered.

Maggie pulled a little box out of the bag. Hercules looked at it, intrigued.

"Organic fish-shaped cat treats," she said, holding up the box so Roma and I could see it. Herc's whiskers wiggled when she said "fish." "Can I give him a couple?"

I sighed. "Yes."

She opened the top of the tiny carton, dumped a half dozen crackers into her hand, set them on the floor and then backed away.

Hercules strolled over, trying to act uninterested. He sniffed the crackers. I wouldn't say that he shoved his face in the tiny pile and started eating like a bear in a picnic basket, but the effect was very close.

Maggie handed me the box. I looked at the ingredients. Roma leaned over to take a peek, as well. No chemicals. Nothing I couldn't pronounce. "Looks fine," Roma said.

I set the box on the counter. Herc gobbled the last fish and licked the crumbs off his face. He walked over to us, stopping in front of Maggie to meow a thank-you.

"You're welcome," she said with a smile. Hercules rubbed against my leg and headed back to the living room.

"So if I bring bribes will the cats like me?" Roma asked.

"They're not bribes; they're gifts of love," Maggie said, squaring her shoulders and sticking out her chin.

"Bribes," Roma repeated.

I took both women's coats. "It's not that Owen and Hercules don't like you . . ." I began.

Roma gave me a skeptical look.

"Okay, so it is that they don't like you, but in their defense, every time they see you, you stick them with a needle."

"I wouldn't like you that much if you poked me with a needle every time I saw you," Maggie said, peeking in my cookie jar to see if I had any brownies. "I guess you'll have to stick to hockey players."

Roma held out her hands and grinned. "I guess so." She seemed to have found her sense of humor about the Eddie rumor.

We moved into the living room and I turned on the lamp. Maggie curled in her favorite corner of the couch. Roma sat in the leather chair.

"You know, if Owen were a guy, I'd date him," Maggie said as the cat came over to sit by her feet.

Roma and I both laughed.

"No, really," Maggie said. "He's cute. He's crazy about me. Why not?"

"Mags," I said. "He has morning breath that would make your eyes water and a major addiction to catnip, and he smells every bite of food before he eats it."

Roma shrugged. "I've gone out with worse."

We all laughed.

"Have you ever thought about getting married again?" Maggie asked Roma.

"Well, not to a cat," she said.

Maggie threw a pillow at her. Roma caught it with one hand and tucked it behind her back. Her smile faded. "I don't even know if I'd be good at marriage," she said. "Luke and I were married only two years—he was killed by a drunk driver." She studied her left hand for a moment. "We were so young and married for such a short time, there wasn't a chance to find out what kind of a marriage it would've been." Then she smiled. "But I have Olivia."

Roma's daughter was a biologist and commercial diver working on a new TV show for the Exploration Channel.

"What about you, Maggie?" Roma asked sweetly. "Ever been married that you know of?"

Maggie stretched her hands behind her head. "No. First of all, I was what people call a late bloomer. I think I was maybe fifteen before I figured out why all my friends were so gaga about boys. Then I was concentrating on school. It was just my mom and me." She smiled down at Owen, still sitting adoringly by her side of the sofa. "In college I was a geek, working in the summer and studying every term, trying to hold on to my scholarship."

"What about you, Kathleen?" Roma asked.

Maggie and I exchanged glances. "I was almost married," I said.

"In Boston?" Roma leaned forward, clearly interested.

"Yes." Hercules appeared at my feet and I reached over to stroke the top of his head. "His name was ... is Andrew. He's a contractor. He specializes in restoring old houses."

"What happened?" Roma asked. She held out both hands palms up. "You chose all of this instead?"

That made me laugh. "In a way. We had a fight. Andrew went away on a two-week trip with his friends. He married someone else while he was gone."

"You're kidding."

I shook my head. "True love, tequila style," I said. Telling the story didn't hurt the way it used to.

"So you decided if he could get married, you could come to Minnesota."

I grinned. "Pretty much."

Roma propped her feet on the footstool. "I think Toby Keith wrote a song about something like that. Was she a waitress at a honky-tonk?"

"Fifties diner, I think."

Roma shrugged. "Close enough."

"Maybe you were supposed to come here," Maggie said. "Maybe you'll meet Mr. Right here."

"I don't believe in soul mates or destiny," I said. "And don't even try to sell me on Marcus Gordon as my one true love."

"What's wrong with Marcus?" Roma asked.

I frowned at her and pulled up my feet. "He arrested Ruby," I said, holding up a finger. "He thought I was having an affair with Gregor Easton and that I might've killed him." Now I was holding up two fingers. "And he's annoying." I added one more finger to the other two.

Roma held up a finger of her own and waved it at me. "He's my best volunteer." She added another. "And he rescued Lucy and Desmond."

I folded my arms and watched her, amused. Now she was holding up three fingers. "And he helps coach the boys' hockey team."

So that's why he was such a good skater. "He arrested Ruby," I said.

"He's a police officer," she said. "He's doing his job. It wasn't just his call. And Marcus won't stop investigating just because Ruby's been arrested. He'll follow the evidence wherever it takes him, and he will figure out Ruby didn't do this."

"You like Marcus."

"I do. He's a good person. Give him a chance."

Owen chose that moment to meow his agreement.

"Not you, too," I said. He flicked his tail at me and went back to giving Maggie googley eyes.

I stood up. "As much as I like listening to you act like Marcus Gordon's cheerleader, I have to go make dumplings." The word "dumplings" got Owen's attention. He turned his head toward me. "C'mon," I said.

Owen kept up a murping commentary while I made

dumplings and set them on top of the stew pot. The phone rang while I had my hands in the dough. "Maggie, would you get that and take a message, please?" I called.

"Got it," she said.

I was just putting the lid back on the pot when Maggie stuck her head in the kitchen.

"That was Rebecca," she said. "Ruby's okay. She has to spend the night in jail, but she'll go before a judge in the morning."

"We expected that," I said.

She leaned against the doorframe. "I don't understand how this got to be such a mess."

Roma came up beside Maggie as I started washing the few dirty dishes.

"How did Agatha die?" Roma asked. "Do you know?"

I hesitated. "I'm not certain." I scraped bits of dried dough out of the mixing bowl I'd used for the dumplings. "She might have been hit by a car."

Roma looked away for a second and Maggie lightly touched her shoulder. "You mean someone ran her down and then ...?"

"Maybe."

"Which proves it wasn't Ruby," Maggie said. "She would've never run someone over and just left them."

"No, she wouldn't," Roma agreed.

"What was Agatha like?" I asked to change the subject. "When she was young, when she was teaching?"

Maggie got out the placemats, and I handed Roma salt and pepper.

"Well, you saw her," Roma said. "She was tiny and as tough as nails. I've seen her face down kids and parents that were twice her size. She was on your side all the way if you were going to give it your best effort. But if she thought you weren't working, forget the excuses."

Maggie nodded. "Karen Anne Peary," she said.

Roma and I both turned to her.

"After Agatha retired she still did substitute teaching. She taught our math class in grade six for a month because Mr. Kavanaugh broke his hand in gym, trying to teach the class how to climb the ropes. Not a good idea if you're afraid of heights." She waved away the mental picture.

"Anyway, Agatha gave us a math test. Two-thirds of the class failed, including me, including Karen Anne Peary. Mr. Kavanaugh graded generously and on a curve. Agatha didn't."

Roma was already smiling. Maggie handed her a fork and spoon. "Day after we got the tests back, Karen Anne's father showed up. Ever seen Mike Peary?"

"I don't think so," I said.

"Bigfoot," Roma said. "Okay, maybe a little bit hairier."

Maggie nodded in agreement. "Back then we were in a portable classroom, like a Spam can with fake wood paneling inside. Agatha goes outside with Mr. Peary. He's a roaring at her, shaking those massive hands. We were all at the windows, watching."

"What did she do?"

"Nothing," Maggie said, centering her placemat on the table. "She let him wind down and then she started to talk, and I swear you could see the man shrinking. All that hot air, gone."

"That sounds like her," Roma said.

"When she came back in she told us we were all going to get our grades up. And she promised Karen Anne in front of the entire class that she would have an A by the end of the year."

Maggie laughed. "The only subject Karen Anne Peary was interested in was boys. Getting an A in math didn't seem very likely."

"But she did, didn't she?" Roma said.

Maggie nodded. "Agatha took a promise very seriously."

I thought of Harry Taylor, adamant about keeping his promise to a dead person.

I got three bowls down from the cupboard and checked the clock. The dumplings were just about done. "What was she like outside of school?"

"Her whole life was school," Roma said. "After she got divorced she threw her energy into David and the school. I don't think I told you she did a six-month stint of volunteer teaching in a school in rural Tennessee. That was Agatha."

Mags and Roma shared stories from their high school days over supper. I spent as much time laughing as I did eating.

"I want to see pictures," I said, pointing my spoon at Maggie.

"Nonexistent." She speared the last dumpling in her bowl. "When my mother moved I got every single one of them and burned them all."

"You didn't."

"Big hair and parachute pants, gone."

"I need to check in at the clinic," Roma said after the table was cleared and I'd turned down her offer to help with the dishes. She looked at Maggie. "Do you want a ride?"

"Yeah," Maggie said. "I don't feel like walking."

Hercules and Owen wandered in to say good-bye. "Call me if you hear anything," I said, giving Maggie a hug.

"You, too."

Owen made a low sound in his throat when the door closed. It was almost like a sigh.

"Just a little too over the top, Owen," I said, walking back into the living room. The house seemed so quiet with Maggie and Roma gone. Then I thought about

Ruby sitting in a jail cell. I picked up the pillow Maggie had thrown at Roma and put it back on the sofa. I sat in the chair and pulled the phone closer. Hercules appeared at my feet as I punched in the number.

"Come on up," I said, patting my leg. He jumped and settled on my lap.

My brother, Ethan, answered on the fourth ring. "Hey, Mom said it was you."

Our mother always seemed to know when it was one of us on the phone. Ethan would be on the road, hundreds of miles away. The phone would ring and Mom would say, "Get the phone, Katie. That's your brother." And the next thing I'd hear would be, "This is a collect call from . . ."

"So, you haven't run off with a yeti or anything yet," Ethan said. I could picture him grinning.

"No," I said indignantly. "We've just started dating."

He laughed and the sound made me catch my breath with homesickness.

"So, what's up?"

"Winterfest."

"What's Winterfest? Some kind of pagan ritual where you all join hands in a circle and ask the gods of winter not to send any more snow?"

"Actually we ask them to send it all to Boston," I countered. That got another laugh. I told him about the sliding hill, my victory at the puck shoot and my first time on skates.

"Are there any pictures? Any cell-phone video?" he teased. "Because I have cash."

"Forget it. The only way you're going to see me on skates is if you come and do it in person."

"You inviting me to visit?"

"Anytime, baby brother," I said. "We're planning a big party for the library in the spring."

"Yeah, maybe I will. When things quiet down. I miss having you to boss me around."

I felt that twist of homesickness again, but I swallowed it away. Ethan and I talked about his band, The Flaming Gerbils—which was spending a lot more time on the road—and his love life, which was always entertaining and way more complicated than anyone's I knew.

Finally Ethan said, "I'd better let you talk to Mom. She's hovering."

"Stay out of trouble," I said. "I love you."

"Love you, too," he said, handing the phone off to Mom.

"I wasn't hovering" were the first words out of her mouth.

"Okay."

"I was lurking," she continued.

"What's the difference?"

"It's all in how you hold your upper body."

I wasn't sure if she was joking or not. With my mother you couldn't always tell.

"How are you, Katydid?"

"I'm fine."

"Tell me about Winterfest," she said. My mother read the Mayville Heights paper online, so she always had a general idea of what was going on here.

I told her all about the winter carnival, including my turn around the outdoor rink. She laughed. "So that's what Ethan was teasing you about."

"Yeah," I said. "It's a good thing there are no pictures. Knowing him, I might end up an Internet star."

"Are there any photos of Maggie's installation?" Mom asked. "I'd love to see it."

"I don't think she'd mind if I took some and e-mailed them to you."

"Thank you, sweetie."

We talked for a few more minutes. Mom and Dad were working on a production of *King Lear* at the school where they both taught. She was directing and he was playing the old king. They were speaking at the moment, but I knew before the production started there'd be fireworks. There always were, which is why they'd been married twice. There were crazy for each other, but they also made themselves and everyone around them crazy, too.

I thought about telling Mom about Ruby and letting her reassure me that everything would work out. But I didn't. I didn't want her to worry that I'd gotten tangled up in another crime, even if only peripherally.

Finally I said good-bye and set the phone back on the table. Hercules lifted his head and looked at me. No matter what I did, I couldn't stop thinking about Ruby. I couldn't let it go.

I remembered what Maggie had said. Ruby couldn't even kill a mouse in her apartment. She hadn't killed Agatha. Not deliberately. Not by accident. I didn't care what evidence Marcus had. Ruby wasn't that kind of person.

If I hadn't found that sliver of glass in my pants cuff, would Ruby be in jail right now? I couldn't help feeling responsible. Was there anything I could say to Marcus to make him see he was wrong? No. He believed in evidence, not feelings. The only way I could convince him Ruby was innocent was to prove it.

I looked into the cat's green eyes. "You know Ruby didn't kill Agatha," I said. "How are we going to find out who did?"

15

Before I could get up, the phone rang. We both jumped. Herc teetered on my lap like a high-wire walker in a windstorm, and almost fell off.

I put one hand on the cat and picked up the phone with the other. It was Rebecca.

"Hi," I said. "Maggie gave me your message from earlier."

"Oh, good," she said. "I'm hoping you can do me a favor. It's for Ruby, actually."

"Of course. What do you need?"

"Her lawyer called. Ruby needs clothes for court in the morning. I have Violet's keys, so I have a key to Ruby's apartment, too."

"And you'd like me to go with you." It was only a couple of days ago that I'd gone with Ruby to find clothes for Agatha.

"If you don't mind. Ruby's style is quite a bit different from mine."

I smiled. "Mine, too, but between the two of us we should be able to find something that will work."

We settled on a time in the morning and said good night.

"This is a sign," I said.

Hercules looked at the phone and then at me.

"All right, so I don't believe in signs," I said. "But if I did, this would be one." He just kept staring at me. "Rebecca wants me to help her find something for Ruby to wear to court. I'm going to meet her at Ruby's apartment in the morning." He still didn't so much as blink. "Ruby's apartment," I repeated. "Where she probably took that bag of Agatha's things Lita gave her. You know," I leaned close to his furry black and white face. "That bag that may have the envelope everyone was fighting with her about."

His green eyes narrowed. "Agatha had that envelope with her, and it seems to have disappeared. Maybe it had nothing to do with her death, but I have to start somewhere."

Hercules lifted a paw and smacked me on the arm.

"Ow!" I said. It didn't actually hurt, but I was trying to make a point. Why did he suddenly have to develop standards about me poking around in one of Marcus's cases?

"Look, all I want to do is look in that bag," I said. "If Ruby wasn't in jail you know she'd let me." Hercules actually seemed to consider that thought. "I'd wait if I had the time"—I leaned in even closer—"but I don't."

I set him on the floor, brushed off my lap and headed for the stairs. He was in front of me before I'd taken more than a couple of steps.

"It's for a good cause," I said. "And I'm not asking you to help me." I closed my eyes and pressed the heel of my hand to my forehead. I'd lost my mind. I really had this time. I was trying to justify to a cat what I was going to do.

I opened my eyes and looked into deep green cat eyes in a cute, furry black-and-white face. He looked like any other house cat, ready to rub against my leg or chase dust balls under the bed. But he wasn't someone's cute, cuddly house pet.

Would I have figured out how Gregor Easton died without Hercules? Or Owen? Herc had found a bead and a piece of very unique musical notation that helped me put all the pieces together. Not only had Easton's killer been caught, but Rebecca and Everett had gotten back together.

And when the house was broken into last summer, Hercules had gone for help while Owen had helped me fight off the intruder.

I imagined for a moment telling Maggie or Roma that Owen and Hercules had helped me find Gregor Easton's killer. They'd laugh. They'd think it was some kind of joke.

But the cats had. Which didn't mean they had to do it again.

"Marcus isn't going to look for another killer," I said to the cat. "At best, all he's going to do is look for more evidence against Ruby." I shrugged. "She's my friend. She's Maggie's friend. We're just going to have to agree to disagree."

I turned and headed for the kitchen instead, trying to ignore the insanity of telling a cat we were going to have to agree to disagree.

I filled the sink with hot water and bubbles and I was just starting to wash the glasses when I heard a noise. What the heck were those two doing now?

I went to the living room doorway. Hercules was coming across the floor, backward, from the closet, dragging my messenger bag, the strap in his teeth. His way, I realized, of telling me he'd help.

I walked over and crouched down to his level. He let go of the woven strap and looked at me. I suddenly had a giant lump in my throat. I kissed the top of his head. "Thank you," I said hoarsely.

Out of the corner of my eye I could see Owen by the end of the couch doing his neglected-cat pose. I reached out my right hand to him. "I love you, too, fur ball," I said. He scooted over and leaned against the side of my leg.

We were the Three Musketeers. We were Batman and Robin and a librarian.

We were probably nuts.

16

I got up Monday morning to warmer weather and no snow. While Hercules and Owen ate, I sat at the table with a cup of coffee.

I was having major second thoughts. Maybe I should wait until Ruby was out on bail, then get her to let me check the bag. *But what if she doesn't make bail?* a voice in my head asked.

Hercules finished his breakfast, walked over to the messenger bag I'd hung over one of the chairs the night before and gave it a swat with one paw.

"No," I said.

He hit the bag again.

I took it off the back of the chair and set it on the seat. "I'm happy you've decided to help," I said. "I really am. But I can't take you with me. How would I explain that to Rebecca?"

He jumped, landing on the chair seat and sending the nylon bag to the floor. Then he turned and stared defiantly at me.

"Oh, like that's going to work." I scooped the bag from the floor and set it on top of the fridge.

I should have known he wasn't going to give up easily. He hopped down and headed for the porch.

"Where are you going?" I asked.

Owen glanced up from his food, decided he had no dog—or in this case, cat—in this fight and went back to eating. I set my cup down and scrambled after Hercules. I knew if he wanted to he could get outside on his own. On the other hand, how likely was that? Outside meant snow, cold and wet feet.

That wasn't going to stop him. He was already in the yard. Hercules had committed to the plan and he was going to see it through. I yanked on my boots and hurried after him. He was halfway around the house, walking slowly, almost gingerly, stopping every few steps to shake one paw or another.

"Hercules, c'mon," I called. It was cold and I didn't have a jacket. I hugged myself, trying to stay warm. He looked back over his shoulder at me. "I can't take you," I said.

He headed for the driveway again.

This was stupid. I lunged for him, intending to scoop him up and go back inside. He darted forward, faster than I'd ever seen him move in the snow. I overreached, skidded on a small patch of ice and went sprawling on the path.

Hercules turned and craned his neck toward me.

"I'm fine," I grumped. I got slowly to my feet, brushing off the snow that clung to my sweater and pants. The heel of my left hand was red where it had scrapped along the frozen snow. I looked down at the cat. "You can come," I said. "This is completely insane, but you can come."

He lifted one front paw and shook it, then gave a pitiful-sounding meow. "Oh, for heaven's sake," I said. I bent and picked him up. "I'm the one who went tail over teakettle on the ice, and you're the one who's getting carried."

He snuggled into the crook of my arm and gave me a self-satisfied smirk.

Inside I set Hercules on the kitchen floor and brushed

off the last bits of snow sticking to my sweater. The side of my hand stung where it had scrapped across the ground. Owen and Hercules exchanged looks, then Owen turned to stare at me. Again I wondered if they shared come kind of cat telepathy. Considering everything else they could do it wasn't that far-fetched.

On one of the shelves in the hall closet I found a piece of orange fake fur. I stuffed it in the bottom of the messenger bag. Hercules came over, looked inside and shook his head.

"It's left over from the mad-scientist costume I wore at Halloween," I said. "It'll be warm."

Maggie had made me a fabulous mad-scientist outfit—part Marty Feldman in *Young Frankenstein*, part Beaker from the Muppets—including a custom hairpiece from orange fake fur.

"Try it," I said. Hercules stuck one paw the bag. Then the other. Then he climbed in all the way. He kneaded the bottom with his paws and finally lay down.

I got my coat, pulled on my boots, and carefully swung Hercules over my shoulder. "We'll be back soon," said I said to Owen, who was watching from under the table. "You got money for bail if we need it?"

He meowed.

"Good to know."

I walked quickly down the hill and over to Violet's house. Between them, Rebecca and Ruby had been keeping an eye on the house. Violet was gone for the foreseeable future. Ruby had moved into the apartment over the converted carriage house just before Violet left.

The steps up to the apartment were at the back of the building. I set the messenger bag down on the floor of the covered porch at the top of the stairs. Herc popped his head out and looked around. "Not a sound," I warned. "Not a meow, not a rumble, not even a burp. Rebecca will be here any minute."

I bent down to close the top of the bag. He jumped out, looked right and left and then and disappeared through the door before I could grab him.

I was never going to get used to that.

I dropped down into a crouch. Hercules was definitely gone. He could pass through any solid object—doors, six-inch-thick walls, concrete foundations. "Hercules, get back out here," I hissed at the door.

Nothing.

"I'm not kidding. You are in big, big trouble. Get out here now."

It was an empty threat. It wasn't like I could go in and fetch him. I took a deep breath and blew it out slowly. Then I leaned in close to the bottom panel of the door and called the cat's name.

Again, nothing.

"Are you looking for secret panel?" a voice behind me said. "Because I can promise you there isn't one."

Startled, I almost fell over. Rebecca was standing in the porch doorway. Heart pounding, I stood up.

"Good morning," she said. She gestured at the door. "It's a lovely door, isn't it? But not nearly as nice as the original wooden one. It had a squeak in the winter and it stuck in the summer." She didn't seem to think it was strange that I'd been "examining" the door.

"I like old houses," I said lamely.

"Me, too," Rebecca said. "But I admit I like doors that close and windows that keep the wind out." She fished in her pocket and pulled out a set of keys.

I stepped back to let her slip the key in the lock, bending to grab the strap of my bag. I crossed my fingers, hoping that Hercules wouldn't be sitting in the middle of the floor, blinking at us, when Rebecca opened the door.

He wasn't.

I set the messenger bag on the floor next to my boots,

close to the door, hoping the cat would take the hint and climb in while we were in the bedroom.

Rebecca held up a small piece of pale green paper. "I have a list."

I took it from her and looked it over. The underwear, and coat would be easy. I knew Ruby had a dark wool coat. She usually wore it with a fuzzy orange hat and scarf. I wasn't so sure about the plain white blouse and I couldn't remember ever seeing her in a dark skirt.

I smiled at Rebecca. "Let's see what we can find." I knew I had a simple dark skirt. If we couldn't find anything that seemed right for court, I'd send that and a handful of safety pins.

The bedroom was painted a soft shade of lilac. And the bed was covered with a deeper violet spread and heaped with pillows. Ruby had painted tiny stars on the ceiling. I looked around. Agatha's bag was sitting on an old nursery rocking chair in the corner. Thankfully I didn't see Hercules anywhere.

Rebecca pointed at an old steamer trunk under the window. "I'll look in there. Would you see if there's anything in that armoire?"

I couldn't find any skirt that wasn't a riot of color in the antique armoire where Ruby kept her clothes, but at the back I did find a plain white blouse.

Rebecca held up a pair of black woolen pants she'd unearthed from the old trunk. "What do you think about these?" she asked. "They're plain and dark and I don't think Ruby has any skirts that are going to work."

I draped the blouse over the waistband of the pants. The combination was serious and sedate—nothing like Ruby, but perfect for court. "Yes," I said.

Ruby's coat was in the hall closet. Rebecca had brought a nylon garment bag with her. We put everything inside and I folded the bag over my arm.

Rebecca made a small sigh of satisfaction. "Thank you," she said.

"You're welcome," I said. "I'll carry this down for you. Did you bring the car?" I couldn't help shooting a quick glance at the bag on the rocking chair.

"Yes, I did," she said. "But first, tell me why you keep looking at that grocery bag over there."

I felt my cheeks get red. "Was I that obvious?"

She nodded.

"You know Ruby didn't kill Agatha."

"Of course."

"The police have a piece of glass they think may have come from Ruby's truck."

"I heard that," Rebecca said.

"I, uh, found it. It caught on the hem of my pants."

"And you feel guilty."

"A little. The police think they have Agatha's killer. They aren't going to be looking for any evidence that will clear Ruby. Someone has to help her." I shrugged. "So here I am."

She smiled and gestured toward the rocking chair. "How is that bag going to help Ruby?"

"Agatha was carrying around an envelope the day she died. It's disappeared. Maybe it's not important, but maybe it is." I turned to look at the bag. "She was carrying that bag around, too. Lita gave it to Ruby. I thought maybe the envelope would be inside."

Rebecca nodded slowly and her eyes flicked from me to the rocking chair and back again. "I don't see why it would hurt to look. I think Ruby would probably say go ahead if she were here."

"Are you sure?" I asked.

"I'd like to help Ruby, too. If we find anything that seems important we'll call Everett and ask him what to do."

I laid Ruby's things on the bedspread and picked up

the bag. Inside were several pair of gloves, a crocheted black scarf, a small, square box of Kleenex, and three packets of ketchup. There was no envelope, no papers at all other than an old postcard from Florida with nothing written on it, and the bottom half of a torn old photograph—what looked to be the legs of a chubby baby sitting on someone's lap. This was clearly just stuff Agatha had collected around town.

"It's not here," I said to Rebecca, trying not to let my disappointment show. "They're things she was saving for some reason—gloves, ketchup."

She peeked inside the bag. "See those green gloves? They were in the lost and found at the community center for months. Someone probably gave them to her." She pointed to the postcard. "Wasn't there some kind of postcard display at the co-op store?"

"I think it came down just a few days ago."

Rebecca let the postcard fall back into the bag. She looked sad. "I think these are just things Agatha picked up walking around town. I'm sorry. There clearly isn't any envelope here and even if there was, knowing Agatha, I don't think you find anything in it to help Ruby."

I wasn't convinced of that, but I nodded. I picked up the nylon garment bag and followed Rebecca out to the kitchen.

My messenger bag was where I'd left it. *Please be inside,* I thought as I reached for the strap. The moment I lifted the bag I could tell Hercules was there. Or else I'd picked up a cat-sized hitchhiker. Surreptitiously, I slid the zipper closed, then put the strap over my shoulder

"Oh, that's a nice bag," Rebecca said. "Did you buy that here?"

"I did," I said. "I only paid five dollars for it over at the thrift store."

"I like it. Are those mesh panels?"

Okay, what was I going to do if she saw Hercules's face through the webbing? "Um, yes," I said. "I have a piece of fake fur in there right now. You can probably see it through the panel." As long as Hercules didn't make a sound, we were okay.

At the bottom of the steps Rebecca gave me a hug. "I'm sorry you didn't find anything helpful," she said. "But things will work out. They have a way of doing that."

I handed her the garment bag, then headed down the driveway, giving her a little wave when I reached the street.

The library was closer than home, so I went in that direction. I needed to make sure Hercules was okay. I let myself into the empty building, and as soon as I was in my office I set the bag on my chair and unzipped it. He climbed out, jumped onto the top of my desk and shook himself.

"Are you all right?" I asked. He looked at me, almost . . . smugly? No, I was imagining that. "That was one of the stupidest things I've ever done," I said. "Letting you come with me. What the heck was I thinking? What if Rebecca had seen you?"

Hercules walked across to my side of the desk. I reached out to stroke his fur, but he twisted his head away, and spit a soggy piece of paper onto the dark polished wood of the desk.

"What is that?" I said.

He looked from the damp piece of paper to me. Then he lifted his paw and started washing his face. As far as I'd been able to figure out, if Hercules had something in his mouth, he could walk through a wall—or a door—with it.

I picked up a pen, flipped the bit of paper over and studied it. It was part of a photograph. It was the missing piece of the photograph that had been in Agatha's bag;

a dark-haired baby in a white sun hat smiled up at me. I couldn't tell if the baby was a boy or girl.

"Did you tear that picture?" I asked him, folding my arms and frowning at him. He continued to wash his face.

I looked at the picture again. There was a bit of yellowed Scotch tape on the break. I held up a hand. "You didn't chew it. I'm sorry."

I held the fragment up to the light. The baby was sitting on a woman's lap. The woman didn't look like anyone I knew in Mayville. On the other hand, it was an old photograph.

I thought about the postcard Rebecca and I had found along with the bottom half of this photo. She was right. Agatha must've taken it from the display that had been at the shop. She'd probably found the photo there, too.

Maggie had had piles of photos in her studio for weeks while she was working on the collage panels for Winterfest. She'd spent days sorting, logging and then copying the ones she wanted. Maybe this had been with them.

A postcard, gloves from the lost and found, a scarf, this photograph. It was clear Agatha had been collecting things.

I pressed the knuckle of my thumb between my eyes and tried to rub away the frown lines I knew had to be there. "This doesn't mean anything, except maybe to show that Agatha's mind was slipping." I was frustrated. "Maybe that envelope is meaningless, as well."

I picked up Hercules and he stretched his front paws onto my shoulder so he could look out the window behind the desk.

"So, now what?" I asked him.

He looked blankly at me.

"Yeah, I don't know, either."

17

I wasn't quite as confident now about the contents of the envelope, since I'd seen the contents of the bag Agatha had been carrying around. On the other hand, it was all I had.

"You have to get back in the bag," I said to Hercules. He didn't move. "You can't stay here. Too risky. And you wouldn't want to miss one of Eric's breakfast sandwiches, would you?"

Hercules jumped down onto the desktop, walked across my files and dropped to the chair, sending it spinning in circles. I leaned over the desk and caught the chair back halfway through the fourth circle.

He looked up at me woozily. I came around to his side and held open the top of the tote. He jumped in and lay down. I closed the zipper and got my coat on again, and we headed back out.

It occurred to me that there was someone else I could ask about that envelope: Peter Lundgren. His law office was just up by the Stratton Theater. "Detour," I said to Hercules.

There was no one at Peter's office. It was probably too early. "Maybe we'll get lucky and Eric will be working," I said to Herc. Well, actually I said it to the bag slung over my shoulder. Thankfully there was no one on the sidewalk.

As we turned toward the restaurant Hercules shifted in the bag. I stopped and peered through the top panel. Two green eyes looked up at me. "Not a sound," I hissed. "And no jumping around. The last thing I need is to have to explain why my bag is moving."

That had happened to me once at tai chi with Owen. Luckily, Maggie had saved me by saying her phone was in my bag, set to vibrate.

The restaurant was almost empty, but Eric was back behind the counter. I resisted the urge to unzip the tote and high-five the cat. Or do a fist-paw bump.

Eric nodded hello when I walked in, but then turned away. He still looked a little ragged, and I wondered how much of that was due to Agatha's death.

Jaeger, who usually worked weekends for Eric, was wiping down the counter. He was a mask maker. I'd seen him a couple of times in his studio at the River Arts Center when I'd gone to visit Maggie. He smiled and gestured around the room. "Anywhere you'd like," he said. "I'll be there with coffee in a second." I picked a table for two in the far corner under the window, but against the side wall.

When Jaeger came over I ordered a breakfast sandwich and set Hercules by my feet, between the wall and my chair. The top of the bag was open a crack. After I'd taken off my coat, I put cream and sugar in my coffee and took a drink. It was good, hot and strong.

I felt the bag moving between my feet. I looked down just in time to see Hercules wiggle out of the bag and make a mad dash along the wall, disappearing down the hall to the restrooms.

Crap on toast! What was I going to do now? I grabbed the bag and bolted from the table, turning the corner just in time to see the cat go through Eric's office door, the door with the PRIVATE sign on it. And I did mean "through."

"Hercules!" I hissed. Waste of time. He was already gone and it wasn't very likely he'd have listened, anyway.

I stood in the small hallway and took several deep breaths. Hercules was in Eric's office, yes, but Eric and Jaeger were still out front. All I had to do was not panic, wait until the cat came out, and get him back in the bag. How hard could that be?

I tried not to think about all the things that could go wrong, like Hercules walking through the very solid-looking door just as someone else was on their way to the washroom.

"Hey, Kathleen."

Or Eric needing to get into his office.

I turned around.

"Is there a problem with the restroom?"

"Um, no," I said. "I wanted to talk to you in private."

His expression was instantly guarded. "This really isn't a good time."

I took a step closer so he couldn't go around me easily. Then I pushed the bag behind me with one foot. "You, uh, you look tired," I said gently. Whatever was wrong with Eric, I didn't want to make him feel worse.

"Yeah, well, I had a tooth that was giving me problems." He wiped a hand on his apron. "Like I said, this isn't a good time." He moved to go around me.

Maybe being gentle wasn't going to work. "It's a heck of a lot worse time for Ruby."

That stopped him in his tracks. He turned. "Look," he said. "I'm sorry that Ruby was arrested. And for the record, I don't think she had anything to do with Agatha's death. But neither did I." He pulled a hand over the back of his head and his eyes slid off my face. "Is that what you wanted to know, Kathleen?"

Since he was being direct, there was no reason for me not to be the same. "The night she died Agatha was in here. She was carrying an envelope," I said. "It was an old brown envelope with a metal tab closure, probably from a report card."

"If you say so."

"You argued with her about it."

"I didn't argue with Agatha about anything." His body language said different. He shifted uneasily from one foot to another.

"You weren't the only one," I said. "It had to mean something."

"We didn't argue," he said again.

"Call it a discussion, then. Call it whatever you want. I think whatever was inside the envelope might have something to do with Agatha's death. And now, very conveniently for someone, it's disappeared."

Eric looked me in the eye then. "Look, Kathleen. I don't know what you think you saw, but Agatha and I didn't fight over an old envelope or whatever might or might not have been inside. You misunderstood what you saw." He looked away just a little too quickly.

I took a couple of steps sideways, trying to turn Eric away from his office door, and waited, hoping the silence would nudge him into saying more.

"After Agatha had that stroke, she got argumentative over things that didn't matter, like how many packets of mayo I gave her with her sandwich."

I shook my head ever so slightly. I knew what I'd seen. Eric hadn't been arguing with the old woman over mayonnaise.

"And she started collecting things—junk, really— things she tore out of the newspaper, things she found around town."

I thought of the collection in the canvas bag—the gloves, the postcard. Maybe he was right. Then I remembered how protective Agatha had been about that brown envelope. She hadn't felt the same way about the bag and its contents because she'd left it behind at the community center. And no matter what Eric was saying now, he had argued with her about that envelope.

Eric crossed his arms and ran one hand up and down his upper arm. "Kathleen, no offense, but you're not from here, and you haven't known us that long. You didn't know Agatha at all."

You're not one of us. I'd heard that before. It used to make me feel left out, but this time all I felt was angry. Eric was lying; that was clear by the way he couldn't look at me for more than a few seconds at a time. He was using the fact that I wasn't Mayville born and bred to avoid being honest with me.

I felt a faint change in the air, in the energy of a small hallway.

Hercules.

Eric didn't seem to notice. He was turned away from the office, and over his shoulder I saw Hercules come through the door. The cat blinked, looked around and then disappeared into the bag.

"You're right," I said to Eric, my heart pounding with relief. "I haven't been here nearly long enough to know everyone. But I do know Ruby didn't kill Agatha and she doesn't deserve what's happening to her." I moved behind him and grabbed the strap of the bag.

"Please think about that, Eric," I said. I walked back to the table, setting the messenger bag on my chair. "You are in deep, deep trouble," I whispered to the cat. I could see one green eye watching me through the top mesh panel.

Jaeger had my order ready. I paid and walked back to the library with Hercules slung securely over my shoulder and my hand on top of the bag.

Inside my office with the door closed, I let Hercules out.

"I can't believe you did that," I said, pulling off my coat and hat. "Twice in the same morning. How would I have explained why I had a cat in Eric's restaurant? Huh?"

His response was to poke the take-out bag with a paw. "I'm not surprised you're hungry," I said, pulling out the toasted English muffin sandwich and fishing out some of the egg for him. "The life of a cat burglar will do that to you."

I ate a bite of the muffin, then pulled out a strip of crispy bacon. Hercules spit a piece of paper at me, snatched the bacon from my fingers and jumped to the floor in one smooth motion.

"Hey!" I yelled. He was already under my desk.

I bent down and peered underneath in time to see the last bit of bacon disappear into his mouth. "This isn't a funny," I said. "No sardines for you for the rest of the week."

He licked his lips. The piece of paper he had swiped from Eric's office had fallen on the floor. I picked it up, straightened it and smoothed it flat on the desktop. There was a rushing sound in my head, like I'd held a seashell up to my ear.

The piece of paper was the top part of an envelope.

An old brown report-card envelope.

18

I dropped into the closest chair, trying to make sense out of something that wasn't making any sense at all.

Agatha had been carrying around an old brown envelope. That envelope had disappeared just before or just after her death. Eric claimed he knew nothing about it.

Except Hercules had found a piece of the same kind of envelope in Eric's office. The same kind of envelope, or a piece of the envelope Agatha had been carrying around?

No matter what Eric said, I was certain of one thing: Whatever had been inside that envelope was important. Important enough that Eric would lie and Old Harry would stay silent.

Hercules poked his head out from under the desk. "Come on out," I said. "I'm not mad." I put the remaining slice of bacon and the rest of the egg on the floor on the waxed-paper sandwich wrapper. I kept the English muffin for myself.

So now what? I didn't know. What I did know was that I knew very little about Agatha Shepherd. Maybe if I learned more about the woman, I'd be able to figure out what secret she'd been holding on to so tightly.

I looked at my watch. I had just enough time to get

Hercules home and come back. I wasn't looked forward to another trip up and down the hill.

I swallowed the last of my coffee. "Come on, Fuzz Face," I said. I picked up the cat and popped him in the bag yet again. I fished the cinnamon roll I'd gotten for Owen out of the paper take-out bag.

I was getting good at dressing for the cold. We were out on the sidewalk in less than five minutes. As I headed to the corner, the strap of the messenger bag securely across my body, I thought for maybe the hundredth time this winter that I really needed a car. Hiking all over the place in a heavy parka and boots was wearing me out.

As I started up Mountain Road, Harry Taylor's truck pulled up beside me. Harry leaned over and pointed at the empty seat beside him. I couldn't help wondering if his driving by again was planned or a coincidence. I decided I didn't care. It was cold. I nodded.

"What are you doing out so early?" he asked as I got in.

"I was at Ruby's with Rebecca," I said, as Harry pulled away from the curb.

"I heard she was arrested," he said, his eyes straight ahead.

"She didn't kill Agatha." I was starting to sound like a broken record—or should that be CD? "I'm afraid the police will stop looking for the person who really did, though."

"Do you think the old man knows something?" Harry asked.

I was surprised by his bluntness, so I chose my words carefully. "I think he might."

Harry glanced over at me. "Like what?"

I told him about the envelope and how his father and Agatha seemed to have had words about whatever was in it. I felt bad about essentially telling on Harry Senior, but I felt worse about Ruby being in custody. "The envelope's missing," I said. "That's way too much of a coincidence for me."

Harry pulled into my driveway and put the truck in park. "You want me to ask Dad? I can't promise you he'll tell me anything."

"Do you think he'd talk to me?" I asked. If Harry Senior understood he might be able to help Ruby, maybe he'd tell me what he'd argued about with Agatha. Maybe it would help. It was worth asking.

"I think he's more likely to talk to you than me. How about coming out tonight after supper?"

I nodded. "All right."

"I'll come get you about seven," he said.

I thanked him, picked up my bag and got out of the truck. As soon as we were in the house I let Hercules out. He shook himself and went for a drink. Owen appeared from somewhere. I gave him two pieces of the cinnamon roll. He sniffed them carefully.

"I'll tell you everything tonight," I said. "Or ask your brother."

Quickly I changed my clothes, fixed my hair and touched up my makeup. I tossed some of the granola bars I'd made and an apple into my briefcase and headed back down to the library, grateful that Mayville Heights was small and the library was downhill.

I was almost at the bottom when I noticed Roma's SUV up ahead at the intersection. I waved my arms to get her attention and half ran, half skidded down the sidewalk. She caught sight of me and waited. Luckily there was no one behind her.

She stuck her head out the driver's window. "Hi, Kathleen. Were you looking for me or just practicing semaphore with your bag?"

"Very funny," I said. "I wanted to ask you something."

"Sure," she said. "Get in."

I climbed into the SUV and fastened the seat belt.

Roma looked both ways and headed down the street. "What did you want to ask me?"

"Remember when we saw Agatha at Eric's?"

"Yes."

"She was carrying an envelope."

Roma frowned. "Yeah," she said, slowly, "brown. Maybe an old one from the school."

I nodded.

"Is that important?"

"Maybe," I said. "I don't know. It's disappeared and I don't have a clue what was in it. She argued with more than one person about that envelope."

"Maybe the police have it."

I shook my head. "I don't think so."

"You think it could help Ruby?"

"Yeah, I do."

"How can I help?" she asked, as we turned toward the library.

"I need to know more about Agatha," I said. "Maybe it'll help me figure out what was so important to her that she was carrying it around everywhere in that old envelope."

"Any coffee at the library?"

"There can be." I held up the bag. "And I have granola bars."

Roma looked at her watch. "I have about a half hour," she said.

Mary and Abigail arrived as Roma turned into the library parking lot. I made coffee, filling a cup for Roma and one for myself, and leaving the rest for the other women. Roma and I settled in the two chairs facing my desk.

"So, what you want to know?" she asked.

"I don't know exactly."

"You know Agatha was divorced when David was young."

I nodded.

"She was a teacher before she was married, but she hadn't taught in years." Roma reached for one of the granola bars and took a bite. "Oh, those are good," she said, her mouth full of oatmeal and chocolate chips. "She went back to school, got her degree, came back here and eventually became the principal of the junior high. She had no other family, no help. I don't how she did it."

"What was she like as a person?"

Roma considered the question for a minute. "She had high standards for everyone, but no more than for herself. She expected a lot, but she gave a lot, too. I told you that she took that time to go work with underprivileged kids." She set her cup on my desk. "Kathleen, what you looking for? I can tell you Agatha was a good mother and a great teacher, but I don't think that's going to help you."

I fingered the seam along the arm of the imitation-leather chair. "I don't know what I'm looking for, really," I said. "Something I can use to help Ruby. The only thing I have to go on is an old report-card envelope. And now it's disappeared."

Roma picked up her cup again and took a long drink. I could see she was weighing her words before she spoke, so I waited without saying anything. She leaned forward in the chair. "Kathleen, one thing I can tell you about Agatha is that she was an extremely private person. She didn't share anything of herself with people. I'm sorry, but I just don't think that envelope is the key to who killed her. I think you'll find out it would've been meaningless to anyone but her. It could've been papers from the rehab center. It could've been something she saw in the newspaper." She reached over and broke off half of one of the remaining granola bars. "Have you talked to any of the people you saw arguing with her?"

"I talked to Eric," I said with a shrug.

"What did he say?"

"That he wasn't arguing with Agatha and he didn't know what was in the envelope."

"I'm sorry," Roma said. "I think you're looking in the wrong place." She stood up, brushing crumbs off her jeans. "I think the whole thing's going to turn out to be a horrible accident."

What could I say? That I was positive the envelope did matter because Hercules had found part of it in Eric's office? "Thanks," I said.

"We'll figure out a way to help Ruby."

My phone rang then.

"Go ahead," Roma said. "I need to get going. I'll see you in class tomorrow night."

I got the phone the fourth ring. It was Maggie.

"I just wanted to let you know that Ruby is out on bail," she said.

I sank onto my desk chair. "I'm so glad to hear that." I felt some of the tension drain out of my body.

"We're going to have a late lunch here at the studio. Could you come? Ruby wants to thank you in person for calling Everett."

I quickly ran over the staffing schedule in my head. I was fairly sure I could take a late lunch.

"I think I can come," I said. We agreed on one thirty and I hung up, swinging around in my chair to look out the window at the clouds, low and heavy and probably full of snow.

I'd talked to Eric about Agatha. I was going to see Old Harry tonight.

It was time to talk to third to the third person I'd seen arguing with Agatha.

Ruby.

19

There were a few flakes of snow blowing around when I headed down to the art studio. Ruby got to her feet and came over to me as soon as I walked into the room.

"Thank you," she said, her voice husky with emotion. "I didn't think I needed a lawyer, which wasn't very smart."

"You're welcome," I said. "But all I did was make a phone call. The credit should go to Everett."

"I already thanked him." She slid a stack of brightly colored, knotted bracelets up and down her arm. "Kathleen, I didn't hurt her."

"I know that," I said. "They'll find out what really happened."

We walked over to Maggie's worktable. Mags was in the middle of an animated conversation with one of the other artists who shared studio space on that floor. She gave me a smile and kept on talking.

"How can anyone think that I would hurt Agatha?" Ruby asked, as I shrugged off my coat. "She changed my life."

"Ruby what were you doing that night? Is there anyone who saw you or talked to you?" I was pretty sure I knew the answer: If Ruby had talked to anyone or been with anyone, the police wouldn't have arrested her.

"I was home by myself, just watching a DVD," she said quickly.

I looked at her without speaking. She flushed and looked away. "That's a lie. I was sitting in the dark, eating cookie dough," she said in a small voice. "I wasn't on my computer. I didn't answer the phone." She let out a breath. "I had a fight with Justin. He drove me home and we got into it. He left, and I was going to walk down and get my truck but instead I just sat around eating half-frozen chocolate chip cookie dough." She finally looked at me. "Pretty stupid, wasn't it?"

I shook my head. I couldn't help remembering my first few weeks in Mayville Heights after I'd left Andrew back in Boston. I'd spent a fair amount of time sitting in the dark, eating raw cookie dough myself. And ice cream and gobs of jam on English muffins. "It's not stupid," I said.

"If I had answered the phone or I checked my e-mail I'd at least be able to prove I was there."

"We'll figure something else out." I looked around the room. Maggie was still talking. Justin was deep in conversation with a man whose suit and tie pegged him as Ruby's lawyer. I was surprised to see Peter standing by one of the tall windows. In his dark suit and white shirt, his hair back in a ponytail, I almost hadn't recognized him. Maybe he was there to represent Agatha's son. I took a deep breath. "Ruby, I need to ask you something," I said.

"Sure, what is it?"

"Last week, I saw you in the parking lot of the library with Agatha."

She stiffened. "You probably did," she said carefully.

"You were arguing about something."

"It doesn't have anything to do with her death," she said with an offhand shrug. "It was nothing."

I knew that wasn't true. She'd answered too quickly. I was getting so sick of hearing that the arguments and the envelope meant nothing when it was so clear they did.

"No, it wasn't," I said. "That brown envelope she was holding on to so tightly? It's disappeared."

The color drained from Ruby's face. "Agatha's death was an accident," she said. "Someone was driving too fast or driving when they'd been drinking and they ran her down, panicked and took off."

"Maybe," I said. "But maybe not."

Ruby looked stricken. "You think . . ." She had trouble getting the words out. "You think someone killed Agatha deliberately?"

"I don't know." What I left unsaid was that Marcus Gordon thought so, and that was what mattered.

"Even if that's true, it couldn't have been because of what was in the envelope." She shook her head emphatically.

"Why?" I didn't even try to keep the aggravation out of my voice. "What was in that stupid thing, anyway?"

"I can't tell you," she said.

"Ruby," I said, leaning closer to make my point. "The police think you killed Agatha. This is a very bad time to be keeping secrets."

"It's not my secret to tell," she said stubbornly.

"Well, whose secret is it?"

She took a long moment to think. "You should talk to Harry Taylor," she said at last.

All roads led back to the old man. "Old Harry?"

She nodded. Harry had a secret. Ruby had a secret. Agatha had a secret. And now it looked like it was the same secret. All this secret keeping was a very, very bad thing to do. You just had to watch a couple of episodes of *The Young and the Restless* to know that.

Justin was looking in our direction and I knew I didn't have much more time to make my point. "Agatha had some secret that Harry apparently knew, that you knew, and who knows how many other people knew."

"No one else knew."

I thought about Eric and realized that probably wasn't true. "Agatha is dead. The police don't think it's an accident. That envelope with whatever was in it is gone. And you, who just happen to be one of the secret keepers, have been charged with Agatha's murder. That's four too many coincidences." *And way too many secrets.*

"Harry didn't hurt Agatha," Ruby said, her mouth set in a tight line, hands on her hips. "First of all, he's too old, and second, he's not strong enough. And even if none of that stuff was true, I can promise you he would never ever hurt Agatha."

"Ruby, I know that," I said. "I know Harry didn't kill Agatha any more than you did. But I can't help but to keep thinking that whatever she had in that old envelope had something to do with her death."

"It didn't. You just have to trust me on this. It didn't." She made a dismissive wave with a hand. "Talk to Harry, Kathleen," she said. And then she walked back to the others.

For a moment I thought about turning around and leaving, but Maggie was on her way over to me. "Everything all right?" she asked,

"Ask me later," I said, watching Ruby go over and hug another one of the building's artists who had just come in.

"Okay." She linked her arm through mine and walked me toward the food. "Come have some soup," she said. "It's tomato vegetable, and there's fresh Parmesan and those sourdough croutons you like."

Maggie got me a bowl of soup and sprinkled cheese and croutons on top. I picked up a spoon and took a stool at the end of her worktable. I'd eaten about half the bowl when Justin came over, hooked the rung of an empty stool with his foot, and pulled it close so he could sit down.

"Hi, Kathleen," he said. "I wanted to thank you for helping Ruby, so"—he held out his hands—"thank you."

"You're welcome," I said.

We sat in silence for a moment. Then he said, "This doesn't feel real, you know. Ruby being arrested and me suddenly getting all this money from someone I didn't know." He shook his head. "I got something that will do so much good from Agatha Shepherd's death, and Ruby—who loved her—got a load of trouble."

So it was definitely true. "No one thinks Ruby killed Agatha."

"The police do."

"And they'll figure out they're wrong and find the real killer."

Justin put his fingers flat on the table. And stared at them. "The funding fell through and I thought it was the end of the project. I was out of ideas. I'd begged for money. I'd literally begged for it. And then I found out a stranger had left me what I needed to get started. A stranger. I thought it was a dream or some kind of sick practical joke." His eyes went to Ruby before giving me his attention again. "I'm thinking about not taking the money."

"Because of Ruby."

"Yeah."

I could actually feel the energy coming off of him. It didn't seem like he ever stopped moving. Some part of him—hands, feet—was always in motion. Right now it was his right foot moving up and down on the rung of the stool.

"Turning down that money isn't going to change anything for Ruby," I said. "And she'd hate your doing it."

He shrugged. "Yeah, I know. But it would ease my guilty conscience." He gave me a small smile.

I could sympathize a little on the guilt.

Justin shifted in his seat, picked up his coffee and set it down again. "Kathleen, what do you think happened in that alley?" he asked.

"I don't know."

"It could have been an accident," he said slowly. He was still playing with his cup. "Maybe it was, I don't know, someone who panicked, someone who was drinking. They ran and now they're afraid to come forward. Otherwise . . . why would anyone want to kill an old woman?"

I shrugged.

"I just don't buy that someone her age, who'd just come from rehabilitation hospital, for God's sake, would have any enemies."

"So maybe it was an accident and the driver panicked."

"Yeah," he said. "That had to be it. And it's a stupid shortcut, you know. I walked through it."

I'd thought the same thing myself. The alley didn't really save any time or any distance, but if someone were driving it would help him avoid the stop sign at the corner.

"I feel bad for Eric, too," Justin said, looking past me toward the high windows of the former school classroom behind us. "This can't be good for business, and he made a hell of a lot of sacrifices to get that place off the ground."

"You two are friends?" I asked. I glanced over at Maggie. She dipped her head in Justin's direction and raised her eyebrows, code for *Do you need rescuing?* I gave a slight head shake.

He shifted on the stool again, pulling it a bit closer to me. His foot was tapping to some rhythm only he could hear. "We go way back," he said. "We used to hang out together." He laughed. "We got into a fair amount of trouble together."

"Eric?" I said. That didn't quite fit with the man I knew.

"Oh, yeah," Justin said. "Kids I work with? Kids I want the camp for? I used to be one of them. I drank; I used. There's a big chunk of time when I wasn't straight for even an hour."

I wasn't sure what to say, although I was starting to see the reason for his intensity. "I was shoplifting," he continued, "swiping stuff out of cars. You know that straight stretch of highway just outside of town, headed for Minneapolis?"

"I do."

"Raced out there more times than I can count or remember. Pretty much every time with Eric riding shotgun." He gave me a wry smile, almost like he had a bit of pride for the memory

"So, what changed?" I asked, leaning my elbow on the table and propping my head on my hand. "I take it you're not still doing that anymore."

He laughed, "Nope. Sober and straight for seven years now. No dope, no booze, although I do admit to still having a bit of a lead foot on the highway. What happened is I got arrested. I got sent to juvie."

"Where you've learned . . . ?" I prompted.

"How to hot-wire a car and pretty much nothing else." He fingered the silver skull bracelet on his right arm. "It took a couple more trips there and a couple of kick-ass counselors to turn me around. It's why the camp's so damned important. Some of us need a kick in the ass and a lot of help to get it all together."

He drummed his fingers on the edge of the stool between his legs. "Eric, on the other hand, he got it together by himself. With Agatha Shepherd's help." He laughed. "Of course, it probably helped that I wasn't around."

His face got serious. "When I drank I was just mostly looking to have a good time, you know, but Eric, he was"—he hesitated—"destructive."

I was still having a problem picturing Eric as the young man Justin was describing.

"He had blackouts when he had no idea what he'd been doing." Justin looked at me. "It's good that he doesn't drink anymore. Period. I just don't want what's happened to mess up everything he's worked so hard for."

I thought about seeing Eric at the rink and how my first thought was that he looked like he'd just come off a binge. "Are you saying that something like Agatha's death could start Eric drinking again?"

"No," he said. "I mean, she was one of the few people who stuck by him when he was still drinking, so her death had to hit him hard. But start drinking? No."

He fiddled with one of the silver skulls again. "Stress is not good for an alcoholic. There's the impulse to have a couple, you know, just to take the edge off." He exhaled slowly and noisily. "But that's not where Eric is anymore. He has a wife and kids." Justin traced the edge of the stool's curved seat with his finger. "And he'd never do something and let Ruby or anyone else take the blame."

Abruptly he got to his feet. "Sorry," he said. "Sometimes I talk too much. I need to go see how Ruby's doing. Excuse me."

I watched him walk over to where Ruby seemed to be saying good-bye to Peter and slide his arm around her waist. I slipped off my own stool and went to Maggie. "I have to get back to the library."

"Did Justin talk your ear off?" she asked.

"No, I, uh, learned a couple of things," I said.

"Anything you want to share?"

"Later," I said.

Maggie studied my face, but all she said was, "All right."

I grabbed my coat and left. As I walked, I thought about what Justin had said, his insistence that Eric wouldn't drink. I thought about Eric's appearance, his evasiveness, and Susan's out-of-character excuses. If I didn't know better, I'd say he had been drinking. And now I couldn't help thinking that maybe I didn't know better.

I stopped at the corner. Peter was farther ahead of me, already on the other side of the intersection. All at once I was frozen in place, watching him making his way down the sidewalk in a black woolen Winterfest hat . . . and Ellis Slater's aviator jacket.

20

I had to remind my feet to move, and by the time I was across the street I'd lost sight of Peter. *I must be wrong,* I told myself as I trudged back to the library. He'd been wearing a jacket that looked like the one I'd seen in Agatha's house, not the actual jacket. Peter wouldn't take something that didn't belong to him. He was a lawyer, after all, and a pretty decent guy, from what I'd heard.

I was glad to get home at the end of the day. I heated the last of the stew and ate with Owen for company. Hercules appeared long enough to let me scratch behind his ears and then he wandered off.

I thought about Hercules' little forays into Ruby's apartment and Eric's office.

"You know what the problem is?" I said to Owen. The cat leaned forward as though he really wanted to hear the answer to the question. "Too many secrets. I'm starting to see connections where there aren't any. I saw Peter Lundgren ahead of me on the street and I actually thought he was wearing a jacket I'd seen in Agatha's house and that had belonged to her brother."

There were a couple of pieces of meat and a bit of carrot left in my dish. I set it on the floor for Owen. "Don't tell Roma," I said. Admittedly, I was telling him to keep a secret when I had been complaining about other people doing it.

I checked the clock. I had about a half hour before Harry came to get me. What was the old man going to tell me? Anything? The more roadblocks I ran into, the more curious I got, and the more convinced I became that the envelope's contents held the key to Agatha's death.

"Ruby knows what Agatha was carrying around with her." Owen had finished eating and started to clean himself up. "And Eric is mixed up in this in some way, too. Why won't anyone tell me what's in the damn thing? What's the big secret?"

It didn't make any sense. What were Harrison Taylor, Eric and Ruby all willing to risk being implicated in a crime for? Had Agatha done something illegal? Had someone else? It wasn't money. I was fairly certain of that. Harry wouldn't keep his mouth shut, promise or no promise, over money. For him it was personal, emotional. Probably for Eric and Ruby, too. The one thing they had in common was they all loved Agatha.

I was going to have to talk to Eric again. I kept trying to push the thought that he'd been drinking out of my mind. But it wouldn't quite go. Justin said Eric had been destructive when he drank and sometimes he blacked out.

I look down at Owen and gave voice to the thought that had been twisting in my head and in my stomach since I'd left Maggie's studio. "Eric did not get drunk, have a blackout and run over Agatha. Did he?"

Hearing the words made me see how preposterous the idea was. Owen didn't even dignify the question with so much as a twitch. I didn't have any real proof that Eric had been drinking, let alone that he had been drunk. And if he had fallen off the wagon and had a blackout I didn't believe that meant he'd turned into someone else. Even if there'd been some kind of accident, I refused to believe Eric could drink enough to turn into the kind of person who would just leave someone to die.

"I'll talk to Eric again after I talk to Harry," I said to Owen as I reached for the bowl on the floor. "If Harry tells me what all the secret keeping has been about maybe I'll be able to find out what's happening with Eric."

I began filling the sink with hot water. "And maybe somewhere in all of this we'll find a way to help Ruby." Owen finished washing his tail and went to get a drink.

"I'm going out to the Taylors to talk to Harry in a little while," I said. "I forgot to tell you." Owen's head snapped up. I could read his little kitty mind. "Forget it," I said. He ignored me, walked over to the door where the messenger bag sat by the heating vent and stuck one paw side.

"No," I said. "You can't go with me." After what had happened this morning I wasn't chancing taking a cat with me to Harry's.

He leaned his head over the top of the bag and peered inside.

"Owen, have you forgotten about Boris?" I asked. His paw came out a lot faster than it had gone in. Boris was Harry Junior's German shepherd. Boris was a pussycat, pun intended, but I couldn't convince the cat of that. The only menacing thing about Boris was his bark, but Owen wasn't taking any chances.

Harry pulled into the driveway at exactly seven o'clock. "Your father knows I'm coming?" I asked as I got in the truck.

He nodded. "I wouldn't ambush the old man."

"I didn't really think you would."

"He knows about Ruby being arrested. He wants to talk," Harry said as he backed out onto the road and started up the hill. "I think there's stuff he's been wanting to get off his chest for a long time." He glanced over at me. "And he likes you."

"As I said before, I like him, too."

"There's no way he's going to talk to me. He still sees me as a kid. Dad keeps his cards pretty close to his vest, but for some reason he trusts you." He blew out a breath as he realized how that sounded. "I'm sorry," he started. "I didn't mean—"

"It's okay," I said, lifting a mittened hand to stop him. "I know what you meant."

"I think the fact that you didn't grow up here makes a difference," Harry continued. "You don't have any judgments about anyone, or any ideas about who they ought to be or how they ought to live."

It was the first time being from away was seen as an advantage. I liked Harry's way of looking at things.

The Taylors lived close to Oren, two roads above the Kenyon family homestead. Young Harry and his kids—a boy and a girl, both teenagers—lived in the main house. I knew Harry and his wife were divorced and she lived out of state, but the town talk was silent on that subject.

The old man lived in a small house, more like a cottage or a guesthouse, behind and to the left of the main house, in a cleared area surrounded by trees, with Harry Junior's shop nearby.

"Your dad still lives alone?" I asked as the truck followed the curve of the neatly plowed driveway.

"Oh, yeah," Harry said. "There's a woman who comes in every weekday to clean up and do some cooking. Paula Stevens—she's a cousin somehow to Lita. You know, Everett's secretary."

I nodded. It seemed like half of Mayville was related to Lita somehow.

"Old man doesn't like it," Harry went on, "but sometimes he lets me win one."

We pulled into a wide, clear area between the little house and the shop and we both got out of the truck. It was a bitingly cold night. The tiny house looked warm and welcoming. An amber light shone in the outside fixture, and a spiral of smoke came from the chimney.

We walked toward the back door. "Dad's been very quiet and thoughtful the past couple of days," Harry said. "Whatever this all is, I think he wants to get it out." He rapped on the back door, then turned the knob and stepped back so I could go in.

Harry Senior was sitting on a chair by the corner woodstove in the kitchen. He smiled at me.

"Don't get up," I said, but he was already pushing himself to his feet.

"I wouldn't be much of a gentleman if I didn't get up and take your coat," he said.

I slipped out of my jacket and gave it to him. His son gave me a quick smile, which his father caught. He dipped his head toward the younger man. "See, Kathleen? My son has already figured out to humor the old man."

Boris padded over for a scratch behind the ears. When I bent to undo my boots, he nudged my hand with his head, much the way the cats did when they felt they weren't getting enough attention.

"Dog's spoiled," Harry said, reaching down to pat him on the head.

"Would you like some coffee?" his father offered. "Will it keep you up?"

"I'll chance it," I said. "Thank you."

"Let me get that, Dad," Harry said, taking off his boots.

The old man shot him a look.

"Or not," his son said, holding out both hands in surrender.

"Coffee cake," I said, holding up a foil-wrapped package.

Harrison smiled at me. "I was hoping I'd get to try some of your cooking." He pointed to one of the cupboards. "Plates are in there. Knives are in the top drawer."

Harry Junior had put his boots back on without doing up the laces. "I'll outside, cleaning up the driveway," he said.

"You don't have to leave," the older man said without looking up from the coffee he was pouring.

"It's okay, Dad."

I cut several slices of cake and put them on a blue bubble-glass plate. Harrison had poured three mugs of coffee. He set them on a wooden tray along with spoons, napkins, cream and sugar. I added the cake plate.

"Would you set that on the table over there, please, Kathleen?" he asked, gesturing at the low wooden trunk in front of the woodstove.

"Of course," I said. I picked up the tray as the old man made his way over to his son, still standing by the door.

Harrison clapped a hand on his son's shoulder. "Sit down and have a piece of cake."

The old man's seat was clearly the chair closest to the fire. There was a plum-colored corduroy pillow against the cushions for his back and a couple of books and a newspaper on the floor. He liked Scottish history and political biographies, I knew. I took the chair next to him. Boris came and lay down with his head against my leg.

"Over here, boy," Harrison said to the dog, patting the side of his chair. "Give Kathleen some space." The dog lifted his head, gave the old man a mildly interested look and lay back down.

"Stubborn," he said, shaking his head.

"Wonder where he learned that," his son muttered.

"I heard that," Harrison said, reaching for the coffee.

The hint of a smile played across the younger man's face.

Boris raised his head again, nose twitching. I took a piece of cake for myself, broke off a small piece, and slipped it to the dog. If the two men noticed, they didn't say.

The old man added cream and sugar to his mug and settled back in his chair. I held on to my coffee with one hand and scratched Boris's neck with the other.

Old Harry smiled at me." You have more questions about Agatha."

"I'm sorry for being so nosy," I said. "But I like Ruby. I truly believe she had nothing to do with Agatha's death."

"The police are idiots. You're thinking they'll stop looking for answers now that they think they have the killer."

"Yes."

"For what it's worth, I agree with you about Ruby." He studied the flames behind the glass window of the wood-stove door. "You want to know what Agatha and I were fighting about," he said, still watching the flickering fire.

"I'm sorry to invade your privacy and hers. But whatever was in that envelope that Agatha was holding on to so tightly, I'm convinced it has something to do with her death."

The old man let out a slow breath. To my left his son hadn't moved an inch. "You don't think Agatha's death was an accident?"

"No, I don't," I admitted. "Even if someone did hit her by mistake and then panicked, they ran and they left Ruby to be blamed. Either way, Agatha's death is a crime."

I set my cup back on the tray and turned toward him. "I saw three very different people argue with Agatha about that old brown envelope. Now it's disappeared."

His face went pale and he closed his eyes for a moment. When he opened them again he looked at me. "Would it be enough if I told you that what was in the envelope had nothing to do with her death?"

I held out a hand. "I need to be sure," I said softly. "I'm sorry. But I need to know why you're so certain."

He sighed. Boris looked over at him. I gave the dog another scratch behind the ears.

Boris got up and moved over to the old man's chair. His hand settled on the thick fur on the back of the dog's neck. "There have been too many secrets," he said, absently patting the dog. "And I've been guilty of keeping them." He looked over at his son. "You know how much I loved your mother." It was a statement, not a question.

Harry nodded.

"I'm not making excuses," the old man began. He stopped and fingered his beard for a moment. "If I'm not making excuses, then I shouldn't be making them, should I?"

"It's okay, Dad," Harry said quietly.

They locked eyes and something stretched between them. For a moment it felt almost the way it did when Hercules walked through a wall or a door. The energy in the room seemed to somehow change.

Finally the old man leaned back and smiled wryly. "You know, don't you?"

I looked from one man to the other, but I didn't say anything. It was clear I was on the verge of learning something important.

"You had an affair with her."

Harrison looked at me. "The boy's right," he said. "I broke my vows."

I hadn't been expecting this.

"My mother had a series of strokes that eventually ended with her in a nursing home," the younger Harry said, as though his father hadn't spoken. "She spent the last two years of her life there." He gestured at his father. "He never missed one single day of visiting her in those two years. She couldn't talk. She couldn't move." He looked down at his hand still holding the coffee he hadn't even touched. Then he met his father's steady gaze. "No one would fault you for taking a little comfort."

"I fault myself," the old man said, his voice harsh. "I had no right to do what I did. How could I offer my heart when I wasn't free to do that?"

His son set his cup on the tray and stood up. "Don't judge the man you were so harshly," he said. "I'm not." He turned and went out the door.

Boris moved a bit closer to the old man's feet and stretched out with his head on his paws. "He's a good man," Harrison said, his eyes still on the door his son had just exited through.

"Yes, he is."

We sat in silence for a few minutes, but it wasn't awkward. I knew now he was going to tell me the whole story. All I had to do was let him do it in his own way.

"That envelope?" he said finally.

I nodded.

"As far as I know, the only thing in it was information about my daughter."

All the pieces dropped into place then.

"Agatha had a baby." I remembered Roma talking about Agatha being away for several months, teaching. It had to be then.

"Yes," he said. "I didn't know for a very long time. She left town, had the baby and put her up for adoption." Boris's head pushed against his hand again and he began to scratch behind the dog's ears. "Kathleen, you know I'm sick."

I nodded again, suddenly not trusting my voice.

"I want to meet my daughter before I die. And I want her to have the chance to ask me any questions she might have." His voice got even quieter. "I hope . . . I hope maybe she'll want to know her brothers, but that's her choice. I just want her to have that choice."

I leaned toward him, elbows on my knees. "Agatha had some kind of papers about your daughter's adoption in the envelope," I said.

He nodded. "I think so. That's what we were arguing about. She thought I was wrong for wanting to meet our child. She said I had no right to push myself into her life." He shook his head, the memory clearly painful. "I was angry because she'd kept everything secret." His eyes locked onto my face. "Kathleen, the only person who cared about the contents of the envelope was me. And I didn't kill Agatha."

I laid my hand on his arm for a moment. "I know that," I said. "Are you certain the information about your daughter was the only thing in that envelope?"

"As far as I know," he said. "Why?"

"Because I'm pretty sure Ruby argued with her about it, too."

He hung his head for a moment. "That's because of me, Kathleen. I knew Ruby's grandfather. I know her mama. Ruby and Agatha were close. In some ways, for Agatha, I think maybe Ruby replaced our child."

He looked at the dog at his feet, smiling when he lifted his head to look at him. "I'm not proud of it," he admitted, "but I went to Ruby and asked her to talk to Agatha. It's my fault she got caught up in all of this. I finally got her on the phone a little while ago. I told her to come clean. Agatha . . . she wouldn't have wanted it to come to this."

"It's not your fault. Ruby has a good lawyer and a lot of friends. She's not going to . . ." I exhaled slowly. "The truth will come out."

Harry studied his gnarled fingers. "I even hired a private detective," he said. "Now with the envelope gone, I don't know how I'll find her." He was talking about his daughter, not Ruby, I realized.

I thought about the piece of paper Hercules had found in Eric's office. I was going to have to figure out how talk to him about it without letting on how I knew he had it.

"I'm so sorry," I said. I didn't want to say anything to Harry until I was sure Eric hadn't destroyed the envelope, maybe out of some misguided loyalty to Agatha.

"I appreciate that."

I tried to imagine what it would be like to have a child you've never seen out there somewhere, but, really, I couldn't. My family—my mother and father, and Ethan and Sara—had always been in my life, even when they drove me crazy.

"Harry, did you ask Eric to talk to Agatha?" I asked.

He shook his head. "No. Why?"

"I saw them that same night. They had words about that envelope."

"No," he said. "The only person I pulled into this was Ruby. Whatever Eric was arguing about with Agatha, it wasn't my daughter."

I could see that he was getting tired, the lines on his face seemingly etched even deeper. "Thank you for telling me," I said. "I know it wasn't easy."

"There never should have been all those secrets," he said. "There never should have been anything to keep secret. I was a married man."

"You were human being. You loved two women."

All he could do was nod.

I got to my feet and went to hug the old man, feeling a lump in my throat at the thought that he might not be around much longer.

"I have to keep nosing around to help Ruby," I said.

"If I find that envelope, if I find anything that will help you find your daughter, I promise you, it's yours."

I broke out of the hug and he put a hand against my cheek for a moment. "Thank you, Kathleen," he said.

Behind me in the doorway his son cleared his throat. "I'm going to see Kathleen home, and I'll be right back," he said. Harrison lifted a hand in acknowledgment.

Out in the yard I took a deep breath of the frosty night air. The stars really did seem to sparkle more out here. We stood by Harry's truck.

"How long have you known?" I asked.

"I figured it out about a year or so back," he said. "I know about the baby, too. I suppose you think it's strange I'm not angry."

"None of my business," I said. "Even though I do seem to be poking my nose in it."

He smiled for a second, then his face grew serious again. "Kathleen, my mother died by inches. She was a beautiful, capable woman who shrank into nothing. And she loved my father fiercely." He laughed. "That may seem like a strange word to describe it, but that's how it was. If she'd been herself ... Well, he didn't see any other woman when my mother was in the room."

Harry looked up at the sky again, filled with stars so far away there was no warmth in them for us. "My mother was gone long before she died, and I can promise you that she would never have begrudged the old man a little love." He stumbled over the last word.

"As far as I can tell, whatever Agatha had about the baby has disappeared," I said. "But if I find anything, I promise you I'll let you know."

"Thanks," he said. "I'm sorry Ruby got caught up in all of this. If I can do anything, you'll call me?"

"I will."

We got in the truck and as I turned to fasten my seat belt, I caught sight of another old vehicle I knew. "Harry, what's Ruby's truck doing here?" I asked. "I thought the police had it."

"What do you mean, Ruby's truck?"

"There." I pointed to it, parked next to his workshop.

"That's not Ruby's truck," he said, putting on his own seat belt. "That's an old truck I mostly use around here and as backup for the plow."

"It looks just like Ruby's truck," I said. As he turned I got an even better look. The old Ford was the twin of Ruby's vehicle.

"Well, it is pretty much the same truck," he said as we started down the long driveway.

"What am I missing?" I asked.

Harry smiled as he reached to adjust the heater. "Years ago one of the car dealers in Red Wing got a half dozen identical trucks from some fleet order that fell through. They were good basic trucks and the price was very good. I bought that one. It's got a hundred and fifty-three thousand miles on it, and it's still running."

"A hundred and fifty-three thousand?"

He nodded. "I've cannibalized a couple of junk trucks over the years to work on it and bought a few generic parts, but it's mostly been a damn good vehicle."

My mind was racing. Maybe that piece of glass hadn't come from Ruby's truck after all. "Are the other five trucks still on the road?"

"Well, Ruby's," Harry said. "Roma was the original owner of that one. Sam wrecked his—must be a couple of years ago. I think the other three are out there somewhere."

"They all look the same?"

"Same model, same style, same paint job. Although I can't guarantee the paint hasn't changed over the years."

Ruby's truck had a broken headlight. Glass from the same kind of light had been caught in my pant cuff. And what had Mary said? Something about paint fragments matching the paint on Ruby's truck? All five trucks would've had the same original paint job.

Harry pulled into my driveway and the motion-sensor light came on.

"Thank you for everything," I said.

"Ruby wouldn't hurt anyone," he said. "I hope you find something. Good luck."

I smiled. "I think you just may have given me some."

21

Hercules was waiting on the porch; Owen was in the kitchen by the door. They trailed me as I hung up my coat and set my mittens by the heat vent.

"Give me a minute," I told them.

I washed my hands, put bread in the toaster and a cup of milk in the microwave. Finally, I settled at the table with a cup of hot chocolate and a piece of peanut butter toast. Both cats positioned themselves directly in front of my feet, as much for a bite of toast as for information.

"I might have something that can help Ruby," I said. Two sets of ears twitched.

I explained about the trucks. "Ruby has one. Harry has one. One's been junked. And there are three others— three identical old trucks. That piece of glass came from a truck like Ruby's. *Like* Ruby's. Not necessarily hers."

I bent to give each cat a bit of toast. It made sense. There were other trucks like that truck. Maybe the glass came from one of them.

Hercules looked up at me. "The headlights were okay on the truck at Harry's," I said. "I checked." With that he bent his head and began licking the peanut butter.

"We have to find out where the other trucks are." I held up a hand even though no one was meowing any objections. "And yes, I know it's a long shot, but it's all we have right now to help Ruby."

Owen, who had finished eating, walked over to the refrigerator and meowed. "Are you still hungry?" I asked. He dipped his head and put a paw over his nose, cat for "You are so dense." Okay, so he wanted to draw my attention to something on the fridge door.

I got up and walked over. "What is it? This?" I pointed at the Winterfest schedule. Owen's response was to look under the fridge. I took that as a no. "Well it can't be this." I gestured to a photo of Sara and Ethan mugging for the camera. Owen didn't even look up.

The volunteer schedule for Wisteria Hill was stuck to the fridge with a gingerbread-man magnet.

"This?" I asked. Owen meowed his approval.

It was like playing charades with someone who didn't speak English. "Well, obviously you don't mean Wisteria Hill," I said, walking back to the table with the sheet of paper.

"Everett? No." That didn't even get a reaction. "Not Marcus?"

Owen tipped his head to one side as though he was considering the idea.

"I don't think he's going to help. He arrested Ruby. He thinks she's guilty."

I broke off another piece of toast and held it out to Owen, who sprang across the room like it was a catnip chicken. I gave another bite to Hercules, too. "I don't see Marcus helping us look for the killer when he thinks he's already found her." I stared at the sheet of paper. "Roma," I said slowly.

Both cats murped at the same time. Although Owen's was more of a mumble, since he had peanut butter stuck to the roof of his mouth.

"She knows everyone in town. She had one of the

trucks. She wants to help Ruby." I looked at the boys. "Very good idea."

I headed for the phone. Roma answered on the fifth ring. She sounded distracted.

"Did I catch you at a bad time?"

"No, I, uh . . . no," she said. "You didn't. Are the cats okay?"

It didn't seem like a good idea to tell her Owen was sitting right in front of me, trying to get peanut butter off of his whiskers, so all I said was "Yes."

"Good."

"I need your help with something that might help me find who really killed Agatha."

"What do you need?" she asked, her voice all business now.

I explained what Harry had told me about the trucks. "Any chance you could help me find out where the other three are?"

"I think so," she said. "I may know where one of them is, and I'll ask around about the other two. Give me a day or so."

I thanked her and hung up. I went back to the kitchen with Owen on my heels. We'd eaten all the toast, and what was left of my hot chocolate was now cold.

I put the feeding schedule for the Wisteria Hill cats back on the fridge. I could feel Owen and Hercules staring at me. I turned around to see them sitting like a couple of statues, one pair of green eyes and one pair of gold eyes locked on me.

"What?" I said.

Nothing. Not a blink, not even an ear twitch.

"You think I should talk to Marcus, don't you?"

Two sets of whiskers twitched.

I folded my arms and stared back at them. "First of all, when did you two become the champions of law and order? And second, what makes you think he'll help?"

They stared.

I stared back.

Never get into a staring contest with a cat, or, even worse, two cats. You can't win.

"Give Roma some time—a couple of days. Then I'll talk to him."

They exchanged looks. Then Owen turned and headed for the living room, while Hercules came over to me and rubbed against my leg. I picked him up.

I'd been thinking about telling Marcus about the trucks since Harry had told me about them. Marcus was so wrong about Ruby, but he wasn't so close-minded a person or a police officer that he wouldn't listen to what I had to say about the trucks. At least I hoped he wasn't.

Carrying Hercules, I went out to the porch to double-check that I'd locked the door. I looked over at Rebecca's house. The lights were on in the kitchen and I could see Everett's car in the driveway. "I'm glad those two are together," I said to the cat. He rumbled his approval. "At least something good came out of that awful mess of Gregor Easton's death last summer."

I picked up my scarf that had somehow ended up on the bench in the porch and took it back inside. "We need a happy ending for Ruby."

Hercules nuzzled my chin. "I want to talk to Susan again," I said. "Before I ask Eric about the envelope."

The piece of envelope Hercules had taken from Eric's office was upstairs with my computer. "You know, maybe we should search the newspaper archives, to see if we can find anything about Eric. Justin said they got into a bit of trouble when they were kids. It might've made the paper back then."

The *Mayville Heights Chronicle* had been around for more than a hundred years. The archives, going back to the early sixties, were online for subscribers. I typed in my customer number and password.

The search system was a little funky, not at all like the one we used at the library that let readers search by author, title, subject, and keywords, and that allowed for minor spelling errors à la Google. The newspaper system required you to first settle on a year and then a category before you could search for keywords.

I did the math in my head and started with the year I figured Eric would've been sixteen. It took two tries to get the category right.

The story had made the front page below the fold. I was a bit surprised the paper had identified the boys. Eric, Justin, and three other young men, whose names I didn't recognize, had been out driving—too fast and without headlights—and passing a couple of cans of beer around the car. Along the road that leads to Wisteria Hill, they hit something.

And ran.

What they'd hit had turned out to be a fifty-pound jute bag of apples. But they didn't know that at the time. It would have been hard not to know you'd hit something, but they hadn't known it was a sack of fruit. It could've been a raccoon. It could've been a dog. It could've been a person. The fact that it wasn't was only luck, and maybe the old saying was true that angels watch out for fools and drunks, and heaven knows those boys were both.

I had to read another paragraph to learn Eric had been the driver and claimed he couldn't remember the accident. He'd had a lot to drink.

My mind raced and my stomach twisted into a knot. I thought about Eric's distracted manner and disheveled appearance the past few days and how Susan had been evasive, not her usual cheery, snarky self.

Was I wrong? Had Eric been drinking? Was he the one who hit Agatha in that alley? Did he have a blackout?

No.

I wasn't going to do that, jump to conclusions about Eric, when all I had was an old newspaper story.

I logged out of the newspaper's Web site and shut off my laptop. I'd talk to Susan in the morning, and after that, well, I wasn't going to think that far ahead.

I would've overslept the next morning if Hercules hadn't lurked over me. I fed the cats, drank two cups of coffee—extra strong—and left early for the library.

Fate or something seemed to be on my side. As I came down the sidewalk I saw Susan cutting across the parking lot, chin buried in the collar of her coat. Moving closer I could see two red plastic take-out forks in the knot of hair on top of her head. She smiled when she saw me, waiting until I caught up with her.

"Coffee?" I asked when we'd stomped the snow from our boots and I'd relocked the library door.

"Please."

I dumped my things in my office and headed down the hall to the staff room. Susan walked around, turning on the downstairs lights even though there was almost a half hour until we opened.

I had the coffee on when she came up. I'd brought the remainder of the granola bars with me on the theory that a little chocolate couldn't hurt.

Susan broke one in half, putting a piece on a blue-flowered plate from the staff room's collection of mismatched dishes and stuffing the other half in her mouth. "These are good," she said. High praise from someone who ate Eric's cooking every day.

"Thank you."

I got the cream, sugar and a couple of mugs and poured the coffee. Then I sat at the table opposite Susan, who inhaled half the cup like a man crawling through the desert who had just come across an oasis.

I was trying to figure out how to start when she

looked at me over the top of her cup and said, "Eric said you asked him about Agatha."

"I did. I'm trying to help Ruby. She didn't kill Agatha."

"I know," Susan said. "She was the reason Ruby became an artist. And Eric probably wouldn't have the café if it weren't for Agatha Shepherd." She set down her cup, picked up a chocolate chip from the plate and ate it. "Kathleen, you didn't grow up here so you don't know much about Eric when he was younger."

"No, I don't. I do know he got in a bit of trouble."

"Agatha changed his life," she said. "Hell, saved it, for that matter." She drank from her cup, then set it back on the table. "Short version: Eric's mom and dad were too young and had too many kids. He was feeding the little ones when he was eight years old. And doing a good job of it. And he was running wild from about that time, too." She gave me a brief smile. "Doesn't sound like the man you know, does it?"

"No. Truthfully, it doesn't."

Susan let out a slow breath. "Eric started drinking when he was twelve, stealing beer from his father and other people in the family. When he drank he lost chunks of time. He had a car accident when he was sixteen. He didn't remember being in the car, let alone driving. And he still . . ." She didn't finish the thought.

She picked at another chocolate chip but didn't eat it. "Agatha saw something in him and she encouraged his love of cooking. Kind of melodramatic to say it, but it is true that she changed his life."

She was stalling, dancing around whatever it was she felt she needed to tell me. She flicked the chocolate chip around the plate like a little hockey puck.

I got up and refilled both our cups, trying to give Susan the time she needed.

"Eric hasn't had a drink in a long time. He goes to

meetings." Abruptly she straightened. "The thing is, Kathleen, the past few weeks he's been helping someone, I don't know who, but someone he acted as a sponsor for in the past. Whoever it was had started drinking, and had the idea he could control it." She shook her head. "It doesn't work that way, believe me."

"You don't know who it was?" I asked.

"No. Eric said he couldn't tell me. But I know he was worried. I told him if he couldn't tell me, he should talk to his own sponsor."

The silence stretched between us. I wasn't sure if she was going to say it, so I asked, "Susan, did Eric have a drink?"

Her left eyelid began to twitch. She nodded. "The night Agatha was killed. The person, whoever it was, called Eric on his cell. He hadn't been home a half hour. I got the feeling from Eric's side of the conversation that they'd talked earlier in the evening. Anyway, this guy was in a bar; at least I'm pretty sure he was. I was standing right beside Eric when the phone rang and I could hear the background noise. Eric said he had to go." She laced her fingers together and stretched her arms in front of her. "He came home after two in the morning. His coat and hat were all snowy. He'd obviously walked, I don't know how far. And he was drunk."

I reached across the table and laid one of my hands on hers. "I'm sorry," I said.

"I put him to bed," she continued. "In the morning he didn't remember coming home or where he'd been."

"He had a blackout?"

"Yes. I don't know what scared him the most: taking the first drink or the fact that he doesn't remember it."

I wasn't sure how to ask what I needed to ask. "Susan, does Eric know anything about . . . about Agatha's death?"

"No." Her mouth moved, then she said, "I'm not sure.

Eric would never hurt anyone, especially Agatha . . . but there's all that time he can't remember."

"And he still won't tell you who he went to meet?"

She shook her head. "No, and believe me, we've been back and forth about it over the past few days. He says the whole program falls apart if you can't trust your sponsor. I don't even know if he's told his own sponsor."

I pushed a stray bit of hair away from my face and tried not to let my frustration show. "Do you have any idea, any hint, who it was?"

"I don't. I'm sorry. I don't. All I can tell you is that it's someone Eric used to know a long time ago when he first stopped drinking." She looked at me, tight lines of anxiety around her mouth. "You believe me, don't you?"

"I do," I said. It was true. I did. Susan was a lousy liar, as I'd seen in the past few days.

"Eric didn't hurt Agatha," she said. "Even if he was having a blackout, he wouldn't hurt another person."

I thought about the news story I'd read. Eric had left the scene of an accident back then. But that hadn't been a person, and Eric had been a kid in a car full of other kids. I could remember what peer pressure was like. "I don't think Eric hurt Agatha, either," I said. "I think Eric would always be Eric even if he couldn't remember."

Susan searched my face and she must've liked what she saw, because she smiled as she stood up. I got to my feet, as well. "Susan, do you remember seeing Agatha with a brown envelope any time before her death? I think it was a report-card envelope at one time."

She thought for a moment. "Yeah, I do. Why?"

I couldn't betray Harry's confidence and I didn't want to tell her that Eric had argued with Agatha over the envelope. "It might be nothing, but Agatha was hanging on to it pretty tightly, and it's disappeared."

"You want me to ask Eric about it? He's really worried about Ruby, you know."

Maybe she'd get further than I had. "Please," I said. "Tell him it's important." *At least for Old Harry,* I added silently.

She nodded and looked at her watch. "I'll go down. It's almost time to open."

"I'll be right there," I said, gathering the dishes and setting them in the sink. I leaned against the counter.

Eric had had a blackout. I'd meant what I said to Susan. Blackout or not, I didn't believe Eric had killed Agatha. Eric would always be Eric. But the fact was, he'd been drinking. He'd had a blackout. And Agatha was dead.

I needed to know who Eric had been with in the missing time and where they'd gone. The question was, How was I going to find out?

22

The smell of chicken soup filled the house, thanks to the slow cooker. I sent a mental thank-you to whomever had invented the pot.

"We were right." I told Hercules, who'd kept me company while I changed into my tai chi clothes and got myself a bowl of soup. Owen had wandered in and out with a loopy expression that told me he'd been into funky-chicken parts again.

"Eric was drinking the night Agatha was killed." I set down my spoon. "We have to find out who he was with and where they were. Eric's in that *what happens in Vegas stays in Vegas* mode. You know, kind of like we do with your little superpower." I whispered the last word.

Hercules suddenly got interested in the back door. I picked up my spoon again. "I'm thinking Eric and his friend wouldn't do their drinking here. Someone would have said something by now." I slipped him a piece of chicken. "Susan said it was noisy, so I'm guessing a bar, like she did."

Hercules looked at me and bobbed his head. Which might have meant he agreed. Or he didn't. Or he wanted more chicken. After all, I was talking to a cat. But I did know a real person who could help me.

"Hi, Katydid," my mom said when she picked up.

"Hi, Mom," I said. "I don't have a lot of time, but I'm hoping you can help me with something."

"Sure. What do you need?"

"Do you remember that choreographer you worked with in *Guys and Dolls*?"

"Chloe Westin," Mom said at once.

"She, uh . . ." I hesitated.

"Was an alcoholic," my mother said bluntly.

"That's the one." Now, how was I going to explain why I wanted to know what I wanted to know? "One of my staff, her husband—"

"Say no more, sweetie," she interjected. "You think he has a drinking problem."

"How do you know for sure?"

"Can you smell it on him?"

"No." I leaned back against the arm of the chair.

"Doesn't necessarily mean anything," she said. "I never smelled alcohol on Chloe's breath. She always smelled like Juicy Fruit gum, which, of course, explains why I didn't smell alcohol on her breath."

"So how did you figure it out?"

"Aside from her showing up drunk at a rehearsal and doing a grand jeté into the orchestra pit?" Mom asked dryly. "She was sneaky, evasive. She disappeared for long stretches of time and no one knew where she was. She used to go to this little hole-in-the-wall bar to drink, where no one in her real life would catch her. She'd lie and then tell a lie to cover the first lie. And on and on."

My head ached. I rubbed my temples with the heel of my hand.

"I remember one time Chloe missed rehearsal. Then she tried to tell me she'd been out researching urban street dancing and lost track of time."

"Where was she really?" I asked.

"An hour and a ferry ride away, drinking homemade wine with some new friends she'd met at the dinky little bar," Mom laughed. "I'm pretty sure that wine was the reason the term 'rotgut' was invented. Oh, the child paid for it, though, believe me. Ever have a headache so horrible it looked like you were permanently cross-eyed?"

"I, uh ... Thankfully, no."

"Am I helping at all?"

"You are," I said. "And I'm sorry I have to go, but I have tai chi."

"Call me soon," she said. "I'll be keeping my fingers crossed. I love you."

"I love you, too," I said, and hung up.

Based on what my mother had just said, I felt that I was on the right track. Eric and his friend most likely had been drinking somewhere other than in town. The thing was, where?

I pulled on my coat and boots and headed for tai chi. I was running late.

I had my head down, watching for slippery spots, which is why I turned the corner at the bottom of the hill and bumped—literally—into Marcus.

"Sorry," I said, pushing my hat up off my forehead and talking a step back. "I wasn't looking where I was going."

"It's okay," he said. "I'm taking up most of the sidewalk. I didn't hit you with my bag, did I?" He had a large black hockey bag over his shoulder.

I shook my head.

"Where are you headed?" he asked as I shifted my own bag from one shoulder to the other.

"I'm on my way to tai chi class."

"I'm headed to the marina. I'll walk with you."

"You're going over to the Winterfest site?" I said, as we started along the sidewalk. Then before he could answer I remembered. "Oh, that's right. It's the all-star game."

Another tradition of Winterfest, I'd learned, was the all-star hockey game, the best of the police and fire departments against the high school stars. "Good luck," I said.

"Thanks." He paused to let a half-ton truck make a left turn in front of us and into an alleyway, automatically putting his arm out in front of me. "You've seen my puck-shooting ability. So I'll take all the luck I can get."

"You're a good skater," I said. "You just need to anticipate a little more with the puck."

He shot me a puzzled look. "Anticipate?"

"When someone has the puck, watch his body language, especially his feet. A guy will fake right with his body, but if you check his feet he's already headed left."

He nodded. "Thanks. I'll try it."

We were almost at the tai chi studio. "How's the case?" I said.

The last bit of a smile on his face disappeared. "You know I can't talk about that with you."

"Ruby didn't kill Agatha."

"You're not the first person to tell me that."

"Maybe you should listen."

"Are you digging around in the investigation?"

"You know I can't talk about that with you," I said lightly.

That brought the smile back out just a little. We stopped in front of the co-op building.

"Have a good game," I said. I took a couple of steps toward the door and then I turned back toward him. He was an irritating person, but he was a good, conscientious police officer. "Marcus," I said. "I don't know if this matters or not, but Ruby's truck isn't the only truck like that in town."

"What do you mean?" he asked, stamping his heavy boots on the snowy sidewalk.

"I mean there's more than one truck exactly like Ruby's. Same make. Same model. And bought at the same time, from the same dealer."

He sighed, "Kathleen—"

"Stay out of the case," I finished. "There were six trucks. Six identical trucks sold to people who live in this area or who did. And at least one of them is still around." I held out both hands, then turned and went into the building. He didn't come after me.

I didn't know what Marcus would do with what I had told him, but I'd played fair. And for some reason that mattered to me.

Ruby was at the top of the stairs, taking off her coat. "Hi," she said. She looked uncomfortable, her eyes darting away from my face.

"Hi." I put my bag on a hook. "I talked to Harry," I said. "He told me what was probably in that envelope Agatha was carrying around, and he told me that he asked you to talk to her for him."

She met my gaze directly then. "So you understand why I couldn't tell you?"

"I guess I do."

She tucked her gloves in the sleeve of her coat. "I wish I knew where that envelope was."

"Maybe it will turn up," I said, thinking of Hercules spitting that soggy piece of paper into my hand. That reminded me about the photo fragment he'd found in Ruby's apartment. Could that be a picture of Harry and Agatha's child? I'd forgotten all about it.

Ruby touched my arm. "Kathleen, you zoned out there for a minute. Are you okay?"

"I'm sorry. It's just . . . I may have a picture of the baby."

"What?" Her mouth actually hung open.

Okay, how was I going to explain this? I pulled her over to the bench against the wall beside the coat hooks. "I was with Rebecca when she got your things for court."

"Okay," she said slowly.

"Remember Lita had given you that bag of things belonging to Agatha?"

Ruby nodded. "I just took it home."

"So you didn't look inside?"

"No. Well, not much more than a glance." She cleared her throat. "The last while, even before she had the stroke, Agatha kind of got a little weird about stuff. She'd pick things up that she thought might be useful. A scarf, napkins—that kind of thing."

"Ruby, I looked through the bag. I'm sorry, but I was looking for the envelope. I thought maybe it would be there or maybe there would be something in there that would help you."

"It's all right," she said. "Obviously the envelope wasn't there."

"No," I said. "But there was part of a picture. Of a baby."

"A baby?"

"A baby," I repeated. Now the awkward part. "Ruby, I kind of walked out with the picture." That was more or less true. I walked out with Hercules and he had the picture. "Do you think you'd recognize whether it was a photo of Agatha's son? I think you said he's working in China."

"Yeah. David." She shrugged "I don't know. Maybe. Agatha did have a couple of pictures of him when he was little in her office. He doesn't look that different now."

I pulled off my hat and scarf. "Are you going to be in your studio tomorrow? I could bring it over."

"Justin is going to pick me up," she said, her eyes sparkling like the old Ruby for the first time in days. "He has meetings tomorrow and the next day in Minneapolis about the camp. We could give you a ride home and I could take a look at the picture."

"If Justin doesn't mind, that would work."

"He won't mind." She stood up. "Maybe we'll have something to give to Harry."

"I hope so," I said.

Ruby headed inside. I hung up my coat and changed my boots for shoes before I went in.

In the middle of the room Maggie was demonstrating a move to Rebecca, Roma and a couple of others. I watched for a moment. It was Cloud Hands. My nemesis.

Maggie finished, smiled at me, then clapped her hands and called, "Circle."

We moved into our usual places. Rebecca smiled at me from one side, and on the other side Roma held up a finger and whispered, "I found one of the trucks."

Thank you, I mouthed.

"Kathleen," Maggie bellowed from across the circle.

It was going to be one of those nights. "I know: bend my knees," I called back.

"Good to see you're paying attention," she retorted.

The class took all my focus. I'd almost learned the complete form, but that didn't mean I had all the different movements completely mastered. Ruby and Maggie were the only ones who could do all 108 movements at the end of class, although everyone else was getting pretty close. One by one we stepped out, letting Maggie and Ruby finish the form.

I glanced at the door and saw Justin standing there. He smiled and I did the same.

As soon as she was done Ruby crossed to where I was standing. "Kathleen, there's something I forgot to tell you."

"What is it?" I asked. Out of the corner of my eye I could see Justin was looking at us, shifting restlessly from one foot to the other.

"Obviously, Justin doesn't know anything about Harry and Agatha."

"I won't say anything."

She ran her fingers along her hairline, damp with sweat. "I'm just going to tell him you found an old picture that you me want to look at. I mean, that's true as far as it goes."

"That sounds good to me." I didn't like lying to people and I thought there were way too many secrets being kept as it was, but it wasn't my place to reveal things Harry and Agatha had wanted to stay private.

I followed Ruby over to where Justin waited. "How was class?" he asked, leaning over to give Ruby a kiss on the top of her head. He looked at me and smiled. "Hey, Kathleen."

"Hi," I said.

"Class was good," Ruby said, moving out to the coats. "Could we give Kathleen a ride home? She found an old picture she'd like me to take a look at."

"Yeah, sure," Justin said. He turned to me. "Where do you live?"

"Up Mountain Road," I said, stepping into my boots. "On the right. The fourth house before Pine."

"I know where that is. Little white farmhouse, right?"

I nodded. "That's it." I stuffed my shoes into my bag, pulled on my coat and hat and followed Justin and Ruby down the steps.

Justin drove a small blue Focus.

Ruby turned partway around as we headed up the hill. "I meant to tell you before. I heard you waxed Detective Gordon's"—she paused and grinned at me—"tail at the puck shoot."

I raised one eyebrow. "Let's just say I was little better than he was expecting."

She laughed. "Considering the past couple of days, I love it."

"You play hockey, Kathleen?" Justin asked.

"Street hockey," I said. Justin turned onto Mountain Road. "Oh, I should warn you about my cats."

"It's okay," he said. "I like cats, although I'm more of a dog person myself."

"My cats were feral. They don't let anyone touch them but me."

"Sure," Justin said with a shrug.

"Is Rebecca still buying them chickens?" Ruby asked. "I met her in the Grainery a couple of times last summer."

"She is," I said. "At least for Owen. Hercules doesn't care."

"Hercules?" Justin asked. "After the strong man?"

"Yes," I said. More or less, anyway. Warrior of myth and legend, and on-screen incarnation of one Kevin Sorbo, if I was telling the truth.

"That's it right there," I said to Justin, pointing out the driveway.

He pulled in by the house and they followed me around to the back door. I had expected at least one cat to be in the kitchen, but there was no sign of either of them. I dropped my coat on one of the chairs. "The picture is upstairs," I said to Ruby. "I'll be right back."

The photo fragment was on the table by the window, along with the scrap from the brown envelope that Hercules had taken from Eric's office. That reminded me: I still wanted to figure out where Eric had been last Wednesday night. I grabbed the torn picture and headed back downstairs. "Here it is," I said to Ruby.

She laid the photograph on the table and studied it carefully. Then she looked up at me. Nothing in her face gave her away except for the smile that pulled at her eyes. "I'm sorry," she said. "I don't have a clue who might've lost this. You could ask Maggie. She's been going through old pictures for weeks."

"Thanks," I said.

"Or you could ask Harry Taylor. He knows everyone in town."

I knew what she meant. "That's a good idea."

"Okay. Let's get going," Ruby said to Justin.

"Thank you for the ride, Justin," I said.

"No problem."

Just then Hercules came in from the living room.

Ruby smiled. "Hello, puss," she said, leaning down closer to his level. "This is Hercules, right?"

"Yes. And that's Owen." He'd just stuck his tabby head around the doorframe to see what he was missing.

Hercules was still studying Ruby. Justin leaned over beside her. "Hey, cat," he said. Herc's head swiveled left. His eyes narrowed and he hissed.

Justin started and straightened. "Whoa!" He looked from the cat to me. "You weren't kidding about those cats."

Behind Hercules, Owen crept closer, his ears flattened against his head.

"Hey, it's okay," Ruby said in a low, soft voice.

Hercules turned back to her, looked into her face and twitched his whiskers almost as though he were saying, *I don't have a problem with* you. Then he took a step toward Justin and hissed again. Justin took about a half dozen steps backward.

I moved between them. "Justin, I'm sorry," I said. "They grew up at Wisteria Hill. They're not always good with people."

He shrugged, but it was just a shade too casual. "Hey, it's okay," he said. "They probably smell dog on me. Like I said, I'm a dog person." He turned to Ruby, but I could see he was still watching Hercules out of the corner of his eye. "We better get going," he said.

"Thanks for looking at the picture," I said to Ruby. "I'll check with Harry."

"Good idea," she said. "I really think that picture will mean something to him."

I walked them to the back door and waited until I

heard the car pull out of the driveway. Then I went back into the kitchen.

Owen and Hercules were sitting by the table. Herc was washing his face. Owen was sniffing who knew what on the floor. I folded my arms across my chest and glared at them. "Okay. What the heck was that all about?"

23

Owen at least looked guilty; he hung his head and slunk over to me. I crouched down and he looked up at me, a cute-guilty combo.

"Why did you do that?" I asked him. "The first time Marcus came here you all but climbed onto his lap. What's wrong with Justin?"

His gold eyes narrowed and his ears went back again. "I get that you don't like him," I said, patting the top of his head. "But why?"

Of course, since he couldn't talk, he couldn't exactly tell me.

I turned to Hercules, who was still washing his face and studiously ignoring me. "You didn't like Justin, either."

Lick, lick, lick, and then the paw wiped the face.

"He's intense—I'll give you that—and self-absorbed, but that whole show with the ears back and the hissing was a bit over-the-top. If you didn't like the guy, couldn't you just, I don't know, ignore him? Like you're doing to me right now?"

The phone rang then and I went to answer it.

"Hey," Maggie said. "You disappeared so fast I didn't get a chance to ask if you wanted to walk down and catch the end of the all-star game."

"Sorry," I said. "Ruby and Justin offered me a ride."

"She seems more like herself, doesn't she?" Maggie said.

"Yeah, she does." I hesitated for a second. If I was going to check out drinking establishments I didn't want to go by myself, and this wasn't really the type of road trip I could take Hercules or Owen on. Plus, I needed a car. "Hey, Mags, do you feel like going out?" I asked.

"The game's probably close to over."

"I was thinking more like going out for a drink," I said.

For a moment there was only silence. Then Maggie said, "A drink?"

"Uh-huh."

"At a bar?"

"Why not? Why not try something new? Meet some new people."

Another silence. Then Maggie spoke again. "Kathleen, if you're being held captive by some freak, winter-loving terrorist, say 'avocado' and I'll hang up and call the police."

I laughed. "I haven't been kidnapped and I haven't lost my mind. I want to check out some of the bars up on the highway. It's something that might help Ruby."

"Why didn't you say so? I'm on my way."

I was so surprised for a moment, I didn't speak.

"You thought I'd say no." Maggie chortled.

"I thought you'd at least want more of an explanation."

"Oh, I do," she said. "You can tell me on the way. Right now go put on some lipstick and wear something feminine."

I looked down at my comfortable exercise pants and long-sleeved T-shirt. "You mean, don't dress like a librarian."

"I didn't say that," Maggie countered. "But yes. You have fifteen minutes." With that she hung up.

Owen and Hercules were both sitting by the footstool. "Maggie and I are going barhopping," I told them. I looked down at Owen. "Your girlfriend wants me to dress cute." He turned and headed for the stairs. I looked at Hercules and shrugged, and we followed Owen up to the bedroom.

I pulled a pair of khaki pants out of the closet. I might have imagined it—he might just have been taking a swipe at something stuck to his fur—but it almost seemed as if Owen put a paw over his face. I took out my favorite black trousers. He sneezed. "There's nothing wrong with those black pants," I said. He disappeared into the far left end of the closet.

"There's nothing back there," I said. I heard an answering meow. I looked at Hercules, who was just sitting and watching the two of us.

Owen meowed again. I started flipping through the hangers. I had two more pairs of black trousers, the gray pants with the cuffs I've been wearing the morning Ruby had found Agatha's body, and way at the back, a pair of slim jeans. I could see Owen's golden eyes gleaming up at me.

"Those don't fit."

He meowed his dissent. I took the hanger off the rod. "Maggie's going to be here in ten minutes," I said. "I'm going to try these on just to show you you're wrong and then I'm going to pick out my own clothes, because last time I checked you didn't have a subscription to *Vogue*."

I tugged on the jeans. The first surprise was that I could get them on. The second was that I could zip them up. They were snug, but not skintight. Hercules walked around me. Owen poked his head out of the closet door.

"Fine. I'll wear them," I said. The last time I'd fit into those jeans was probably more than a year ago. My sister, Sara, had talked me into them. I couldn't help checking out the rear view in the mirror. Maybe all that walking up and down Mountain Road was paying dividends—which still didn't mean I didn't need a car.

I rifled through my tops and found a cranberry sweater. Sara had bought that for me. It had a deep V-neck and the soft knit hugged me all over. It wasn't me at all. Which probably meant I should wear it.

I put on lipstick and dangling earrings and tousled my hair. Not only did I not look like myself, but I didn't feel like myself, which probably indicated I was on the right track.

I was ready when Maggie tapped on the porch door and came in. I held up my arms and did a little twirl.

"Not bad," she said approvingly.

Owen walked in as I got my coat. Maggie bent down and he stopped maybe three feet from her. "Hey, Fur Ball," she said. He got all squirmy but didn't get any closer. Maggie kept talking softly to him, and I grabbed my purse and boots.

"Hey, do you have any other boots?" she said over her shoulder.

"What's wrong with my boots?"

"Well, they're kind of . . . sensible."

"You think they're ugly." She was wearing brown suede boots that molded to her legs. I swear my first thought was that they probably didn't have a very warm lining.

Maggie looked me up and down. "I don't think they go with your outfit." She turned back to Owen and gave him a conspiratorial grin.

I went fishing in the living room closet and pulled out a pair of black dress boots with heels. I'd bought them in Boston and brought them with me when I moved to Mayville. The first time it had snowed here, I'd worn them to work. I didn't make that mistake the second time it snowed.

Maggie said good-bye to Owen. I locked up and we

got in Maggie's bug. Before she had even fastened her seat belt she turned to me. "Before we go, where are we going and why are we going?"

I handed her a piece of paper on which I'd copied the names of the bars I wanted to check out.

Maggie's face was unreadable as she scanned the list. She looked at me again. "Now I know where we're going. Why are we going?"

"You know Eric doesn't drink?" I said.

"Uh-huh." She nodded and gave a slight shrug.

I hated violating Eric's privacy, but there wasn't any way around it that I could see. "He was drinking Wednesday night."

Maggie blinked a couple of times, then frowned. "Are you sure?"

I picked at loose thread on my glove. "I'm sure."

She began to slowly shake her head. "Kathleen, no. I'm sorry. You're wrong."

I held up a hand. "Maggie, I don't think Eric ran over Agatha. Wherever he was, he walked home. But he definitely drank. What I want to know is where he was and, more important, who he was with."

She exhaled slowly. "Why don't you ask him . . . or Susan?"

"I did," I said. "Whoever this person is, Eric used to be his sponsor. He won't violate that relationship for anything."

"You think the person Eric was with might have hit Agatha."

I nodded.

"Kathleen, that's a real long shot."

I peeled off my glove before I picked that loose thread into a hole. "I know," I said. "It's not the only thing I have to go on. I found out that there may be as many as three trucks identical to Ruby's on the road."

"So who owns them?"

"Roma is checking that out for me."

Maggie stared out the windshield. "Kath, what about talking to Marcus?"

"I already did."

That got her full attention.

"I bumped into him on the way to class."

"And?"

"And he didn't exactly do a Perry Mason and declare it was clear that Ruby was innocent."

Maggie opened her mouth, but I spoke before she could. "Look, I know you think Marcus and I would make a great couple, and I do think he's a decent cop, but he thinks he has the person who ran down Agatha—Ruby. I could find all of those trucks and line them up in front of the police station, and unless I had the person who really killed Agatha trussed up with duct tape in the back of one of them, I don't see him changing his mind."

Maggie looked thoughtfully at me. "So, you want to do this alphabetically or by location?"

"You're not going to argue with me?"

She stuck the key in the ignition and started the car. "Nope."

I was at a loss for words.

Maggie smiled as she backed out of the driveway. "Look. You're right," she said. "I think Marcus is an excellent detective, but he's probably already handed the file on Ruby's case on to the county attorney. It's going to take more than just the possibility of there being another truck or even three to get Ruby out of this mess. This is a long shot, but it's better than no shot."

She glanced at my list on the dashboard. "We may as well go to the Brick first," she said. "Did you bring a picture of Eric?"

I pulled a snapshot out of my purse. It had been taken at the library picnic. Eric was at the grill, squinting into the sun. I held it up and Maggie glanced at it briefly. "That's good," she said.

I'd heard that tone in her voice before. "You have a plan, don't you?" I asked. Watching her, I could feel the energy as all the neurons fired in her brain.

"I have a couple of ideas."

That wasn't good. The last time Maggie had one of her ideas we'd ended up hijacking Roma and her SUV. Part of Maggie was laid-back and Zen. She truly believed that what you put out into the world would come back to you, positive or negative. She thought Matt Lauer from the *Today* show was sexy.

On the other hand, she could keep a secret better than anyone I'd ever met. And she'd seen every Dirty Harry movie Clint Eastwood had ever made, more times than even she could remember.

"Watch for the sign," Maggie said once we were on the highway out of town, headed for Minneapolis–St. Paul. "The last time I was by, the B and the R were burned out in the sign."

"So what I'm really looking for is the Ick," I said.

"Probably in more ways than one."

The Brick was a strip club. It was dark and loud and we had to pay a cover charge to get inside. Maggie put her mouth close to my ear. "Follow my lead and try to look uncomfortable."

I was uncomfortable. There was a woman dancing on the T-shaped stage. At least she had all her clothes on— "all" being a hot pink, feather-trimmed bikini top and matching bottom. She actually looked like she was having fun. She did a slow twirl around the pole, and I caught sight of her face.

"I know her," I said, grabbing Maggie's arm. "She brings her little boy to story time."

Maggie looked past me. "Yeah, that's Jenna. She's in my yoga class."

"I didn't know she was an exotic dancer."

"She's not," Maggie said. "It's amateur night. If we're here very long you'll probably see some other people you know." She climbed on a stool and smiled down the bar at the female bartender.

I took the stool next to her and turned my back to the stage. There was a long list of people I had no interest in seeing in feathers and spike heels.

It wasn't at all hard to follow Maggie's instructions to look embarrassed. I kept picturing people I knew in town up on the small stage. Abigail. Lita. Rebecca. How would you look someone in the eye after seeing her swing around a pole while wearing next to nothing?

"You want wine," Maggie whispered as the bartender approached.

"Hi. What can I get you?" she asked. She was about Maggie's age, blond hair in a ponytail, serious dark-framed glasses, and arms that suggested a regular work-out with weights.

"I'll just have coffee," Maggie said. "I'm driving."

"I'll have a glass of red wine," I said.

"No problem," the bartender, whose name was Zoe, said. She put a basket of pretzels between us. I grabbed one and popped it in my mouth. If I was going to have to drink, I wanted to eat something.

The pretzel was good, crisp and lightly salted. The wine was not good. I had another pretzel.

Maggie had paid for our drinks and was talking to the bartender, leaning forward, elbows on the bar. I saw her eyes flick sideways a couple of times at my glass. I was guessing she wanted me to drink a little more or at least look like I was. I took a swallow and chased the taste with a couple of pretzels.

I wasn't sure what Maggie's plan was, but it didn't seem to be working. I was tired, the music was too loud and I was afraid of what I might see if I turned in the direction of the stage. I was about to tell her this had all been a bad idea when she looked at me and said, "You got his picture?"

The picture. I'd put it back in my purse. I pulled it out. Maggie took the photo from me and slid it across the bar. "Were you working last Wednesday night? Did you see this guy?"

The bartender studied the picture, then looked up at Maggie. "What did he do?"

"Well," Maggie said, holding out both hands. She looked at me and raised her eyebrows.

I felt my face getting red. I ducked my head, took another drink and followed it with pretzel.

Zoe smiled knowingly and looked at Eric's photograph again. "No, he wasn't here. It was very quiet last Wednesday night because of that auction."

She gave me a look of . . . pity? Sympathy? I wasn't sure which. Then she turned to Maggie. "He wasn't here. Is that a good thing?"

"Maybe," Maggie said. "But everybody has to be somewhere, so maybe not. Thank you for your help."

"No problem," she said. There were a couple of guys at the far end of the bar, trying to get her attention. She grabbed another basket of pretzels and headed toward them.

Maggie picked up her coffee cup, drained it and set it down again. She looked at my wineglass. "You want one for the road?"

I grimaced. "No. I think the windshield-washer fluid would taste better."

"Let's go, then," she said, slipping out of her seat.

We were halfway to the door when Maggie caught my arm and said, "Please tell me that's not who I think it is." She was gurgling with laughter.

I put a hand up to the side of my face. "I'm not looking."

She grabbed my wrist and pulled my arm away from my cheek. "If you don't look I'm going to describe what I just saw in teeny, tiny detail."

I took a quick look at the stage. Then a longer one. Then I grabbed Maggie's sleeve and dragged her out of the Brick so fast she tripped over a step and almost landed in a heap of snow in front of the building.

"So was it?" she asked, one arm wrapped around a railing post so she could get her balance.

"I don't know," I said. "Maybe. Probably. I think so."

She started to laugh. She laughed so hard her feet started to slide on the icy parking lot and she had to wrap her other arm around the stair post. From a distance she looked drunk.

I glanced back at the building. I could hear the music—Bon Jovi belting out "You Give Love a Bad Name"—and I could still see the dancer in my mind's eye. A black corset, fishnets, heels and a harlequin feather-trimmed mask, all worn by Mary, the kickboxing grandmother who worked at the library and hand-made all those luscious pies for the Winterfest supper.

Because it was her. The mask didn't hide enough of her face. Maggie was still laughing, hugging the stair post like it was a giant teddy bear.

"It's not funny," I said. "I work with Mary. What am I supposed to say when I see her tomorrow? Nice corset?"

"Well, it was a very nice corset," Maggie laughed. "Where do you think she got it? Not around here."

I started for the car. "I'm not asking her, so don't even think about it."

"I didn't think you were such a prude, Kathleen," Maggie said as we got in the bug.

"I'm not a prude," I said. "And what people do for fun is their own business. It's just that Mary was the last person I expected to see in a strip club. She's someone's grandmother."

"She looked hot," Maggie said. "All the kickboxing means she's in great shape. Why shouldn't she flaunt her booty once in a while?"

I glared at her. "Thanks for putting that image in my mind."

One thing was for sure: When I saw Mary at the library tomorrow I wasn't going to ask her how her evening went.

24

We repeated the process at the next bar, The Hill-top, only with a waitress and with the same result. Now that I knew my role as cuckolded girlfriend, I played it up a little, looking morose and sighing. Apparently Maggie thought I was turning it up a bit too much. She elbowed me in the ribs. Hard.

It didn't matter. The place had been deadly quiet Wednesday night and Eric hadn't been in.

At Barry's Hat, which was more of a jazz place than a dive bar, Maggie charmed the male bartender. It was a side of Mags I'd never seen before. I couldn't exactly figure out what she was doing. It was nothing blatant.

The guy had gone from businesslike to goofy in about three minutes. By now I had the wronged-woman routine down pat. When Maggie pulled out Eric's photo, all I had to do was think about the quick glimpse I'd gotten of Mary starting to undo the laces on the front of her corset, and my cheeks burned.

We weren't any luckier at Barry's Hat. The smitten bartender even had one of the waitresses look at the picture. No one remembered seeing Eric on Wednesday night.

As we were standing up to leave, the bartender asked, "Have you tried the after-hours club back that way?"

He pointed the way we'd come. "The Drink," he said, and rolled his eyes. "Really creative name. Your guy might be doing his drinking there."

He gave Maggie directions and she gave him a smile that probably made him forget his own name for a moment. "Come back in sometime," he said.

"I just might," she said.

"Where did you learn to flirt like that?" I asked.

"I wasn't flirting. I was just talking."

"Of course you were," I said, pulling on my gloves. We hadn't found out anything about Eric, but I'd had an educational night. I'd learned that Mary had some smooth moves as a stripper, and Maggie had some smooth moves period.

"You want to go check out this Drink place? We're going to pretty much be driving by it, anyway."

I leaned my head against the back of the seat. "Why not?"

The parking lot of the Drink was jammed with cars. Maggie squeezed the bug in at the end of a row. I hoped she'd be able to back it out when we were ready to leave.

The Drink was noisy, smelled like smoke and bodies and was jammed with people. Maggie scanned the space.

"How are we going to do this?" I shouted.

She turned toward me but kept her eyes on the people dancing and drinking. "I don't know." Then something caught her eye. She started to smile. "This is going to work," she said. "This is going to work just fine. Come on." She started making her way through the crowd.

I kept my eyes on the back of her head and followed. She stopped beside a young woman with hair the color of lime Jell-O and a nose ring. "Jamie?" she asked.

The young woman, whose little apron marked her as a staff member, turned. When she saw Maggie, her face split with a huge grin. "Hi," she said. "What are you doing here?"

Maggie tipped her head toward me. "Helping a friend."

After Barry's Hat she'd put Eric's photo in her pocket. Now she pulled it out. "Were you working last Wednesday night? Was he here?"

"What did he do?" Jamie asked suspiciously.

"It's more like who," Maggie said. She looked from the waitress to me and back again.

Jamie looked at me and shrugged. "Sorry." Then she took the picture from Maggie. "He was here."

"Are you sure?"

"Oh, yeah. He was a good tipper and he got really, really drunk."

Maggie and I exchanged looks.

"But he wasn't with any girl. He came in by himself."

My heart sank.

She gave me an apologetic half smile. "He seemed really nice. Way nicer than his jerk of a friend."

Maggie held up a hand. "Wait a second. I thought you said he came in by himself."

"He did," she said. "His friend was waiting for him."

"What did the friend look like?" I asked.

"He was cute." A guy two tables away snapped his fingers at her. "Yeah, yeah, I'm coming," she called. She turned back to us. "Like I said, cute. Bit of stubble, dark hair all slicked back in a ponytail and one of those jackets sailors wear."

Maggie looked blankly at me.

"A peacoat?" I asked.

"Yeah, that's it. But he was a jerk. Figured he knew way more than me because I'm just a dumb waitress. And he stiffed me on a tip."

"Thanks, Jamie," Maggie said. "Any time you want to come for a few classes, they're on me."

She gave Maggie a one-armed hug. "Thanks. I might do that."

Finger-Snapping Guy was at it again. Jamie made a face. "Your guy's nice, you know, for what it's worth."

"I'll keep that in mind," I said. "Thanks."

We elbowed our way back out and slid across the parking lot to the car.

"How do you know her?" I asked Maggie.

"Jamie? She was in my tai chi class last winter. She has great balance. I think her hair was blue then, though."

I waited while she negotiated the car out of the cramped parking spot before I said anything else. "Any idea who the other guy was?" I asked.

"No," Maggie said. "I was hoping you did."

"Problem is, whoever it was doesn't even have to live in Mayville anymore. All Susan knew was that Eric used to be our mystery guy's sponsor."

Maggie nodded. "Stubble, a ponytail and a peacoat isn't much to go on."

"Maybe Roma will come up with something as far as the trucks," I said.

"What if you just laid it all out for Eric?"

"He won't tell Susan who he was with," I said. "What makes you think he'll tell me? And when I did talk to him I didn't get anywhere."

"What kind of support group is this where you can cover for someone who's committed a crime?" Maggie asked, flicking the switch for the heater up a notch. The inside of the car began to get warmer.

"I think it's more Eric's thing than any group's thing," I said thoughtfully. "Have you noticed how important loyalty seems to be to him?"

"What do you mean?" she asked, eyes glued to the road. A few flakes of snow were blowing around.

"Look at the staff of the café. He hires the same students in the summer. His regular staff's been there for years. He's done the library barbecue forever, according to Abigail. Even the year Susan was pregnant with the twins and couldn't get out of bed."

"Good point," Maggie said.

I sighed and shifted in the seat. I couldn't wait for Susan to talk to Eric. "Maybe if he understands this is going to help Ruby . . ."

We talked about Winterfest the rest of the way home and how the rumors about Roma and Eddie Sweeney wouldn't die. But I was really giving the conversation only half my attention. I kept rolling Jamie's description of Eric's friend around in my mind. It could have been anyone. Anyone.

So why couldn't I shake the feeling that I should know exactly who it was?

25

The next morning I was at the table, feeding Owen crunchy peanut butter, when Harry Taylor—the younger Harry—knocked on the back door. Owen was in an extra-good mood because Rebecca had stopped in for a minute to bring my newspaper, which had somehow ended up at her house instead of mine.

"Hi," I said to Harry. "I was going to call you this morning." I'd changed shifts with Abigail, so I wasn't due at the library until lunchtime.

"Is something wrong?" he asked.

"No. Something might be right. Hang on a second." I hustled into the living room for the baby-picture fragment. I'd put it in a small envelope. I handed it to Harry. "This is for your father. There's no way to know for sure, but it's possible this is a picture of his and Agatha's child."

He swallowed a couple of times. Slowly he slid the image from the envelope. "Where did you get this?"

"Ruby ended up with a bag of Agatha's things. It was inside. It doesn't seem to be a picture of her son, David; it's not that old. I asked Rebecca"—I held up a hand—"without telling her why, and she didn't recognize the child. Maybe—and it's a big maybe—it's the baby."

"Thank you, Kathleen," Harry said, his voice suddenly husky. "Dad will . . ." He stopped and cleared his throat, then looked at me. "Thanks."

"You're welcome," I said, suddenly feeling my own throat tighten.

Harry shook his head. "I almost forgot myself." He held out a set of keys. "These are for you."

"For what?"

"For the truck sitting in your driveway."

"Harry, I can't take a truck from you."

"First of all, it's not from me; it's from the old man. And second of all, if you really don't want it you're going to have to tell him, because there's no way I'm doing it." He swung the keys back and forth. "He wants to do this for you. Do you really want to tell him he can't?"

"I . . ." I looked at him helplessly. "All right," I said, holding out my hands in surrender. "But only until I find something for myself." I took the keys.

"It's not fancy," Harry said. "But it runs well and has new tires. You'll have to call Gunnar about insurance."

I nodded. "Okay."

Carefully he slid the envelope with the baby picture into an inside pocket of his jacket. "Thank you for the picture."

"I hope it helps," I said. "Thank you for the truck."

"I hope it helps," Harry said with a smile.

After he'd gone I pulled on my jacket and boots. I didn't have to coax either cat to come with me. We walked around the house, and there was the truck in the driveway. It was identical to Ruby's, sort of an ugly brown color. The only difference was that the right front fender had been replaced and it was primer red. I opened the driver's door. The inside was sparkling clean—no surprise, since the truck came from Harry's.

Both cats were craning their necks to see. I bent down and picked up Owen and set him on the seat. When I reached for Hercules he wrinkled his nose. "It's clean," I told him. "No Boris cooties."

I set Hercules on the seat next to Owen, who was alternately sniffing and poking a paw into everything. Then I leaned in and studied the dashboard. What I really wanted to do was dance around the truck, squealing. The truck was a wonderful gift.

I pulled my head out of the inside and checked the tires. They were big with heavy, knobby treads. More than enough for Mountain Road in the snow. Harrison's generosity made me even more determined to help the old man find out about his child.

"Let's go," I said to the boys. Owen came to the edge of the seat, looked at the ground and jumped. "Nice," I said.

Hercules came to the end of the seat, looked down and looked at me, meowing pitifully. I scooped him up in my arms and shut the door with my hip just as Roma pulled into the driveway.

She got out of the SUV and pushed her sunglasses up on her head.

"Why do you have my old truck?" she asked. Then she stopped, studied the old Ford and said, "It's not mine, is it?"

"Nope," I said. "For now it's mine. Want a cup of coffee?"

"Please."

We walked around the house. Owen was on the top step. There was no sign of Hercules, which meant he'd decided not to wait. Why wait to be let in when you can just walk through the door?

Inside I poured a cup of coffee for Roma and another for myself and we sat at the table. Owen had disappeared but I could see Hercules' whiskers as he lurked by the living room doorway.

"So, how do you have one of the trucks like my old one?" Roma asked.

"Harry Taylor. It's his. He loaned it to me." I ran my finger around the rim of my cup. "Tell me you found something useful," I said, although I knew she hadn't. If she had, she would've said so the minute she saw me in the driveway.

Roma shook her head, confirming what I'd suspected. "Nothing. Truck number one is out of state. Truck number two is driven only in the summer—trust me, I saw it. It's covered in bird droppings. And truck number three has been cut down to drive in the woods. It doesn't have a roof anymore." She leaned back in the chair. "It's covered with a tarp, sitting in a snowbank."

I squeezed my forehead with my thumb and two fingers. I was so sure I'd been on to something.

"For what it's worth, I thought we were going to find something."

"Me, too."

"Maybe there was another truck?"

"Do you really think so?" I sighed, which sent my bangs airborne.

"Not really."

I raked my fingers through my hair.

"Rebecca did a great job with your hair," Roma said.

"Yeah, she did. I can finally get it back into a ponytail. And I admit I've eaten the occasional sardine with the cats. Susan claims sardines will make their fur shiny. Maybe it works for my hair."

Roma made a face.

"Well, I wouldn't expect you to eat sardines," I said. "Especially since you're so hot and heavy with Eddie Sweeney."

Her face turned a cute shade of pink. "I don't think there's a single person in Mayville Heights who hasn't heard the story of my torrid affair with Eddie Sweeney, the famous hockey player." She shook her head, drained her cup and set it on the table.

"Winterfest is almost over," I said. "As soon as Fake Eddie is out of the community center, gossip about you and the real Eddie will stop."

Roma stood up. "I need to get to the clinic," she said. "Call me if there's anything else I can do to help Ruby."

I promised I would and thanked her for the help. As soon as she was out the door Hercules stuck his head all the way around the living room trim.

"She's gone," I said. He walked over to me. "We're back to square one."

I pulled my hands through my hair again. Roma was right. Rebecca was a great hairdresser. All I had to do most days was wash my hair and put a little gel in it.

And then it was as though all the little pieces fell into the proper slots. What had the waitress said about Eric's friend? He was cute. He needed a shave. He was wearing a peacoat and his dark hair was slicked back in a ponytail.

I knew who it was.

I grabbed the edge of the table. I knew who Eric had been with. I knew who'd killed Agatha.

A feeling of dread, like I'd swallowed a concrete block, settled in my stomach.

Not only did I know who'd killed Agatha. I was fairly sure I even knew why.

26

I drove to the café. I was a little rusty shifting gears, but I only ground the transmission once and got safely through all the stop signs. I left the truck at the corner, near the alley where Agatha had died, so I wouldn't have to ease my way out of a tight parking spot when my clutch skills were still rusty.

I'd seen Peter having breakfast a fair number of times at the café. If I was lucky, he'd be there and I could talk to him before I spoke to Eric.

Luck was on my side. Peter was sitting at the same table he'd been at the night Agatha had come into the restaurant. I shook my head at Claire and walked over to him. The leather aviator jacket was hanging on the back of his chair. I wasn't wrong. It was definitely the jacket I'd seen at Agatha's house.

"Why did Agatha fire you?" I asked. I probably should have at least said hello, but I was in a hurry.

He looked up at me. "Why would that be any of your business, assuming she did fire me?"

"Was it because you tried to talk her out of leaving all her money to Ruby's boyfriend?"

"Again, why would that be any of your business?" he said. The only thing that gave him away was the briefest twitch at one corner of his mouth.

"It isn't," I said. "But I don't want to see Ruby go to jail for something she didn't do, and since I can't come up with any other reason for you to have been at her get-out-of-jail lunch, I don't think you do, either."

He picked up his coffee, took a sip and set the cup down. Then he looked at me again. "Hypothetically speaking, if Agatha *had* come to me, wanting to leave her money to Justin Anders, I would likely have strongly advised her against making that change."

"Agatha didn't like to be told what to do."

"No, she didn't," he said.

I stuffed my gloves into my pocket. "And if she went somewhere outside of Mayville to have a new will made—hypothetically, of course—someone would have had to take her. And maybe whoever that was figured out what she was going to do."

His expression changed as he got what I was suggesting. He looked down at the table, his fingers squeezing the edge of the mug. "Can you prove it?" he asked.

"Not yet," I said.

"How can I help?"

I shifted from one foot to the other. I needed to talk to Eric before it got busy. "You could call the lawyer Agatha went to see. You could ask if anyone there saw who drove her. And you could call Detective Gordon if you find out anything."

"I could," he said.

I hoped that meant he would.

I had to know about the jacket. "Why did you take the jacket?" I asked, gesturing to the back of the chair. "I know it was Agatha's brother's jacket. Were you that angry with her?" I waited for him to tell me it was none of my business.

He didn't.

"I didn't take the jacket. I asked David for it. The last time I saw Agatha—the night she died—she told me that old peacoat I was wearing wasn't warm enough," he said, his voice surprisingly thick with emotion. "She wanted me to go over to the house with her to get this jacket. I ... I said no." He swallowed hard. "I've wondered since then, Would she have even been anywhere near that alley if I'd gone?"

He shook his head and looked around for Claire. "I have to go. I have phone calls to make." He gave me an appraising look. "Don't do anything stupid, Kathleen," he said.

I walked over to the counter. Eric looked like himself again. His hair wasn't poking up every which way, his eyes were clear and the dragging tiredness was gone. His face went closed and tight when he saw me.

"I need to talk to you," I said, deliberately keeping my voice neutral

"Susan told me," he said. "I don't have the time right now."

"I was at the Drink last night," I said. I didn't add anything cutesy like, "heard of the place?"

The only thing in Eric's face that shifted were his eyes. They narrowed and met mine directly for a change. He beckoned Claire over. "Cover for me, please. I need to talk to Kathleen for a minute."

"Sure," she said.

I followed Eric into his office, trying not to be too obvious as I looked around for Agatha's envelope. I didn't see it.

He faced me in front of the desk. "Kathleen, I know you know that I had a drink—well, a lot of drinks—the night Agatha died."

"I don't think you had anything to do with her death," I said.

"But you think the person I was with did."

"Yes, I do."

He shook his head. "You're wrong."

"No, I'm not." I shifted uncomfortably from one foot to the other.

He shook his head again but didn't say anything.

I squeezed my hands together for a moment; then I took a deep breath and said it. "It was Justin."

The only thing that gave Eric away was the brief flick of his eyes toward the floor. It was enough.

"You and Justin go way, way back," I said. "Back to when you were teenagers, back to when you were both drinking. Back before Agatha saved you."

His expression hardened, his lips a tight, thin line.

"Justin was like you. He'd been sober long time, but something made him take that first drink again." I stuffed my hands into my pockets. "I don't know why. Maybe it was the stress of trying to get the camp off the ground. Maybe it was the loss of his funding. It doesn't really matter why he started drinking again."

I wanted to move, to walk around, but the office was too small. "Eric," I said. "Agatha died alone in the alley just down the street. She didn't deserve that. No one deserves that."

I couldn't keep the frustration out of my voice. "And Ruby doesn't deserve to be blamed."

His jaw clenched.

"Eric, please," I pleaded.

He stared past me and I waited, the silence stretching out between us. Finally he looked at me. "Yes, I was with Justin. And yes, he did start drinking again. He thought . . ." Eric stopped for a moment. "He thought he could control it. He thought he could drink and not get into trouble." Anguish was etched into every line on his face.

"It doesn't work like that," I said.

Eric slowly shook his head.

"You met him at the Drink."

He nodded. "I walked down here and called a cab."

"Why?"

"I didn't want Susan to know where I was going, or that it was Justin I was meeting. It seems stupid now."

"Justin was drinking?"

He nodded.

"And what about you? What got you started?"

He swiped a hand over his face and leaned back against the edge of the desk. "I ordered a Coke and I tried to talk some sense into Justin. He kept saying he could drink and not have it mess up his life. He said he'd been drinking for a couple of months and he'd kept it under control."

He rubbed his palm over his mouth as if he were trying to rub the words away. "I went to the can. When I came back I must've picked up the wrong drink." He stared at his feet. "I had the drink and I knew . . . I knew but somehow I didn't . . . I couldn't put it down, and Justin was talking the whole time about how he could keep it together, and I thought about all the times I'd seen him in the past two months and he'd seemed normal and it did look like it was working." His voice dropped to a whisper. "And I took the second drink. And then I couldn't stop."

He looked away, and when he looked back his voice was stronger. "We ordered another round. And then another. And then . . . And I don't remember much after that."

"You have no idea how you got home?"

"I woke up on the cot here. It was maybe two a.m. I . . . stuck my head in the sink and ran cold water over it, and I walked home."

"Did you talk to Justin?" I asked.

"Yes. He came in not long after Agatha's body was found and the police were everywhere." Eric threaded his fingers through the back of his hair almost, as though pulling it out by the roots. "He said we had a few drinks, we talked about old times and then we walked down here."

"Walked?"

Eric nodded

"That would've taken an hour at least," I said. "Are you sure Justin didn't have Ruby's truck?"

"I'm not sure of anything, Kathleen."

"There's something else I need to ask you," I said.

"What?"

"You did argue with Agatha about the envelope the night she died, didn't you?"

He nodded. "You saw us." He pointed toward the main part of the diner. "What you didn't see was we fought about it again. She was outside later that night. I got her to come in again to get warm."

"Why did you argue? What did you think was in the envelope?"

He put both hands on the surface of the desk on either side of himself. I could see he was struggling with how to answer.

"Eric, what was in that brown envelope is really important. Anything you tell me is going to help."

He looked at me warily. "You know, don't you?"

"Yes." I said. There didn't seem to be any point in dancing around it.

Whatever he saw in my face seemed to convince him he was right. He studied his feet for a moment. "Last week—Monday, I think it was—I picked up Susan after work. I overheard Agatha having an argument with Ruby about the envelope. About the baby."

He tipped his head and looked at me. "My old man took off when I was about thirteen. I have no idea where he is. Hell, he could be dead, for all I know. Harry Taylor wants to know this child. I told Agatha she was wrong. I thought she should give him that chance, give both of them that chance."

He sighed. "She wouldn't consider it. We were standing right here. I tried to grab the envelope and the corner tore."

The piece Hercules had found. I couldn't help feeling let down that he didn't have the entire envelope.

"She was angry. She told me she was disappointed in me." He gave me a twisted smile with no warmth in it. "And what did I do? I went and got drunk. She would have been even more disappointed if she'd known that."

"You made a mistake, Eric, and you fixed it and you're still fixing it. I think Agatha would be proud of you for that."

"I'm not drinking," he said.

"I know. Susan said you've been doing the meetings. What about Justin?"

"I don't know. I've only talked to him that one time. I have to stay away from him if I'm going to stay sober. But . . . but I'm pretty certain he's still drinking."

He wiped his hands on his jeans. "If he is, everything he has, his whole life, is going to be destroyed."

I just nodded. I didn't say what I was increasingly convinced of. That Justin had already destroyed someone's life.

Agatha's.

27

I promised Eric I'd let him know what else I found out, and walked back to the truck. I wasn't due at the library for several more hours, so I drove home, feeling a little pinch of pleasure at not having to climb Mountain Road by foot. I made a new pot of coffee and sat at the table, trying to figure out what to do next.

Owen came wandering in and I scooped him up onto my lap. "Justin killed Agatha," I said to him. "I'm sure of it." He looked at me and I stroked the fur under his chin. "It's just a little too convenient that he steered me toward Eric. He tried to set me up and I almost fell for it."

I remembered how both cats had reacted to Justin. "You and your brother weren't fooled that easily." That got me his fake-modest, pseudo-embarrassed head bob. Then he jumped to the floor to investigate something by the basement door that looked suspiciously like a disembodied funky-chicken part.

I slumped in the chair as Hercules came in and wound around my legs. "How do we prove Justin took Ruby's truck?" I asked Hercules. "She left it in the studio lot. She told me Justin had driven her home and then they got into an argument and she didn't feel like going back and getting it."

I closed my eyes and tried to picture the parking lot

behind the studio building. Ruby's truck had been there when Maggie, Roma and I had left for the community center. And Maggie had said it was there when she'd headed home. So Justin had taken it sometime after Maggie had left for the night. If it had been any other night somebody might have seen Justin. But the entire town had been at the auction or over working on the Winterfest site.

That parking lot was tiny, squeezed in behind the building. Each tenant had a parking spot, and that was it. It couldn't be seen from the street, so it would have been surprisingly easy for Justin to take the truck and return it unseen.

"Unless," I said aloud. Both cats turned to look at me. I was already on my way to the phone.

"Does the studio building have surveillance on the parking lot?" I asked when Maggie answered her phone.

"Why, hello, Kathleen. So nice to hear your voice," Maggie said sweetly.

"Hi, Mags. How are you? Does the building have a surveillance system?"

"You mean a camera? No."

"Crap on toast," I said, grinding my teeth together.

"Why do you want to know if there's a camera on the parking lot?"

I looked at my watch. I didn't have a lot of time, but I had enough.

"I'll tell you later, I swear. I have to go now." I hung up over her protests and went back to get my coat.

"I have an idea." I told the cats. "Cross your ... paws. I'll be back."

I drove downtown again. The universe, karma, someone was smiling on me, someone was on my side. How would I have done all of this without the truck?

I drove along Main Street and checked out the building to the right of the old school that was now the River

Arts Center. There was no sign of a security camera. I cruised the block again. Same for the building to the left.

The third time around, I pulled into the lot, into Ruby's empty parking spot, and got out to look around on foot. There were no cameras. I smacked the side of the truck with my hand and said some very unlibrarianlike words.

The truck was hard and cold and my hand hurt. I stood there rubbing it and looking around in frustration, when I realized I could see part of Everett's office building. If I could see the office, then the office could see the lot.

I got back in the truck, turned around successfully in the small lot, and drove up to Henderson Holdings' offices.

Lita was at her desk. She smiled when she saw me. "Hi, Kathleen. You're about five hours early for the meeting."

I smiled back. "Hi, Lita," I said. "This is going to sound a little strange, but do you have security cameras on the building?"

She nodded. "Yes, we do."

How was I going to explain that I wanted to look at the footage to see if Justin had taken Ruby's truck?

"You want to see the footage from last Wednesday night," she said.

"The police were already here, weren't they?" I dropped onto the chair in front of her desk.

"The cameras don't show the old school at all. I'm sorry. There was nothing recorded that could help Ruby."

I rubbed the space between my eyes. Nothing was working. I couldn't exactly go to Marcus and explain that I knew Justin killed Agatha because he had elastics on his arm and smelled like hair gel.

I stood up. "Thanks, Lita," I said. "I'll see you this afternoon."

There was a plaque by the door and I would have missed it if I hadn't dropped my gloves and bent to pick them up. I had the same simple plaque in the library. The school gave one to every business that participated in the student work-experience program.

I stood there with one hand on the door, my thoughts falling over themselves. Kate, my co-op student, had been working on a mixed-media art project with a couple of her friends. The kids had mounted webcams on a rotating base at various spots around town and were editing the footage to create a dizzying 360-degree look at Mayville Heights.

That's why there had been a camera in the second-floor storage room for the past ten days. They kept having trouble with the signal and feed. They hadn't been able to get all the cameras working at the same time.

"Kathleen, are you all right?" Lita asked.

I turned around and walked back to her desk. "I'm fine," I said. "Lita, do you have a co-op student?"

"Yes. Brandon."

I let out the breath I'd been holding. The universe was back on my side. Brandon was one of Kate's friends.

"Did he ask you about setting up a webcam for a school project?"

She laughed. "That child is persistent."

"And did you say yes?"

"I did," she said. "He was extremely persistent, Kathleen."

"Where's the camera?"

Lita pointed up over our heads. "Up in a little closet we use to store office supplies." Her expression changed then. "Do you think that camera might have recorded the parking lot down at the studio?"

I held out both hands. "I don't know."

Lita stood up. "Let's find out. I'll get Brandon."

Waiting for her, I thought about calling Marcus. What would I tell him? I didn't know if the webcam had recorded anything useful at all.

Lita came back with Brandon, whom I remembered from the setup in the library.

"Hello, Ms. Paulson," he said. "Mrs. Gray said you want to look at what we've been recording."

"Please, Brandon. I do."

He shrugged and set his laptop on Lita's desk. "Sure thing." He hit some keys and muttered to himself, then tilted the screen back a bit more, shifted sideways and said, "There you go."

Lita and I both leaned in. The live image feed was clear and mostly showed an area of the downtown and the water.

"There," Lita said, pointing to the bottom right corner of the screen.

I could see a slice of the studio parking lot. "That's it," I said. I touched the corner of the screen. "That's part of the back wall of the building."

She nodded. "There is the edge of the door. Those are the first three parking spots." She turned to me. "Which one is Ruby's?"

"Two," I said. I turned to Brandon, who seemed to be trying not to look bored. "Brandon, were you recording last Wednesday night?"

"Yeah," he said.

"Is there any way to look at what you recorded?"

He gave me that pitying look that computer-savvy kids give to adults like me. "Sure. What time?"

Agatha had died sometime between two and three a.m. Eric had met Justin about ten.

"Try nine thirty," I said. Brandon started hitting keys again.

Lita gave me a smile and held up two crossed fingers.

"Okay, here is Wednesday night at nine thirty."

Lita and I exchanged glances and I looked at the screen. There it was. Ruby's truck, or at least the back end, in the bottom corner of the image.

"Can you fast forward that?" I asked.

"You mean advance the time?" Brandon said.

I nodded.

"Where to?"

"Fifteen minutes ahead."

"Sure," he said, but I caught the eye roll as he ducked his head over the keyboard.

Ruby's truck was still there at the forty-five-minute mark. I felt a flicker of excitement. "Show me ten thirty, please," I said.

The quality of the image from ten thirty wasn't as clear, and it cut out for a minute.

"We've been having problems with the Wi-Fi signal," Brandon explained.

"How about two a.m.?"

The truck was still in the spot.

"Two thirty, please," I said. I could feel my heartbeat thumping in the hollow at the base of my throat.

Brandon looked up at me. "Sorry, no two thirty. The signal cut out."

"What about three?"

He turned back to the keyboard. If he was curious about what we were looking at in his footage, he wasn't asking. At three o'clock the truck was still in that spot. I stepped away from the computer, trying to sort things out in my head.

Lita stood silently, hands clasped in front of her. Ruby's truck hadn't moved. There were gaps in the footage, but it sure looked to me like reasonable doubt. I turned to leave. "Lita, could you do something for me?"

"Of course," she said.

"Call Ruby's lawyer and Detective Gordon. Please tell them what we found."

Brandon's head snapped up. "'Detective,' as in 'police'?" he asked.

"Yes," Lita said.

His eyes darted from Lita to me. Then he shrugged. "Cool." He turned back to the computer.

I headed for the door. "You're not staying?" Lita asked.

"There's something I have to do," I said. "I'll see you this afternoon or I'll call you, or something."

I hurried out to the truck. My mind was jumping from thought to thought faster than I could sort them into anything that made sense. But overriding everything was the thought that Ruby's truck hadn't moved. It hadn't moved. Which meant there *was* another truck.

All I had to do was find it.

28

Hercules was sitting on the bench in the porch, almost as though waiting for me. Which he probably was.

"There's another truck," I said kicking off my boots and unlocking the kitchen door at the same time. I dropped my bag and jacket on a chair and raced into the living room. Hercules followed. "What did I do with the brochure Justin gave me about the camp?" I asked the cat.

It wasn't on the table next to the phone. I took the stairs two at a time and burst into the bedroom, almost giving Owen, who was stretched out on the chair by the window, a kitty coronary.

He jumped down and hung his head. "I don't have time to yell at you," I said. "So we'll all just pretend I didn't see you."

I went through the papers next to my computer. Nothing. The brochure wasn't in the drawer, either.

"There's another truck," I said to Owen. "I don't care what Roma found out. Justin didn't drive Ruby's truck. So there has to be another truck. And he has it." I sat on the edge of the armchair. "Harry said that Sam's old truck was junk. But what if it wasn't? Or what if somehow Justin ended up with it?"

Owen seemed to be thinking about what I was saying.

I stood up and walked around the bed. "If Justin had or has the missing truck, it's not in town. Maybe it's out at the campsite. That would be the perfect place to hide an old truck. I just need to find that brochure so I can figure out where the camp is."

I turned to pace back around the bed, and Hercules was standing in the doorway with a piece of paper in his mouth.

"You found it?" I said.

He walked over and dropped the folded paper at my feet. I bent down, cupped his black-and-white face in my hands and kissed the top of his furry head. "You're a genius. Thank you." He stretched forward and licked my chin.

The paper smelled of garlic and tomato. Clearly I'd stuck it in the recycling bin.

I scanned the brochure for the camp's location. It was there in the last paragraph of the last page, "several acres on Hardwood Ridge."

Where the heck was Hardwood Ridge?

I had a map of the area in the drawer. I pulled it out and spread it on top of my laptop. There was no Hardwood Ridge on the map.

I smacked the top of my head with my open hand in frustration.

This was one of the idiosyncrasies of Mayville Heights. Like having two different Main Streets. It seemed charming until you were trying to get directions to somewhere. Just because the place was called Hardwood Ridge didn't mean it was going to show up on the map under that name.

"I'm going to have to call Maggie," I said. Owen immediately looked at the phone. I wasn't sure if she was home, at the studio or at tai chi. So I called her cell.

"Hello," she said, sounding out of breath.

"Hi," I said. "Did I take you away from something important?"

"Just burpees. What's up?"

"Do you know where Hardwood Ridge is?"

"Yes." She still sounded a bit breathless. She was probably working out and talking to me at the same time. "Remember there was a road just this side of the Drink? Well, you just—" She suddenly stopped. "Why do you want to know? Does this have anything to do with you wanting to know about security lights on the studio?"

"I was looking at the proposal Justin gave me and I wondered where the camp was going to be."

"No, you didn't," she said. "You figured something out. You should call Marcus."

"I did figure something out. One of the kids from the co-op program has a webcam at Everett's offices. It picked up part of the parking lot down at the studio building. And it doesn't look like Ruby's truck moved at all the night Agatha was killed."

"That's wonderful. Did you tell Marcus?"

"Lita did."

"So why do you want to know where Hardwood Ridge is?"

"I'm just curious. It's no big deal. Forget it."

"Kath, you can't walk that far."

"Yes, I know," I said. "Go back to your burpees. I'll talk to you later."

"Okay," she said slowly. "Promise me you won't try to walk way up there."

"I promise I won't walk up to Hardwood Ridge," I said solemnly.

"Fine. I'll talk to you later."

I hung up the phone. Two furry faces were at my feet glaring at me. "Don't look at me like that," I said. "I told Maggie the truth. I'm not going to walk up to Hardwood

Ridge." I gave them the Mr. Spock eyebrow. "I'm going to drive."

Both cats followed me downstairs. Ruby had said Justin was going to be in Minneapolis for a couple of days. Now was my chance to look for the truck.

I got my old jacket and snow pants from the closet, pulled on an extra pair of heavy socks and got my big boots. As I put on the snow pants I looked up to see both cats standing by the messenger bag.

"No, no, no," I said, shaking my head. "I can't take you with me." They exchanged some kind of wordless cat telepathy. Then Hercules walked over to me while Owen used a paw to push open the top of the bag and climb in. "Very funny, Owen," I said. "But when I said 'I can't take you with me' I meant 'I can't take *either* of you with me.'"

Owen gave a snippy meow and pulled his head down inside the bag. I finished putting on my things, put my wallet and phone in my pocket. And started out. Hercules stepped in front of me. I moved to go around him and he did it again. This time with a loud yowl.

"What do you want?" I growled. He looked over at the bag. "I'm not taking Owen. All I'm going to do is look for the truck. That's all."

I went to step over him and he darted backward so quickly I almost fell trying not to step on him. "You're crazy," I said in frustration. "Both of you are crazy, and you're making me crazy because I'm standing in the middle of my kitchen in twenty pounds of clothes, arguing with one cat about another."

I stalked over to the bag and grabbed the strap. "Happy?" I snapped. A small meow came from inside.

There was a flashlight on the floor by the vent. I'd used it when the bulb had burned out in the porch light. I picked it up and slipped it into the bag next to the cat. "Here, hold this," I said.

Inside the truck I slid the messenger bag along the seat. Owen immediately climbed out and put his paws on the door to look out the window. I leaned over to double-check that the door was locked, and I set the bag on the floor.

"I take it you're riding shotgun," I said. His response was to come back over, sit angelically on the seat and look straight ahead.

I started the truck, backed out of the driveway and headed for the highway, hoping the same karma that had given me a truck on the one day I really needed it would also help me find another truck.

I overshot the road to the camp the first time and had to turn around in the bar's empty parking lot. We bounced over the icy ruts and a wide-eyed Owen went sliding across the seat. I thought I was on the wrong road and was about to give up and try to turn around when I spotted the handmade sign with an arrow pointing down a dirt track nailed to the tree.

I stopped in the road—there was no one behind us—and looked down the trail. It was plowed, but I didn't dare chance getting stuck. "We'll go up there and turn around," I said to the cat, pointing to the slight rise ahead. "And I'll be able to pull off to the side."

So we did that. I got the truck off the road as far as I could. "What are the chances of you staying here?" I asked Owen. He jumped off the seat and dove into the bag. About what I had figured.

I picked up the bag, locked the truck and made my way to the turnoff. One benefit of the cold temperatures was that the road was dry and frozen, although the ruts were more like trenches.

I stayed close to the edge just in case someone did start down, although I couldn't see who would. Justin was the only person working out here and he was in Minneapolis.

The road cut into the woods in a slow arc, coming out into a cleared area amid the trees. There was a small log cabin and in back of it, off to one side, some kind of old metal-sided storage building

No one was there. I walked slowly around the cabin. The truck was behind the storage shed. Justin hadn't even made the effort to hide it. I wasn't sure if it was stupidity or arrogance.

I didn't touch the truck, but even from a distance I could see the broken headlight and the front-end damage. It looked exactly like Ruby's truck, even more so than the truck Harry had loaned to me, which had the primed replacement fender. This truck was dented and dirty and old.

"We got it," I said to Owen. I pulled out my cell phone and took three pictures of the front of the truck. Then I called Marcus's number. Nothing happened. I looked at the phone. The reception was almost nonexistent. I'd have to walk back out to the road and try there. I slung the bag back onto my shoulder and started around the building, past the cabin. Something stopped me.

Justin had killed Agatha. Had he taken the envelope? Whatever documents Agatha had in the old brown envelope could be Harry's only chance to find his daughter. And as soon as the police came to the cabin the envelope would be part of the investigation and anything inside would be off-limits.

"We have to take a look inside the cabin," I said to Owen. "If Justin has that envelope . . ."

The question was, How was I going to get inside? The answer was apparent as soon as I walked closer to the back door of the log cabin.

The back door was fastened with an old-fashioned padlock. I could pick a padlock in my sleep. It was one of the many skills I'd learned hanging around backstage at all those theaters my parents had performed at, along with street hockey, counting cards and a pretty decent fake British accent.

I hesitated. No matter how good my motives were, I was still breaking into Justin's place. I remembered Agatha's body, lying crumpled in the alley while tears slid down Ruby's face. I swallowed and fished in my pockets. There was a paperclip in my jeans and another in my coat, along with Roma's roll of duct tape that I kept forgetting to give back to her.

The back door opened into the kitchen. There was a small, round table with two chairs against the back wall, squeezed in between the refrigerator and a propane stove. Justin was clearly not spending much time at the cabin. There was nothing on the old wooden table. I checked the drawers and cupboards.

Nothing. I stepped out of my boots and went into the next room.

A sofa was against the end wall in the living room, along with a rocking chair and a banged-up rolltop desk. I went through everything on the desk, checking each piece of paper. All of it had something to do with the camp. Maybe Justin didn't have the envelope. Maybe it really was gone.

There was one more room. The bedroom. The only things in the room were a mattress and box spring on a metal frame. There was no sign of the envelope.

Unless . . .

"What do you think?" I said to Owen, setting the bag on the floor. I lifted the edge of the tan blanket and slipped my hand between the mattress and box spring. *Please don't let me feel anything creepy,* I thought.

The envelope was at the top edge of the bed. My hand shook as I slid it free. I did a little fist pump in the air and grabbed the messenger bag.

"Let's go call Marcus," I said to Owen.

I stepped into the other room just as Justin came through the front door.

"What are you doing here?" he said.

I slipped the hand with the envelope behind my back and pasted a smile, albeit a fake one, on my face. "Oh, good. You are here," I said. "I'm sorry for just walking in, but the door was open and I've been looking for you." I held the envelope against my back with my index finger and tried to use my thumb and middle finger to fish out some of the papers.

"Looking for me in my bedroom?" he said.

"I'm sorry. I didn't know it was your bedroom. I thought this was some kind of office for the camp. That's why I walked in. I wouldn't have done that if I'd known you were living here."

I had some of the papers out of the envelope. I twisted my wrist to slide them under my coat and then behind the back of my snow pants. It was hard to move my hand without giving away the movement, and the envelope slipped to the floor.

"What's that?" Justin was across the room in a few steps. He grabbed my wrist and bent to pick up the envelope. Most of the papers had at least made it under the waistband of my snow pants, the top edges hidden underneath my jacket.

Justin straightened and smiled at me, but it wasn't friendly. "Where did you get this?"

There was no point in bluffing. "Under the mattress, where you hid it," I said. "It doesn't belong to you."

He squeezed my wrist, twisting outward just a little. I bit my cheek so I wouldn't make any sound.

"Yeah, well, it doesn't exactly belong to you, either, does it?"

The front door was in front of me, across the open floor. The back door was behind me, through another room. If I ran out the back door Justin could easily go out the front and head me off.

I glanced down. He was wearing heavy boots, much like the ones I'd come in with, so stomping on his instep in my sock feet wasn't going to work. I swung my foot, connecting with the side of his left knee. He shouted an obscenity and let go of my arm.

I hugged the bag close to my body and ran for the front door, knocking Justin off balance and onto the floor. I grabbed the doorknob, twisted it hard and pulled, but the door didn't give. I twisted it in the other direction, pulling with both hands, but nothing happened. Justin was already up. I bent my knees, braced my feet and frantically twisted the knob, willing down the panic that was spreading throughout my body.

Justin caught me by my hair and yanked me back from the door. He winced as he shifted his weight onto the leg I'd kicked, and pulled a key from the pocket of his jeans.

He dangled the silver key in front of me. "Ah, gee. I locked up behind myself."

My eyes flicked for a second from him to the back of the cabin. Justin pulled on my hair, hauling my head back so hard, my teeth came down on my tongue.

"Oh, see, you've been thinking you should have gone for door number two," he whispered, his mouth so close to me I could feel the warmth of his breath on my neck. "Just to make you feel better about your choice"—he turned my face toward him—"it's only fair to tell you, I locked that one, too."

He kept his fingers laced through my hair, gripping tightly on my scalp, and frog-marched me to the sofa. He gave me a push and I landed sideways on the couch, shifting my weight at the last minute so I wouldn't land on Owen in the bag.

Justin sat on the arm of the sofa, slapping the end of his closed fist against his palm. "Who knows you're here?" he asked.

"Lots of people," I said.

"Now, you see, I don't think so." His tone was conversational. "Because if lots of people knew, then lots of people would be here with you, and they're not." He extended his arms and looked around the room with that same unsettling smile. "Ruby told you I was going to be out of town, didn't she?"

I didn't say anything.

He tossed the key up in the air and caught it. "Yeah, I lied about that. Sometimes I just need a little space."

"How did you manage to get a truck just like hers?" I asked.

Justin laughed. "The fact that my old truck is like Ruby's is just bullshit luck." He held up his hands like a doctor who had just scrubbed for surgery. "The fact that it's running is because I'm good with my hands. I told you that when I was in juvie I learned how to hot-wire a car. I learned a few other things, too."

"You killed Agatha," I said.

"Miss Marple." His eyes narrowed. "You didn't think I was that well-read, did you?" He shook his finger at me. "The village busybody. I should have guessed it would be you. You are a librarian." He said "librarian" like the word left a bad taste in his mouth.

Suddenly his hand shot out, pulling the strap of the messenger bag from my hand. "What's in the bag, Miss Marple?"

I swallowed hard. "A flashlight," I said. I hoped the cat was invisible, but if he wasn't, I hoped he'd launch himself out at Justin's face, because I wasn't going to waste another chance on either door. I was going to grab the old chrome chair in front of the rolltop desk and launch it through the window.

Justin peeked in the bag and then tossed it back on the couch. Owen didn't make a sound, but I was guessing he was mightily pissed. And he was probably plotting his revenge.

"Why did you kill Agatha?" I asked. I was going to have to stall him until I figured out what to do. My voice didn't shake, although I was struggling to keep the rest of me from trembling.

"I didn't kill her. Not on purpose. It was an accident."

The creepy joviality was gone like that. He was still fidgeting.

"People will understand that."

"What the hell was she doing in that damn alley in the middle of the night, anyway?" He yanked both hands through his hair. "It was dark. She was wearing that big, dark coat. How the hell was I supposed to see her?"

I nodded. "It was an accident." The taste of something sour filled my mouth. Even if Justin had hit Agatha by accident, he was drinking and driving and he had literally left her there to die. "You took Eric to the restaurant rather than home. That's why you were in the alley."

"I didn't know she was going to leave me the money in her will." His eyes darted around the room. I wasn't sure I believed him.

"But you knew she had money," I said. "How? No one else did."

He started smacking his hand with his fist again. "Post office was holding a bunch of mail for her. Ruby picked it up. I saw the return address on one of the envelopes and I knew it was an investment firm. Didn't mean anything to Ruby."

"You opened it."

He shrugged. "You'd think a fancy place like that would spring for envelopes with better glue."

Maybe if I kept him talking he'd let down his guard and I could make a break for it. "You told Ruby how worried you were about losing your funding, banking on her telling Agatha. What were you planning to do? Use Ruby to convince Agatha to invest?"

"What if I was? What the hell was she going to do with all that money?" he said derisively. "She was just sitting on it."

I shifted on the sofa, moving a little closer to the edge. "And the truth is, you took the envelope Agatha wouldn't let out of her sight, because you figured if she was holding on to it so tightly, it had to have something to do with the money."

He looked past me, out the front window. "You know what's true? Some people really can't drink, and Eric is one of them."

"You spiked his drink."

His eyes came back to me. "Very good. Yeah, I did. I was trying to make a point." His jaw tightened. "It didn't work out quite the way I hoped. Eric's not like me."

"You can have a drink or two. You can stop."

"What? You don't believe me?"

"You've had a drink or two since the accident," I said. "Haven't you? I couldn't tell."

He came down off the arm of the sofa and paced in front of me. "That's because I'm not an alcoholic. That's a load of crap they've been trying to feed me since I was sixteen. I'm not like Eric. For God's sake, he doesn't even remember Wednesday night."

"So why don't you just explain what happened to Agatha? Explain it was an accident."

"Yeah. Yeah, I can't do that." His hands were everywhere. "I'm really sorry about the way things worked out for other people. But I can't do that."

"You mean Ruby." I pulled the bag closer. "And Eric."

"Like I said, I'm sorry, but sometimes stuff happens. Sometimes people have to make sacrifices."

"Or be sacrificed," I said softly.

He stopped in front of me. "Yes, or be sacrificed." He wiped his hand over his neck. "Do you know how hard and how long I've worked to make this place"—he gestured around the room, but I knew he meant the camp, not the space we were in—"a reality?"

"I probably don't."

"No, you don't," he said. "There are so many kids who need a place like this. And everywhere I turned people got in my damn way."

I nodded.

"This place is going to change lives. It's going to save lives." He pulled the chrome chair out from the desk and straddled it. "So that makes it worth it. The needs of the many outweigh the needs of the few."

Aristotle.

"Does it have to be that black-and-white?" I asked.

He laughed. It was a harsh sound in the almost-empty cabin. "You're one of those people who see shades of gray, aren't you, Kathleen?" His long, strong fingers were beating out a rhythm only he could hear on the chair back.

I swallowed, my mouth suddenly very dry. "Not always, but a lot of the time."

"That's what's wrong with the world; too many shades of gray and not enough black and white. Not enough clear decisions. Not enough absolutes." He shrugged, swung his leg over the chair and got up.

"I have to do what's best for the most people. I'm sorry about Ruby and Agatha. I'm sorry about Eric. Hey, I'm even a little sorry about you." He bent down and hauled me up by my elbow, yanking my arm up behind my back so hard that I whimpered as the pain shot from my elbow to my shoulder.

"Justin, what you doing?" I said, as he dragged me into the kitchen.

"I'm doing what I have to do."

There was a trapdoor in the kitchen floor. I hadn't noticed it.

Still holding my arm with one hand, he bent and lifted it. Crude wooden stairs disappeared down into the darkness. The hairs rose on the back of my neck and for a second the room whirled around me. Tight, dark places and I were not friends.

Justin patted the pockets of my coat and pulled out my cell phone. "I'm sorry, I can't let you keep this," he said. He dropped the phone and then stomped on it with the heel of his heavy boot. Then he pushed me on to the first step.

"Please . . . please don't put me down there," I stammered. "I . . . I . . . I'll help you with the police. I'll help you with Ruby. I don't . . . I don't like small spaces. Please just don't put me down there!"

He studied my face, looking at me with something close to pity and regret. "You shouldn't have come out here. You really shouldn't. There are so many kids who need help."

He sighed. "I can't let you ruin that. I don't have a choice." He let go of my arm and at the same time gave me a shove. I tumbled down the stairs, instinctively holding Owen in the messenger bag close to my body.

The trapdoor slammed shut over my head.

And I couldn't breathe.

I was sprawled on the steps, about two-thirds of the way from the bottom, as far as I could guess. I couldn't tell for sure because it was so dark.

My chest was tight and my breath came in ragged gasps as my lungs tried to suck in air. There was a rushing sound in my ears, as though I were trapped under the tumbling water of a waterfall.

Owen twisted in the bag and pushed his head out the top. He laid it against my chest, over my racing heart. I slid my hand up the bag and onto his fur. He kept his head against me, and slowly I could breathe again.

I was in a small, dark basement but I wasn't alone. I had Owen. He was fierce, he was loyal and he had claws. I knew from past experience that when something bad happened Owen would fight back.

"We have to get out of here," I said. "I have to see if I can get the trapdoor open."

I worked my way up the stairs, step by step, bumping from one riser to the next, holding Owen with one hand and feeling my way with the other.

A couple of steps from the top I stopped and reached over my head for the outline of the trap. "Okay we have to get you out of the bag." I said.

Owen started to pull himself up, and I remembered the flashlight. "We have a flashlight." I fished it out of the bag, held on to the cat and let the bag fall over the side of the steps. I turned on the light with my free hand.

Owen blinked his golden eyes at me. "We're going to get out of here," I said. He meowed softly. "I'm going to put you on the steps so I can use both hands on the trapdoor."

I set him on the step below me, shrugged out of my jacket, braced both feet on the wooden stair and pushed the trapdoor over my head with all my strength. The muscles in my neck and shoulder strained and sweat popped up along my hairline.

The hatch didn't move.

I dropped my arms, hung my head and caught my breath. And muttered a couple of swear words. Then I took a deep breath and tried it again. I leaned back and the edge of the step dug into my back as I pushed with everything I had.

It wasn't moving. My best guess was that Justin had latched or locked the trapdoor in some way.

I edged up another step and turned on the flashlight.

The hatch was a solid piece of plywood and it fit flush into the hole. We weren't getting out that way.

My throat squeezed shut and the darkness began to blacken. Justin wasn't just holding me in the basement. He'd left me there to die.

I pressed my head between my knees and put my hands over the back of my head. I wasn't going to die in this damp, dark basement in the middle of nowhere. Neither was Owen.

I felt behind me for the papers I'd managed to get out of the envelope. They were still safely tucked in my waistband. And they were the only shot Harry had of finding his daughter.

"Okay, puss," I said. "We have to figure something else out."

I looked down at the stair below my feet. Owen was gone. He wasn't on any of the stairs below either.

"Owen, c'mon," I called. Now that my eyes had adjusted to the darkness, I could see the steps went down to a dirt-floor cellar. I couldn't see the cat at all. In fact, nothing moved in my range of vision at all—both a bad thing and a good thing.

"Owen," I called again, leaning forward. This time I got a faint meow in return.

"Come back here."

He meowed again. That meant I was going to have to go get him.

I eased down a couple of stairs. My skin crawled as I concentrated on not looking at how close over my head the floor beams were.

The basement smelled musty with a sweet, fetid odor, like something had started to rot. I made myself think of rotting apples or rotting potatoes with dark mold and soft white patches. I didn't let myself think of all the other things that might be decomposing down there.

I worked my way to the bottom. The dirt floor was cold even through my heavy socks.

"Owen, where are you?" He meowed from the back wall of the cellar. "You had to pick a spot over there," I said as I made my way over the cold ground. "What are you doing? Did you find some way out of here?"

I kept talking because there were things I didn't want to chance hearing, and as long as I was talking, I wasn't screaming. And there was no way that could be bad.

I kept my eyes fixed on where I'd heard the cat's meow. I didn't look at any of the boxes or discarded piles of junk. If I didn't look at it, it couldn't scare me.

Owen was sitting on a discarded metal bedspring, probably from an old bunk bed. "This is what you wanted me to see? Why?" He pulled at one of the coiled metal springs with a paw. I could feel tendrils of panic creeping up the base of my skull.

I took a couple of deep breaths. "I'm going to have to drag this over to the stairs," I said. "You think we need it, okay with me."

The spring framework wasn't as heavy as I'd thought. It wasn't that difficult to pull it over to the bottom of the steps, where I felt more secure—relatively speaking.

I dropped onto the second step and wiped my hands on my snow pants. And then I saw it, above me in the cement-block wall: a small, grimy window almost completely boarded over. A window with just a small sliver of light showing. For a moment it felt like I had two Slinkys for knees.

I grabbed Owen and hugged him in relief, a tad too hard, and he squeaked his objection. "I'm sorry," I said. "But there's a window. We can get out of here."

I scrambled up the steps and got the flashlight from where I'd left it and grabbed my jacket, too, because I was cold.

I shone the light on the window. The small bit of glass

I could see was black with encrusted dirt. Weathered gray boards had been nailed over the top of the window into the frame.

When I stood on tiptoe I could get a grip on the top length of wood. I pulled with every bit of strength I had, but it didn't so much as wiggle. I tried the board below it, but it was nailed tightly, as well. My right foot slid out from under me and I lost my balance and banged my leg against the steps.

I sank to the basement floor. Tears filled my eyes. I held on to my leg, rocking from side to side for comfort. Owen climbed onto my lap and licked away one tear that had gotten out and rolled down my face.

I stroked his fur with one hand. "We're going to get out of here," I told him. "All we have to do is find something to pull off those boards."

I set him on the dirt, struggled to my feet and swiped away the tears. "Come on. There's got to be something."

Except there wasn't.

We looked in discarded boxes that were full of moldy paperbacks and old issues of *National Geographic*. There was a broken toaster and a tangle of cutlery.

I don't know when exactly I first smelled the smoke. It was faint, barely more than a hint, but as we got closer to the back corner of the basement the odor was stronger.

Justin had set the cabin on fire.

I jammed half my hand in my mouth so I wouldn't scream, because I knew if I started I might not be able to stop. Owen went back to the stairs and I ran back, as well, trying to ignore how cold my feet were.

"We've got to get those boards off," I told him. I pulled frantically at them, but nothing happened. I kept yanking, splinters slicing into my hands.

I beat on the wood in frustration, my eyes burning again with unshed tears. Then I couldn't help it; I dropped to the dirt and let the tears run down my face. "I should've called Marcus," I whispered. "I should've told Maggie or Lita or someone I was coming here."

I kicked the bedsprings in anger and frustration. The frame slid across the dirt and one of the metal slats came loose from its spring, whipping into the air, the sound and movement sending me back against the stairs.

I looked at the window. I looked at the thin piece of metal. It was very flexible and very strong. Would it work? I had no other options.

I knelt on the cellar floor and grabbed the end of the slat. Twisting and pulling, I managed to get it free from the other spring. I took it over to the window. Stretching over my head, I eased the length of metal under the edge of the top board near where it was nailed and pulled up on the other end. The rough edge of the strip cut into my left hand.

This wasn't going to work.

Breathing hard, I leaned my forehead against the cement block wall. *Think, think.* I remembered Roma saying chocolate or duct tape could fix just about anything.

Roma's roll of duct tape was still in my jacket pocket. I pulled it out and tore off a long piece, winding it around the metal bar for a handgrip. Then I pulled with everything I had, Owen at my feet, seemingly cheering me on. The wood groaned. I ground my teeth together, braced one leg against the block wall and pulled. There was a splintering sound as the dry old wood gave way. I left it hanging by one nail and went to work on the second board.

"We are getting out of here," I told Owen through clenched teeth. "And the next time I see Justin . . ."

I channeled my fury into pulling, the muscles in my arms shaking.

The smell of smoke was getting stronger. I coughed,

shook my head and pushed in the edge of my makeshift pry bar just a little bit more.

It was enough. The wood cracked and I was able to pull it loose the rest of the way with my hands.

"Yes!" I shouted, nearly out of breath. I made a small shooing motion to Owen. "Get up there a little bit." He moved up the stairs about halfway. I turned my head, put a forearm in front of my face and smashed the three small windowpanes with the metal bar, beating out the wooden dividers between the squares of glass.

There were needlelike slivers of glass everywhere. They cut into my feet through my heavy socks as I moved to the window. The icy air had never felt so good.

I used my sleeve to brush away the worst of the glass. Then I turned around and grabbed Owen. I reached through the window and set him in the snow outside, grateful that it had drifted away from the house on that side of the cabin.

"Go," I said. I pointed toward the trees at the far end of the open yard. He crouched down and looked back through the window.

I coughed again. There was way more smoke coming down through the floorboards now. I put my face close to Owen's. "Go. I'm right behind you, I swear. Please go."

I think he heard the urgency in my voice. He started across the snow. I braced my palms on the window ledge and tried to pull myself up. Bits of glass cut into my hands and the gash in my left palm began to bleed. I didn't have time to do anything about that. I had to get out while I could.

"Keep going," I called to Owen, who looked back at me. "I'm coming."

On the third try I got up on the window ledge. I stuck my head and shoulders out through the window. I could see Owen almost to the cleared parking area. At least he was safe. I stretched my arms out over the snow and try to move forward, but I couldn't.

I couldn't get through.

I clawed at the frozen snow, but I couldn't get a grip on anything. I twisted and kicked my feet, but the window was just too narrow.

I pushed myself back in and dropped to the floor. I could see the smoke now, swirling in the basement. Panic warred with anger, and anger won.

"I am not going to die in this place," I yelled.

I hauled off my coat and peeled away my snow pants, tearing the button at the waist. I folded the papers from Agatha's envelope as small as I could and jammed them into my bra. Off came my sweater and my long underwear. I was down to tights, a T-shirt, underwear and my heavy socks.

I braced my hands on the windowsill and pushed myself up. I dug my hands into the frozen snow. My feet kicked. I blew out every last bit of air and sucked in my stomach, and I started to move.

I didn't think about my hands or the cold. I pulled and I scrambled and I flailed, and in some miracle of physics my hips pulled loose from the window and I was free.

I half ran, half fell over the snow. The icy crust cut through my tights. I kept going, scrambling for purchase on the snow.

I was almost at the tree line when the propane tank blew up.

The impact propelled me into the brush. I wrapped my hands over my head as branches whipped my upper body. I landed flat on my back in a pile of snow, under a tree, cocooned in silence.

There was truly no sound, not so much as a rustle of pine needles. I pushed up on my elbows. Where was Owen? I couldn't see him.

The cabin was a ball of fire and smoke. And then I caught sight of Owen coming toward me, bits of tree bark and snow crystals clinging to his fur, meowing his anger all the way. I lay there in the snow, trying to catch my breath. The cat climbed up onto my chest and licked my face.

I blinked away tears and grinned at him. "We did it," I said. The cut on my hand was still bleeding. Looking at it made me dizzy. So I didn't look. I could see blood soaking through both socks and there wasn't anything I could do about that, either.

Shaking with cold, I got to my feet, holding Owen against me with my good hand.

"We have to stay in the trees," I told him, "just in case Justin comes back."

I might've been bruised and bloody and cold, but if Justin suddenly appeared I was pretty sure I would've beaten him into unconsciousness with just my good arm, assuming Owen didn't get to him first.

Every part of my body shook and I couldn't feel my feet. I looked around and decided which way the road likely was, and we started in that direction. It felt like someone was driving those slivers of glass into my feet with every step. But I took each one, anyway.

I talked to Owen, my face against his fur as I walked, although I did't have a clue what I said. The snow was above my knees but I kept on walking, slowly and painfully breaking a trail to the road.

I have no idea how much time passed. When I heard my name called, I thought hypothermia had caught up with me. I thought I was hallucinating.

Then I heard it again. It wasn't Justin.

"Here," I called. Yelling made me almost double over with coughing.

"I'm here."

"I'm coming," a voice answered. "Stay there."

In a moment I could see Marcus coming through the trees, his long legs breaking easily through the snow, his eyes locked on me. If I were hallucinating, he was the best damn hallucination I'd ever had.

"Kathleen, are you all right?" he asked as he got close to me. Was I imagining the slight catch in his voice?

I nodded, because all of a sudden I couldn't speak. He unzipped his parka and put it around me, zipping it up with my arms tucked inside instead of in the sleeves. It smelled like Marcus and it was so, so warm it made me dizzy.

"What the hell happened?" He bent over and looked into my face.

"Justin . . . Justin killed Agatha," I said through chattering teeth.

"I know."

He knew? How did he know?

My hand was still bleeding. I eased the zipper down with my thumb because I wanted to stick my arm out and not get blood all over Marcus's coat. I watched the blood run down my arm like a tiny river.

He was still talking, but I couldn't hear him for some reason. It began to get dark from the edges in. Those big hands reached out for me. And that was the last thing I remembered.

I woke up on a stretcher in an ambulance down on the road. I was wrapped in blankets, a paramedic was sitting beside me and a very pissed-off Owen was perched on my stomach. Below the foot of the stretcher, another paramedic was cleaning several long gouges on the back of a police officer's hand.

The paramedic beside me smiled. "Hi," he said. He leaned sideways. "Detective Gordon."

Marcus poked his head into the ambulance.

"Hi," he said. I was ridiculously happy to see him smiling at me. What the heck had that paramedic given me?

"What did Owen do?" I croaked.

"Don't worry about that." He pointed at the police officer. "I told him not to touch the cat."

The young officer and Owen glared at each other like a couple of grizzled gunfighters.

"Justin had the missing truck," I said hoarsely.

Marcus nodded. "I know."

Then I remembered the explosion.

"It's gone, isn't it?" I said.

"Yeah, it is, but we've got him, anyway."

I struggled to get up, and the inside of the ambulance swirled like a kaleidoscope. The nice paramedic eased me down, careful to keep his hand away from Owen.

"You got him?"

"We got him."

I let myself relax against the pillow and felt the papers inside my bra crinkle. Ruby was in the clear, and maybe Harry would find his daughter.

Marcus started telling me how stupid it had been for me to come out here without telling anyone where I was going, but he couldn't seem to stop himself from smiling every time he looked at me. I closed my eyes.

I didn't even hear him.

29

They kept me at the hospital overnight, against my objections. Roma came and coaxed Owen into a cat carrier, with some help from Maggie and two Fred the Funky Chickens. Maggie took Owen home and fed both cats. Since I was missing two cans of tuna and a fair amount of peanut butter, I could pretty much guess what they ate.

Everyone just assumed Owen had stowed away in the truck and I hadn't wanted to leave him there in the cold, so I'd taken him to the cabin with me. Since it was pretty close to the truth I didn't say anything.

The papers I'd taken from under Justin's mattress, from Agatha's envelope, were about the baby. Harry Senior and Junior had come to the hospital and I got to put the documents in the old man's hands. He hugged me so tightly I squeaked, and he insisted I keep the truck.

It turned out that Marcus had been suspicious of Justin from the moment he'd found out about the half million dollars. It had seemed like too much of a coincidence that Agatha would leave Justin, whom she barely knew, so much money just when he needed it. It was enough to get Marcus to start digging. And he had taken what I'd told him about the other trucks seriously. He'd tracked down the junkyard owner that had sold Sam's wreck to Justin.

Had Justin been lying when he said he didn't know about the will? It looked that way. The manager at Agatha's new lawyer's office described the young man who'd picked Agatha up. It sounded a lot like Justin. It seemed like he'd somehow been able to capitalize on Agatha's love for Ruby and convince her that changing her will in his favor was something Ruby wanted.

Had he run her over on purpose? I didn't like to think about that, but Marcus was certain he had.

I'd expected a long lecture about butting into the case, but all Marcus had said was, "You could have been killed." That and his troubled expression had made me feel worse than anything else he could have said.

Eric closed the café early on Thursday evening and Maggie canceled tai chi class. We gathered at the restaurant to celebrate Ruby's freedom. She was still grieving for Agatha and I knew she had some work to do over Justin. I'd seen Eric talking to her, and whatever he'd said seemed to help.

I sat at a table by the window, my bandaged feet on a pillow on the chair. Maggie dropped onto the seat beside me. "You okay?" she asked. She'd been asking that pretty much steadily for the past twenty-four hours.

"I am," I said. I patted her arm with my good hand. Suspicious over my questions about Hardwood Ridge, Maggie had called Marcus when I didn't answer my cell phone. Surprisingly, he'd also had a phone call from Peter Lundgren.

"You know, when I saw Marcus coming through the snow, I thought I was hallucinating," I said.

As if he knew we were talking about him, Marcus turned from where he was standing across the room with Rebecca, smiled and lifted the hot chocolate he was holding in a toast.

I smiled back.

"He likes you," Maggie said.

"He's not my type," I began, but I really couldn't muster much of an objection.

The door opened and Roma came in. It was a good thing I was sitting down and had my feet up, because she was holding hands with Eddie Sweeney.

The real Eddie Sweeney.

"Am I hallucinating now?" I asked Maggie, as they made their way over to us.

"Nope," she said smugly, looking like the Cheshire cat.

"You look a lot better," Roma said. "How's Owen?"

"He's fine. Thank you for getting him home." I looked at Maggie. "You, too."

"I like the little fur ball," Maggie said. "He's got cojones."

"Kathleen, this is Eddie," Roma said, turning to smile at the big hockey player beside her.

"Hi, Kathleen," he said. "It's nice to meet you."

"It's nice to meet you, too," I said. I couldn't stop staring at him.

He turned his million-dollar smile on Roma. "Would you like some hot chocolate?"

"Please," she said.

Eddie looked at Maggie.

"I'm fine," she said with a little shake of her head. She was enjoying my shock.

"Kathleen?" Eddie asked.

My mouth was hanging open and I had to close it to answer. "Um, yes, please." I handed him my cup.

"I'll be right back."

All three of us watched him go. Eddie looked just as good going as coming.

Roma pulled up a chair and sat with just a tiny sigh of satisfaction. "So, how are you really? How's your hand?" she asked.

"How's my hand?" I sputtered. "Roma! You? Eddie? How?"

She grinned like a teenager. "The rumor about Eddie and me hit the Internet. He happened to see it. He e-mailed me. I e-mailed back. We e-mailed maybe two dozen times. Then we had coffee."

Her smile got bigger. "We talked for two hours."

"Some of those sightings of you and Eddie were—"

"Real," she finished. "I'm sorry I didn't tell you two. It's just that I told myself I was crazy. He's younger than I am. We're so different. Then one day I just decided, Why the heck not? And here we are."

Eddie was on his way back with the hot chocolate. Maggie was saying something about playing match-maker.

I could feel Marcus looking at me before I turned my head to lock eyes with him. I remembered how I'd felt when I'd seen him coming through the trees toward me, how he'd been there to catch me. I remembered how he couldn't stop smiling at me in the ambulance. He kept looking at me, and then he started across the room, and I couldn't help thinking, *Why the heck not?*

Read on for a special preview from
Sofie Kelly's next Magical Cats Mystery,
coming soon from Obsidian.

I'd never heard a cat laugh before—I didn't think they could—but that's what Owen was clearly doing. He was behind the big chair in the living room, laughing. It sounded a little like hacking up a fur ball, if you could somehow add merriment to the sound.

I leaned over the back of the chair. "Okay, cut it out," I said. "You're being mean."

He looked up at me, and it seemed as though the expression in his golden eyes was a mix of faux-innocence and mirth. "It's not funny," I hissed.

Okay, so it was kind of funny. Owen's brother, Hercules, was sitting in the middle of the kitchen floor, wearing boots. Specifically, black and white boots, to match his black and white fur, in a kitty-paw-print design with fleece lining and antislip soles. They were a gift from my friend Maggie.

"Stick a paw in it," I said to Owen. "You're not helping."

I went back into the kitchen. Hercules gave me a look that was part acute embarrassment and part annoyance.

"They are kind of cute," I said. "You have to admit it was a very nice gesture on Maggie's part." That got me a glare that was all venom.

"I'll take them off." I crouched down in front of him.

He held up one booted paw and I undid the strap. "You're just not a clothes cat," I told him. "You're more of an au naturel cat."

I heard a noise behind me in the doorway. "And Owen is very sorry he laughed at you. Aren't you, Owen?" I added a little extra emphasis to the last words. After a moment's silence there was a soft meow from the other side of the room.

I took the second boot off, and Hercules shook one paw and then the other. I stroked the fur on the top of his head. "Maggie was just trying to help," I said. "She knows you don't like getting your feet wet."

Hercules was a total wuss about wet feet. He didn't like going out in the rain. He didn't like going out in the snow. He didn't like walking across the grass in heavy dew. Maggie had seen the cat boots online and ordered them. I didn't know how I was going to explain to her that boots just weren't his thing.

I stood up, went over to the cupboard to get a handful of kitty crackers and made a little pile on the floor in front of Herc. "Here," I said. "These'll help." Then I scooped up Owen. I could tell from the way his tail was twitching that he'd been thinking of swiping a cracker.

"Leave your brother alone," I warned, carrying him upstairs with me. "Or I'll put those boots on *you* and I'll tell Maggie you like them."

He made grumbling noises in his throat. I set him on the floor, and he disappeared into my closet to sulk. I pulled on an extra pair of heavy socks, brushed my hair back into a low ponytail and stuffed my wallet in my pocket.

Hercules had eaten the crackers and was carefully grooming his front paws. "I'm going to meet Maggie," I told him, pulling my sweatshirt over my head. "I'll figure out something to tell her."

I locked the kitchen door behind me and walked

around the side of the house to the truck—my truck. Sometimes I still got the urge to clap my hands and squeal when I saw it. It had started out as a loaner from Harry Taylor, Sr., and when I'd manage to retrieve some papers about Harry's daughter's adoption, he'd insisted on giving me the truck.

When I'd moved to Mayville Heights about a year ago to become head librarian and to oversee the renovations to the library building, I'd sold my car. The town was small enough that I could walk everywhere I wanted to go. But it was nice not to have to carry two bags of groceries up the hill. And with all the rain we'd had in the past week and all the flooding, I never would have been able to get to the library—or a lot of other places—without the old truck.

The morning sky was dull and the air was damp. We'd had a week of off-and-on rain—mostly on—and the downtown was at serious risk of major flooding. The retaining wall between Old Main Street and the river was strong, but it had been reinforced with sandbags just in case. We'd spent hours two nights ago moving those bags into place along a human chain of volunteers.

This was the second day the library was closed. The building was on relatively high ground, a rise where the street turned, and the pump Oren Kenyon had installed in the basement was handling what little water had come in, but both the parking lot and the street were flooded.

Maggie was waiting for me on the sidewalk in front of the artists' co-op building. The old stone basement had several feet of water in it, and we'd spent most of the previous day moving things from the first-floor store into the second-floor tai chi studio, in case the water got any higher. There were still a couple of her large collage panels that needed to be carried upstairs.

"Hi," I said. "How late did you stay here last night?"

"Not that late," she said as she unlocked the front door.

I followed her inside. Mags and I had met at her tai chi class and bonded over our love of the cheesy reality show *Gotta Dance*. She was an artist, a tai chi instructor, and she ran the co-op store.

Her two collage panels were up on a table, carefully wrapped and padded. We carried them up the steps without any problems.

I was about to suggest that we walk over to Eric's Place for coffee and one of his blueberry muffins, when we heard someone banging on the front door.

"Please tell me that isn't who I think it is," Maggie said. Before I could ask who she meant, she was on her way downstairs.

Jaeger Merrill was outside, his back to the door. Maggie let out a soft sigh and went to unlock it. He turned at the sound.

"Good morning," she said.

Jaeger stepped inside. "The window in my studio is leaking," he said. There were two deep frown lines between his eyebrows. Jaeger was a mask maker. He sold both his masks and some of the elaborate preliminary sketches he made for them in the store.

"Ruby told me," Maggie said. "Someone's coming to take a look at it this morning."

"I wanted to get some work done and instead I had to waste a lot of time sticking my stuff in boxes. Again." He dragged his fingers back through his blond hair. A couple of weeks ago he'd cut off a good six inches. It made him look more serious, less bohemian. "The building needs a manager."

"River Arts does have a manager," I said. "The town owns the building."

"Too much bureaucracy and too little money," Jaeger

said derisively. "The center should have a corporate sponsor. So should the store."

Maggie placed a loosely closed fist against her breastbone and took a slow deep breath. I knew that was her way of staying calm and in control. "The artists own and run the store," she said, "so they can make the decisions."

He gave his head a slight shake. "Like I said before, what the hell does the average artist know about running a business?"

Maggie was the current president of the co-op board. I thought about how hard she'd worked to promote the artwork and the artists at the shop in just the year I'd known her.

"I'm sorry about the leak," she said. "There isn't anything anyone can do about all the rain. Everyone is frustrated and tired, Jaeger."

He crossed his arms over his chest. "This is a ridiculous way to run a business," he started.

"The weather and how we run the co-op are two different things," Maggie said. Her tone hadn't changed at all but there was something just a little intimidating about the way she stood there so perfectly straight and still. "If you have problems with River Arts, go to the town office, call public works, call the mayor. Save everything else for the meeting later this morning."

She tipped her head to the side and looked at him. If it had been an old Western this would have been the point where the audience did a collective "Ohhh." Maggie could outstare anyone, even my Owen and Hercules, who were masters of the unblinking glare.

Jaeger's mouth opened and closed. He shook his head. "This is stupid," he muttered. He pushed past us and headed upstairs.

"What was that?" I asked once he was out of sight.

Maggie gave me a wry smile. "Mostly Jaeger being Jaeger. Did you know he's been pushing for the co-op to find a patron almost since he first got here?"

I nodded.

"With the flooding and having to move everything in the store, he's just gotten worse." She let out a breath, put one hand on the back of her head and stretched. Then she looked at me. "I should check the basement."

"Okay," I said. I followed her through the empty store to the back storage room. She flipped the light switch and unlocked the door. Three steps from the top of the basement stairs she stopped, sucking in a sharp breath.

"What is it?" I asked.

"Is he dead?" Maggie asked in a tight voice.

I leaned around her to get a better look at the body. "Yeah, he's dead."

"Are you sure?"

I moved past her on the steps so I could see better. The corpse of a large gray rodent was floating on its back near the stairs railing, in the four feet of muddy, smelly water that filled the basement. "He's not doing the backstroke, Maggie," I said. "He's dead."

She shivered and ran a hand through her short blond hair. "I'm not touching that thing."

"I'll get it," I said. It wouldn't be the oddest thing I'd ever done in the name of friendship. I grabbed the yellow plastic snow shovel that was hanging on a nail to the right of the cellar door and went down a couple more steps so I could scoop up the dead rat. Behind me I heard Maggie make a faint squeaky noise in her throat, probably afraid that it had just been floating, eyes closed, in the filthy water, like some rodent spa-goer, and was now going to roll over and run up the steps.

It didn't.

I tightened my grip on the shovel handle and turned, swinging it in front of me. "I'm coming up," I warned.

Maggie took a step backward. I grabbed the railing and something sliced into my hand. "Ow!" I yelled, yanking my hand back. There was blood welling from a small gash on the fleshy part of my hand below my little finger.

The end of the shovel dipped like a teeter-totter, and the plastic blade banged hard against the wooden step. The rat corpse somersaulted into the air like a high diver coming off a tower. I swiped my bleeding hand on the leg of my jeans and lunged with the shovel, but the rat had gotten a surprising amount of height and distance. It arced through the air and landed with a soggy splat on Maggie's foot.

She shrieked and jerked backward, banging into the doorframe. I scrambled up the stairs. "I got it. I got it," I said. "It's okay." I scooped up the dead rodent and squeezed past Mags, keeping the shovel low to the ground.

Out in the hallway I looked around. Okay, so what was I going to do? I couldn't exactly drop the rat in the metal garbage can in the corner.

Holding the shovel out in front of me, I cut through the empty store, opened the street door, and tossed the body of the rat out toward the street. It didn't do any elegant somersaults this time. It hit the sidewalk with the same wet splat as when it had landed on Maggie's foot. Except this time the rat rolled over, shook itself and scurried away. I said a word well-mannered librarians didn't normally use and then realized that Ruby Blackthorne was standing by the streetlight. The rat had gone whizzing right by her head.

Crap on toast! "Ruby, I'm sorry," I said, holding the door for her as she came across the sidewalk.

She looked at me. "Inventing a new sport?" she asked. "Because I don't think it's going to replace discus in the Olympics. And I'm pretty sure you just violated at least a couple of cruelty to animal laws."

"It was floating in the basement." I gestured behind me.

"And that was your version of rat CPR?"

I wasn't sure if she was joking or serious. Then I noticed just a hint of a smile pulling at the corners of her mouth. She was growing out her usually spiked short hair and it stuck out from the sides of her head in two tiny pigtails, one turquoise, one pink.

"I really thought it was dead," I said. "It was on its back in the water. It didn't move." I went to swipe my hand across my sweatshirt, which is when I remembered it was bleeding.

"Hey, are you okay?" Ruby asked. "It didn't bite you, did it?"

I shook my head and felt in the pocket of my hoodie for a Kleenex. "No. I did that on the railing."

Maggie came out through the store then, holding a length of old pipe like a club, scanning the space as though the rat might come walking by. It didn't seem like a good plan to tell her it was possible it could.

"It's okay, Mags," I said. "It's gone." That much was true. "I put it outside." Also true.

She looked around again, then tucked the piece of pipe between her knees.

I shot Ruby a warning look, hoping she remembered how Maggie felt about small furry things.

"Is Jaeger still here?" Maggie asked, glancing at the stairs.

"I don't know," I said.

"I just saw him putting boxes in his car," Ruby offered. She rolled her eyes at Maggie. "So, what was it this time? The we-need-a-corporate-sponsor speech? Or the we-need-to-expand-our-horizons rant?"

"The first one," Maggie said. Then she noticed my hand. "Did you do that on the railing?" She caught my wrist and rolled my palm over. "I think that needs stitches."

"I don't need stitches," I said. "It isn't even bleeding anymore. All I need is a Band-Aid."

Maggie shook her head and mock glared at me. "C'mon upstairs. I'll fix it."

Ruby and I followed her up the steps. Mags knew I hated hospitals. It went back to when I was a kid. Blame it on a weak stomach, a dark examining room, an artificial leg and way too many cheese curls.

"So, it seems like Jaeger is really pushing this corporate sponsor idea," I said to Ruby, while Maggie cleaned my cut.

Ruby made a face. "He thinks we should find some big business to subsidize the co-op, kind of like a patron of the arts." Ruby painted huge abstracts and also taught art.

"What's in it for the business?" I asked. "I'm guessing something more than just goodwill."

"The use of our artwork for commercial purposes, among other things," Maggie said, fastening a big bandage on my hand. "I'm not against that necessarily. But I'm not about to give up the right to choose how my art is used. Jaeger thinks I'm wrong." She looked at me. "How's that?"

I opened and closed my hand a few times. "Perfect," I said. "Thank you."

"He's an asshat," Ruby said.

"A what?" I asked.

"Asshat," she repeated. "You know—someone whose head is so far up his . . . you know . . . that he's wearing it for a hat."

"Sounds uncomfortable," Maggie said.

"Does Jaeger look like anyone else either of you have seen?" Ruby asked.

I shook my head. "No."

"Uh-uh," Maggie said. "Why?"

"I can't shake the feeling I've seen him somewhere before, especially since he cut his hair."

"Maybe a workshop or an exhibit," I said.

"No, I don't think that's it." She shook her head and all the little hoops in her left ear danced. "Anyway, it doesn't matter. I just came to see if you guys wanted to go get something to eat at Eric's."

I glanced at my watch.

"Is this a cat morning?" Maggie asked.

"Uh-huh." I was one of several volunteers who helped tend a feral cat colony at Wisteria Hill, the old abandoned Henderson estate just outside town.

"Going by yourself?" She was all innocent sweetness.

"Maybe," I said. I knew where the conversation was headed.

For months Maggie had been trying to play matchmaker between Marcus Gordon and me. Marcus was a police detective, and we'd gotten off on the wrong foot the previous summer when he thought it was possible I had killed conductor Gregor Easton, or at the very least been involved in some intimate hanky-panky with the man who was twice my age and a . . . well . . . pretentious creep.

But last winter Marcus had rescued me when I was left dazed and wandering through the woods in the bitter cold after an explosion. We'd gotten closer since then, though not close enough to suit Maggie. She was indirectly responsible for our friend Roma's relationship with hockey player Eddie Sweeney, and it had just made her worse where Marcus was concerned. Maggie believed in happily ever after and she had no problem with giving it a nudge, or even a big shove.

"Meeting anyone out there?" she continued.

"Don't start," I warned.

"Start what?"

Ruby grinned. She'd heard us do this before. "Start on Marcus and me getting together. We're friends. That's all. He's not my type. He doesn't—"

"Even have a library card," Maggie finished. "Is that the only thing you can find wrong with him?"

Okay, so I had probably used that excuse too much. I thought about Marcus for a moment. He was tall, with dark wavy hair, blue eyes and a gorgeous smile that he didn't use nearly often enough. He was kind to animals, children and old people.

I caught myself and shook my head. I was supposed to be thinking of what was wrong with the man, not what was right. Maggie was smirking at me as though she could read my mind. I stuck my tongue out at her.

"So, how about breakfast?" Ruby said.

Maggie nodded. "Sounds good to me."

"I have to get out to Wisteria Hill," I said. "But I'll drive you two over and get a cup of coffee to go."

Maggie picked up the length of old pipe again.

"Are you taking that with you?" I asked.

"Would it look stupid?"

"Well, not exactly stupid," I said. "More like you're about to start looting and pillaging."

"You know, I really do believe every creature has a right to exist. It's just . . ." She blew out a breath. "I don't want some of them for roommates." She set the pipe on the floor against the wall at the bottom of the stairs.

Maggie locked the building, and then we piled in the truck and headed for Eric's Place, farther up Old Main Street. Even though I knew the town pretty well now, I still found the whole Main Street versus Old Main Street thing kind of confusing.

"Is it ever going to stop raining?" Ruby asked, looking skyward as we got closer to the café.

"There's more rain in the forecast," I said.

"It could be wrong."

"It could." I rubbed my left wrist. It had been aching for days, and not just from slinging sandbags. I'd broken it the previous summer and now it was pretty good at predicting bad weather. Maybe the fact that it didn't hurt so much today meant the forecast was wrong.

The restaurant was warm and dry and smelled like coffee, a nice change from the scent of wet feet. Eric's wife, Susan, worked for me at the library, and I knew they had a heavy-duty sump pump in the basement.

I crossed to the counter. "Hi, Kathleen," Eric said with a smile. "What can I get you?"

"Just a large coffee to go. Thanks," I said.

He reached for a take-out cup, poured the coffee and added just the right amount of cream and sugar. As he passed me the coffee, he noticed the overly large bandage with which Maggie had wrapped my hand. "That doesn't look good," he said. "How did you do that?"

"She was scooping up dead things with a shovel and throwing them at me," Maggie said.

"New hobby?" Eric asked dryly.

"More like a side job," Ruby said with a grin. "Rodent wrangler."

Eric nodded. "Yeah, the rain's driving them out of their hiding places."

Maggie put her hands over her ears and started humming off-key.

"Maggie has a hear no rodents, see no rodents, speak of no rodents policy," I said.

"We tried that with the twins when they went through their streaker stage," Eric said.

I handed him the money for my coffee.

"How'd that work?" Ruby asked.

"About as well as you'd expect. They may be four, but they have the tactical skills of Hannibal getting those elephants across the Alps. They always managed to be stark naked at the most embarrassing moments."

He handed me my change. "Thanks, Eric," I said.

Maggie dropped her hands. "Have fun with . . . the cats," she said. Her lips were twitching as she tried not to smirk at me.

"Nothing's going to happen out there," I hissed at her. "Nothing."

Of course, I was wrong.

ABOUT THE AUTHOR

Sofie Kelly is an author and mixed-media artist who lives on the East Coast with her husband and daughter. In her spare time she practices Wu-style tai chi and likes to prowl around thrift stores. And she admits to having a small crush on Matt Lauer.